Sunfun Calypso

A Novel

by

Julian Putley

Virgin Island Books

Acknowledgements

Many thanks to the following persons:

Jeremy Putley for long hours spent proof reading the manuscript and correcting spelling and grammar and making other useful suggestions.

Foxy of "Just One Dyke" for endorsing certain parts
Liz for advice
Julia for editing tips
Ina for cover suggestions
Rob for computer help in mermaid research

N.B. The Obeah and the Jumbi both pertain to sorcery and spirit worship with roots in African history.

A portion of the proceeds from this book will be donated to the Caribbean charity KATS (Kids And The Sea).

Cover art: Les Anderson

Sunfun Calypso

Contents

1

The Vacation

JC was in the process of removing the sail covers from the rather battered 50 foot yacht, *Sunfun Calypso* when he heard a West Indian voice, "You expecking four guests, well dey jus' comin' now, I jus' bring dem from de earpart. Where you want de bags?" It was Quickly, the taxi driver for Carefree Yacht Vacations, and possibly the slowest taxi driver on the island, preferring to preserve his beloved mini-bus rather than ruin it by racing through the island's many pot holes.

"Just leave them there on the dock," said JC. "I'll stow them aboard."

JC was the captain for a week. A week of sailing around the Caribbee Islands on what normally was a "bareboat", a yacht that people rented and then sailed themselves, unless they were not experienced enough or preferred to be shown around. JC was one of the best in the business and although he hated to be called a chameleon he could get along with almost anyone and was good at tailoring his week's charters to suit the temperaments and desires of his guests. He was a fit and tanned blonde haired lad of 34 and was an expert free diver as well as scuba instructor. He got his name from the many times friends had uttered the expletive Jesus Christ! and he would look down his nose, loftily and reply "Yes, my son."

"JC, this is Harold and Jackie Mcphereson from Devonshire in England, and Roy and Shirley Blake from Florida. We'll leave you to explain the operational details of the yacht's systems, chart briefing and provisioning details." It was Bob and Virginia, managers of CYV's 10 yachts.

"No problem." said JC. "Welcome aboard, folks. Hope you're ready for the best vacation of a lifetime."

"How do you do," said Harold, in a very English accent. "What a beautiful vessel." His florid complexion was beaded with sweat and his walrus moustache drooped in sympathy with the bags under his eyes. The heat of the sun coupled with the humidity was intense.

"Good ta know ya," said Roy and Shirley in unison and everyone stepped on board.

JC passed the bags below and showed them their cabins, "We can go over most of the systems as we go along but I'll run through the basic important ones now, for your convenience and the yacht's safety. First the head, that's the marine term for a toilet. Nothing must go down it that hasn't been eaten first." Then, pointing at the levers on the pump, he explained the mechanics. "Paper should go in the waste paper basket, here," he said, opening a locker door.

"Very third world," said Harold. "Won't it stink after a while?"

"Harold, you agreed on this boating holiday, you'll just have to get used to being primitive for a time," said Jackie.

"Well, actually I was thinking of you darling. Now when I was in the army we were issued with one square of paper per day and . . ."

"Thank you dear, I'm sure I'll manage just fine. Now Captain, please continue."

"The shower is here and the sump pump is here. The shower sump should be emptied after every use and the main thing to remember is to please conserve water." The orientation went on for about half an hour. When everyone was familiar with the buttons, bells and switches below, JC explained the use of the deck gear from the windlass forward to all the winches and lines in the cockpit.

The man from Nature's Hamper, the gourmet grocery shop, knocked on the hull to announce that the provisions had arrived and JC started handing down the boxes. He noticed with dismay that the drinks of choice were light beer and diet cola. He preferred light rum and Heineken. It seemed that there was plenty of food: lots of rich cheeses and a funny looking multi-coloured vegetable paté that wouldn't even have to change colour before it came up over the (hopefully) lee rail. "Just one thing before we get going," said JC, "don't forget your snorkelling equipment. It's in the bin at the end of the dock. Pick fins that are a bit on the loose side so your feet don't cramp."

"Snorkelling!" said Harold, "Sounds terribly dangerous to me. What about the bends?"

"Don't worry, we'll take everything step by step." said JC with a re-assuring smile and an inner feeling of "here we go again." Just then Roy poked his head up through the companionway.

3

"We're all battened down and ready below." He maneuvered his huge bulk into the cockpit and slumped onto the seat; he was sweating profusely. Roy was a large man of about 6' 3" and 280 lbs. His orange T shirt that fell short of covering his massive stomach said, "This isn't a pot belly, it's a fuel tank for a sex machine." His red and green striped shorts revealed skinny white legs which ended in a pair of brand new, polished topsiders. His nose and lips were covered in a thick white paste. He was ready!

Then Shirley came up and sat beside him – what a contrast! She was small with straight, blonde hair and had hills and valleys in all the right places. Her skin-tight white shorts left little to the imagination and her breasts were about to pop out of a bikini top that was probably one size too small. She had a slight lisp which was strangely sexy. "Well, isn't thith juth fun," she said happily.

JC, behind the wheel, fired up the engine whilst Jackie clambered aboard clutching flippers. With practised ease the lines were loosed by Bob who had come over to wish his clients bon voyage. JC expertly reversed out of the slip and soon they were motoring out of Roadstead.

There was a good trade wind of 20 knots with fleecy clouds skudding across the sky and the morning sun made a sparkling, silver highway on the blue Caribbean sea. They spent the next twenty minutes driving to windward towards the pretty, palm-fringed sandy bay at Cooper Island. "It all seems a bit hectic at first," explained JC with a grin, as spray cascaded over the whole boat, "but once you become familiar with the gear it's nothing but fun." During the first five minutes a line had somehow become wrapped around Shirley's leg and the resulting slight abrasion had given JC a chance to rub an ice cube on the offending red mark, much to the obvious delight of the lithesome girl.

Jackie, who had been sitting wedged in the corner cockpit seat, spoke up. "This is all rather lovely. Why do they call it Cooper Island?"

"Well," said JC, "It all started in the 1690s when an old Quaker family fell in love with the island and decided to settle here. He was a barrel maker by trade and found plenty of work making oak casks for the rum distilleries at Cane Bay and Distillery Bay in Tortuga. He had three beautiful daughters and before long pirates infested the place hoping to assuage their lustful desires with the Quaker's fair maidens whilst acquiring casks for that essential part of any ship's stores, rum. One particularly ardent scoundrel, a tall, dark-haired rogue by the name of Silver had had one leg amputated above the knee and old Mr Cooper, a very handy carpenter, offered to make him a wooden leg in order to befriend the pirate and hopefully forestall his lascivious intentions. This was not to be, though, and one day the pirate and one of the fair maidens sailed away into the sunset, Silver sporting a very fine, polished oak leg cleverly carved with a skull and crossbones at the kneecap. Word spread among the pirate community and soon there were pirates of all nationalities hobbling up to Cooper's workshop. The anchorage is still called Peg Leg's Landing." JC looked around to see if they liked his tale: story-telling was an essential part of his job and he was good at it.

"Long John Silver was the name of the principal pirate in Robert Louis Stevenson's 'Treasure Island'," said Jackie knowledgably. "I wonder if there's any connection."

"Sounds as though rape, pillage and plunder was the way of life back then. We'd better lock the boat at night." said Harold, with a worried expression.

"OK," said JC ignoring Harold. They were

approaching the anchorage, "We'll drop the sails and motor in. Roy, head her up into the wind." The sails were furled and lines coiled and JC took the helm while Roy went forward to grab the mooring line. When all was secure they settled back to relax. It had been an exhilarating first sail and the consensus was that they all deserved refreshments. JC went below and before long returned with ice cold rum punches that he served in the cockpit. Peg Leg's Landing was a picture perfect bay – coconut palms rustling in the breeze, the turquoise water lapping onto white sand and the yachts swinging gently to their moorings.

The first round of drinks seemingly evaporated so JC went below and fixed another batch of rum punches. He passed them around and then went to sit discreetly on the cabin top. He scanned the beach and noticed that the little beach bar was beginning to fill up. It was approaching "happy hour" when drinks would be half price. He put the swim ladder down and suggested to his guests that perhaps they would like to go for an evening dip. Then he went below to his cabin, stuffed some dollars into a plastic baggy and into his shorts pocket and dived over the side. In five minutes he was perched on a bar stool with a frosty beer. Next to him was Memnon, a local skipper, employed by Golden Sunset Charters or more popularly GSC.

"How many guests on your boat?" enquired JC.

"I got a family of five Americans. Dey seems OK but I can't eat de food. It all tin wegetable an' process meat. Me eat fish an' rice or maybe goat water or bull foot soup but I can't eat dat American process food. It don' agree wid me stomach."

They sat there chatting while pelicans dived for an evening meal just off the rocky promontory. Then Roy and Harold came up to the bar, having just swum ashore from *Sunfun*. Roy was still wearing his red and green shorts and his large white belly hung down over the front of them. His face was a healthy pink from the afternoon's sail and his eyes twinkled, probably from the rum punches. "From now on I'm going to follow our captain. Seems like he knows the best spots. Two rum punches, please bartender. Would you boys like to join us?"

They both nodded pointing at their empty beers. "Thanks Roy, this is Memnon," said JC, introducing his friend and fellow captain to his guests. "He knows the islands better than anyone in the Caribbean."

"Really," said Harold. "Perhaps you could tell us more about old Mr Cooper and his leg manufacturing business? What a fascinating story."

For only a fraction of a second Memnon looked befuddled, and then a quick wink from JC and he got the picture. JC was renowned for his stories. "Oh yeh, mon. Dat be a good story for true. Ol' Mr Cooper, heh, heh, heh. Well, I got to get back, tanks for de beer." Memnon made a quick exit.

"Seems a pleasant enough fellow," said Harold. "Little short on conversation, though." They finished their drinks and headed back to the boat where Jackie and Shirley were busy fixing a salad. The barbecue was sizzling away with aromatic smells emanating. Roy, after a quick shower, came up with a bottle of red wine and soon they were sitting around the cockpit table.

"Juth look at thothe starth," said Shirley, "Ith tho romantic." She had changed into a semi transparent, tropical sarong cleverly folded and tied to expose a healthy cleavage. She had managed to squeeze in next to JC who had showered and changed into cutoffs and Hawaiian shirt. For some reason he couldn't explain, he had dabbed on a little of his expensive patchouli aftershave.

Jackie served up steaming plates of chicken and

ribs with a savoury rice and they helped themselves to tossed salad. "The Coach and Horses couldn't produce the warm breezes and star studded sky but Jackie's food is always excellent." said Harold, who went on to explain their life story. It transpired that Harold had retired from the Royal Fusiliers as a major, and after a couple of years as a whisky salesman they had decided to buy The Coach and Horses, a small hotel and pub in Devonshire, England. Jackie was the driving force in the business, having been to hotel school. Her excellent cooking and management skills had made the pub a great success. Harold was the archetypal publican with his walrus moustache and tweed jacket. He had a repertoire of war stories that everyone took with a pinch of salt. Jackie explained that although Harold did the ordering of supplies and took charge of the banking, his main job was public relations, which meant standing at the bar with a half pint or single malt whisky regaling his customers with stories ranging from the Falklands War to the latest grouse shoot with the Duke and Duchess. It was here that they had met Roy and Shirley.

Roy had a brother doing time in Dartmoor prison for armed robbery of a transatlantic plane, and he took it upon himself to visit there three times a week during his month long annual vacations. He could see no reason, though, why this familial duty should be a total burden and always booked the best room at The Coach and Horses. It was also revealed, whilst the third bottle of red was being opened, that Roy had had a different lady friend on each of his three visits and although Shirley seemed to be the flavour of the moment, Roy was undoubtedly a philanderer. It was late one night in the lounge bar of the hotel that the subject of a Caribbean sailing holiday had come up. While leafing through colour brochures, a few evenings later, they had all got excited about it. Harold was the only one not quite convinced until Jackie had painted a picture of "sailing under the flag, a British colony, pink gins on the poopdeck, visiting the governor's mansion." Soon it had all been arranged.

Shirley hailed from Florida and had graduated from high school with straight D's. She had spent three months at modelling school but hadn't progressed further than modelling swimsuits and underwear for multi-national catalogues. She had met Roy in a topless bar in Fort Lauderdale where she had been a waitress, and whether she had fallen in love with him or his lifestyle was obscure, but probably it was the latter – there must have been thirty years between them. Roy had a string of hardware stores in South Florida called "Mr Fix It" and was a wealthy man.

" What about you, JC? What brought you down to the islands?" said Roy, slightly slurring his words.

"Well," said JC, "I was brought up in Guernsey in the Channel Islands. Always was around boats 'cos my ol' man was manager of the yacht club there. Sailed here 21 years ago, 1977. Before the boom of the early 80s. 18 day passage from the Canaries to Barbados."

"Must have been a grand adventure," said Harold, puffing on a large cigar.

"There were no satellite navigation systems back then and the captain of the 90-foot yawl I'd hitched a ride on hadn't a clue about celestial navigation. He had a method that worked, though, and by God he brought us through right as rain." JC paused for effect.

"Sounds damned foolhardy," said Harold, shaking his head.

"Don't judge too quickly," said Jackie. "The proof of the pudding is in the eating."

"Well," said JC, "I'll tell you the secret. It was all done with the north star. You know the north star is one star that doesn't move, just sits there over the north pole. That means it's the perfect star for judging latitude. When you're on the equator its on the horizon; when you're at 45 degrees, it's at 45 degrees. So what old Captain Cecil did, that was his name, Cecil. He had us steer south-west from the Canaries to the latitude of Barbados. He was fairly confident in this because he had an old protractor. Then, he had this wooden ruler and he'd hold it at arms length and measure the north star. It was four and a half inches off the horizon. We'd just run down the latitude and every night, after dusk and before dawn we'd measure the distance off the horizon of the north star. If the measurement increased to, say, closer to five we'd know we were heading a little too northerly so we'd just steer a little south of west to compensate. If the measurement decreased to four inches we'd steer a little north of west to get back on our latitude. Well, it worked a treat except we had no good way of figuring our longitude except by dead reckoning. We played it really cautious and slowed right down to two knots when we thought we were about 200 miles off. We picked up the local AM station on a little plastic radio. I'll never forget it because it was playing a steel band version of 'She'll be coming round the mountain when she comes'. We came in on the signal. You know we were almost bang on the latitude."

"It would seem to be a rather hit or miss method of navigation," said Harold. "What about if there had been a couple of days of cloudy weather?"

"Seldom happens in the trade wind belt. Besides, there's nothing out there to run into anyway. The secret of navigation is to know where you're not, not where you are. As long as you know you're not near that rock or that reef and you've got plenty of sea room, no problem."

Shirley was starting to nod off and JC decided it was bed time for him so he said goodnight and went forward to his cabin. He'd had odd couples before but this time his guests were a couple of odd couples and amazingly enough they seemed to get along fine: pompous Harold, reckless Roy, sexy Shirley and sensible Jackie. Time will tell, he thought and he dozed off dreaming of Shirley without any clothes on.

The next morning the sun rose into a cloudless sky. JC was up first and after putting the kettle on, he dived in for his morning dip. The water was calm and clear and he decided that a snorkelling expedition should be the first event of the day.

Breakfast was a simple affair with hot croissants, yoghurt, fresh orange juice and sliced tropical fruit accompanied by freshly ground Colombian coffee. Harold was the only one who begged to differ and helped himself to bran flakes and prunes and a large mug of hot, sweet tea. Everyone agreed that a snorkelling trip would be a wonderful way to start the day provided that they could practice from the beach first and JC pointed out the dangerous things to watch out for, like fire coral and sea urchins and emphasized not to touch, break or kick any flora or fauna. Soon they were all sitting on the sandy beach trying on their equipment.

"You have to walk backwards when you're wearing flippers otherwise you'll fall," explained JC. "The other way to do it is to sit in the shallows and put your flippers on there and then just swim off when you're ready. Don't forget to spit into your mask and wipe it around to prevent fogging." Harold muttered something about uncouth habits but soon all five of them were splashing around in the shallows and then off into deeper water out over the reef, JC leading the way. The water was crystal clear with probably 100-feet visibility and since they were only in about 15 feet the colours, in the early morning sunlight, were astonishingly beautiful. They came, first, to a bed of elkhorn coral and swimming between the branches were fish of many varieties: sergeant-majors, yellowtail snappers and phosphorescent blue chromis. On they went through stands of golden staghorn with turquoise parrot fish nipping at the coral and a French angel fish swimming effortlessly by. This was a different world. There was a different rhythm here and the four newcomers were becoming entranced. They were just approaching a patch of brain coral interspersed with waving, purple sea fans and gorgonians when JC heard a commotion behind him. He looked up and there was Roy some 20 feet behind him, coughing, kicking and splashing and shouting an unintelligible noise. JC was beside him in an instant, but Roy was still back-pedalling furiously.

"Did you see that! A monster shark, didn't move an inch and kept opening and closing its mouth. Had fangs and looked nastier than a wolf," said Roy, breathlessly and still spluttering.

"That was only a barracuda," said JC. "They look frightening but are actually harmless. Are you OK?"

"Oh God," said Roy, shakily, "It scared the bejabers out of me. I'll be all right. I just swallowed some sea water that came down my snorkel. It's nothing, I'll be fine."

"There's nothing out here to be afraid of. Just keep calm and don't touch anything. Do you want to go back or shall we carry on for a while?"

They were all treading water in the area around Roy. "Oh, let'th go on for a while," said Shirley, "It'th juth tho pretty. Do you think you can carry on, Roy?"

"Oh, hell yes," said Roy, suddenly realising that his manhood was in jeopardy. "It was just a little water that got down my tube."

So on they went with Roy so close to JC that they kept bumping into each other, much to the annoyance of JC, whose eyes kept wandering over to the sylph-like form of Shirley, in a brief, white bikini. The highlight of the trip was when two, spotted eagle rays swam, in unison, right underneath them.

Back at the beach the talk was animated. "Wasn't that just fabulous!" said Jackie, whose sometimes quiet demeanor had been given a sudden boost by the magic of the reef. "Those rays, they were poetry in motion, so graceful, flying underwater like that. And their beautiful, spotted markings and long tails, unforgettable!"

Harold put his arm around her, "You did very well, darling. Your mask didn't leak, did it?"

"Not at all. I want to snorkel every day, it's so fascinating. Whatever happened to Roy? Did I hear him say a shark attack?"

"Oh, no my dear, if he'd had a heart attack he'd be in real trouble."

"Shark attack, Harold. I heard something about fangs and a shark!" said Jackie with exasperation. "Of course I didn't believe it. I know Roy tends to exaggerate."

"Very dangerous to exaggerate," said Harold, "Now, when I was in the Malayan jungle . . ."

"Yes, darling , I've heard all your war stories a thousand times. My God, look at those two over there. They seem to be getting on famously."

JC was crouching under a palm tree and in one hand he held a magnificent queen conch shell. Shirley was lying down with her head propped up with one hand and the other was caressing the shiny pink inside of the shell. JC was explaining that the conch was known throughout the islands as an aphrodisiac.

"One thing I don't need ith an aphrodithiac," said

Shirley, looking up at JC with a lascivious smile, "Thpecially with you around. Would you mind rubbing thome thun tan lotion on my back?"

JC glanced up the beach. Roy had immediately walked off after the snorkelling trip in order to distance himself from any embarrassing comments. JC felt he couldn't, ahem! refuse his guest's request so he seized the moment and with deft fingers applied the oil with the expertise of a Thai masseuse. He was rewarded with groans and sighs of pleasure and was just getting ready to do the backs of her thighs when he noticed Roy coming back.

"Right, are we ready to continue?" said JC to no-one in particular. "We can head back to the yacht and then, when we're all showered and ready, we should have a great sail down to our next anchorage at Pinnace Bay. There are some caves there where once treasure was buried."

"Oh, JC," complained Shirley, "I wath juth getting comfortable."

"Now, now," said Harold, "we can't be lolling about in the middle of the day." Then Roy strolled up and seemed anxious to go sailing. So it was settled and they all climbed into the dinghy and headed back to the yacht.

The sail down to Pinnace Bay was a Caribbean dream, just like the brochures. It was about seven miles of smooth downwind sailing in a 12 knot breeze. The sky was clear with little fluffy clouds, the water navy blue. They sailed past Booby Island with palms swaying behind a pink, powder sand beach. On they went past Arawak Island with its green rolling hills, and in the corner of Monkey Bay was a village of gingerbread houses, all with brightly coloured roofs of different pastel shades and little fishing boats swinging to their anchors.

JC had set the genoa, a large lightweight foresail, and in the quartering breeze it was filling nicely. Shirley was lying on the foredeck, topless and Roy, on his second ice cold Heineken, was happily horizontal in the cockpit. Harold and Jackie were sitting opposite absorbing the scenery. It was just one of those picture perfect days.

They rounded up at the entrance to Pinnace Bay and furled up the genoa without a hitch, Harold doing the winching. The colourful cliff face was awe-inspiring with the yellow and red rock reflecting the sun. Goats were grazing on the sparse bushes up on the ridge. They picked up a mooring right at the entrance to the "Treasure Caves". "Well, what's the story here?" asked Roy, "There must be a wooden-legged, hook-handed pirate with a parrot and an eye-patch giving guided tours."

"As a matter of fact there used to be," said JC, "but one day the parrot pecked at his only good eye, he stumbled and stabbed himself with his hook. Now, there's only me to tell you the real story." Everyone laughed.

"Well, let's go and investigate these caves. Do we have to snorkel in?" asked Roy.

"Yes", replied JC, "and take care not to damage any undersea life. By the way, as captain, I take 50 per cent of any gold recovered."

While waiting for his snorkelling guests to return JC decided to prepare lunch as a surprise. This was not part of his job but extra little services like this tended to influence his tip. He took two fresh French baguettes, cut them in half and sliced them open. Then he carefully skinned four portions of smoked mackerel fillets and laid them on the bread. Next he made a dressing of mayonnaise and horseradish with generous additions of freshly ground black pepper and crushed garlic. This was spooned onto the fish and the whole thing topped with sliced gruyere cheese. He put these aside for popping under the grill just before serving and continued with a mushroom and spinach salad that would be served with vinaigrette. Then he put two bottles of Chardonnay in the fridge and went out to lay the table in the cockpit. Roy and Shirley were first back and were rinsing themselves off with the fresh water shower on the stern platform. "Oh, JC, you've laid the table for lunch, you muth be thtarving, you thweetie."

JC gave a mock salute, "Aye, aye, m'am." He went below to finish his preparations. He heard the others return and with perfect timing he arrived back on deck with four chilled wine glasses and proceeded to serve a gourmet lunch.

"You are a man of many talents," said Harold, "This is as delicious as the reefs are beautiful and by God they are beautiful. I swam the length of every single cave. Then on the way back I dived down and picked up that." He pointed to a Triton's trumpet lying on the deck, an uncommon shell made famous by Greek legend. Harold had found a piece of treasure.

"No sign of the bends yet?" asked JC, with a grin. It had been only yesterday morning that Harold had made a fatuous remark about this painful and sometimes dangerous ailment common amongst scuba divers who decompress too quickly, producing swelling in the joints.

"You can't be too careful on the sea, or in the sea, for that matter," replied Harold solemnly, and then changing the subject, "I must say the caves look a perfect hiding place for treasure. What an intriguing story."

JC disappeared below and came up with a ripe brie and a wedge of stilton neatly arranged on grape leaves and decorated with a bunch of plump red grapes. "I took the liberty of making dinner reservations for four at The Hispaniola, the floating bar/restaurant anchored in Great Bay," he said, and went on to describe the restaurant made famous by the lusty libation, "the body shot."

"Oooooh, I'd love to thee it, JC. It thounds like tho much fun. But you'll join uth, surely, won't you? I'd like to buy you a drink," Shirley giggled and looked at JC out of the corner of her eye. Roy frowned at her, obviously not amused.

There was an awkward silence and then Jackie came to the rescue. "You would be most welcome to join us for dinner, JC. So far we have had a wonderful time, largely thanks to you."

"Thank you," said JC, "Very kind of you, but this evening I have some letters to write. I'll make myself a snack on board. If you like I can run you across to the restaurant when you're ready and then I'll stand by on the radio and bring over the dinghy to pick you up when you've finished. Just call on Channel 12." JC would have given a week's pay to do "body shots" with Shirley but he felt he had to be discreet.

Shirley was pouting but Roy was obviously relieved, "You've probably seen the place a hundred times. I'm not surprised that you want a peaceful evening alone. Hey, sounds like we should have a great time. Have you ever done a 'body shot', Harold?"

"To be quite honest, Roy, I haven't. And there is little chance that I ever will. Tequila is a Mexican liquor made from a type of cactus, I do believe, and purported to have hallucinogenic properties. Probably put you in the psychic ward of the nearest hospital. No, I'll stick to Scotch."

They motored round to Great Bay and anchored in a secure spot. After a nap and a shower, smells of deodorant, after shave, and perfume filled the cabin as preparations were made for an evening of revelry. Harold was first on deck, scrubbed and polished and looking smart in a blue blazer and grey flannels. Everyone managed the descent into the dinghy with only Roy causing an anxious wobble.

JC couldn't help but admire Shirley as she stepped out of the dinghy onto the small dock alongside the restaurant She was bra-less and her skin-tight black dress was so short, a mini skirt would have looked long by comparison. She was wearing Aztec sun earings and a gold scarf was carelessly thrown around her neck with one end at the back and one end in front. She was starting to get a slight, but healthy sun-tan that accentuated her platinum blonde hair. She caught him staring at her and threw him a wide smile and then a quick pout as if to say, "Why aren't you coming with me?"

"Channel 12," shouted JC to Roy as he motored the dinghy back to *Sunfun*.

The four of them headed towards the stern of *The Hispaniola* and into the Quarterdeck bar where a pirate theme created a West Indian, island ambience. Pirate flags of skull and crossbone motifs festooned the ceiling. Cutlasses, swords, daggers and pistols decorated the walls. Old bottles stood on shelves and flagons in wicker casings hung from hooks. Cannons pointed seaward from gun ports cut into imaginary bulwarks and cannonballs were stacked in pyramids next to them. Ship's blocks, anchors and coils of hemp rope were displayed around the bar, all well secured against present day pirates. An old sailing ship's yard arm was slung diagonally under the deck head and it provided a walkway for a blue and yellow macaw. Antique copper running lights, red and green, supplied subdued lighting. It was comfortable and on

18

hot evenings side panels opened up to allow ventilation. Roy ordered the first round of drinks, a single malt whisky for Harold, a banana daiquiri for Jackie and two large body shots. When the bartender heard the order for body shots he flashed the lights on and off three times and then turned on a spot light that shone on to a long table just forward of the bar on the main deck. Roy led Shirley to the table, rather reluctantly it seemed, and a small crowd appeared from no-where to witness the spectacle. The body shot required a person to lie horizontal while a shot was poured into the exposed belly button – accessories, like salt and wedges of lemon, were often put in even more suggestive places. There was much screaming, laughing and shouting and flashes of camera bulbs as Roy stripped down to briefs and exposed his huge belly. But when Shirley's turn came and Roy placed the lime practically inside her cotton panties, a roar of approval went up from the mostly male spectators. Shirley didn't know whether to laugh or cry – she was desperately covering her top with her skimpy dress and there was Roy trying to pull a piece of lime out of her panties with his teeth. All of a sudden she grabbed a full bottle of Heineken from a lecherous gawker and poured it over Roy's head. This led to more wild applause.

In the meantime Harold and Jackie had struck up a conversation with George Cleary and wife Anne at the next table. He was a tall and distinguished looking man with silver grey hair and she was a good match for him: a tidy figure in yachting whites and a good tan. George and Anne were owner/operators of Golden Sunset Charters and had sailed over to Great Bay for a couple of days respite from their busy schedule. They were both Bermudians, and as such, British subjects; their accents, however, were mid-atlantic. They had sailed down to the Caribbee Islands in the late 60s. George took an instant liking to Harold – he, too, was a retired regimental man and soon they were engrossed in old war stories, regimental successes and failures and R and R excursions in places like Bangkok and Manila. Anne was telling Jackie of some of the "must see" places of interest. "Don't forget the Emerald Pools on Sage island. They're a photographer's dream . . . and the beautiful hike around Coco island, through 'The Valley of the Palms'. There's a tiny, secluded beach on Coco island, just off the trail, called Honeymoon bay."

Another commotion was heard from the 'body shot table' just as a waiter, with pirate headband and droopy moustache, announced that their table was ready. They bade goodnight to the Clearys, with promises to meet again, and Harold rounded up Roy and Shirley and they went into the Upper Deck restaurant. Their table looked out over a shining, silver sea, highlighted by the rays from a crescent moon, and Harold was prompted to say that this was turning out to be a most delightful vacation. Everybody agreed. Both Roy and Shirley were looking slightly flushed after three large tequilas and Harold was in a jovial mood too, "I hear they're having a limbo competition after dinner," he said.

An hour and a half later Jackie put her spoon down, "I hate to waste Chocolate Mousse Grand Marnier but I can't squeeze in another ounce." On the main deck a four piece reggae band was starting up and the four of them decided to stay for another half an hour.

They were just deciding where to sit when a West Indian man approached, "Mr Harold, nice to see you again. Everyting fine?" It was Memnon and he acknowledged the rest of the party with a toothy grin and a nod. "Where JC?" he said.

"JC's on the boat. He decided to stay aboard while we came for dinner. Can we give him a message?" replied Harold.

"Well, it jus' dat dey havin' a gourmet evenin' at de Royal Palms Yacht Club an I was goin' to sugges' it for you all to go. It nex' Friday. Here's de programme," He handed a sheet of paper to Harold.

"Looks like a very grand affair," he said, after a quick glance. "The chief minister and the governor are going to be present," he showed the programme to Jackie.

"A steel orchestra will play after the dinner. It sounds like it might be fun."

"Yes, and a six-course dinner with several vintage wines. Where can we buy tickets, Memnon?" asked Harold.

"It jus' happen dat I have some tickets. My uncle is de minister for tourism an' he axe me to promote de evenin'. The proceeds are goin' to teachin' islanders to be chefs so it all for a good cause. De tickets $75 each. How many you like, Mr Harold?" Harold turned to ask Roy what he thought of the idea, but he had disappeared. Then he saw him and Shirley gyrating on the dance floor.

"We'll take two tickets please Memnon, and you might check with our friends on the dance floor to see if they are interested." He handed Memnon $150 in travellers cheques.

"Yes sir, tank you sir."

It was 1:30 a.m. when they finally returned to the *Sunfun* with Shirley clutching a bottle of rum – first prize in the limbo contest. Actually she had been second but had been presented with the prize by the real winner, a local fellow called Spiderman who said, "Dey all lookin' at you anyhow an' you get de mos'

21

applause."

A brisk wind was up by the following morning and fluffy cumulus were scudding across a hazy sky. Everyone had decided that the Emerald pools would be a fine destination, allowing for about five hours of upwind sailing and then a chance to explore the geological wonder sheltered by huge granite boulders. *Sunfun* was dipping her lee rail and driving into moderate six-foot seas. All of a sudden, Shirley, who was sitting on the weather cockpit coaming, made a deathly groan, "Eeeeeaaaaaaah" and made a half hearted effort to lean over the windward side. Too late – she erupted in a mass of yellow-brown spew; a mixture of scrambled egg, fruit yoghurt and coffee. This was immediately whipped across the cockpit by the 20 knot breeze and caught Roy on the cheek where it started to ooze down his neck, some of it hanging off his chin by strands of dangling mucous. Roy had not been feeling too perky that morning but had pretended to be fine and had heroically taken the wheel with a bon vivant that belied his grey-green complexion. But even a man in the pink of condition could not have survived an onslaught such as this. Roy almost doubled over and deposited the contents of his stomach in Harold's lap, at the same time losing control of the ship, which came up into the wind with sheets flapping. The lazy sheet, now whipping in the wind, caught Jackie a couple of good lashes before catching her sunglasses and tossing them into the sea. JC rushed to the helm to try to rescue the situation, but slipped on a pool of vomit and careened into Harold, who was shouting, "Ready about, steady as she goes." and then, "God dammit, lookout man. You'll have us all in the drink."

It took JC a precarious five minutes to sort everything out and sluice down all offending areas.
After another two hours of vigorous sailing, the

boulders at Emerald Pools hove into view and soon the wind and waves eased as they came up under the lee of the land.

When they were finally moored in a secluded spot behind the giant rocks, JC said. "Well, I hope everyone enjoyed the morning's sail."

As usual there were nods of approval and affirmative grunts, "Magnificent stuff, very exciting," said Harold and even Shirley, now back on deck, seemed to have forgotten her nightmare of only a couple of hours ago.

The plan was to spend the afternoon exploring the famous Emerald Pools, an unusual geological formation where soft volcanic rock had been eroded away from harder granite to form concave dish-like shapes. Here, crystal clear Caribbean sea collected in pools and rays of sunlight filtered through cracks between overhead boulders and reflections danced on the speckled granite surfaces.

"Let's find the beginning of the trail," advised Jackie, once they were ashore. So off they went through the opening – a tight fit between two boulders which forced them to crawl on all fours. The Emerald Pools were all that they had been led to believe. The rock formations were nothing less than awe-inspiring, often with hundreds of tons of boulder precariously balanced on an impossible upright or pinnacle. The pools were warm and still and perfect for a quick dip. The trail wandered up and down, over and under and through, sometimes helped by wooden ladders or handholds thoughtfully provided by the Tortuga National Parks Trust.

Finally they emerged onto the beach at Skull Bay, a beautiful crescent of sand, and there was JC, standing by the dinghy in the shallows with the snorkelling equipment. "I can point out some of the finest underwater scenes if you'd like to follow me on a short tour."

For the next 20 minutes JC led his guests along a fascinating underwater trail with myriads of fish, so colourful, so exotic, so mesmerising that it overshadowed anything they had seen so far. Eventually they came across some cannons strewn haphazardly on the bottom, and here and there was a cannon ball or two. From underneath one cannon poked the ugly head of a large green moray eel, a serpent of the deep with a reputation that belies its gentle nature.

They had all dried off and were sitting in the shade of a seagrape tree. JC had thoughtfully brought a cooler of drinks ashore. "Well, I think I could retire down here," said Jackie, "It's just so beautiful – the green islands, the tradewinds blowing to keep things cool and provide wonderful sailing conditions, the friendly islanders. And now you have shown us the magical underwater world. Thank you so much, JC."

It was time to get going. JC had decided that Distillery Bay would be the most suitable overnight anchorage. It was not only well protected but put them within easy reach of The Royal Palms Yacht Club where Harold and Jackie were attending the gourmet evening the following night. Roy had declined to buy tickets for himself and Shirley and it seemed to JC that the rift between them was growing wider. Shirley had hardly said a word all day.

They motored the short distance and found the bay almost deserted – only one other boat was anchored there, way up in the corner They had an early dinner and went to bed. Everyone was bone tired.

The next day the wind had decreased to a gentle 10 to 15 kts and they had a wonderful sail up to The Royal Palms. They picked up a mooring within easy access to the clubhouse and the four of them spent the afternoon relaxing on the beach. They were half way through their vacation and so far hadn't had a minute to relax. JC found a tennis partner and enjoyed a well deserved break.

At 7p.m. Harold and Jackie were standing on the stern of *Sunfun* awaiting the arrival of the club launch to take them to the reception and dinner. The remnants of a beautiful sunset were casting pink and mauve rays across a clear sky and the first of the evening stars were twinkling in the east. JC, standing in the cockpit, caught a wiff of Jackie's expensive French perfume. She was wearing an ankle length, deep blue lamé dress complemented by a pink coral necklace and matching ear-rings. Harold, with blue blazer and grey flannels, had, at the last minute, discarded his regimental tie and now looked quite dapper in a blue bow tie with white spots.

After a careful, splash-free ride to the yacht club's main dock, they made their way up a red carpeted walkway lined with royal palms. A liveried doorman took their tickets and ushered them into a reception area where a long table was covered in crystal glassware, silver ice buckets and rows of bottles. Exotic displays of bird of paradise flowers decorated each end. Another table festooned with bougainvillea held tempting plates of hors d'oeuvres. Expensively dressed couples were milling around eating and drinking.

"Look, there's George and Anne Cleary," said Jackie. "Over there by the steel band." A waiter approached with a tray of dry martinis and they each took one. Then the two couples spotted each other and waved.

"It's all a bit pompous," said George to Harold, "but it can be a lot of fun. Last year the minister for public works fell in the pool and when he climbed out he announced that he was just inspecting the plumbing!" They all chuckled, "I hope you've been enjoying the islands."

A tray was presented to them by an immaculate waiter. It held cornets of smoked salmon with a cream cheese filling on diamonds of crispy toast. "We've had an absolutely fantastic time," said Jackie, "and the more I think about it the more I think we should spend more time enjoying life. You're so lucky being able to live here."

"Well, it's not all a bed of roses," replied Anne, "but there's nothing to stop you relocating here if you want to. The Caribbee Islands' government actually welcomes expatriates, especially if you start a business that will employ some of the islanders. Of course you must make a considerable financial investment and the more money you invest the easier it is. Like anywhere else, money talks."

"The lifestyle is very tempting," said Harold. "One can get really involved in healthy, invigorating pursuits because the climate is so conducive to them; sailing, cruising, racing, diving and snorkelling. Splendid stuff!"

Just then the crowd hushed and the doorman announced, "Ladies and gentlemen, the Honourable Chief Minister, Mr Lionel Bradshaw." The head of the islands' government swept into the room followed by his entourage. He was wearing a dark blue pin-striped suit complemented by a plum red waistcoat; a white handkerchief at the breast pocket and a red carnation in his lapel gave him a flamboyant appearance appropriate for the occasion. Tall and lean, with African hair and moustache shining, he looked imposing as he walked across the room accompanied by his attractive ebony-skinned wife. Two policemen stationed themselves at the entrance and soon the party atmosphere continued with laughter and chat.

Harold continued, "I've been involved with the hospitality industry ever since I retired from military service. Jackie and I have a little pub in Devonshire in England, but somehow I can't see myself pulling pints until I die. Our two daughters are grown up so our responsibilities are only to ourselves. We must plan on more sun and fun in the Caribbean." George nodded, smiling. The grass is always greener . . . he thought to himself. Then he noticed the governor standing by the buffet table.

"Look over there, Harold," said George, conspiratorially, "That's our governor, Roger Clement-Jones. He's either been snubbed, arriving unannounced like this or he's sneaked in through a back door. Probably the latter – he hates protocol." Harold looked across and saw the Queen's representative take a large swallow of martini. He was a tall man, slightly stooping, in a rumpled, fawn linen suit. He had a jovial countenance and his twinkling eyes were topped by bushy grey eyebrows only just underscored by a mass of unruly grey hair. "Come on, I'll introduce you."

"Good evening , Your Excellency. We have a good crowd here tonight."

"Ah, hello there, George. Yes, I expect we shall all be well fed tonight. Is your lovely wife here?"

"Yes, she's over there attacking the buffet table. May I introduce Harold Mcphereson, ex major, Royal Fusiliers, presently enjoying a yachting holiday in the islands."

"My pleasure," said Clement-Jones, shaking hands warmly. "I spent a year at Sandhurst many years ago before my career was diverted to the diplomatic service. Are you enjoying sailing the islands?"

"Very much indeed," said Harold. "Wonderful tradewind weather, beautiful waters, splendid yacht and a great captain and now a gourmet evening. What could be better?" A white gloved waiter came by with more martinis and they each helped themselves to another. Mrs Clement-Jones appeared, freshly made up, from the powder room and Jackie was instantly at Harold's side when the introductions were made. The conversation and laughter increased proportionally as the martinis decreased. The chief minister and his wife, roving the floor, paid their respects to the governor and his party. Harold was grandly introduced as president of a leisure conglomerate in Britain. Then a bell rang and an MC announced that dinner was served.

Jackie was delighted when they were asked to join the governor's table. There were eight all together: the Clement-Joneses, the Clearys, the Mcpheresons, a Miss Primby, the governor's aid and a Mr Talbot Winston, a well-educated islander and not only Miss Primby's escort but also a spy for the chief minister's office, according to George. The chief minister tolerated the governor but every year financial aid to Tortuga diminished and occasionally the subject of independence surfaced in the islands' council. Britain, however, was determined to control the constitution of The Caribbee Islands in order to maintain stability and there were inevitable conflicts.

The first course was an iced gazpacho and this was served with an Amontillado sherry, slightly chilled. This was followed by grilled Caribbean dolphin fillets with a tarragon-nut butter and accompanied by miniature duchesse potatoes: the wine was an '86 French Chablis. Harold spent the first part of the dinner quizzing George, sitting opposite him, on the ins and outs of the yacht chartering business. Harold was informed that you just had to love the islands and the lifestyle to engage in such a business and that there were easier ways to make money elsewhere but Harold, half full of martini, was mesmerised by pink sunsets, balmy tradewinds, tropical fish in gin-clear water. As soon as they had finished a course waiters quickly cleared away and prepared the table for the next. Nobody was on "island time" tonight – but of course, this was the governor's table. Next came a salad of sliced avocado, tomato and kiwi fruit drizzled with orange vinaigrette, glasses were topped up with more of the excellent Chablis. Small cups of mango sorbet to clean the palate marked the half way point and some gourmands disappeared outside for a quick smoke. Harold wandered over to where the steel drums were temporarily lying idle to inspect the unusual instruments. Jackie came up behind him and slid her hand in his, "Oh Harold, I am enjoying the evening," she said. "The governor's wife has invited me for an afternoon at the botanical gardens followed by tea in the official residence. Wouldn't that be fun?"

"It sounds very civilised, my dear. You should accept tentatively and confirm later. We still have a lot of sailing and exploring to do." They sat back down just as the fillet of beef Wellington was arriving. It was cooked perfectly, moist and pink in the middle and a Madeira sauce was served separately in silver gravy boats. A South African claret was offered with this dish, an '89 Pinotage.

"What do you think, Harold?" said the governor, holding up his glass, "A rather unusual wine, don't you think?"

Harold was not unfamiliar with wines. "The Pinotage is unique to South Africa," he explained. "The Pinot Noir grape vine and the Hermitage grape vine were grafted together and found to do very well on the slopes of the Paarl valley near Cape Town. The result . . . Pinotage, one of my favourites." He took a large swallow and let out a sigh of satisfaction. Clement-Jones was impressed.

The meal continued in five star fashion to the end. Dessert consisted of individual key lime tarts decorated with half moons of glacé lime and orange and topped with rosettes of Chantilly cream. Small glasses of Trochenbeeren Auslese were served with it. Harold declined – he had just spotted a whole stilton on the buffet table with bottles of Taylor's port adjacent

Brief speeches were made during the coffee. The chefs were congratulated and after lengthy applause came out and took a bow like artists should after a great performance. The Clearys invited Harold and Jackie to visit and stay the night at the end of their cruise. They said goodnight and slipped away – they had to work the next day. Harold and Jackie wandered out onto the tiled patio – the moon was shining down brightly so that the wavelets reflected silver sparkles and the breeze rippled the palm fronds. Then the steel band started up with a version of Yellow Bird. It had been a memorable evening.

After farewells to the Clement-Joneses, Harold managed to squeeze inside the chief minister's circle and congratulate him on a most successful evening. Even though he knew that the chief minister had nothing whatsoever to do with the planning of the evening, he thought it might help him be remembered. After all, in England a high profile at gala events always worked wonders for the careers of politicians and showbiz glitterati.

When the launch dropped them off on *Sunfun* it was 12:30 a.m. They were both asleep before their heads hit the pillow.

JC was up early the next morning and as usual he dived off the stern to swim a few laps around the yacht. On his second turn he glanced up at the transom and there was Shirley looking at him with the hint of a smile playing at the corners of her mouth. She was wearing a new bikini, a shiny, turquoise-blue fabric and cut high at the thigh. The top was suitably brief to match – a pair of little spinnakers. Suddenly she grabbed the top and pulled it off, her firm breasts bouncing out to meet the morning sun. With a big leap she jumped into the water, splash! right next to JC, "Rathe you to the bow," she said, and before JC could get his wits together she was half way there. They both arrived at the mooring line, huffing and puffing like a couple of race horses.

"The element of surprise is a good tactic in competition," he said, smiling. He looked down at her perfect breasts, shining in the water, nipples hard.

She caught him admiring her and moved to his side. She stretched up and breathed hotly in his ear, "Ith it true that boyth get the biggeth hard-onth in the morning?"

He looked into her eyes and he knew he couldn't resist. She had a primal, hungry look; a look of wantonness, open and undisguised. She was a ripe peach, full and juicy and ready. Her lips parted and she offered them to him and as gentle as a butterfly they kissed . . . then more hotly, more passionately, more urgently with tongues exploring. They were both hanging on to the mooring rope and suddenly she let go – she needed both hands she decided. Both her legs were entwined around JC's torso and now their combined weights were too much so he let go too and they both submerged.

They disentangled and surfaced, "Let's go to the beach," he said, and off they went, swimming hard, to a sandy spit with a grassy verge at the end of The Royal Palms' property. It was a swim of about 100 yards and JC got there first and lay in the shallows waiting for her. When she reached the shore they both scrambled out and tumbled onto the grassy bank. There were some sea grape trees that offered a bit of privacy but at that time in the morning there weren't many people about. He lay there, momentarily looking up at the sky and she came to lie next to him. Then he reached over and plucked a bunch of the wild grapes and laid them on her venus mons, "Should I eat the forbidden fruit?" he said.

She cuddled up next to him and started kissing his neck. "I wanted you from the very first day we joined the boat," she said. She raised up her leg and started to caress JC's thigh. Then she slipped her hand inside his swimming shorts.

He rolled over onto his side and gently squeezed a breast and then with his tongue he massaged her nipple, occasionally enveloping the whole areola.

She started panting with desire, undulating her pelvis. He moved down and with the tip of his tongue circled her navel whilst both hands caressed her breasts and nipples. She started moaning, which developed into a high pitched whimpering. Then with his strong hands he cupped her firm buttocks and his fingers caressed the inside of her silken thighs. She groaned, her breath out of control now, "Fuck me, fuck me, fuck me," she pleaded . . . He did.

By mid morning they were sailing fast down the north side of Tortuga. JC had dug out the cruising chute and, with the sun behind them, the colours of this large billowing sail were spectacular. It was cut in a radial fashion with stripes of red, pink, yellow and orange and in the centre was a large smiling sun with the letters F.U.N. in a semi circle above it. The island was more green on this, the lee side, and the steep slopes and valleys with lush growth gave a much more tropical feeling than the arid windward side. Groves of banana trees, patches of sugar cane and the ubiquitous palm trees, bowing and dipping to the sea, all came and went as *Sunfun* sailed majestically westward, pushed by a balmy tradewind breeze. Their destination was Cane Bay and the crew were thinking of hiking the meticulously maintained mountain trail above the bay. "A good walk will be just the ticket," said Jackie, "Both Harold and I overindulged last night and a bit of exercise will do us good. Harold grunted something unintelligible. He had been thinking that a large gin and tonic would be more his cup of tea. "I think you'd enjoy it too," she said, looking at Roy and Shirley. "There are supposed to be teak and mahogany trees up there in the rain forest and just think of the views from that elevation."

Surprisingly, Roy agreed. He'd been getting a bit bored ever since he'd lost interest in Shirley, "Excellent idea. I can try out my new telephoto lens. Feel like modelling for some shots, Shirley? I could entitle them 'Babe in the woods.'"

"Well," she said, "I wath thinking of thtaying here and rethting. I think I thprained my ankle." She shot a quick look at JC who frowned and imperceptibly shook his head. He didn't want any suspicions to be aroused. She got the message, "Maybe, though, some exercise would do it good." So it was arranged.

They sailed into Cane Bay in glorious colour, the spinnaker drawing the whole way in. Harold was stationed on the foredeck and handled the sock or protective bag perfectly and Roy, in charge of the sheet, eased it just at the right time so it didn't have a chance to wrap itself around the headstay, "Well done crew!" shouted JC. "America's Cup, here we come!!" It was one of his favourite lines when a maneuver had been successfully performed; it made the guests feel good. Unfortunately he wasn't able to use it often.

No sooner had they got the anchor down than a

dinghy came up alongside and a big islander wearing a battered straw hat stood up and shouted, "Welcome to Cane Bay. JC, Mr Harold. How you all doin'?" It was Memnon and he was grinning from ear to ear.

"Memnon, you wily devil," exclaimed Harold. "What on earth are you doing here?"

"Me drivin' cab for a couple days till de nex' charter come up. Can I help you wid anyting? Shoppin' in tung maybe?"

"Well, the four of us were thinking of walking the trail up on the ridge. We'd need a cab to take us up the mountain and then a ride down again afterwards. How much would that be?"

"Up de mountain, wait a hour den back dung," Memnon mumbled to himself scratching his head, "Dat be dirty dolla'."

"Thirty dollars!" exclaimed Harold, "That's a bit steep isn't it? Can't you give us a better price?"

"Farty dolla," said Memnon, "And dat widout de tip."

"Forty dollars!" said Harold, completely bewildered. "But you just said thirty dollars.

"Well," said Memnon, "De real price be farty dolla but since I a friend o' yours I give you a special price, dirty dolla'." Another wide grin appeared.

Harold was about to argue again when Jackie interrupted, "That would be fine Memnon. We'll meet you on the beach in 20 minutes." Memnon drove away in the dinghy, smiling to himself.

It was four o'clock when the four of them clambered into Memnon's battered minibus for the trip up the mountain. There was a strange collection of paraphernalia on the dashboard, a gold coloured crown being the centrepiece. From the rear view mirror hung a cardboard Christmas tree that emanated some sort of sanitising odour; a grinning stuffed monkey hung next to it. Stuck to the windshield was a sticker, 'Jesus Saves'. Another read, 'Sex Me Up, Honey' and yet another, 'Feed De Cat.'

Memnon turned to Harold, "How you enjoy de dinner, Mr Harold?"

"We enjoyed it immensely. The Royal Palms is an excellent resort and the food was first class. Thanks to you Memnon we had a great evening."

"Yeah, dat for true. De Royal Palms a real fancy place." They were winding there way up the narrow road past sugar cane fields and banana groves. They turned a corner and there by the side of the road were some ruins. "Dat were de ol' mill for de bigges' plantation in Tortuga, de Penn plantation. Dat windmill would crush de sugar cane into juice for sugar an' rum. Dat were de economy o' de islands in de ol' days."

"And nowadays you crush the tourists for dollars, instead," said Roy, sitting in the back.

"Heh, heh, yeah, dat's a good one, heh, heh, heh." Memnon laughed his head off. "Well, we all got to make a livin'."

They came up behind an old VW that was meandering along and suddenly Memnon changed down and accelerated passed the old car round a blind corner, "Aaaaaahhhhhh," cried Jackie, as her whole life flashed before her eyes.

"By jove, that was a bit risky," said Harold with the typical understatement of the English.

"No problem," said Memnon and tapped the 'Jesus Saves' sign with the large gold ring he wore on his pinky. "Keep de faith, you be fine wid me." He grinned widely.

They drove on up, the road getting steeper nearer the top. The foliage was getting greener and more lush now. They slowed for a herd of cows and Memnon expertly weaved his minibus through them. Another hairpin bend was navigated on the wrong side of the road and finally, with great relief, they were there.

The view was breathtaking. The fleecy white clouds scudded by, casting shadows on the deep blue sea far below. Tiny, toy boats sailed towards emerald islets with their bays and coves offering inviting sanctuary.

Roy started dashing around with his camera taking shots from different angles. He found some bright pink bougainvillea to frame a panoramic shot. Then he got Memnon to take a group shot of the four of them – these were memories not to be lost.

"Come on Roy," said Shirley, "We haven't got long, so let's get going." Off they went along the path passed elephant ear vines and tropical creepers climbing around mahogany tree trunks. They had been walking for about ten minutes when they came to a clearing offering another magnificent view and the National Park Trust had supplied a bench, facing west towards the setting sun. Harold and Jackie sat down, "You two carry on," shouted Jackie. "We're going to rest for a while."

Shirley was some way off along the path. She had been posing for erotic shots using vines and tree limbs as props. Roy was in his element, camera clicking away.

"Harold, these islands are Shangri-La. The climate, the sea, the flowers and the trees. The islanders are easygoing and the governor and the business community seem pleasant enough. Why don't we move here and start a business?" Jackie clasped her husband's hand tightly and looked into his eyes.

"I've been thinking of nothing else for the last couple of days," said Harold, "The economy of the islands is largely tourism based and that's the area of our expertise. A small hotel with a restaurant, somewhere rundown that needs revitalising. That's what we should look for. The challenge of creating something out here in the colonies that would improve the islands and help the people. Something that we could be proud of. Something that we could build together and when it's all running smoothly we could sail the islands in our spare time. Take time to visit other islands to the south; The Grenadines, Martinique . . . " Harold had a far-away look. He had a healthy tan and the bags under his eyes had all but disappeared. As he talked of his dream his shoulders squared and his jaw took on a determined set

Jackie leaned over and kissed him on the cheek. They were both entering the autumn of their lives and needed a new challenge, "When we get back to the marina I have an appointment with Mrs Clement-Jones and we both have an invitation to stay with the Clearys. We must make enquiries and search out opportunities."

"You're quite right, Jackie my love. You're quite right." They walked back with a new vigour in their stride.

They got back to the minibus where Memnon was dozing in the back seat, "How long have we been gone, Memnon?" said Harold.

"Jus' 'bout a hour, What happen to de udder two. Dey ain' lost, I hope."

At that moment Shirley came running down the path, panting and rather dishevelled. "That Roy. He'th thuch a devil. He wanted Penthouthe thentrefold shots.

Then Roy appeared, camera in hand and sweat running down his face, "Nothing I haven't seen before," he said.

"Thats right, tell the whole world," said Shirley sarcastically and rather embarrassed.

"Now, now you two, calm down," said Jackie

soothingly, "It's time to be getting back to the boat. Memnon, would you mind driving a little slower. We would like to watch the sunset."

"Sure ting, Ms Jackie, no problem." They sped off and were back at their starting point in 15 minutes.

Harold was in a jovial mood. He'd been dreaming of a new life in the islands the whole way down the mountain. He reached into his shorts pocket and handed 50 dollars over to Memnon, who was holding the door open for the ladies, "Keep the change," he said, "No doubt we'll meet again soon."

"Yes sir, tank you, Mr Harold," Memnon got back into the driver's seat, smiling and shaking his head. He would never understand the white man. First they argued about the fare, then they complained about the driving and then they gave you a huge tip.

The next day was their last day of sailing on the *Sunfun* and they'd decided to sail to the Isle of Pines. The island was home to Bimbos bar, famous for its loud and raunchy, reggae band and its sometimes lewd and debauched dance floor action. It was a favourite amongst islanders and tourists alike.

Like many good things in life Bimbos had happened almost by accident. Its owner was Sonny Stone, more popularly known as Rocky, and in the late 60s he had a small fisherman's shack at the end of the sandy beach in Grand Harbour. During the pioneering days of yacht chartering sail boat crews would stroll the beach and often at sunset would find themselves at Rockys buying a fish or lobster and sharing a glass of rum. When he wasn't there he would leave the bottles out on a wooden bench with a few paper cups and crews would help themselves and pay 50 cents a drink on the honour system. Often they'd be there well into the evening and Rocky would sometimes show up and tell a sea story or fishing tale. Occasionally at weekends some of the locals would stop by with a guitar or two and an impromptu jam would spring up. Many lies were swapped at Rockys in those early days.

By the early 70s bareboating began and Rockys became a "don't miss" attraction on the weekly itinerary and it was then that Rocky decided that he didn't like tourists – they were more demanding than his usual bunch of sailing cronies and he didn't have the time to run after their demands. He was in his 20s then and he had more important things to do like fishing, drinking and the horizontal bop. But try as he might to dissuade the tourists, the more they became attracted to him and his place. He would be rude to them, he would make fun of them, he would laugh at them but still they would flock to his shack and of course the wild weekend jam sessions soon became famous. So Rocky decided, after a year or so had gone by, that if you couldn't beat them, then join them. After all, the writing was on the wall and tourists were coming in ever increasing numbers, it was an irreversible tide. Rocky got hold of a guitar and learned about three chords. He also learned the words to "Yellowbird", "Mr Tallyman", "Red Sails in the Sunset" and a couple of other "trademark" Caribbean songs and he would sit in his shack in the afternoons and play and sing. Slowly all the tourists disappeared.

It was then that he changed the name of his place from Rockys to Bimbos. Someone had told him that it was a reasonably objectionable name. He went back to berating and belittling tourists and became good at making up derogatory songs about them on the spur of the moment. Soon business was booming again. It was not uncommon to see Rocky being slapped on the back and invited for drinks by a pink, pear-shaped tourist who had just been mocked and ridiculed by a Rock Song in front of a crowd of like minded holidaymakers. Rocky loved it – and he was making money too.

The sail across was fast and fun and trouble free. JC felt he'd done a good job with his guests. From green novices to a crew who, at least, were competent enough not to be a danger to themselves. On the sail over they had decided to spend the day on the beach and browse the few shops that sold island handicrafts and souvenirs. They'd have lunch ashore, Harold said. Jackie collected beach towels and snorkelling gear. Snorkelling was her new passion – she couldn't get over the beauty of the undersea world and the relaxing feel of the warm, buoyant Caribbean sea.

JC dropped them ashore in the dinghy. He noticed that Roy was showing renewed interest in Shirley, who as usual was doing her best to avoid him. At least that was good, he thought to himself. When he picked them up at five o'clock he noticed that they were not talking again.

The music at Bimbos, on a Friday night, was now legendary. There were at least 30 yachts in the anchorage and it seemed that the whole of the local population of "The Pines", as it was called, was there. JC had driven Roy and Shirley to the waterfront bar in the dinghy. Harold had made a jug of martinis and he and Jackie had decided to stay on the boat and watch the stars.

Bimbos bar was situated just beyond the high water mark and over the years had escalated to a series of shacks, all surrounding the famous original. On one side was the band with amplifiers and speakers. At the back was the bar with bottles stacked so haphazardly that only the bartender knew where anything was; on the other side, tables and chairs surrounded the small dance floor. Over the passed 25 years or so nearly every guest who had visited Bimbos had left a memento; a business card, a bra, or a cap that was usually signed and pinned up on the ceiling or supporting posts. This was what gave the place its character. The whole place was open; there were no walls, just roofs on posts, so a pleasant breeze flowed through, and out in front hammocks were slung and they were seldom unoccupied.

"Let me buy the first round," said JC. "What'll it be Roy?"

"I'll have a 'Between the Sheets' and a 'Black Russian' and to drink I'll have a Heineken," he said with a straight face. Then he burst out laughing and slapped JC on the back. "Just the beer, thanks."

"Shirley, what about you?"

"Pina Colada, pleathe JC." They were all standing at the bar and Shirley was attracting quite a bit of attention. She was wearing the tiniest white cut-off shorts and a halter top with no bra underneath. When their drinks arrived they sat down and surveyed their surroundings. The band was tuning up and more and more people were coming in and milling around. Bob Marley's *No Woman No Cry* started the evening's music with a slow reggae beat but the tempo soon increased and by the third number the dance floor was packed, "*Back to back, belly to belly, hope you like my guava jelly,*" the singer boomed. The drummer was great, using cow bell, cymbal and bass to great effect.

It was amazing that this bar with its low ceilings, sand floor and rustic construction caused people to lose all their inhibitions. Just to watch the dancers, gyrating with reckless abandon, was good entertainment. A pretty black girl with an extremely large derriere had caught the attention of Roy. She was over in the corner dancing by herself, slowly revolving her huge hips in an enticing, sexy manner. He was on his third rum and Coke and feeling no pain. She caught him staring at her and sidled over to him,

"Come on honey," she said, "let's dance."

JC and Shirley looked at each other and grinned. Now they could be together, "Let's take a walk along the beach," he said. "I'll get a couple more drinks to go." When he came back from the bar, JC glanced over to where Roy was dancing. The girl had her arms around Roy's neck and she was slowly gyrating, this time hip to hip with Roy, who seemed to be having no trouble getting the hang of it. Her large breasts were squeezed against his chest and he was looking off into seventh heaven. JC and Shirley quietly slipped out.

They walked up the beach holding hands. A crescent moon had just risen over the hill to the east and the wavelets out in the harbour glittered silver whilst the breeze rustled the palm fronds overhead. At the end of the beach they found a grassy patch amongst some bushes and sat down to finish their drinks, "I'm going to mith you tho much, JC. I'm not going to have anything more to do with Roy, I promithe."

JC laid down on his back and looked up at the moon, the rays of which shone on his thick blonde hair, "As the moon circles the earth and the earth circles the sun so all things change. We have had some beautiful moments together, so let's not worry about the future but enjoy the present. 'Be Here Now,'" he said, quoting from a hippy gospel of the 60s. He leaned down and kissed her tenderly.

"I don't know what I'm going to do in Florida," she said. "I hate working ath a waitreth and modelling work is tho hard to get."

"You must leave me your phone number and address. I overheard Harold and Jackie discussing some kind of business venture in the islands. There may be a position for you especially if you did a course and became qualified in business administration or something similar."

"Oooohh, do you really think tho?" she said. "I wish it were true. I'm going to apply for a college courthe as thoon as I get back." She caressed the flat of his stomach and muscular chest with her small fingers.

"Let's go in for a swim," he said. "The water's really warm." He slipped out of his jeans and pulled his T shirt over his head. "Ready?" he said and ran into the shimmering water, ending in a shallow dive. He turned around to see if she was following and splash! she dived in right beside him. They swam out together a little way and then he pulled her to him and they kissed, gently at first and then more aggressively as their passions rose.

"Oooohhhhh, 'Be Here Now,'" she repeated, "I'm going to remember this 'now' for ever," and she swam back to the shallows and waded out.

"Wait," he said and she stopped and turned, looking back at him inquisitively. He gazed at her in the moonlight. She was standing in profile, water glistening on her proud breasts and muscled thighs, and running down her belly in rivulets, forming shining pearls that clung to her downy pubescence.

He strode out of the water and they ran back, hand in hand, to their grassy cushion. They lay down and he leaned over and devoured her, she the willing supplicant, melting under his powerful lust.

After they had rested for a while they got dressed and were walking back, hand in hand, towards the bar when they heard some rustling and animated talking from behind a large bush, "Sssshhhhh," said JC into Shirley's ear and they crouched down and peeped around the side of the undergrowth to see what was going on. They must have been 50 feet away but they could just make out the dark shape of a large person being helped to lie down. Then the other person

43

turned slightly and the moon shone briefly on his face. It was Roy and his shorts were down by his ankles. They burst into giggles of laughter and then they ran down the beach as fast as their legs would carry them.

Meanwhile, back on the boat, Harold and Jackie had been dreaming of a new life in the islands. As the martini jug had slowly diminished Harold's knowledge of the stars increased: the big dipper, the little dipper, some of the astrological constellations. Then he had managed to pick out Venus and he thought it was in the constellation Aries which happened to be the sign that Harold was born under. He leaned over and whispered something in Jackie's ear.

. "You just behave yourself," she said. "You think you're some kind of teenager!"

Harold put his hand on her knee and whispered something else in her ear. She slapped his hand playfully and got up and walked down the companionway to their cabin. As she opened the door, Harold, following close behind, gave her a round smack on her ample rump. Ten minutes later they were both giggling like a couple of kids.

Love was in the air that night.

At breakfast the next morning everyone seemed to be in a good mood – except Roy, perhaps, who complained that the local kids were a nosy bunch of rascals. Harold and Jackie were chattering away about how the islands and the sea air were so rejuvenating. Roy suggested that a bloody Mary would be more likely to rejuvenate him and JC obliged by mixing a large jug.

Everyone was anticipating an exhilarating last day of sailing. It was about a three-hour sail back to the Carefree Yacht Vacations base at Roadstead. The breakfast dishes had been cleared away and the boat made ship-shape for sea. JC hoisted the anchor and they motored out of the harbour.

With 20 knots of wind JC tucked one reef in the mains'l and soon they were doing eight knots rail down, close hauled with spray flying, "She can smell the barn," said JC as *Sunfun* romped along, slicing through the waves. Every tack was performed flawlessly, with Harold and Roy handling the sheets. The last of the cold beers were being consumed at a steady rate, especially by Roy. Nobody was getting seasick.

They entered Roadstead harbour and furled the sails. Dock lines and fenders were rigged and they motored up to their slip and tied up. As soon as they were alongside, Roy stepped ashore, rather unsteadily, Heineken in hand. The manager and his wife were there to greet them. "Good to see ya again, Bill, Georgia," he said, shaking hands vigorously. "Ha, Ha, I never forget names," he explained. "Technique I learned at business school to avoid embarrassing clients. When you're introduced to someone remember something about their name so it sticks in your mind. Bill's a shortened form of Robert. Georgia's the name of an American State. Works every time," Roy was prattling on, the alcohol obviously working. Then he took two unintentional steps sideways, hicupped loudly and almost fell off the dock into the water.

Bob and Virginia turned to each other with a wink and a smile, "Well, it looks like you all had a great time. Those suntans will keep the memories alive for a few weeks. Before I forget I have a message for Mr and Mrs Mcphereson to confirm a dinner invitation from George Cleary," said Bob, giving them the number.

"We all had a wonderful time," said Harold. "JC certainly knows the islands and the best spots for evening entertainment.

"Not to forget the snorkelling and diving locations," added Jackie. She looked around for JC but he was down below. She peered into the cabin and saw

JC and Shirley in a clinch, Shirley was crying. "Mmmmmm," thought Jackie, her suspicions confirmed. She certainly couldn't blame the poor girl – JC was far more compatible than Roy.

Harold walked up to the public telephone to call the Cleary number. Yes, they'd love to join them for dinner. It was all arranged and George would pick them up at the boat at 6 p.m.

Roy disappeared to the marina bar and Shirley went into her cabin to start packing. She and Roy were due to fly out at 10 the next morning and Bob had said he'd confirm their flight reservations. Harold and Jackie's return flight was open. JC continued tidying up, coiling lines and stowing gear. This was usually the time when his guests handed him a fat envelope along with their thank yous but JC had noted that Harold and Jackie were English. His hopes were not too high.

"Don't forget to leave us your address and telephone number," said Harold to JC. "We want to keep in touch." Then just as JC had anticipated, Harold handed him an envelope, "We would like to show our appreciation for your fine service and good company."

"Thank you very much. It was my pleasure," said JC and stuffed the envelope into his pocket. He was discreet enough not to open it in front of them but was surprised and delighted to find, later on, that it contained $600. He would invite Shirley to his favourite island restaurant, the Calabash, for their last evening together. Roy would probably be legless by sundown, he thought.

2

The Acquisition

Harold and Jackie were getting their things together when there was a knock on the side of the boat. It was Bob and Virginia and they invited the Mcpheresons to join them for lunch up at the Pink Hibiscus. "How very hospitable, thank you," said Harold.

Over cold beer and curried goat, Bob was saying how pleased he was that they'd all had such a wonderful time and would they mind taking a pile of brochures with them back to England to drop off with an agent friend of theirs? Harold agreed. There's no such thing as a free lunch, he thought.

"I heard that you may be moving out here to start up a business," said Bob. The statement caught Harold by surprise, until he realised that both they and the Clearys were in the charter yacht business and probably conversed together. "Yes, we have been discussing the possibility," said Harold, and Jackie nodded smiling. She had instigated the idea.

"Well, I'll tell you right now. It's not as easy as you think," said Bob. "A quarter of new businesses started by ex-pats fail. Everything is contingent upon variables. You've got the vagaries of the American economy, the local crime scene, the weather, the hurricane season. Then there are the politicians with their permits and licenses that can be revoked on a whim. I wouldn't invest a penny of my own money in the place, too risky. You should think about it very carefully."

"Yes, always wise to weigh up the odds," said Harold. "But I like the motto of the SAS, 'He who dares wins.' Come on dear, we've got our packing to do. Thank you for lunch." He hurried Jackie away before the cynical couple dampened their previously high spirits.

At 6 p.m. on the dot, George Cleary was at the dock to pick up his guests and before long they were navigating the coast road in George's air conditioned Land Cruiser. "We're going to stop at our own little marina bar for a drink. Anne will be there and I'd like to show you our operation," said George. "We'll go up to the house for a bite to eat afterwards. Anne managed to get some fresh grouper at the fish market."

"Mmmmm, sounds wonderful," said Jackie. "I believe one should always eat food indigenous to the locale." On they drove along the twisting, pot-holed coast road until, finally, they crested a hill and came to a well protected bay. Its name was Rum Cove and it had a small marina running along one side. At the bottom of the hill a dirt road branched off and a sign pointed to Golden Sunset Charters. Another sign nailed underneath it read The Rusty Pelican. George pulled up in front of the marina office and then led his guests along a small path to the bar. Anne came running out of the office and caught up with them.

"Welcome," she cried, "how nice of you to come. George is dying to show you around. Let me order us all some drinks. Jackie, Harold, what'll it be?" They all decided on tall, ice-cold gin and tonics and sat down at a table. The bar was simple, a half round affair with stools in front and there was a roof of palm fronds. Like most island bars it was completely open, and bottles were locked in a cupboard at night. At one side were two island style barbecues made from disused 55 gallon drums. These had been sliced in half lengthwise and then hinged along one long side – half was the base and half the lid. Four propane burners and a large stainless sink sitting on a wooden trestle made up the primitive kitchen.

One essential piece of Caribbean bar equipment that was clearly in evidence here was the boom box, a large portable radio, situated above the bottles in the middle of the bar. Someone had painted this one in the Rastafarian colours of red, yellow and green. At each end of the bar and high up under the roof, but angled down towards the customers, were the speakers.

When the drinks arrived, George and Harold strolled off down the dock, deep in conversation. "We have 10 slips here to accommodate 14 yachts that we charter," said George, pointing to the rather dilapidated finger piers that ran at right angles to a bulkhead running along the shore. "All are serviced with electricity and water and we have our own fueling station there." He pointed to the end of one of the jetties where there was a T pier with a rusty pump sitting in solitary desolation, a hose snaking this way and that, abandoned. The service outlets for fuel and water were in sad disrepair too, Harold noticed. Just then a huge cockroach ran out from a crack in the jetty, just in front of them.

"It seems as though a little renovation here and there would not be amiss," said Harold in a casual, conversational tone – not wishing to offend his host.

"Yes, you're quite right. We only lease the property and the owner doesn't want to spend the money to fix it up. In fact he expects us to refurbish the property at our expense. At the moment it's a bit of a standoff but we soldier on. We're planning on a boutique this year and a scuba station next year. A sailing school is also in the planning stages. It's all looking very positive."

"Yes," said Harold, trying to sound cheerful, "it would seem to have potential." Actually it needed a vivid imagination to see how this could ever be a thriving business.

There were five yachts tied up to the jetties at one end. Each one was a different size and type. "The rest of the fleet are out earning their keep," said George, gesturing to the empty slips. They walked back past the boat shed where there was a row of outboards on a wooden horse. Dinghies were stacked up on the grassy bank behind the shed.

They rejoined the ladies who were busy chatting away about the wonderful time they'd all had on the *Sunfun*. The Rusty Pelican was empty except for a well-oiled local who was making his amorous intentions clear with the pretty barmaid.

"Let's go on up to the house. Some fish and a glass of wine would sit well with me at the moment," said George, and Harold readily agreed. They walked up a path bordered by hibiscus and bougainvillea, through a well-manicured garden to a large, colonial style house, solidly built of local stone. The entrance way opened into a large, tiled room – a dining room and lounge with a library raised up and accessed by some steps to one side. A long kitchen ran along the back wall.

George threw open the heavy wooden shutters and invited his guests to sit. The ornate rattan chairs contrasted effectively with the green Italian tile and it was pleasantly cool.

"I hate to mix business with pleasure," said George, "but I'll come straight to the point. We have decided to sell GSC, lock, stock and barrel and move back to Bermuda. We have a large house there where Anne's ailing mother lives all alone. Anyway, the point is that as soon as we heard you were looking for a business opportunity here in Tortuga we thought, how ideal, this would suit the Mcpheresons perfectly."

Harold looked at Jackie with raised eyebrows. This was a total surprise. "You have caught me completely off balance. I thought you were planning on renovations and expansion," said Harold. "Besides we know nothing of boats and yacht chartering. We are in the hotel and restaurant business."

"It's the same thing, only the rooms are floating. It's a customer service industry," said George, convincingly.

All through dinner the conversation concerned GSC. The terms of the lease were discussed, the rent, the location and much more. Later on in the week they could go over the figures. Harold and Jackie would be welcome to stay at Sunset Lodge, as the residence was called, if they wished.

It was all rather mind boggling; events had happened at roller coaster speed and on the drive back in the Land Cruiser, Harold explained to George that they would need time to collect their thoughts and discuss the proposition. Yes, they would definitely give it some serious thought and get back to the Clearys in a day or two. "Of course, I don't have to tell you that opportunities like this don't come up every day on Tortuga," said George as he grasped Harold's hand in a bone-crushing farewell shake.

Next morning Harold and Jackie moved into a small hotel by the beach, co-incidentally the Calabash, adjacent to Roadstead. They had said goodbye to Roy and Shirley with promises to keep in touch. Both Shirley and Roy had looked rather red-eyed and tired, and each for different reasons. In fact they looked as though they needed a good vacation. Quickly had been on hand to take them to the airport.

Over lunch Harold said to Jackie, "Last night I was really getting some mixed signals from George Cleary. One minute he was being so positive about his business plans and the next minute it was up for sale and we were the perfect new owners. It's very strange. He seems such a nice chap, not like a con man at all."

Jackie, as usual, was practical. "First we must decide if we should seriously consider this business and then we must scrutinise every facet of it." For her part she had decided already, it seemed. "It could be that they are being perfectly genuine."

"The place looks so run down and dilapidated," said Harold, shaking his head.

"But that's exactly the type of place we're looking for," said Jackie. "Something that we can build up, something where our creative expertise can grow and bear fruit."

"Oh yes, well from that point of view I quite agree. Plenty of room for improvement there. We'd probably have to employ a manager for the yacht rental operation. I must say I love the location. It'll all come down to the figures." Harold started warming to the idea.

During the next two days little else was spoken of or discussed except GSC and it was the afternoon of the next day, when Jackie was walking around the botanical gardens with Mrs Clement-Jones, that the subject of yachting came up and Jackie was immediately able to steer the conversation to Golden Sunset Charters and the Clearys. "Lovely people and great friends of ours," said the governor's wife. "They've always had an excellent reputation and they have a wonderful location. I believe they're a bit strapped financially though, just between you and me. They pay a huge rent to that old miser, Hodge, and he refuses to maintain the property. At least that's the scuttlebutt."

"Confidentially, Harold and I are thinking of buying the business," said Jackie, confidently. "Can you think of any reason why we shouldn't?"

"Really!" said Mrs Clement-Jones, surprised. "I know that George and Anne often talk of returning to Bermuda but I didn't know they were seriously offering their business for sale. I don't know much about the yacht chartering business but the integrity of the Clearys, to my knowledge, is without question. Socially they will be a great loss to the island, but of course you will be here to replace them."

The two ladies continued their stroll round the grounds of the botanical gardens, the governor's wife proving to be very knowledgeable about tropical fruit trees. One of her hobbies was making chutney and she had donated six mango saplings to the gardens, specially flown up from Trinidad.

Later they were comfortably seated in the drawing room of the official residence, enjoying afternoon tea. A maid, clad in black dress with white frilly apron, was hovering over them with a plate of fairy cakes. "May I refill your cup, madam?" she said to Jackie, holding the long spouted, silver tea pot.

"Yes, you may indeed," said Jackie. "A most refreshing cup of tea."

"Darjeeling," said Margaret. They were on first name terms now. "My husband insists on the best. Thank you, May," she said, turning to the maid. "You may leave us now, we'll look after ourselves."

"Yes, madam," said the maid with a little bow.

"It will be delightful if you and your husband do come to live with us here in the islands. Of course it's not quite like it used to be in the old days. I mean we don't have the same powers that we used to."

"Oh, really," said Jackie with raised eyebrows, quietly curious.

"Yes, it is the policy of the British government to allow the island to develop its own democratically elected council to govern the islands by means of district representatives. My husband, as the Queen's representative, has no say in the day to day running of the territory. Her Majesty's government dictates the island's constitution and we do our best to see that it is adhered to but we have no say in internal policy. Sometimes grave injustices are brought to our attention by angry expatriates and we are powerless to do anything. We are advised to maintain a hands off policy when it comes to internal affairs. We often advise expats with problems, on an informal basis, and my husband has a working relationship with some of the ministers. On the other hand, some of them hate him and try to avoid him at all costs. It can be difficult.

"I don't wish to alarm you," continued Margaret with a smile. "Most problems are overcome with patience and diplomacy. We must never forget that the islanders were victims of cruel servitude for many generations. Now that they hold the reins of power it is only natural that they enact laws that benefit themselves. It is unfortunate that corruption sometimes prevails but that is a fact of life the world over and that it exists here is perhaps more understandable since they were denied opportunity, money and power for so long."

"Harold will not stand for any bribery," said Jackie.

"Once in Malaya an argument with a minor government official almost led to a duel. I can see that I shall have to deal with any government paperwork involved with our business acquisition. Harold has a short fuse when it comes to dealing with bureaucrats."

"I'm quite sure everything will work out perfectly," said Margaret, getting up. "I do hope your arrangements work out satisfactorily with the Clearys."

Jackie got up. The cue that tea time was over had been given. "Thank you so much for the afternoon and for showing me around the gardens. I thoroughly enjoyed it," said Jackie honestly.

"My pleasure entirely. Do give my kindest regards to your husband. We must get together again soon." They were both standing by the front door of the residence. "I have arranged a lift home for you," said Margaret, gesturing towards an official-looking, shiny black car. The chauffeur-driven three-litre Rover was waiting in the driveway with a Union Jack flying from the bonnet. Jackie had never felt so grand as she was driven back to the Calabash.

When Jackie entered their breezy seaside bedroom Harold was sitting at a table covered in papers with columns of figures, balance sheets, statements and budgets. He turned to Jackie. "All looks in order with the books but the problem with the business lies in the rent. It's just too high. I've located an accountant from the Yellow Pages and will get a second opinion. How was your afternoon at the botanical gardens?"

"I had a very pleasant afternoon and Mrs Clement-Jones was most hospitable. She even arranged a lift home for me in the official car." Jackie didn't mention anything about the rather worrying hints of corruption in the local government.

"I've spent nearly two days going over these figures, and it seems that although we could live off the business, healthy profits are all but impossible with such huge overheads. Then I thought . . . What if we could re-model the old colonial lodge that the Clearys use for their home into a country style inn, then the possibilities would be limitless."

"That is a brain wave, Harold my darling. There could be elegant chandeliers, four poster beds, sunken bath tubs in the rooms. Then an open air dining area overlooking the bay, with flowers, lots of flowers. I can see it all in my mind's eye." She clasped her hands together, her eyes skyward.

"Yes, the idea has possibilities. We must talk with the Clearys and negotiate a price. First, though, we should see old Mr Hodge and discuss the lease agreement and the rent. The huge amounts paid by the Clearys would only be justified if the place was maintained in tip-top condition at all times."

They made an appointment to see Hodge and to their surprise the old man was not interested in discussing maintenance, leases or any other business proposal except outright sale of the property, freehold. He was a thin, stooping man and his African hair was completely white.

"What sort of price did you have in mind?" asked Harold.

"1.8 million in U.S. dollars," replied the old man. "You'll have to deal with my lawyer regarding all the details." It was a lot of money but for the size of the waterfront property with all the buildings and docks it did not seem extortionate. The problem was that it was more than the Mcpheresons had planned to invest in the islands and they still hadn't got a price from the Clearys.

The next day Harold contacted the architect, Alan Stanborg, and together they drove down to GSC to examine the buildings and docks. Harold also took the inventory of the offices, boat shed, the Rusty Pelican and Sunset Lodge.

It turned out that the Clearys wanted $250,000 for the business which included that dubious commodity termed "goodwill." The charter contracts for the yachts in the fleet would all be turned over to the new owners without any trouble, according to George. Harold, after tallying the stock and accepting a large chunk for improvements and goodwill, offered $150,000 and they finally settled, fairly amicably, on $200,000 with the proviso that the property purchase went through without a hitch and that all the necessary permits and licenses were granted by the government.

Next Harold made an appointment with a Mr A. Reephoff of Hannover, Bigsum, Reephoff and Blarney, a local firm of solicitors. Harold took an immediate disliking to Reephoff. He had shifty eyes that never looked you squarely in the face and at the corner of his mouth was an intermittent twitch. His accent was east European and he said yah instead of yes. Someone had once said that the Caribbean was a sunny place for shady people and Reephoff brought the phrase immediately to Harold's mind. Reephoff was handling the sale of the Hodge property and had "no authority whatsoever to make any offers." After a lengthy discussion Harold stood his ground and made a formal offer of 1.5 million U.S. dollars and even though it would be "rather embarrassing" for Reephoff to present such an offer he finally agreed to do so, and said he would be in touch.

It was a week since they had stepped ashore from the *Sunfun* and they were immersed in negotiations that far exceeded their original plans for a small island enterprise. They were not despondent, however; in fact they were full of optimism. Jackie, though, was worried about the financial side.

"The Coach and Horses is worth a million in sterling at least," said Harold confidently, "and when it is offered for sale, which will be as soon as we return to England, the stables will not be included. They can be converted into a cottage for our use later or for rental."

"Harold, the Coach and Horses is still forty per cent mortgaged. Even if we use our savings we'll still need a sizable loan. We'll be paying the bank for years." Jackie said, shaking her head with a forlorn expression.

"There is something in what you say," said Harold, "and I do not intend overextending ourselves. In fact I have an idea. We could ask Roy if he would be interested in joining our venture. He would be perfect, what with his construction knowledge and 'Mr Fix It' hardware outlets in Florida. There can be no doubt that he has the available funds."

"But his ideas for our project might not be identical with ours. He's such a coarse man," she said, making a face. "I can imagine him turning the Rusty Pelican into a brothel with him directing the traffic."

"Well, that is a problem that will not materialise if we offer him a minor shareholding in a private company – say one third. That way our votes on any major decisions outweigh his – providing that we both see eye to eye."

"First you must see if he's interested before we go any further," said Jackie, somewhat mollified.

As it turned out Roy was immediately interested in the proposition. He loved the Caribbean and its laid-back lifestyle and when the accountant had sent him projections for the next five years there had been no hesitation. Jackie rather cynically suggested that he would probably love to have a means of hiding money in the islands for tax avoidance purposes and although Harold didn't say anything he wondered privately if perhaps she wasn't right.

Reephoff, the solicitor, had contacted Harold at the Calabash and informed him that Mr Hodge had requested a meeting in the lawyers' offices the next morning. Harold hardly slept that night. He knew that in the morning he would have a fight on his hands and that large sums of money were at stake. But he would not be squeezed. He could walk away from the whole thing tomorrow, he told himself.

That morning Harold drank two cups of strong black coffee and decided to walk the mile or so to the lawyers' office. The route took him along The Waterfront of Roadstead and the early morning breeze and the view of the yachts swinging to their anchors put him in a good mood. The brass plaque which read Hannover, Bigsum, Reephoff and Blarney, Solicitors had been recently polished and shone brightly in the morning sun. Harold walked in and a receptionist smiled pearly white teeth at him through purple lipstick. She ushered him into an inner office.

"Goot mornink," said Reephoff standing, and the three others in the office stood as well. Mr Hodge was there looking very formal in a rumpled black suit that smelled of moth balls. A well-built black lady was introduced as Sonia Hodge, and Talbot Winston, a handsome young man who Harold thought he knew but couldn't quite place, shook hands but didn't smile.

"Meester Odge ees very pleased wiz your offer," said Reephoff without preamble, "but woult like to counter your offer with a reduced price of 1.65 million. A reasonable compromise – don't you agree?"

"I'm afraid my absolute best offer is 1.5 million," said Harold adamantly.

Reephoff leaned over and whispered into Hodge's ear, "I advise you not to budge on your new price." The lawyer turned and smiled a yellow-toothed grin at Harold.

It occurred to Harold that Reephoff was in this for a sizable commission and the bigger the price, the larger would be the lawyer's share. "The property requires considerable repairs and renovation. I have an estimate from the architect," said Harold, pulling a sheaf of papers from his briefcase.

Reephoff was not prepared for such solid bargaining on Harold's part. He scanned the papers briefly and saw that the figure on the bottom line was $300,000. Exactly the amount that made up the difference between the asking price and the offered price. He handed the papers over to old Mr Hodge, who took out a pair of rather worn reading glasses from a waistcoat pocket. But it was obvious that the old man had difficulty understanding the documents and he said, "What do you suggest, Reephoff? I am retaining you for your professional advice here."

The lawyer was visibly irate. "Stant your grount. Don't put up wiz any treeckery. Your original asking price eez very fair."

Harold got up. "I wish you all a very good morning," he said, "and I'm sorry to have wasted everyone's time." He was at the door when old man Hodge jumped up, more sprightly than one would have imagined.

"Don't be too hasty here," he said. "Perhaps we can still reach a compromise."

"I'm not really interested in compromises," said Harold, "I've made my best offer. But what do you have in mind?"

"I am almost ready to agree to your offer but on one condition. My daughter Sonia," and he gestured to the lady sitting next to him, "wishes to lease the Rusty Pelican and a small piece of land adjacent for a boutique. Of course she would pay a reasonable rent."

Harold could sense that he almost had the property of his dreams but he had no intention of leasing what he thought would be two very lucrative parts of his business. But he had to appease the old man and his daughter. "It is too early for me to make decisions on leasing arrangements such as these but I can promise you this: I will be needing a business manager to handle all retail outlets. That will include the inn, restaurant, bar, shop and watersports. This will be a very responsible position with a good salary, expenses and bonus scheme. If Miss Hodge has the qualifications, she will be at the top of the list for consideration for the position." Harold spoke with authority, as if he already owned the business. Sonia Hodge beamed with delight and looked at her father, who was not smiling. Harold felt that this was one of those pivotal moments that happens on only a few occasions in a lifetime. Then, slowly the old man smiled, got up and shook Harold's hand.

"You drive a hard bargain, young man," said Hodge. "But I think you will make a success of the business. Be sure of one thing, though. I shall be expecting you to keep your word regarding my daughter's employment. She not only has a degree in business administration from the London School of Economics but she also knows the islands, their people and the ins and outs of island politics. She will be a valuable asset to you."

Harold nodded and smiled at the white-haired islander. He hadn't been called a "young man" for a very long time and he admired the concern the old man had for the welfare of his daughter.

Hodge turned to Reephoff. "Have all the documents prepared and we'll sign right away."

"There will be a deposit of five per cent of the sale price payable immediately upon signing. This is to show good faith and, of course, is deducted from the sale price. The balance of the funds must be paid within 90 days," said Reephoff. Harold managed to get the time period extended to 120 days. He needed a little more breathing room. Only Reephoff twitched and muttered something under his breath.

In less than an hour all the paperwork was signed and sealed and Talbot Winston, thus far silent, witnessed the signing of all the documents. Sonia handed Harold a folder. "Here is my CV, references and particulars," she said with a smile. "I am looking forward to working with you."

Mmmm, forthright and forceful, thought Harold. He liked her attitude already.

It was lunchtime when they departed the lawyers' offices. Only old man Hodge hung back and Harold overheard him berating the lawyer. "Your lack of diplomacy almost cost me that sale," shouted Hodge. "Our future business is terminated. Have the files ready by morning." Then the door slammed and he heard no more.

Harold was in a jaunty mood as he walked back along The Waterfront. Things could not have gone more smoothly. He almost felt he belonged to the island community already. After all he had just signed a cheque for $75,000.

Back at the Calabash, Harold notified Roy by fax and told him the news. Then he booked the best table in the restaurant and told the head waiter to put a bottle of Dom Perignon on ice. When Jackie heard the good news she was ecstatic and that night they celebrated in grand style.

They were both keen to get back to England to sell their property there and make all the necessary arrangements for their move to the islands. Before they left they had to put in applications for a business license and work permits to the labour office, "a mere formality" according to Reephoff. Although they had decided to retain the name Golden Sunset Charters,

"Limited" would now be added at the end. GSC would be a limited liability company.

It was three days before they were due to leave when a message was handed to them at the front desk of the hotel. Mr and Mrs Mcphereson were cordially invited to attend a meeting with the chief minister, Mr Lionel Bradshaw at the Administration Building, 9 a.m. prompt. the next morning. It must be a formal welcoming, they thought. After all, their business would be a major revenue earner for the islands.

The taxi pulled up in front of the Administration Building at five to nine, and a uniformed policeman opened the front door of the imposing building and directed them up to the top floor where the chief minister's office occupied four large rooms.

A pretty, well dressed secretary looked up from an empty desk as they entered the reception area. "We have an appointment with the chief minister at 9 a.m.," said Harold, who was smartly dressed in his blue blazer, regimental tie and pressed, grey flannels "Mr and Mrs Mcphereson."

"Yes," she said, "he's expecting you. Follow me." She led them down a corridor to an ornate mahogany door. The skirt of her business suit was so tight and the pins of her high heels so high that she had difficulty walking, it seemed. But the conspicuous wiggle of her bottom was not lost on Harold. She knocked on the door and opened it and ushered them in. Chief Minister Lionel Bradshaw got up from behind a huge polished desk and came round to greet them.

"Good morning, good morning. How nice of you to come," said the chief minister, beaming. He extended his hand and after the initial pleasantries, invited them to sit. Harold noticed that they had been offered rather uncomfortable plastic office chairs and that the chief minister's desk and throne-like armchair were positioned on a dais some 12 inches higher than the rest of the room. Bradshaw's interviewees would be looked down upon. Behind the desk three large picture windows looked out over the harbour of Roadstead.

The chief minister steepled his arms and leaned forward. "I would like to take this opportunity, on behalf of the government of the Caribbee Islands and its people, to welcome you to our territory and to wish you every success in your new venture." His voice was deep and resonant. "These islands have had a steadily increasing economy for the past 30 years, mostly thanks to the tourist sector, of which a large part involves yachting. My government and I support the yachting industry in many ways, with tax incentives and free advertising provided by my tourist board. For these reasons, your business has an excellent chance of thriving.

"Now, apart from being chief minister with overall control of government, my other portfolio is minister of trade and labour, and although my office normally processes business licenses. I take great pleasure in personally seeing to the more important applications. Now, you have made application for a business license for GSC, or more properly, Golden Sunset Charters and that is fine but you will also require one for the Rusty Pelican, the watersports operation, the boutique and the hotel. You are planning a small hotel, aren't you?"

Harold looked at Jackie in disbelief. They couldn't believe their ears – they had only just thought of the idea a few days ago. "Well, yes," said Harold, "but we thought that all the spin-off businesses would come under the same umbrella. We plan on incorporating GSC as a limited liability company."

"Good! Excellent!" replied Bradshaw, smiling.

"Now, let me explain. In the old days we used to allow business licenses to cover all manner of different enterprises but the system was abused. We found a boutique owner selling paint to the marine industry. A restaurant owner in Tortuga opened a beach bar at Cooper Island. It just got out of hand so we had to change the system and now individual licenses are required. Of course the government got the blame, as usual. There is a saving grace though and that is a hotel business license includes a bar and restaurant as long as they are under the same roof or within very close proximity." Harold nodded but looked worried. "Now, if you'd be good enough to complete these four other applications we can proceed. Immediate payment will be required for your licenses – $1,500 each for the hotel and GSC, and $1,000 each for the other three. $6,000 in total and make the cheque out to 'The Treasury.' Then, of course, there will be the donation."

"The donation?" said Harold, completely non-plussed.

"Yes," said the chief minister. "We expect all of our new friends who wish to reside with us here in the islands to make a small donation to the church – the All Saints Baptist Church."

He buzzed an intercom on his desk and a female voice said, "Yes, Chief Minister."

"Send in Mr Winston, please." Almost immediately Talbot Winston walked in from an adjacent room. The chief minister said, "I believe you are already acquainted with my general assistant, Mr Winston. Please excuse me." Bradshaw walked quickly from the room, closing the door behind him. Harold's memory came flooding back. Talbot Winston had sat with them at the gourmet evening at the Royal Palms, "a spy for the chief minister," someone had said. Then he had been at the lawyers' office to witness the signing over of

Hodge's property. So that was how Bradshaw had become privy to all their business dealings.

Winston didn't smile but said, "I am here to collect your donation of $10,000 for the church."

Harold jumped up out of his chair. "How much?" he said, "I don't believe I heard you correctly."

"10,000 in U.S. dollars," said Winston curtly.

Harold started to go red. "I shall give you $200 for the church, young man, and you will be grateful for it. A donation is a voluntary gift, in case you didn't know the meaning of the word."

Winston sighed. "That is a shame, now all these applications will gather dust in the basement. Without business licenses you cannot apply for work permits or immigration approval. What a waste."

Harold's face went from red to purple and little beads of sweat glistened on his forehead. "This is nothing less than out and out bribery! I will not pay you a penny and you can keep your permits and your damn islands." He was shaking with rage.

Winston continued languidly. He was sitting on the corner of the large desk with one leg swinging. "Of course, the $75,000 deposit for the Hodge place is non-refundable."

Harold spluttered something unintelligible and Jackie thought he was going to have a heart attack. She went over and whispered in his ear. "We must pay it, Harold. You can write a cheque and then cancel it later after we've taken advice from a lawyer." Harold calmed visibly but was still breathing heavily.

"Please bring us some water, Mr Winston. This request for a 'donation' has come as something of a surprise." Jackie had always been the diplomatic type, with patience being one of her main virtues. Winston buzzed the secretary and made the request and she dutifully brought three glasses, a jug of cold water and a bottle of sparkling Perrier.

By the time Harold had finished a refreshing drink he had stopped shaking. "And to whom shall I make out the cheque for this 'donation'?" said Harold, accentuating the word donation.

"Mr Lionel Bradshaw," said Winston without much interest.

"But I thought this was a donation to the church?" said Harold, beginning to boil up again.

"Oh yes, you're quite correct," said Winston, "but you see, Mr Bradshaw is a member of the cloth. He was ordained many years ago and still gives a sermon at the All Saints Baptist Church at Christmas here in Roadstead."

Harold was becoming confused. He signed the cheque and handed it over. "Thank you," said Winston, with a smile that was more like a sneer. He buzzed the intercom, and without waiting for a reply, walked nonchalantly from the room through the same door he had entered.

The secretary came in. "The chief minister has been called away to a meeting and sends his apologies. He asked me to tell you that your paperwork will be processed in all haste and thanks you for your co-operation." She ushered them out.

As Harold and Jackie walked down the steps of the government building, Harold breathed in deep lungfulls of air. It was a relief to be out in the Caribbean tradewind breezes again. He felt as though he had just been rescued from a snake pit. He had expected to part with not more than $2,000. Instead he was $16,000 poorer.

They decided to walk over to the Pink Hibiscus for large gin and tonics and Harold immediately called Roger Clement-Jones for an appointment and was pleased that the governor could see them that afternoon. After another round, they ordered conch roti for lunch and after the spicy, curry dish had been consumed they felt better.

It was 3 p.m. and they were sitting in Roger Clement-Jones's office at Government House. The governor sat listening patiently as Harold told him the whole story. When he got to the part about the $10,000, the governor raised his eyebrows in surprise. "We have known about this donation business for some time, but the amounts are generally much less. Of course, with such a valuable property, they must have just decided to stick it to you. You do realise that you got the business and the property for a bargain, don't you? I have a feeling that those 'in the know' were envious of your good deal and would have been happy if you had refused to pay the donation and subsequently lost your new acquisition."

"Well," said Harold, "I don't believe that justifies the chief minister's office or vindicates the chief minister. Do you have any knowledge of what happens to the money?"

"Unfortunately, we have no way of knowing exactly, but we do know that at weddings and funerals, he provides all the flowers and he also provides caskets and gravestones for parishioners who can't afford their own. It's a clever way of getting votes at election time.

"Officially, there is nothing we can do about it because no wrong can be seen to have been done. As Winston said, if you had declined to pay the donation, your business applications would never have been processed. 'In the pipeline' is a favourite phrase here, and then things can 'get lost.' After your 120 days were up to complete the payment on the property, you would forfeit it and it would go back to Hodge. You made a smart decision to pay.

"The government here is very cunning, especially in

the wording of its laws. There is always a loophole that allows the government to win. For instance, there is a subsection, in fact subsection 43A, in the immigration laws that states that 'if a person appears undesirable in temperament or manner or by way of appearance, long hair or dreadlocks he/she may be denied admission into the territory or be summarily extradited if already residing here.' That means that the immigration department can arbitrarily kick out anyone it feels like at any time, except citizens, of course. This is very discriminatory, yet it remains as part of the law of this territory. About half of the population of this country are temporary residents and this one law makes them very uneasy. It says, in effect, that Jesus Christ would be denied entry!

"I have been trying to get the government to debate this question in council for the last twelve months but although it's put on the agenda it always gets shelved. They like to have this safety valve of being able to kick out anyone they don't like. Then of course they quote the low crime rate, low drug abuse statistics, increasing tourism and the whole thing is forgotten.

"As far as your own recent nasty experience is concerned, you should forget it and put it behind you. You have made an excellent start to your future in the islands and you will never be asked to make further 'donations.' As far as I know, it is only ever asked for at the initial application interview. However, I will recommend an excellent fellow for you to see and perhaps do business with in case of future altercations. His name is Mike Broadrite. He's been in the islands for nearly 20 years and is a member of the Caribbean Bar Association. He's ex-Cambridge and did his articles with a prestigious London firm in the 50s. He sailed out here on his father's yacht in the mid 70s and decided to stay. He was instrumental in solving a lot of the island's early legal problems – even advised Reagan on the Grenada situation some 15 years ago. Broadrite is a highly respected lawyer and sometimes plays golf with Bradshaw. You could do no better than to affiliate yourself with him." Clement-Jones opened a desk drawer and handed Harold a business card.

"Thank you very much for your valuable time and sound advice," said Harold, getting up, "and on such short notice. It makes me feel much better knowing that perhaps some of the 'donation' money goes to charity."

"Yes, you have been very understanding and helpful. Please give our regards to Margaret," said Jackie, silently relieved now that Harold had been somewhat mollified. Miss Primby, the governor's aide, showed them out.

Back at the Calabash they decided to have a dip in the pool, and that evening at dinner they were both talking animatedly about their new yachting resort. Harold had just ordered two large planter's punches when he noticed JC walking through the restaurant towards the bar. They seemed to lock eyes at about the same time and JC came over with a wide grin. He was wearing his island uniform: blue jeans, Jimmy Buffet T-shirt and baseball cap on backwards. "Congratulations," he said. "Hey, you don't have to be crazy to move here, but it helps." They all laughed. The coconut telegraph had obviously spread the news. "The only thing that moves fast on this island is gossip," he said, and they all nodded.

Harold turned to face JC. "Jackie and I will be leaving for the U.K. the day after tomorrow, but when we return, around the beginning of November, we will be looking for an operations manager for our charter boats. Later on I plan to have one or two large catamarans in the fleet with full time crews. One way or another, I'll have a good position for you."

JC's mind started racing. If he was offered a full-time crew position on a large catamaran then he would need a hostess/cook. Shirley loved the water and the snorkelling but he didn't know if she could cook – and then there was the sea-sickness problem. He had missed her so much since she had left, and he knew that she would jump at the chance of returning to the islands. Catamarans were relatively stable so perhaps she wouldn't get sick. As far as the cooking went – well, the tourists that came to the Caribbee Islands were mostly Americans and anybody could fix a hamburger or hot dog or barbecue a steak. "I'm interested already," he said. "Initially I can help you organize the fleet and then later I would be most interested in running a catamaran." He would call Shirley right away and suggest she take cooking lessons.

"Excellent," said Harold. "Well, keep in touch." They said goodbye and Harold reflected on his business progress. He felt that he was getting a solid nucleus of people behind him. Jackie was his 'number 1,' of course, with her qualifications and experience in hotel and catering. She would take control of the Sunset Lodge. Sonia Hodge would be in charge of business and administration. Roy would be responsible for rebuilding and remodelling, and JC could take charge of the small charter fleet. Or could he? thought Harold, maybe he was too young, a little irresponsible. Then he would take the governor's advice and make Mike Broadrite the company's lawyer. That reminded him – he needed to see Broadrite the next day to give him all the papers for the company's incorporation as well as the land title and deeds.

The next morning Jackie phoned the Clearys and invited them to dinner at the Calabash. Harold made an afternoon appointment with Mike Broadrite and spent a total of three and a half hours with the distinguished lawyer. He too was rather surprised at the amount of Harold's 'donation' and confirmed everything the governor had said. "The islanders regard Bradshaw as a kind of modern-day Robin Hood. It is true that he does help the poor, elderly and underprivileged – mainly in his own district, though, where he needs the votes for re-election." They talked on all subjects of island life and politics and Mike agreed to keep an eye on GSC and hire two security personnel to watch the property in the Mcpheresons' absence.

The Clearys met Harold and Jackie at the bar of the Calabash restaurant that evening. The Mcpheresons had expected it to be a convivial, farewell dinner party. But right from the beginning Harold could tell that George had something on his mind. During the meal it transpired that the Clearys had been short of cash and had offered their business for sale because they had no possibility of raising the funds needed to carry out the necessary improvements. They could move back to Bermuda but employment for George could be a problem there – at 55 years of age he was no spring chicken. For the last 15 years George had been involved with yachts and the charter yacht industry. He knew the business inside out. But there was no yacht chartering in Bermuda. Things could be difficult now with all this uncertainty.

Finally Harold said, with a smile, "I'll be looking for an experienced operations manager as soon as we return and the boutique will need a manageress. Do you know anyone on the island who might be interested?"

"Thank you," said George and Anne, with nods and smiles and there was a collective, tangible sigh of relief. George whispered something into the waiter's ear and when the dessert arrived – coconut ice cream with chunks of fresh pineapple, drizzled with dark rum – a bottle of ice-cold Charles Hiedseick accompanied it. When it was poured, Harold stood up, and squeezing Jackie's hand, said, "To Golden Sunset Charters and prosperity!" Everyone drank.

3

The Renovations

Roy had received a fax from the Mcpheresons saying that the plans for the re-modelling of Sunset Lodge had been completed by Stanborg, the architect. Would Roy fly down right away and organize a construction crew? They wanted to be operational by December, when the season started, and it was already the end of September. The new lodge would have eight self-contained suites – Harold and Jackie would occupy one of them, they hoped, when they returned in about six weeks.

Roy arrived at the Tortuga airport with an old hold-all stuffed with clothes, three trunks full of assorted tools, pumps, valves and odd yacht fittings. With him was a female companion whose black mascara eyes, pink fluorescent lipstick and tousled blonde hair gave her the look of a lady of the night. She was approaching middle age and was slightly overweight. Her name was Betty and she was a travel agent. Besides being able to get both of them discount air fares, Roy hoped that she would book sailing vacations and rooms at the Sunset Lodge.

The immigration desk was giving them a thorough interrogation until Roy showed them a fax that proved he was a director of GSC. Betty was almost refused permission to enter but was finally allowed in as a tourist when she produced $2,000 in traveller's cheques and a return ticket. A fat immigration officer waved them through the barrier with surly impatience. They felt most unwelcome.

"Don't worry," said Roy to Betty, as they were bumping along the pot-holed road towards the Calabash Hotel in Roadstead, "Most of the islanders are friendly but the immigration officials have so much power it goes to their heads – that, coupled with a lack of education and public relations training turns them into neo-nazis."

Quickly, their driver, laughed. As usual he was driving slowly and deliberately so as to avoid the holes. "You seem to know the Caribbee Islands well," he said. "Yes it true. Dey do what dey want an' if dey does kick you out, ain't nuttin you can do 'bout it."

Roy explained that he had recently been down to the islands for a week of sailing and had got to know the place and really enjoyed it. Betty was in awe of the beauty of the islands and the sea, as they twisted and turned along the way to their hotel.

Quickly was saying that the island's immigration officials used to be very casual but so many criminals and drug traffickers were coming in that they were tightening up their procedures. All of a sudden the front of the mini-bus jolted into a big pot-hole. "Lawd amighty," exclaimed Quickly. "It time de govmint tightened up de road buildin' procedures too. Dey spen half o' deir time puttin' in speed bumps when de whole islan' one big speed bump!"

They arrived at the Calabash and checked in as Roy and Betty Blake and by that evening the whole place was buzzing with the news that Roy was the new owner of GSC.

In the morning Roy gave Mike Broadrite a call and introduced himself on behalf of Harold Mcphereson and Golden Sunset Charters. He asked him if he knew of a good man who could "head up a small construction crew." As it happened, Broadrite knew just the man, "an excellent and sober fellow," Elroy Stevens, hailing from Grenada.

Before Roy could hire a construction gang he had to make sure his shipment had arrived at the commercial port. After confirming by phone that indeed there was a container waiting for him, he went over there to check his consignment and pay the modest import dues. He had dealt with the export order himself, making sure that none of it went through the books. There were nine turquoise-blue, porcelain bathtubs with matching wash basins, toilets and bidets accompanied by gold-plated taps and shower heads. There were 4 cubic meters of Italian marble tile, 6 cubic meters of Venezuelan patio tile, door frames, ceiling fans, light fittings – the list went on and on. Perhaps the bulkiest items were the four poster bed replicas complete with box spring mattresses. There were eight of them and even disassembled they took up a lot of room. Finally there was a half-ton pickup truck with a diesel powered, industrial cement mixer strapped in the back. This had come separately as deck cargo.

Everything had arrived safely and undamaged and Roy was elated. The whole shipment, except for the truck, had been purchased through his company, "Mr Fix It" in Florida, and was worth close to $25,000 even after a good discount had been allowed to Golden Sunset Charters Ltd. When he was finally paid by GSC, he would put the funds into a personal account in the islands and as far as "Mr Fix It" was concerned, the merchandise was still in stock in the warehouse in Florida. Roy figured he would save a fortune in taxes this way.

He made arrangements for the container to be trucked over to the property in Rum Cove the next day and then drove back to the hotel in the pick up truck.

Betty was down by the pool soaking up the sun. Roy went up to their room for a quick rinse and they met at the poolside bar for lunch. They ordered hamburgers and fries and cold Heineken beer. While they were waiting, Roy excused himself and went off to make a phone call to Elroy Stevens. Yes, he was available and he even knew the Golden Sunset Charters property – he had built the Rusty Pelican. Roy explained that he thought he needed a mason, a plasterer – both of whom, he hoped, could lay tile – a plumber and a carpenter. Yes, they could have a meeting at GSC that afternoon at 3 p.m. Roy then called Alan Stanborg and asked if he could join them and it just happened that Alan would be passing by on his way back from a field trip that very afternoon.

Lunch had just arrived when Roy rejoined Betty at the table. She was on her second cold Heineken. "How do you like my new sarong?" she said, twirling around and showing off the tropical printed fabric tied low on her hips.

"Very sexy," he said. "You seem to be getting into the island swing of things. Where did you buy it?"

"Over there, in the boutique," she said, pointing. "I just love it here. It's so relaxing by the pool." She let out a sigh of satisfaction. Roy could understand that she was enjoying herself. A beautiful pool under the palm trees, the warm Caribbean sun, cocktails at the click of her finger, and a comfortable lounge chair to lie on. He wondered whether he had made the right decision when he had offered to pay for it all.

"I have a meeting at three," he said. "You stay here and relax and recover from the flight and I'll show you around the island tomorrow."

"Thanks Roy. You're a doll," she said, and, mouth full of hamburger, kissed him on the cheek. Roy, in fact, was anything but a doll, but he looked more comfortable dressed as a construction boss than he did as a tourist. His huge frame was clothed in long, fawn coloured pants and a blue work shirt and his craggy, nut brown face was topped with a red baseball cap, the peak of which was decorated with a naval style gold leaf.

He got into his truck and drove out of the hotel parking lot on the wrong side of the road. A delivery van came at him fast, head on with horn blaring, swerved and missed him by inches, the driver waving his hand furiously and shouting, "Mudderscunnnn," the epithet becoming lost in the breeze as the van disappeared in a cloud of dust. Roy suddenly realised that not only was he on the wrong side of the road, that he didn't have a driver's license or insurance. He parked the truck and took a cab.

The taxi crested the same hill that offered the beautiful view that had so inspired Harold and Jackie. "Dat's Rum Cove," said the driver, "and dat's Golden Sunset Charters." He pointed to the marina off in the distance. They drove down the hill, took the fork to the right and pulled up in front of the marina office. A security guard ambled over.

"De place all close up. Dey ain plannin' on openin'

up till de season. Sometime in December," said the guard.

Roy got out of the cab. "I'm one of the owners of GSC," he said, shaking hands with the guard, "I'm meeting an architect and a Mr Elroy Stevens here at 3 p.m. Please tell them to meet me up at the lodge and I'll need the keys to get in. In the meantime, I'm going to inspect the property."

"Oh, yes sir, very good sir," the man handed over three keys and walked back to his chair outside the office.

Some kind of security guard thought Roy, disgustedly. Didn't even ask for any ID. He wandered past the boat shed and the Rusty Pelican, noting that they seemed to be in good condition. He walked out along the docks and was soon taking copious notes – this was where most of the work was needed. He was leaning over the edge inspecting the concrete support pilings when he heard a whistle. He walked up the path to the lodge and saw Stanborg and Stevens waiting for him.

After cordial introductions they moved across to a patio table and the architect spread out the plans. "We'll have to extend the foundations here and here and here," he said, pointing at the plans and then walking over to the actual location. "Then the retaining wall will be built up to the level we're standing on and the whole area filled. When it's settled we can concrete the surface and then the tiles can be laid." He went on explaining details to Elroy who looked on and asked appropriate questions when he felt he didn't understand something.

They moved inside the building and discussed the remodelling there. The sunken bathtubs looked good on paper, but Elroy doubted that the construction suggested by the drawings would be practical. He suggested that each suite be built on two levels, then there would be room to inlay the bathtub on the upper level. Alan agreed and would make the necessary changes to the drawings.

It was a useful meeting and Roy had a chance to discuss with Elroy his requirements: sand, gravel, bags of cement, plywood, concrete block and so on. "What about the men," asked Roy, "can you round up a good team?"

"Yeh," said Elroy, "I got some good men. An' don' worry 'bout one bein a plasterer, one bein' a mason an' all dat. Dung here in de islands we don' have unions. My men can put deir hans to mos' any job. Shaw, some does specialise in stone wuk and some is only carpenters but mos' o' de time we switch arung to get de job done."

Roy was impressed with this philosophy. "When can you start?" he said.

"We can start Monday mornin.' Hours will be 7 till 4 wid a hour for lunch, five days a week."

"Good," said Roy, "I'll be here at seven on Monday morning to meet the men." He shook Elroy's hand, strolled down to the marina office and cadged a ride back to the hotel with Alan Stanborg.

"You've got a great property there," said Stanborg. "Lovely old colonial building, too. It was built as a plantation great house in the early nineteenth century and I believe it had major renovations around the 1920s. You're very lucky to get it. No one knew it was for sale."

"Well, I'm only a minor shareholder in the business, but everyone's been saying the same thing. I threw in my bit sight unseen. Just lucky, I guess."

When Roy got back to the Calabash the sun was almost setting. He went straight to his room. There was a note from Betty, "Gone to the Pink Hibiscus for happy hour." That wasn't unusual, he thought – she was a free spirit. He was bone tired. He lay down on the bed, only just managing to shake off his boots, and was asleep in seconds.

The sun was streaming in through the window when he awoke next morning. It was 8:30 and suddenly he realised that Betty wasn't there and it didn't look as though she'd slept in the bed. Then he remembered the note and stopped worrying so much. She'd probably met someone at the Pink Hibiscus' happy hour and then gone on to a party, and then one thing had led to another and goodness knows what might have happened. One thing was for sure, though. He wasn't going to pay for her vacation if she was going to run around with every Tom, Dick and Harry on the island.

He went into the bathroom and took a wonderfully refreshing shower. As he walked back into the bedroom the telephone rang. It was a message from the front desk. "Please meet me at Cane Bay. I will explain everything. Love Betty." Apparently he'd been in the shower when she rang.

He slipped on shorts and a cotton shirt and went down to the front desk and ordered a rental jeep for the weekend. Yes, they could provide a temporary license. The vehicle would be there in half an hour.

Roy was absolutely famished – he'd missed dinner the previous night and lunch had been a burger "on the run." He walked into the restaurant and helped himself to fruit salad, yoghurt and granola from the buffet bar, and then ordered pancakes with maple syrup and an order of bacon, sausage and eggs. He swilled down the whole meal with two large cups of coffee, burped loudly and returned to the front desk to await the arrival of his vehicle.

"Don't forget to drive on the left," said the rental

man, as Roy signed the agreement. "Have a nice weekend."

Roy was not about to make that mistake again. Yesterday he had barely escaped with his life. Driving a left hand drive vehicle on the left side of the road seemed more than a little odd, though.

He stopped at the local supermarket and bought a portable cooler. Then he bought a six-pack of beer, a bottle of tequila, a bottle of margharita mix, some plastic cups and a bag of ice cubes. He arranged the drinks carefully in the cooler and covered the whole lot with ice. He stowed the cooler securely in the back of the jeep and headed over the mountain to Cane Bay.

He parked the car just behind the crescent shaped beach and walked barefoot onto the sand. It was a glorious morning and the waves gently lapped onto the white sand. There was nobody much around. A young girl was jogging up the beach with two labradors scampering along behind and an old native, wearing a wide-brimmed straw hat, was raking up leaves from around the beach bar. Then he saw Betty running towards him. "Roy, oh Roy, am I glad to see you." Betty collapsed onto his broad chest and large stomach. She was breathless. "I've had an adventure I don't ever want to repeat. Yesterday evening I went to the happy hour at the Pink Hibiscus – you got my message, didn't you?" Roy nodded and Betty continued, "It was really packed and a reggae band was playing. After a while I noticed this big black guy staring at me and before I knew it he was asking me to dance. Well, we started dancing and he kept grinding his hips into me and all the while looking around to make sure all his friends were watching. Every now and again he'd smile at one of them with a wink – you know, really showing off. He didn't let me go between dances and he never even spoke more than 'where you from?' After about the third dance he somehow managed to get me into the darkest corner of the room and it was then that I felt he was getting really excited – you know – hard. And he was rubbing himself all over me. So I grabbed hold of my rum and coke – and it had plenty of ice in it – and I pulled open the front of his pants – he was wearing cotton pants with elastic at the waist – and tipped the whole drink in. That was when all hell broke loose."

Roy had been listening intently and smiled when she got to the bit about the drink. Up till then he hadn't felt much sympathy. It was exactly the sort of thing he would do. "What happened then?" he asked.

"I managed to pull myself loose and pushed myself through the crowd. He was shouting out, 'You honky bitch – wuthless white trash,' and on and on and coming after me. A lot of people who'd seen what had happened were laughing at him and he was really embarrassed. Finally I got out to the road and these two couples were getting into a jeep to go home and I begged them for a ride. 'Anywhere, just anywhere,' I pleaded, 'I've got a crazy guy chasing me.' They brought me to a house at the edge of the hill over there," she pointed. "They're on vacation and have rented a villa for two weeks. They're really nice – their settee made into a double bed . . . I tried to call you but no reply."

"Sounds like you handled the situation perfectly," said Roy. "I was so tired last night I must have slept through the phone rings."

"I'm scared, Roy. What do you think will happen if I run into this guy?"

"I think you should stay within the hotel grounds and not go gallivanting around the islands on your own. Make sure you're with someone, that's all. The guy will probably forget about it – he was probably drunk anyway." Roy dismissed the whole episode with a wave of his hand. Betty wasn't so sure.

"Today, though, I am your escort. I've rented a jeep and we'll do a grand tour of the island." Roy bowed ceremoniously and Betty laughed, her tension easing. Roy's talents did not usually include theatrics.

After a swim in the limpid waters of Cane Bay, they jumped into the jeep and toured the island. They explored the old rum factory and Betty bought a couple of bottles of the locally brewed fiery spirit, just because of the pretty labels. They walked the National Park trail and Roy smiled to himself, remembering Shirley posing for erotic pictures on his last visit.

Close to lunchtime, Roy spotted a grassy slope under a copse of palms, just off the road, and he pulled over. He mixed margaritas and they sat under the trees to enjoy them. "What do you think of the place so far?" said Roy.

"I think it's the most beautiful place I've ever seen," she smiled, and let out a sigh of satisfaction.

"And tomorrow I'm going to take you to Barney's Seafood. It's the best fish restaurant on the island. They're famous for their conch chowder and whole broiled lobster with lemon and butter."

"Mmmmm, I'm getting hungry already. I just love fresh seafood. Can I have a re-fill? Those were delicious," said Betty, handing Roy her paper cup.

"One of these days I'm going to rent a fishing boat and we'll go out and see what we can do. There are banks not far from here just teeming with fish. We could stop at a beach and barbecue up all the fresh fish we can eat." Roy was lying on his back looking up at the sky, dreaming.

"You're being a bit presumptuous, aren't you? I mean counting your chickens before they're hatched."

"Don't worry," said Roy, "you'll be along for luck. There's a Chinese proverb that goes, 'Young girl go out with fisherman, come back with red snapper.'"

She looked at him blankly for a second, and then caught the innuendo. She burst out laughing and cuffed him on the chin. Betty was not above a raunchy joke. They were peas from the same pod.

They continued on around the island and made a quick stop at Golden Sunset Charters. Roy wanted to make sure his container had been delivered and placed where he had stipulated. He showed Betty round the property and she was duly impressed They ended their trip with a refreshing dip in the hotel pool back at the Calabash.

It was not until 11 a.m. on Monday when Roy pulled into the GSC property. He had woken late and had a slight hangover. He had drunk most of two bottles of white wine that they had ordered to accompany their lobster lunch at Barney's the previous day. Then, that morning, he had tried to get insurance coverage for his truck, but everyone in the office was on 'island time' and he had to wait and wait. Then they couldn't find the right forms; the girl who dealt with vehicle insurance was off sick. Finally he drove out to GSC in the jeep in a thoroughly bad mood.

When he arrived at the lodge he found the crew digging out the foundations for the new retaining wall with pickaxe and shovel. Elroy climbed up the slope to meet his boss. "Dis gonna take a week jus' to dig de trench. Best to hire a backhoe an' a operator."

"Quite right, I'm going to make some calls now down at the office. Call off the men and put them to unloading the container. I don't want any damage to the porcelain."

They all walked over to the container, and Roy unlocked the padlock. Although Elroy was in charge of his crew, Roy felt he should get to know the men.

"Roy Blake," he said, and stuck out his hand to the

first man, who came forward somewhat hesitantly.

"Isaac," he said, nodding.

The second man came forward, and when their eyes met Roy immediately recognised the smiling Memnon. "Memnon!" exclaimed Roy, "there's no keeping you down. You're like Houdini."

"Pleased to be workin' wid you, Mr Roy. I can lay block quicker dan any man. Dey can't make de cement quick enough." Memnon laughed, tipping back his straw hat.

The third man was a Rastafarian. He was tall, thin and wiry, and on his head he wore a red, yellow and green tam: a woven beret as large as a small sack, to contain the natural, uncombed, matted hair or 'dreadlocks' of the cult. When Roy looked at him, expectantly he just stared back. Then he spoke suddenly, "Hell, fire in Babylon, Jah rules. Power to de spirit of Africa's Haile Selassie, Ras Tafari." He paused and everyone looked at him. Then he gave the black power fist-in-the-air salute and said, "Irie." Roy looked confused. He didn't know what the man was raving about. Elroy, Memnon and Isaac were laughing quietly to themselves and Roy didn't know if they were laughing at him.

"What's your name?" said Roy.

"Dey call me Toshi," said the Rasta. "After my dead brudder, Peter Tosh."

Then he said, "Redemption will come."

Roy walked over to Elroy and together they went down to the office. "I don't know what to make of that last guy. Is he any good?"

"He's de best stone mason on de island. Not only dat – he works fast and he never gives any trouble. Jus' now he was jus' testin' you. If he didn't like you he would have walked off. He might seem strange at first but we're lucky to have him."

Roy called up for a backhoe and luckily he could get one that afternoon. Roy checked with Elroy, and yes, the operator was good and the machine was his own. This was the ideal combination; owner-operators were best.

Elroy walked back up to supervise the men and Roy stayed in the office to peruse his lists of materials, quantities needed, prices etc. When the backhoe arrived, he sent him up to Elroy and then he drove the jeep back to town for a late lunch. Nearly the whole afternoon was spent organizing his truck insurance, but by 5 p.m. he had the policy in his hand. God help me if there's ever a claim, he thought.

During the days and weeks that followed, Roy spent a good part of nearly every day at the site, and progress was quicker than he expected. Roy was no slouch when it came to pitching in and lending a hand, and the men respected him for it. Then on Friday afternoons, Roy would bring a case of cold beer and they'd quit a bit early and sit around and yarn for a while.

Betty, meanwhile, spent her time at the hotel pool. She was apprehensive about venturing too far from the hotel after the episode at the Pink Hibiscus, and after a while she became bored. She developed a routine: she would start her day with a late breakfast, long after Roy had left, and then about mid-morning she'd go to the pool for a couple of hours. She'd have a long lunch with several cocktails and then have a nap. When she awoke, she'd run several laps around the hotel grounds and finish up at the pool again. It was not an unpleasant regimen but there was nothing in it to even remotely stimulate the brain – not that Betty was particularly well endowed in that area, but still . . .

Roy would come back to the hotel at different times in the afternoon but on this particular day he came back earlier than usual and when he walked through the door of their hotel room he smelled the unmistakable, pungent aroma of marijuana. Just as he walked in, Betty waltzed into the bedroom from the shower, wearing a brief, black bikini covered only by a colourful, cotton kimono. Between a thumb and forefinger she delicately held a smoldering marijuana cigarette. "Roy!" she said, surprised, "you're back early. Ooooooh, goody, maybe we can have some fun."

"What the hell do you think you're doing smoking that stuff," exclaimed Roy. "Don't you know it's totally illegal? They can revoke my business license, impound my property, fine us and kick us off the island."

"Ooooooh Roy," said Betty, "don't be such an old stuffed shirt. It's just a bit of fun. Nobody'll find out." She took a couple of puffs, inhaling noisily. Then she giggled – "I'd like a large bowl of vanilla ice cream with chocolate sauce, nuts and whipped cream." She handed him the joint but he waved it away.

"Where did you get it, I mean who . . . ?" Roy was obviously edgy.

"Just relax . . . Let's have some fun." She pulled at his belt, managing to loosen it, and his pants fell to the floor. Then she pulled him down on top of her on the bed and started kissing him with wet kisses, first his neck and ears and then she stuck her tongue in his mouth.

Roy's tension began to ebb away and he started to caress her breasts. All of a sudden Betty cried out, "Roy, something's burning!"

Roy got up off the bed and noticed immediately that a small patch of carpet was smouldering where the cigarette had fallen. He moved towards it and, forgetting that his pants were down around his ankles, fell heavily into the wardrobe with a resounding crash. He recovered quickly and was just staggering to his feet when two suitcases on top of the wardrobe came crashing down on top of him and flattened him once again, The sight was so comical that Betty, still lying on the bed, couldn't contain herself and let out a gale of hysterical laughter, kicking her legs in the air with uncontrollable delight. Roy was not without a sense of humour and joined in the laughter. He doused the smouldering patch of carpet with a glass of water and then jumped back onto the bed and started wrestling playfully with Betty. Soon they were both completely naked and making love, more physically than usual, what with Betty's heightened sensual desires. As the crescendo of their lovemaking reached climax, the headboard of the bed started knocking loudly against the wall and the bed itself began squeaking and creaking.

Then during the final moments Betty joined in the cacophony. "Oooooohhh, AAaaaaaaah, OOoooohh, Ah, Ah, Ah, Ah, Ah, ... AAaaaaaaaaaaaaaaaaaaaah!"

They were lying there panting and bathed in sweat when a sharp rap, rap, rap on the door brought them back to reality. "Inside! Inside!" came a loud, commanding voice.

"Ssshhhhh," said Roy. He quietly slipped off the bed and tip-toed over to the door and looked out of the peep-hole. "It's the cops," he whispered.

Betty grabbed her bag from the dresser and headed towards the toilet.

Again came a loud rap, rap, rap and a deep voice of authority. "Inside, inside, open up."

Roy had turned the air conditioning up to full and was waving the atmosphere with a towel, trying to disperse any lingering smell. "Yeah, coming, just a minute." He heard the toilet flush and hoped that every last remnant of the dope had been washed down the toilet. With only a towel around his waist, he opened the door and stood there in the door frame preventing access. "Yes, what can I do for you?" he said. To Roy's relief the man standing there in uniform was the hotel's security guard – an old man with greying temples under a rather battered military cap and an odd assortment of clothes that made up his uniform.

"We had several calls to the front desk," he said. One said there was someone breaking in, another said it sounded like assault and battery and yet another reported a rape. You Mr Blake?"

"Yes," said Roy, "there's absolutely no problem. I tripped and fell and knocked some things over. That's probably what the people heard."

"Is Mrs Blake all right?" he said, somewhat suspiciously. "I'll have to have a quick look at the room."

"Be my guest," said Roy and stepped back to allow the old man to enter. By now, Betty was lying on the bed reading a magazine.

"You all right, Mrs Blake?" he said.

"I'm fine," she said, "just a little tired, that's all." She yawned as though this intrusion was a major inconvenience. The guard scanned the room quickly and Roy's eyes followed his gaze. Then, horrified, Roy saw the soggy end of the joint lying on the carpet next to a small, black hole. The guard, though, was looking at the furnishings, fixtures and fittings and seemed not to notice it, and Roy adroitly moved and stood on the offending evidence to hide it.

"Well, sorry to have bothered you," said the guard, "I'll report that everything's fine."

Roy reached for his wallet that was on the dressing table and handed the man $10. "Thank you for your concern," he said. "It's good to know we are being well looked after."

The guard touched the peak of his cap with his forefinger. "Thank you, sir," he said and walked away.

Roy closed the door and let out a sigh of relief.

"That's the last time you ever bring dope into this room," said Roy, stooping to pick up the soggy roach. "It's just too risky. Where did you get it, anyway?"

"The bartender sold me a 'dime bag.' It's grown right here on the island," said Betty, as though that made it all right. Roy was shaking his head in disbelief at the stupidity of the woman. He had to admit, though, she was great in bed.

Back at Sunset Lodge, the work was progressing well. The new extended patio was complete and the centrepiece was a three-tiered freshwater fountain. At night the jets of water would be illuminated by coloured lights and there would be water lilies and tropical ferns. Roy particularly liked the placing of a pair of cherubs on the top layer that would pee down to the bottom layer when the water was turned on.

The attractive red tile had been skillfully laid by Toshi and Memnon, who had also finished the surrounding wall with local stone, brain coral and conch shells here and there facing inward showed off their striking pink colouring. A blue and white striped awning covered the area, and garden furniture of wrought iron with marble topped tables was arranged to take advantage of the beautiful view that overlooked the bay. This would be the dining area in all but the worst weather.

The interior of the lodge was almost finished. The kitchen had been relocated at the back, leaving plenty of room for the reception desk and lobby. This area would be tastefully furnished with good quality rattan, and cushions upholstered with colourful tropical prints. The existing Italian green tile would remain. Upstairs the suites were about half finished. The bedrooms looked bigger than had been first supposed and there was ample room for a recessed TV and VCR in front of each four-poster bed. In order to keep the authentic feel of a nineteenth-century inn, the recessed entertainment centres were hidden behind panelled doors that matched the rest of the wall. Other attractive features included concealed lighting and night lights at floor level, and provisions for a refrigerator, tea and coffee service. There was air conditioning, and ceiling fans in all suites.

When Roy got back to the Calabash there was a fax waiting for him. Harold and Jackie would be flying in to the island at the end of the week. The other news was that tropical storm Fred was three hundred miles east of Barbados and "conditions were favourable for the storm to intensify." It was travelling north west at 15 m.p.h. and if it continued on that course it would come close to the Caribee islands in 24 hours. A hurricane warning was expected to be issued soon.

Roy had a quick shower and headed down to the bar where there was a TV. CNN was giving six-hourly updates. Betty had heard the news earlier in the day and now, with warnings imminent, she was petrified. She had survived hurricane Andrew in '91 in Florida, but had lost the roof of her house. A lot of her belongings had been ruined. The worst memory she had, though, was of her neighbour's three-year-old daughter. She had run out of the house during the height of the storm and was struck by a piece of flying galvanised iron roof that severed her leg above the knee. Betty had stayed with the mother and daughter throughout the remainder of the storm, watching the child get weaker and weaker from loss of blood. There was no electricity and no telephone, and they had spent the night huddled around a small portable radio as the wind howled and bits of roof came flying off. Finally, as the storm abated, they managed to get word out and an ambulance was called, but the child died on the way to the hospital. It had been a nightmare.

They sat on stools at the bar. Roy ordered a rum and Coke and Betty a large brandy. "If I can get a flight out in the morning I'm out of here," she said with determination.

"No need to be too hasty," said Roy. "It's only a tropical storm at the moment, and if it increases to a hurricane it will probably only be a Category One." That's the least dangerous of hurricanes with maximum sustained winds of 85 m.p.h.

"I'm taking no chances. Hurricane Andrew was the worst experience of my life. If I can get a flight out I will." Betty sounded adamant. Roy couldn't blame her – he knew what she'd been through. The 9 p.m. update showed the storm to have intensified to 70 m.p.h. maximum sustained winds, with higher gusts and still on its northwesterly track. The local radio station informed everyone that a hurricane warning was now in effect for the Caribbee Islands and that marine interests should finalise all preparations. It sounded ominous.

They returned to their room and Betty started packing. Roy phoned up Elroy and got Memnon's number.

"Memnon, Roy here. Would you go down to the docks at GSC in the morning, with a helper, and make sure the boats are secured properly. It's an emergency so I'll make sure you get a little extra pay."

"No problem, boss. I be dung dere first ting. But de storm goin' sout'. De Bermuda high pushin' sout an' dat keep de storm trackin wes'. I jus' bin discussin' it wid JC an' we both agree."

"Well, I hope you're right, but we can't take any chances. I just heard that hurricane warnings have been issued for this area. Double up all the dock lines

– well, you know what to do better than I do. I should be there sometime around late morning." He put the phone back on the hook.

"Roy, will you be able to take me to the airport in the morning, or should I take a cab?" said Betty, acting somewhat neurotically.

"I'll take you, don't worry," said Roy, putting his arm around the stressed-out woman. Roy was not a sensitive man, but he liked Betty more than he had liked any lady for a very long time. She had an adventurous spirit, and an almost impulsive nature, but she was the exact opposite of a designing woman, and not manipulative at all. Roy admired that. "I'll make sure you're at the airport as early as possible, so you'll have the best chance of getting a seat."

She stood on tiptoe and kissed him on the cheek. "Thanks, Roy, you're a doll."

At daybreak the weather was gorgeous. The cloudless sky was a deep blue and there was hardly a ripple on the sea, the wind was so light. The visibility too was exceptional, with the outer islands standing out clearly in the morning sunlight. The famous "calm before the storm," thought Roy. It was 7 a.m. when they reached the airport. There were a few people milling around waiting for ticket counters to open, but it certainly didn't seem like a mass exodus was about to happen. Roy had a busy itinerary that day, so he kissed Betty goodbye with promises to visit her the very first time he stepped foot in Florida. She, in turn, would energetically promote Golden Sunset Charters and Sunset Lodge. Her business was affiliated with travel agents nationwide, and Roy was going to see that she was sent ample brochures and promotional material.

It was still early when he drove his truck into the GSC parking area. He had just heard on the radio that Fred was now a fully fledged hurricane, with sustained winds of 100 m.p.h. Further strengthening was likely, especially during the day when the heat from the sun accelerated convection. The good news was that Fred had changed course to a more west-northwesterly direction and the Caribbee Islands were not now in the direct path of the storm. As he got out of the truck, he looked at the sky and noticed high white cirrus clouds in the pattern commonly referred to as a "mackerel sky," usually a portent of bad weather. On the horizon to the southeast, cloud activity was increasing.

Memnon, JC and Luther were down on the docks preparing the boats for the storm. All the sails and Bimini tops had to be removed and stowed below. Lines were being doubled up and chafing gear installed where there was any risk of dock lines rubbing through. Memnon and JC were working on the bow of a Sparkman and Stephens 49. "It an amazin' ting how dey does track storms and measure deir strenth dese days," said Memnon. "I were jus watchin de CNN an' deir radar chart las' night sometin' else. It even coloured in blood red where de danger zones is. Now dat's technology!"

"Yeah, they actually send planes with satellite navigation instruments into the middle of a hurricane to measure its exact location. Then they measure wind speeds and barometric pressure. Just think of this: 60 years ago they didn't even have radar – 30 years ago they didn't have satellite navigation. It was all calculated guesswork." JC tied on the last piece of fire hose for chafe prevention.

"Well, I'll tell you sometin' – you wouldn't get me in one o' dem planes for all de tea in China. Jus' imagine if de wings tear off or de whole plane jus' disintegrate. Den you fallin' and swirlin' an head over heels dung an' dung. No suh! dat ain't for me at all. If you fall off a boat you fall in de water an dat ain't so good neither but at leas' you ain't fallin' dung an' dung. It make me giddy jus' to tink 'bout it."

Roy walked up the dock and stopped next to the boat where the men were working. "Morning guys. Thanks for coming down at such short notice. It seems that your prediction last night may be right. The hurricane has taken a slightly more westerly turn. We're not out of the woods, though. The diameter of the storm is so large that tropical storm force winds extend nearly 200 miles from the centre in the northern semi-circle."

"Dat de worse semi-circle, too," said Memnon. "We gonna get a lot o' rain an' dat for shaw. It good for de lan' an' it fill up everybody's cistern. Got to tink positive – every cloud have a silver linin'." Memnon was becoming philosophical.

The wind was starting to pick up and low cumulus clouds were scudding across the sky. "I've got to get back to town," said Roy. "Memnon, before you go, there's that new awning that's just been put up at the lodge. It'll have to come off and be folded up and stored in the office. Make sure all the dinghies are tied down behind the shed. And lock up before you leave." He tossed Memnon the keys. "Good luck."

Roy stopped at the General Store in Roadstead and picked up a couple of kerosene lamps, a tin of kerosene, two flashlights, a large box of kitchen matches and a portable radio with spare batteries. The shop was becoming crowded and certain items were being sold out. Roy saw a yachtsman with some plastic, five gallon jugs – yes, he thought, he'd need something to hold water in as well. If the electricity went off, the pumps that ran the hotel's water supply wouldn't work. He was lucky enough to get the last two that were left. He picked up a tin opener, plate, bowl, cup and a set of cutlery, paid for his purchases and headed to the grocery store.

By the time he got back to the Calabash, it was mid afternoon and the wind was coming in blustery squalls. He took his emergency supplies and rations up to his room and filled his jugs with water. Then he had a long, hot shower, "perhaps my last for a while," he thought. He turned on the radio and almost immediately got an updated weather report. The hurricane was 150 miles southeast of the Caribbee Islands and moving west at 15 m.p.h.. Maximum sustained winds were now at 110 m.p.h. and hurricane-force winds extended 75 miles from the centre in the northern semi-circle. The centre of the hurricane would pass about a hundred miles south of Tortuga in the early hours of the morning. Heavy rain could be expected that night and most of the next day and wind gusts, especially on higher elevations, could approach 100 m.p.h.. There was a reference to wave heights and a storm surge and those people living in low lying areas and beach-front properties exposed to the east were advised to evacuate immediately to a recognised shelter. Yes, they'd be in for a soaking and a lashing, but hopefully they'd escape the worst of it.

At 6 p.m. he went down to the reception area and bought a couple of paperbacks from the rack. Then he went into the nearly empty restaurant and ordered a T-bone steak, rare, with all the trimmings, and a bottle of Medoc. It was done just how he liked it, tender and juicy, and he helped himself generously from the pot of French mustard. Before he'd finished, a waiter approached. "We're closing the kitchen at seven tonight to give the few remaining staff a chance to get home. I can get you a coffee if you like." Roy ordered a large pot and sat there drinking it and reading Steinbeck's *Cannery Row*. Oddly, he found that reading depressing books cheered him up when he was feeling down. He was surprised at how much he was missing Betty – she'd be back in Florida by now. A rather bedraggled couple, yachtsmen perhaps, shuffled by his table and smiled and nodded on their way out. Strange how people became more friendly in emergency situations, he thought. He signed his bill and went up to his room.

Roy awoke at 3 a.m. to an irregular knocking sound on the shutters. The wind was shrieking and the rain was driving horizontally, it seemed, judging by the cacophony. He reached over to turn on the bed-side light but the power must have been switched off. He grabbed one of the flashlights and opened the door to the verandah to investigate. He was almost forced back in by the powerful gusts of wind, but he clung on to the door jamb. The beam of his flashlight picked out the limb of a tree that was lodged between his bedroom wall and the verandah railing, and the branches were beating an eerie tap, tap, tap on his shuttered window. In the few seconds that he'd been outside he was already soaking wet and shivering, standing there in nothing more than a pair of underpants. He bent down to pick up the tree limb but it was firmly wedged in place. He leaned over the railing to try and dislodge it from the outside but suddenly his feet slipped on the wet floor and he felt himself going over. He made a desperate grab at the railing but missed and the last thing he knew was that he was falling.

One of the foremen at CTC, Caribbee Telephone Company, was Benjamin Gumbs. He was driving to his office in the early morning before sunrise, and had been diverted by the co-ordinator who had called him by cellular phone to check out a fallen pole adjacent to the Calabash Hotel. He had driven into the hotel grounds and there, not far from the entrance that was all closed up and in darkness, his headlights illuminated the body of a large, almost naked white male lying face down in the mud. He stopped his Land Rover and ran over to the prostrate figure. Winky, Benjamin's helper, followed behind and stood over the horrifying spectacle. Roy's body was covered in lacerations and the blood was mixing with the mud in a gooey mess. Benjamin bent down to listen for any signs of life, and after careful scrutiny, detected shallow breathing. In the back of the Land Rover, among other things, was a step ladder and some sheets of plywood. They made a crude stretcher, carried it over to where Roy was lying and carefully rolled him onto it. Benjamin took off his rain slicker and covered the man's top half and Winky found a couple of towels in the back of the vehicle that would help keep him warm. Roy was a heavy man, but together they managed to get him into the back of the Land Rover. It was still pouring with rain and the wind was howling so loud that he could hardly hear the hospital receptionist when he called to advise them of the emergency. When Roy was whisked into the emergency room the grey light of dawn was creeping into the eastern sky.

All that day it rained and by evening many low-lying areas were flooded. The local public works department was out trying to keep the main roads open – there were mud slides and rock falls to contend with and some trees had fallen. On the advice given on the local radio, most people stayed at home. Apparently there wasn't much property damage and the marine community had survived with only a few casualties. Maximum winds of 90 m.p.h. had been recorded and the storm was now abating as it moved off to the west. Every 15 minutes the radio broadcast messages and it was one of these that Memnon heard whilst he was sitting in his rocking chair, drinking a cup of hot tea and listening to the radio. "Would Memnon Brathwaite please report to the Caribbee General Hospital."

"Dat's me," he cried, "what dey want me dere for? Oh, Lawd, I hope it ain't nuttin serious." Memnon ran upstairs and pulled on a clean shirt and was starting up his minibus in less than 10 minutes.

The road was in a terrible condition and twice he thought he wouldn't make it; once through a raging torrent of muddy brown water and another where he had to skirt a rockfall. Then just before he reached Roadstead, the police were diverting traffic. A huge almond tree had fallen across the road, and even though two men were working with chain saws, it would be hours before the road would again be passable. A policeman stopped him, "Emergency vehicles only. Return home please."

"No, No!" said Memnon, "I got to be at de hospital. It were on de radio." The cop eyed him shrewdly and waved him through. Memnon was out of breath when he reported to the hospital reception 10 minutes later.

"Memnon Brathwaite? Yes, General Ward, second bed on de right. Next," said the receptionist.

Memnon ran up the stairs to the General Ward and anxiously peered at the second bed on the right. "Roy! What happened?" said Memnon. He could hardly believe it. His imagination had been running wild on the drive over but he never once thought that Roy would be the one lying in the hospital.

Roy told Memnon the whole story, except the part about getting to the hospital, which he couldn't remember because he had been unconscious. "The emergency room put me on oxygen and after a short time, I came to. They examined me all over but couldn't find anything except cuts and bruises. But I know I've damaged my back – it's so painful I can hardly move. The problem is the X-ray machine has broken down, so I can't get a proper diagnosis. One of the nurses dug out this orthopaedic corset from an old trunk and helped me strap it on." He pulled up the surgical singlet they had dressed him in to show Memnon. "I asked her whose it was and how much should I pay for it but she just said, 'Don't worry about it, the guy died last week from spinal complications.'" Roy was not happy.

Memnon was very concerned. "Can you walk OK?" he asked.

"I can just make it to the toilet on crutches, but it's so painful I nearly passed out last time."

Roy's neighbour, listening in intently, was an old man in dirty pajamas and a cloth cap. He was completely toothless and was sitting up in bed and eating soup noisily from a tin cup. Every now and again he'd fish out a piece of meat and pass it under the bed where a very obedient island sheepdog was tied to a leg of the bed.

The hospital was packed and the general hubbub of people crying out in pain, some talking, others shouting across the ward and a radio somewhere in the distance broadcasting a cricket commentary was more reminiscent of a market place than a hospital. On the floor just up the ward from Roy's bed, a large cooking pot caught drips from the ceiling, the paint of which was peeling off in sheets.

"You've got to help me get out of here," said Roy. "I'm supposed to stay for 48 hours for observation according to the emergency room doctor, but I'm going to sign myself out in the morning. Memnon, I've got no clothes, no wallet, no washing things – nothing. I want you to go to the Calabash Hotel right now and bring me my things. Would you do that for me?"

"Yeah, shaw, Mr Roy. No problem. I'll be right back." Memnon drove his minibus to the Calabash in record time, especially considering that the sea was still washing over The Waterfront. He explained the situation to the hotel receptionist and she nodded knowingly.

"I knew something like this was going to happen – you should have heard them fighting the other evening. She probably pushed him over."

"It weren't quite like dat," said Roy, "she flew out yesday marnin'." He went upstairs and gathered up Roy's things and threw them in his holdall. He was back at the hospital a total of only 40 minutes after leaving.

"You're a champ, Mem," said Roy. "Can you be here tomorrow morning at 8:30?"

"No problem, I'll be here," said Memnon. "You was real lucky. I saw where you fall an' it was a tick hedge dat broke de fall.

Roy wasn't feeling lucky at all. "Bring JC, if you can contact him," said Roy. He had cursed himself several times for not having taken down the captain's telephone number.

Memnon was just leaving when a large, very dark woman wearing a green apron over her white uniform came charging around the corner, brandishing a straw broom and trying to coax out a chicken and about six chicks that must have somehow strayed into the hospital. The mother hen was taking great offence at being swept about with a broom and was clucking and flapping furiously, the little chicks running in all directions. The excitement was not lost on the dog that was tied under the bed next to Roy's and he gave a giant snarling leap towards the hapless chicken. Such a forceful leap that he managed to snap the restraining line and shot out into the passageway in pursuit and directly into the path of a nurse who was carrying a full bed-pan to the toilet for emptying. Fortunately this nurse was something of a gymnast – she tripped and fell forwards heavily but with three giant steps managed to regain her balance, at the same time holding the pot with its noxious contents and preventing it from spilling. On her last desperate step, her heel came down on a wet spot and she slipped, but again, with two controlling sideways steps she managed to prevent a disaster, slopping only a small quantity. After a couple of seconds she stared across the ward at nobody in particular and exclaimed petulantly in staccato, "Dat's it! Dat's it! Dat's it!"

Nobody knew what the 'Dat' or 'it' referred to, but a loud cheer went up from the ward. "Way to go, sister," and "What a save!" and "The West Indies cricket team needs you." Everyone was shouting and clapping except the toothless old man, who was opening and closing his mouth silently and pointing to the end of his bed where the slop had landed. There was a wet, yellow stain and a large piece of fecal matter.

Memnon was laughing uncontrollably as he walked down the steps and out of the building, but poor Roy just sighed and covered his head with a pillow. He wondered if he would survive until morning.

It was lunchtime the following day when Roy finally lay down on his bed back at the Calabash. It had been an ordeal to get him there. First, they had managed to rent a wheelchair from the hospital, but one of the wheels had fallen off on the steps on the way down to Memnon's minibus and the severe pain caused by the jolt had made Roy utter a string of profanities that would have offended the devil himself. Instead, it offended a little old lady who was walking past and she came at him with a folded umbrella, calling him the 'son of Satan.' Memnon and JC practically carried Roy to the minibus and exchanged the wheelchair for crutches. When they got out of the vehicle at the Calabash, Roy was hobbling along towards the hotel entrance when one of his crutches sank into soft mud and he toppled over – again with profanities – and they carried him up to his room.

The following morning Roy flew to Miami. He had contacted Betty and she had agreed to meet him at the airport. Roy had given JC a $100 bill to pass on to Benjamin Gumbs after he had found out from the hospital who had admitted him. He had also offered $100 to Memnon for all his time, trouble and service, but the exuberant islander had refused to accept it. "I ain't take advantage o' people when dey dung," he had said. Later on in the afternoon JC had been given folders and files, notes and numbers to pass on to Harold, who was expected in three days. Then he called Mike Broadrite and told him of the circumstances before falling into a deep and long sleep.

4

The Business

The day before Harold and Jackie were due to fly in JC drove over to GSC in his newly acquired VW convertible. The day was picture-perfect, calm and serene, but the landscape and road showed signs of the recent storm. There were many more pot-holes and mud and rocks had to be avoided at every turn. Trees were down too, but at least the road was passable. He pulled into the parking area at GSC and walked down to the docks. The whole bay was a muddy brown from the runoff, and there were coconuts and palm fronds, tree limbs and other floating debris in the water. He checked the yachts and they all seemed to be undamaged, except one that had got badly scraped on its starboard bow.

He walked back along the path and up to the lodge and noticed that the landscape had been badly gouged by what must have been a torrent of water. The raging flow of water had come down the slope and branched at the back wall of the lodge, some of it going down either side. JC walked on, around and then up to the new patio, but could find no-one. He noticed the fountain with its three tiers tapering towards the top and was impressed. Then he remembered it was Saturday and was not surprised that the place was empty.

He continued on down the path and on to the office. A security guard was now sitting there where before there had been no-one. I wonder what kind of hours these guys keep, he thought. He nodded good morning and the guard nodded back; they both knew each other. JC had got the keys from Memnon and decided to check the office for storm damage. He went in and splashed through a huge puddle in the middle of the floor. He found a mop and cleaned it up. The whole place smelled musty and he opened some windows to air out the room. Suddenly, a whirring noise behind him made him jump, until he realised that a fax machine was on. He went over to it and noticed a ream of faxes cascading onto the floor. He glanced at a couple of them: enquiries for charter yachts for the upcoming season. Jackie was going to have her work cut out he thought, not knowing that George Cleary had been tentatively re-instated as manager of the charter yacht division.

On Sunday morning Harold and Jackie flew in to Tortuga and took up temporary residence at the Calabash. They were treated with great courtesy at the front desk and taken to the best room in the hotel. Not only did everyone know who they were, but also they were becoming very good clients, having, together with Roy, spent a small fortune there.

Their business dealings in England had gone extremely well – they had managed, with the help of a very astute estate agent, to get considerably more for their business than they had first thought. Jackie, who had been on a strict diet and slimmed dramatically, had immediately gone out and bought a new wardrobe of tropical clothing, and at bargain prices too, as it was approaching winter there. It was one of these cotton, tropical dresses that she was wearing now. This, coupled with a new shoulder-length hair style and white button earings made her look 10 years younger. Harold looked much the same but had a more positive air to his presence, perhaps the result of a new miniature hearing aid he had had fitted. He had trimmed his walrus moustache to look less conspicuous and had taken to wearing cloth caps. He imagined wealthy yachtsmen would be wearing similar headgear.

The first thing on Harold's mind was to call a meeting on Monday morning at the GSC office. He realised that it was rather short notice, but he was anxious to get his new business in motion – after all, the season was only about 12 weeks away. He called up the Clearys, Sonia Hodge, JC, Memnon and Mike Broadrite and set the meeting for 9 a.m. George and Anne would pick up the Mcpheresons at 8:30 by the front desk and they'd drive over together. JC gave Harold a quick rundown of the events leading up to Roy's accident, and he called Roy in Florida immediately but, according to a maid who answered the phone, he was in the hospital.

On Monday morning they all pulled up chairs and sat down around the conference table at the Golden Sunset Charters office. Sonia Hodge looked outstanding in a red business suit, gold earrings and hair piled up high. The air conditioning provided a pleasant ambient temperature, and the concealed fluorescent lighting gave a daylight feeling to the room. The only absentee was Memnon, who was working with the construction crew up at the lodge. He had been called because he had been the senior captain when the Clearys ran the business, and Roy wanted him to remain in that position. But everybody knew Memnon, so there was no need for his presence during the introductions. In fact everybody knew everybody there anyway, so the meeting got off to a friendly start.

Harold started the meeting and kept things informal. The immediate priority was to get all enquiries and bookings sorted out. There would be two bank accounts set up so that deposits on charters and hotel bookings could be kept separate from final payments. A massive advertising campaign would begin this week, targeting summer business. Sunday newspapers, travel agents and yacht clubs would be sent material aimed at winter and Christmas and more immediate clientele. George Cleary was asked to give a status report on the condition of all the yachts, and work in close co-operation with Sonia, who would make up a bookings chart in graph form. This would tell at a glance when yachts were going out and coming back.

The hiring of staff was also on the agenda, and Harold had a budget for that based on an analysis of previous business. For the yacht chartering end, he would need a good all round mechanic – "not necessarily a fat man," he said, to polite laughter – a helper/cleaner, and a part-time chambermaid-laundress.

The way Golden Sunset Charters was run, all the yachts for charter were privately owned. Revenues from charters were split, roughly one-third to the owner of the boat and two-thirds to the company. The rates for a medium-sized yacht might average $3,000 a week throughout the different seasons of the year, and the boat might be booked for 20 weeks. So from the $60,000 revenue, the company took $40,000 and the owner $20,000. You didn't need a rocket scientist to work that out.

But there were other aggravating problems that even a rocket scientist couldn't work out. And one concerned the cost of repairs, often a bone of contention between an owner and the company because owners had to pay for repairs. Harold told everyone present that yacht owners had to be kept happy if they were to keep their yachts with GSC. "Without yachts we have no business," he said. Harold then asked George to tell everyone the story that George had told him on the drive over.

"We had a very sleek French yacht in the fleet a few years ago and installed in the bilge was a modern automatic bilge pump. One day it broke down so I sent the mechanic in to remove it for repair. It was screwed down to the floor of the bilge, right under the back of the engine. The mechanic could just reach the screw heads with a short handled screw driver by contorting his body into a U shape and standing on his head in smelly bilge water. Unfortunately the pump had been installed with screws of mild steel which had deteriorated badly in the salt water of the bilge. So much so, in fact, that the heads of the screws became badly chewed up as the mechanic became more frustrated. Eventually they became unworkable. The only alternative was to drill out the obstinate screws but there was no room to get the drill in the small space. This meant that the bell housing on the transmission had to be removed and to get this off, the propeller shaft had to be uncoupled and slid back a foot or so. Then all the fastenings on the French engine were metric so metric wrenches had to be found. Well, to cut a long story short, the seemingly simple procedure of replacing a bilge pump took 14 hours of the mechanic's time at $30 per hour and the bill to the owner for installing a new $85 pump was $505. The owner wasn't happy and no amount of explaining could change his attitude. He just thought he was getting ripped off." George ended his story with a sigh and a shrug. "Of course you can't tell an owner that he's bought a boat with an in-built problem and that the yacht builder had not given enough thought to maintenance. It's a situation that we have to deal with all the time."

"We'll have to keep careful tabs on costs of repairs. Perhaps we can absorb a portion of some of the most horrendous charges if it means keeping owners appeased. I will keep an eye on that personally," said Harold.

The meeting got back to a more general tone of overall company policy. "Our charter management programme includes dockage for the yachts, one haulout a year with anti-fouling, and insurance. Owners get four weeks of sailing time per year free and we stipulate what seasons they can come in. They can come for longer if they want to but they must pay us our share. George, you'll organize yacht haulouts over the coming weeks. Any questions so far? Right, we'll have a break for coffee." Harold got up and walked over to the coffee machine. Anne had had the foresight to bring some fresh coffee, milk and sugar and soon the machine was bubbling away.

JC was amazed at how much Harold seemed to know about the business. He'd really been doing his homework and JC was impressed.

After 10 minutes Harold called the meeting to order. "Concerning our policy towards our staff, unlike most companies we will offer salaries and benefits not only above the minimum but above the average and every employee will have full life and medical insurance and a pension plan. This will encourage staff to stay with us and should there be a termination of employment for whatever reason, we should be able to get a good replacement." There was a murmur of approval around the room. "I would like to discuss individual salaries and bonuses privately in my office at the end of this meeting. Mike, I will have to meet with you privately as well to discuss the overall company insurance plan." The meeting continued and plans for the Rusty Pelican, the Sunset Lodge and a boutique were all discussed. "Our target date for opening is the 15th of December and you can be sure it will be a gala event.

"Now, I will finish this meeting with some excellent news that should really kick-start our charter yacht division. Just before I left England, I signed a contract for three 50-foot catamarans that are presently being completed in South Africa. These are luxury, five cabin catamarans and will be operated by a full time crew of two. The accent will be on gourmet cuisine and a complete line of watersports.

"We are fortunate to get these vessels. Ironically it's all a product of South African politics: many businessmen there are disillusioned with the economy since apartheid ended, and although there is a ban on exporting large amounts of cash, it is virtually impossible to stop someone sailing away with a half-million dollar yacht. This is partly the reason that we are seeing so many South African yachts and particularly catamarans in the Caribbean. However we are not really concerned with the political ramifications, and I think we can look forward to good business with these vessels. They have huge advantages over traditional yachts, with their space and stability."

Harold was rambling on a bit and Anne couldn't suppress a yawn.

"The flagship of our fleet will be one of these catamarans and JC will be the captain," said Harold, grandly. The name of the yacht will be '*Sunfun Calypso II.*' The name has special meaning for us." Harold smiled at Jackie.

The meeting was brought to a close and the individual meetings began. Mike Broadrite was invited to step into Harold's office. He looked very formal in a light grey suit and blue tie.

"First, thank you for coming," said Harold. "The question of insurance, for the property, the yachts and the personnel, is a big one and we may get a better policy and discount premiums if we use the same company for everything. What sort of choices are there on the island?"

"There aren't any choices on the island when it comes to insurance companies. Caribbean Mutual Benefit has it all tied up. It is something that the Federation of Caribbean Insurers is examining right now, but the government is adamant that only one company is necessary in a territory with only 15,000 people. If you look in the yellow pages you might think that there are quite a few choices but the three or four names there are all subsidiaries of the same company, specialising in different aspects of insurance – one for vehicles, one for medical, etc. etc. There are about 5,000 private vehicles on the road, so you can imagine that just the car insurance branch is a huge business. Rumour has it that large 'donations' are paid to the government to ensure the monopoly remains." Mike smiled at the irony and shrugged.

"Who owns the business and who are the underwriters?" asked Harold.

There are three partners: Reuben Winston, Charles

Mcguire and Sebastian Durmile. They founded the company in the late 60s and are all very rich now. Winston is the older brother of Talbot Winston, that unscrupulous government employee without portfolio, Mcguire is of Scottish descent, but a U.S. citizen, and Durmile is British. The underwriters are National Allied Insurers of New York. They have billions of dollars in assets and are very solid."

"Good," said Harold, "then I'll leave it to you to make all the arrangements. You already have the land titles and deeds. All the building specs are in the office and Stanborg the architect has the new drawings for the lodge. I suppose they'll want a surveyor to inspect it."

"Yes," said Broadrite, "the insurance company will probably want a complete survey of the whole property. Then the yachts will have to be surveyed by a marine surveyor. I'll set those two projects in motion immediately and get back to you on the policies later. There will undoubtedly be a lot of choices to be made."

They dealt with other matters and Jackie was brought in for the signing of the company incorporation papers. Sonia came in to witness the signings as well. Copies would be sent to Roy in Florida.

5

The Mermaid

Harold and Jackie had been dying to take a closer look at the renovations to the lodge ever since they arrived. They had had a quick glance on their way to the meeting but now they had time for a closer inspection. The reception area, with its green tile and tropical furnishings, looked inviting and Jackie could visualise some impressionist paintings in the alcoves. The bar behind a bamboo latticework partition was almost complete, as was the library. They would serve afternoon tea there, she thought, as well as on the patio. The kitchen needed a bit of re-arranging to facilitate traffic flow, but all the major appliances looked in the right place. Jackie poked her head into the pantry and larder areas where the large walk-in freezer-refrigerator was. It was a mess with sawdust, wood chips, cardboard boxes and paper strewn everywhere. She made a note to get cleaners in there pronto. They went upstairs and looked at all the suites and were deciding which one they would move into when Memnon knocked on the door. "Elroy axe me to say for you to come dung," he said. "Nice to see you back on de islan' Mr Harold, Ms Jackie." Memnon was smiling his usual wide grin.

They went down to the back of the building and met the construction crew. They were busy repairing the damage caused by the raging torrent of water from the storm. "We was jus' clearin' de mud away from de back o' de buildin' when we saw a gap between de fungdation stones. It look like at one time dey were a kind o' cellar or sometin' here." He pointed to a gap in the wall that appeared to open into a large open space, but it was too dark to see much.

"Well, that must be the cistern for the freshwater," said Harold, but Elroy disagreed.

"No suh, de cistern end here," and he pointed to a spot on the side wall. If you look in trew de hole you can see de back wall o' de cistern." It was very dark but Harold could barely make out a back wall.

"Wait a minute, I'll bring a flashlight from the office." He was back in five minutes. "By Jove, I think you're right," he said. "There must be an access somewhere. I mean nobody would just box in an empty space would they?"

They all trooped into the lodge and made their way to the back: one room was a bathroom, walled off from the pantry and larder. The floor was wood but it had been covered with linoleum at some stage. They took their bearings from the outside walls and then started examining the floor. They looked and looked but could find no indentation. "Looks like we have to peel back de lino' to fin' de openin'," said Memnon.

Elroy started peeling up a corner of the linoleum,

but it was fastened down with a potent mastic and it looked as though there had been some kind of thin plywood laid over the original floor. "De bes' ting to do is we cut a hole in de floor jus between de joists an' climb dung in. Den we will be able to see de original opening from de underneat'."

"Excellent idea," said Harold. "We must be careful not to cut a hole too big or it will weaken the whole floor. Just big enough for a man to climb through." Isaac ran down and got an extension cord, an electrical circular saw and a crow bar. Elroy tap, tap, tapped with the iron bar to ascertain where the floor joists were positioned, and marked out a hole between them. Then he plugged in the saw, set the blade to a two inch depth and in no time had the hole cut. He smacked the cut out with the crow bar but there was slight resistance at the corners. The heel of his foot did the job though, and the section of floor went crashing down to the basement.

Elroy lay on the floor with his head down the hole but couldn't see a thing – it was too dark. He reached up for the flashlight and shone it down and around. He saw a couple of rats scuttle into a corner and then he raised up his head and said, "Dere's all kind o' stuff dung dere but it look dark and dirty. Dere's an inspection lamp in de cold room. We can plug it into de extension cord and pass it into de cellar. Dat should give us plenty o' light."

"How high is the cellar, from floor to ceiling?" said Harold. He was getting excited. "Can you jump down in?"

"Shouldn't be a problem at all," said Elroy. "It look to be no more dan 'bout eight feet." He took the lamp from Isaac and dropped it into the hole. Then he swung down himself. Memnon followed and Harold shouted to him to wait under the hole, he was coming in too.

They dusted themselves off and looked around. Along one wall were resting a row of casks. They were covered in dust and Harold looked around for something to wipe them off. In a corner was some old sack cloth and he grabbed a piece, but it disintegrated in his hand. "Throw down a towel or a cloth," he shouted up, and a minute later a kitchen towel fell to the floor. He carefully wiped one of the small barrels and written on one end, in burnt-on letters, was the word 'Jerez' and then underneath 'Produto de la Frontera.' "Sherry," thought Harold, how strange, but what a wonderful find. He wondered if it was still good.

Next to the barrels were some wooden crates and Elroy was bending over and opening one. Suddenly he jumped back with a start as a mass of giant cockroaches jumped, ran and flew out in all directions, some landing on him. Elroy was not squeamish though, and he brushed them off calmly enough and stared into the box. It was full of bottles that had at one time been full of wine but the corks had either rotted away or been eaten away by the roaches and a kind of black, sticky residue had dribbled out.

On the opposite wall and hanging up from nails were some coils of rope and on two hooks hung a pair of ship's running lights. The copper housings were green with corrosion but the glass was visible through the dust: red and green. Rows of rusty horseshoes hung from three other nails. Harold noticed that they were hanging in such a way that the luck would run out. In the corner was an old anvil and several blacksmith's tools.

In another corner and extending out into the middle of the cellar were short planks of wood scattered haphazardly about on the floor with two longer pieces almost parallel. Memnon was first to figure out their origin. "Dat used to be de ladder," he said, "and look up dere – see de notches in de joist where de steps used to fasten in to." They all looked and sure enough Memnon was right.

In the third corner was another heap of what looked like a wood pile with a cloth over it, but it was so dusty it was hard to tell. Elroy started to pull off the covering but it too just fell apart in his hands – completely rotten. But underneath was a heavier canvas, and it was wrapped around what appeared to be a large wooden object. It was hard to unwrap because the object was heavy to lift, but they found that the canvas was so old that, with a little persuasion, it came away in strips. Harold uttered a gasp. He had unwrapped a carving of a giant female head. His immediate thought was that it was an Egyptian mummy. At first glance, both Memnon and Elroy stepped back and cowered into the far corner.

"Me ain't like dat at all," said Elroy. "We messin' wid ting from dead people long time back." And that about summed it up for Memnon, too. He was scrambling out of the hole and back up to the worldly lights of the pantry. Harold, though, was not deterred. Mesmerised, he continued unwrapping the huge female carving. The naked breasts were beautifully formed and nipples stood out conspicuously. As he unwrapped the last pieces of canvas, he saw that the bottom half of the statue was a shapely fish tail, complete with scales. It was a giant mermaid!

"Incredible!" exclaimed Harold. "Come and have a look at this, you chaps."

Elroy and Memnon came forward cautiously and then Memnon's eyes lit up. "Dat's a figurehead from an ol' sailin' ship. Look where it used to attach to de bow of de ship." He pointed to the large bolt holes.

As usual Memnon was right. Figureheads on sailing

ships were a common sight in the golden age of sail. Not only were they decorative, but were considered good luck and "the eyes of the ship." They were always positioned above the cutwater and beneath the bowsprit. This particular one was a beautiful specimen and probably at least a hundred years old. The hair was painted a golden yellow and cascaded down the back of the torso, which was a light pink flesh colour. The face had a knowing half smile, and the eyes were bright blue and piercing, but the cheeks were perhaps slightly too rosy, being almost cherry red. The breasts were full and voluptuous and the body tapered down to a slim waist, the arms ending in delicate fingers at the body's side. The bottom half was painted a turquoise blue, and each scale was highlighted in white as though wet and glistening in the sun. It was a magnificent work of art, and although there were chips and scrapes here and there, the colours had stood the test of time amazingly well.

"Right," said Harold, "I want to photograph the entire area before we move anything. Then I want to get this figurehead up to the main house where we can clean it and examine it more closely."

Jackie walked into the pantry from the kitchen. "I'll run down and find JC. He always has a camera with him."

"We gonna need a rope to hoist up de statue," said Elroy.

They all climbed out of the hole and Memnon gazed up at the ceiling. "If we drill a hole trew de upstairs floor joist right above de hole we can tie a pulley dere an' reave de line trew. Make de hoistin' real easy dat way."

"Yeah, you right," said Elroy. "Better go dung to de boat shed an' get de tackle."

Ten minutes later Harold, Memnon and Elroy were

all back in the cellar and posing with the mermaid whilst JC took photos. Before he'd finished, JC had taken three rolls of film from just about every conceivable angle. He was as excited as Harold at the amazing find.

Isaac and Toshi had everything ready by the time the photo session was over, and all that was needed now was for the men in the cellar to manhandle the figurehead under the hole and fasten the rope securely to it. This they did with several wraps around the mermaid's neck: she would come up head first. Everyone climbed out of the hole to help with the pulling and delicate task of guiding.

Three men grabbed the hoisting rope and heaved. With the mechanical advantage of the pulley, the mermaid came up without much trouble and the head reached floor level fast. "Easy does it," shouted Harold, and he guided the head through the hole. When he came to the breasts he shouted, "Slowly now, steady as she goes. I don't want to break off the nipples." The shoulder and chest area only just made it through, with both sides touching the perimeter of the hole. They thought they were home and dry but in fact they had underestimated the craftsman's generosity when it came to the hips and buttocks, and it was here that the mermaid stuck.

"Wiggle a little to the left," shouted Harold, but she didn't budge. "A little to the right," shouted Harold, but still she wouldn't budge. "A little more tension on the hoist and we'll wiggle in a circular motion," but still she hardly moved, perhaps an inch at most. "Stop," he shouted "I don't want to break her head off." Harold was sweating and tense with frustration. Why didn't I measure the thing first, he thought. "OK, let's lower it back down into the cellar," but that was not an option at this stage. The men let go of the hoisting line and with a little slack in the line, they tried to persuade it back down, but even with a lot more wiggling, the mermaid wouldn't move.

"Only ting to do, cut a bigger hole roun' de existin' hole," said Elroy, "but we gonna need a special saw for dat cos we gonna have to cut clear trew de joist."

Harold had to agree. He thought that perhaps soaking the obstinate area with oil might help, but he really didn't want to risk damaging the figurehead. "Can you find an appropriate saw?" he said wearily.

"Yeah," said Elroy, "I bring one in de marnin'."

It was getting late. The men had already put in an hour of overtime and Harold just remembered that he hadn't eaten any lunch.

"Right," said Harold, "we'll leave everything as it is and continue in the morning. I want to thank you men and you will all be well rewarded." There were nods and smiles all round. Then they packed up and went home.

Beulah and Lynette Leonard lived in the village called The Bluff, which was tucked around the lee side of the western headland that overlooked Rum Cove. They were mother and daughter and lived alone, barely existing on money made from part-time menial labour, so when Beulah got a call from a Mrs Mcphereson at GSC with a cleaning job that would possibly develop into full-time employment, she was excited. Beulah was a big lady with a big personality and lots of laughs. In contrast to her meagre existence, she embraced her world, and whether feeding the chickens or herding her goats, she could often be heard singing gospel songs in full voice.

Lynette, her daughter of 16 years, was rather the opposite. She was at that pubescent stage of life involving transformation from girl to woman and presented the world with a somewhat gawky appearance that made her shy.

They both set off early that morning to start work at GSC. Mrs Mcphereson wanted the lodge to be cleaned from top to bottom. The security guard in the office gave them the key and they entered the lodge through the reception area and went through to the kitchen. Beulah pushed the door open to the pantry and stopped in her tracks. Then she let out a horrifying scream, "AAAAaaaaaaaaaaahh!" Her eyes opened wide and then rolled up into her head and she fell backwards into a dead faint onto the floor, with a loud crash.

Lynette was putting away her lunch bag in the kitchen when she heard the awful scream and went running into the pantry. She looked once, did a double take and then looked again. In the dim morning light she saw the naked torso of a giant, yellow-haired white woman, seemingly without legs, hanging by a rope from the rafters. Then she saw her mum lying face up on the floor with only the whites of her eyes showing. She was overcome with shock and stood there paralysed for several seconds. Then she took to her heels and ran, shouting and screaming gibberish as she went. She ran out of the lodge, down to the office, out of the property, along the road and up the hill to The Bluff. As she ran, she waved her arms in the air and screamed, "De jumbi kilt me mammy! Help! Call de police! Murder! Help! Jumbi in de ol' Hodge place! De jumbi kilt me mammy! Help! Mammy! Mammy! Mammy!"

As she reached the top of the hill, Elroy and his crew of workmen were coming the other way in the pick-up and they pulled to a halt beside the distraught girl. Elroy got out of the truck and took both the girl's hands in his, "Wha' happen girl?" he said, "How you vex, so?"

"De jumbi kilt me mammy," she said, breathing in gasps and tears streaming down her face. "Dung in de ol' Hodge place."

"What you talkin' 'bout girl. Come, get in de truck an' show me." Elroy helped her into the front seat and they drove down into the GSC parking area.

"I ain't goin' in," said the girl, "I frighted too much," and she started sobbing again. "You go in an' check it out. It in de kitchen."

The men looked at each other in amazement and walked up to the lodge and then into the kitchen. They saw nothing and then Memnon pushed open the pantry door. Beulah was still lying on the floor but she was coming round, it seemed. Her eyes were wide but the pupils were back where they belonged. She was mumbling some kind of prayers, every few words being interspersed with 'Oh Lawd' or 'Oh God.' Memnon bent down. "Come now, Miss Beulah, what you doin' dung on de flaw."

"I can't move," she said, then she turned her head and pointed at the mermaid. A look of terror shadowed her face.

"Dat ain't nuttin," said Memnon, gently. "Dat only a statue an' jus now we gonna move it anyhow. Come, I help you up." With Memnon's help, she got to her feet. He guided her out of the pantry and found a seat for her in the kitchen. Just then Harold and Jackie walked in.

Elroy and Memnon explained the whole story and Harold couldn't suppress a smile but Jackie was more sympathetic – after all she had hired the two women and felt somewhat responsible. "Go and bring the girl in," she said to Memnon. "I'll make you both a nice cup of tea."

"Tank you ma'am," she said, "I sorry, but I were real

frighten." Beulah was sitting there with her head bowed, looking miserable.

Meanwhile Harold and the construction crew were back in the pantry confronting the problem of the obstinate mermaid. Harold had brought with him a gallon of vegetable oil. "Before we start cutting more of the floor away, I want to try a little lubrication," he said, and started pouring the oil generously around the perimeter of the hole and torso of the statue. Then Toshi, Isaac and Elroy hoisted and Memnon grabbed the mermaid's upper body and started revolving it in a quick, circular motion.

"More strain on the hoist," said Harold, and went over to help Memnon. The statue came up another inch and he poured on more oil. Then finally the men were pulling and pulling and the mermaid was out. The men let out a cheer and swung the figurehead over to one side and brought it to rest on the pantry floor. Everyone rested for a moment. Harold walked over to inspect the magnificent carving and was pleased to find that there was only slight damage to the paintwork.

"We'd better cover her with a blanket or two," said Harold, "I don't want to frighten the cleaning ladies again." There were chuckles around the room.

Just then a police siren was heard coming from the direction of the parking area and a few minutes later two policemen entered the kitchen. They walked over to Harold, who was stirring a cup of tea. "Good morning, sir," he said, "this is Officer Bungell and I'm Sergeant Balzup. We've had a report of a homicide. Can you show us where the body is located?"

"Ah," said Harold, "well, the problem was in the pantry . . ."

"Right," said Balzup to Bungell, before Harold could finish. "Cordon off the area of the pantry. The area is now off limits, we don't want to compromise any fingerprints. Secure the entire area with yellow tape."

Outside on the patio a reporter had arrived from the *Island Times* and was talking to Memnon, who had gone out for a cooling glass of water. He had introduced himself as Godfrey Allbright, and was an apprentice journalist from England. "OK," said the freckle-faced young man, "let me read it back to you just to make sure I've got the facts right.

"'You found a large, bare-breasted mermaid under the building. There were five of you all together and you all decided that you wanted to get it up. You wrestled her in place and after a lot of panting and sweating you couldn't get it up because the hole was too small. Then with a lot of pushing, pulling and wiggling you managed to get it up a part of the way. Finally, after pouring oil around the hole and rubbing her hips and buttocks she came and you all had a release. Everyone cheered and now she is lying on the pantry floor on her back. A cleaning lady witnessed the incident and fainted. The leader of the gang was Harold Mcphereson.' Is that pretty much the way it happened?"

"Yeah, you got it," said Memnon and walked back into the kitchen, followed by Allbright, who wanted to see the crime scene and get a photo of the body, but was barred by Balzup, who told him it was a restricted area.

"Absolutely disgusting," said the reporter, looking at Officer Bungell. "What a bunch of perverts!" He walked out whilst the cops looked at each other vacantly.

Ten minutes later Harold was still trying to explain the situation through all the interruptions. "Wait!" he cried, "will you all stop and listen!" He shouted so loudly that everyone turned and looked in his direction. Then Harold calmly explained the whole story and finally the two policemen realised that there had been a misunderstanding.

"I'm going to have to take a statement," said the sergeant. He turned to Beulah and Lynette, who both seemed to be recovering quickly. "And you two ladies will have to make a statement as well."

"I sorry," said Beulah, "I did'n' mean to make no trouble for nobody."

"Don't you worry about a thing," said Harold. "You were here for work at the crack of dawn and you will both be paid for a full day. Now let's go in and have a look at this magnificent carving." They all went in to the pantry and looked at the figurehead with all the lights on.

Beulah let out a shriek and Harold looked at her, momentarily worried, but it was an expression of self-ridicule. "AAyyyeeeee, I don' believe I were ever scare' o' dat," she said, tapping the wooden object and laughing loudly.

Then Harold made an announcement: "This amazing find will pre-determine some choices that I have made. One of those is that the bar of the Sunset Lodge will now be named the 'Mermaid Bar.' The mermaid will be mounted above the front door."

By now the two policemen had taken their statements. They apologised for any inconvenience and left. Harold was anxious to bring up the rest of the contents of the cellar. The first job was to cut open the original access door to the cellar and from the underneath, the outline of the old one was clearly seen. Elroy had brought a "sawsall," so the work was relatively easy. A new ladder would have to be constructed but for now they would swing themselves up and down as before.

There were nine 10-gallon casks sitting on the

pantry floor by lunchtime. They had lost one when Toshi had rested it down rather too roughly and the rusty and corroded hoops that held together the staves had disintegrated. The whole floor had been swamped with a golden liquid and it was then they realised that the barrels' contents were not sherry at all, but rum. Here was another unexplained mystery. How did rum get into clearly marked sherry casks? The ship's two running lights were brought up and so were the crates of wine. Unfortunately, none of the wine was any good, but the bottles were clearly old and worth saving.

By 4 p.m. the cellar had been cleared and Harold and Elroy had discussed making it into a proper storage area with white walls and fluorescent lights. Shelves would be built, air conditioning installed and a stout new ladder built. The holes and the cracks caused by the storm would be repaired and reinforced and a drainage gut built behind the property with storm drains.

Beulah and Lynette had worked like Trojans all afternoon. Encouraged by Jackie and Harold's kind words and consoling attitude, they had swept, vacuumed, tidied and polished and the complete downstairs of the lodge sparkled like a new pin. Harold and Jackie had decided to move into suite 1 in the morning and Jackie had been busy making lists of necessities all day.

Before they all went home, Harold tapped one of the barrels of rum and the golden elixir was so smooth that not one of the construction crew declined Harold's offer to take a bottle home and although Toshi "did'n' drink de pizen," he'd still take a bottle for a friend. Harold carefully decanted the golden spirit into four of the wine bottles and together with a cheque for $200 for each man as a bonus, they went home happy.

On the drive back to the Calabash that night, Harold was as excited as a little boy at the fairground, and he wasted no time explaining his theories to Jackie. "This rum is almost undoubtedly 80 years old and maybe more," he said. "Alan Stanborg told me that the last major renovations to the building were in the 1920's and that must have been when the cellar was sealed off. With a mermaid for a figurehead it would seem likely that the name of the ship might have been *The Mermaid*. I'm going to make enquiries through Lloyd's register of shipping. Perhaps *The Mermaid* was in the rum exporting business – after all, the bay is called Rum Cove.

"I'm going to have special bottles made for that rum," he said, "and the labels will have a beautiful mermaid painted on them. The name for our rum will be 'Mermaid's Gold' and it will sell for not less than $100 per bottle! Where else can you buy 80-year-old rum, matured in oak casks?"

"Well," said Jackie, "you'd better make sure that rum really is as old as you think or you'll be had up for sharp practice."

Harold paid no attention. Nine barrels of rum with 10 gallons per barrel – that was 90 gallons or 360 quarts. "It should take care of any more 'donations' the government might spring on us," he said, bitterly. Harold had not forgotten the bribery incident.

At dinner that night Jackie suggested to Harold that she fly to Miami to buy the items on her huge list of necessities for the business. Everything from glasses, cutlery, linens, crockery, kitchen utensils, appliances, and more – the list seemed endless. Harold agreed and suggested that she get together with Anne Cleary and go over the inventory of the Rusty Pelican and decide on a startup inventory for a boutique that wasn't even built yet. She decided she'd go up on the Monday of the following week and take Anne Cleary with her.

In the morning they moved into suite 1 at the lodge. Harold spent the afternoon at Caribbee Motors taking delivery of the company vehicles. He had ordered a Land Cruiser for himself and Jackie which might also be used for taxiing guests in an emergency and he had been offered a recent model station wagon that he "couldn't refuse," because the price was so cheap. This would be an excellent second vehicle and perfect for the yacht division, too. It had enough space in the back for sails, outboard motors etc. The company was also going to buy Roy's pickup truck. They had arranged to use the Clearys' vehicle too, with expenses paid on a mileage basis.

On Saturday afternoon all the staff had gone home and Harold was in the office looking at the yacht bookings chart and reservations for the lodge. The Christmas bookings were looking quite good.

The phone rang and he answered it. It was Miss Primby, the governor's aide, and she sounded sombre. "The governor asked me to call you regarding the article on the front page of the *Island Times*. He said if there's anything he can do, just call." She put the phone down before the bewildered Harold could reply. He jumped into his new car and drove up to the village shop at The Bluff. The weekly paper came out on Saturday morning and he bought a copy and started to read the front page. His first glance revealed nothing that concerned him. Then on closer examination he read the headline: "Alleged Gang Rape. First ever in Caribbee Isles." Then a sub-headline read: "Peaceful charter yacht resort scene of grisly crime." The article went on to describe Golden Sunset Charters and how it had been recently taken over and then it came to the part that made Harold's head spin. "A tourist was sunbathing topless on the grass at the base of the newly renovated lodge. Five men approached the girl, whose nickname is believed to be Mermaid, and started touching, pawing and generally manhandling the defenceless girl. Then the five men reportedly raped the girl one at a time whilst the others watched and cheered. It has been reported that the new owner of the property, Harold Mcphereson, was the ringleader. The police were quickly at the scene."

Harold's head was reeling and his knees felt like jelly. This was outrageous and the more he thought about it the more incensed he became. He returned to the lodge wondering who on earth could have spread such a malicious rumour and why. Could it be that someone was trying to sabotage his new business? He must call Mike Broadrite, the company lawyer.

"Hello, Mike, this is Harold Mcphereson. Have you read today's *Island Times*?"

"Yes," he said, "tell me what really happened."

"The whole story is a complete fabrication. This is severe defamation of character – the governor phoned me up and the whole island has probably read this bogus story by now. I want you to throw the book at them! Sue them for all they've got!" Harold was red with rage and shaking.

"Have you any idea what was the basis of this story?" asked Broadrite.

"Some workmen found a hidden cellar under the lodge and in it, amongst other things, was a carved wooden ship's figurehead. The carving was of a mermaid."

"That's all?" said the lawyer, astounded. "No gang? No live girl? No nothing?"

"The whole story is total fiction," said Harold wearily.

"Right," said Broadrite, "leave it to me. I know the editor of the *Island Times*. I'll call him up and get to the bottom of this. I know this must be very embarrassing for you but try and stay calm and don't talk to anyone."

"Do your best and keep me informed," said Harold and put down the phone. He sat down and slumped forward, head in hands.

Mike Broadrite immediately called up the police station to verify whether there had been a police investigation at GSC the previous Tuesday. The sergeant at the desk confirmed that there had been an enquiry but that there was nothing to report and the call had been a false alarm. Statements had been taken and were on file.

Broadrite then called up the paper's editor, an acquaintance of his, Neil James, and demanded an explanation for a completely fictitious story that implicated his client. They arranged to meet at 9 a.m. on Monday morning at the editor's office.

Mike was a sympathetic and compassionate man and he decided to go over to see Harold and try and console him. The paper would have a lot of explaining to do – it was implicating an ex-officer of the British army, a mature man of high morals with a grownup family. When Mike arrived, he found Harold and Jackie in the kitchen drinking coffee. They invited him to join them and Harold told him the complete story of the cellar and its contents and the trouble they had had getting the mermaid out. "How this story got turned around like this I can't imagine," said Harold. "I shall want a complete apology in writing and on the front page of the paper's next edition."

Jackie went and stood behind Harold in a supportive pose with her hands on his shoulders. "My husband has never ever been even remotely connected with any scandal. This is a great shock."

"Well, I have an appointment with the editor on Monday morning and I shall pull out all the stops. I'll keep in touch." Broadrite finished his coffee and departed.

On Monday, Neil James wished Mike a cheery good morning and ushered him into his office and offered him a cup of coffee. The lawyer declined – this was not a social visit, he said. They sat down. "This is about the rape case you reported in last Saturday's edition," said Broadrite, without preamble. "It is completely without foundation and my client is out for blood."

"On the contrary," said James, "this is a tape recording of an interview that my junior reporter did out at GSC last Tuesday." The editor turned on the miniature cassette player. Godfrey Allbright was clearly audible, as was Memnon, but the island dialect was broad and it was obvious that the boy had misinterpreted it.

"This is confusing and ambiguous at best and certainly not sufficient evidence to implicate Harold Mcphereson in a rape case."

"Mike," said James, consolingly, "the article said 'alleged' and 'reportedly,' in other words it was secondhand information to us. That's all part of journalism."

"What is part of journalism is to report the facts," said Mike with hostility. "You didn't even check the police blotter to see if any charges had been brought or even if there were any suspects, or even if there was a case. You didn't even check to see if there was a victim or what her name was. The only thing you wanted to do was print a scandal in order to sell more papers and without regard to the truth or my client. Thanks to you, Harold Mcphereson's name is now about as clear as a glass of mud. I'm afraid your 'journalism' is going to cost you a lot of money. In fact, it's going to cost you millions! See you in court!" He walked out and slammed the door.

The lawyer walked back to his office, made himself a cup of coffee and waited for the phone to ring. It did, 10 minutes later. It was Neil James on the phone, of course. "There's been a terrible misunderstanding," he said. "On closer examination of Allbright's material, I have to agree that he misinterpreted some of the facts." James was backpedalling fast. He knew that Mike Broadrite was a very powerful lawyer.

"Misinterpreted facts!" said Broadrite. "'Misinterpreted facts' is a gross understatement for what can only be described as malicious distortion of the facts and irresponsible reporting, the blame for which lies squarely on your shoulders as editor. There is only one way that you can avoid a very costly lawsuit and that is to print on the front page of the next issue a full and complete apology – the wording of which will be dictated by me. Then, since this will only partially heal the wounded character of my client, you will make available to him a half page of free advertising every week for six months."

"Now, just a minute," spluttered James. "That is excessive compensation for some rather over-zealous reporting by a junior staff reporter."

"You are personally responsible for the contents of your newspaper," continued Broadrite ebulliently. "So don't try and pass the blame onto the reporter. You can never fully repair the damage done to Mr Mcphereson's character and you should be very grateful that I am letting you off so lightly. It will take quite a bit of persuasion on my part to appease Harold Mcphereson and get him to accept an apology. Personally, I have no doubt that we could win huge damages from your paper, so if you prefer we'll go to court."

"No, no, I accept your proposal," said James. "Might as well calm troubled waters as expeditiously as possible. I'll write to Mr Mcphereson personally." Neil James was weaseling out of a corner that he knew he was backed into.

Broadrite still wasn't finished. "You'll send me an agreement, immediately and in writing, outlining the available space in the newspaper that you will give to Mr Mcphereson for the next six months and state clearly and unequivocally that a quarter of the front page of the next issue will be reserved for a written public apology. I'll get the text over to you in the next day or two. Goodbye!" He slammed the phone down.

Mike then called Harold at Sunset Lodge and explained the events of the morning. "I've got you $10,000 worth of free advertising and a guaranteed apology in writing to be published on the front page of the next issue. It's up to you if you want to accept that or press for further damages in a court hearing," he said.

"That damned newspaper is getting off lightly," said Harold, "but I'm inclined to accept it. The whole island knows that the story is nothing more than a joke – Memnon, Elroy and the rest of the construction crew who were also implicated have all been having a good laugh and the *Island Times* is being properly ridiculed. They've destroyed their own credibility. The other paper, *The Beacon*, sent a photographer and reporter down here yesterday and they are doing a feature on the real news of the amazing find in the cellar. It seems as though we shall get a bit of free advertising from them as well."

"I think you're wise to accept a printed public apology. Court cases, especially civil suits, take an inordinate amount of time here in the islands, and even though you're innocent of the charges, the publicity would be harmful."

"Thank you for your time and effort," said Harold,

"I'm glad you're on our team. By the way, would you mind calling the governor and explaining the situation? I believe he may have got the wrong impression." He rang off with a sigh of relief. He had to admit to himself that the timing was just right for a bit of free advertising.

6

The Opening

It was the second week in December and Golden Sunset Charters was in high gear. The official grand opening was in five days and a barbecue and dance were planned at the Rusty Pelican. A dinner was arranged for the lodge restaurant and tickets were $40 each. Dress was to be informal but "casually elegant."

Down at the dock the construction crew, under the capable guidance of Elroy Stevens, was just completing the repairs and renovations. All the service outlets had been restored to working order, and the wood skirting to the dock had been finished off with a white rubber strip for protecting yachts' topsides. There were new bollards, rows of lights and the fuel dock was clean with new garbage disposal facilities. GSC's yachts were lying alongside. They looked ship-shape and Bristol fashion and ready for action. All the varnish work had been freshly done, sail covers looked neat and tidy, and topsides had been waxed and shone in the noonday sun. There were 10 yachts in total: two were out on charter and two were still in the boat yard. The three brand new catamarans were all expected to arrive within the next two weeks and there was anxious anticipation since they were all booked for Christmas charters.

JC was waiting in anticipation too, but in excited anticipation. Shirley was due to arrive the following day. Harold and Jackie had finally agreed that she could team up with JC as captain and cook on *Sunfun Calypso* after they had learned that she had passed a Cordon Bleu cooking course.

JC had been employed by GSC for the last month. His job was temporary operations manager until he took over his new captaincy. He had been doing chart briefings and yacht orientation for guests, and in between he had been supervising maintenance projects of all kinds.

For people to charter a yacht they had to send the company a resumé of prior sailing experience. This was not really for the company's benefit since charter yachts had to be insured and a security deposit or credit card had to be supplied to cover any deductible in case of an accident. It was for the safety of the clients, who might underestimate the skills needed to run a large yacht. Many rather unscrupulous companies, though, tended to disregard the capabilities of questionable customers in favour of putting money in the bank. More and more charterers were out there with sails flapping around, or sitting on the bottom aground, or otherwise embarrassing themselves.

Regardless of any resumé or questionnaire, JC

prided himself in being able to judge the capabilities of clients within an hour of his yacht briefings. If they looked doubtful he would insist that they take a captain, an experienced local yachtsman, with them for at least the first two days. Sometimes guests were tense when it came to these pre-charter briefings so JC had devised a method of breaking the ice by means of a nautical 15 question test.

Give the correct meaning to the following phrases by circling A or B.

1) Heave to
    A. *Be seasick.*
    B. *Stop the ship at sea.*

2) Swing the compass
    A. *Throw out faulty navigational instrument.*
    B. *Make a deviation card.*

3) Do the bottom
    A. *Scrape and paint the underwater area of the vessel.*
    B. *Engage in act of buggery.*

4) Ship's draft
    A. *A cold breeze.*
    B. *Depth of vessel below waterline.*

5) Wind is up
    A. *Obnoxious flatulence rising from below.*
    B. *Increase in wind speed.*

6) Haul in the sheets
    A. *Adjust the sails.*
    B. *Change the linens.*

7) Heave the lead
    A. *Manually find the depth.*
    B. *Remove the ballast.*

8) Wear ship
    A. *Put on gold yacht earrings.*
    B. *Jibe.*

9) Tie the painter
    A. *Make fast the dinghy line.*
    B. *Securely bind the person painting.*

10) Yard arm
    A. *Arm three feet in length.*
    B. *Horizontally slung spar aloft.*

11) Anti foul
    A. *Chicken resistant paint.*
    B. *Poisonous paint for ship's bottom.*

12) Ratchet	A. *Toothed wheel and pawl mechanism as found in a winch or windlass.*
	B. *Fecal matter deposited by rodent.*
13) A preventer guy	A. *Line used to prevent boom or pole from swinging.*
	B. *Maritime security guard.*
14) Dead reckoning	A. *Method of navigation.*
	B. *Estimating a seaman's life span.*
15) Jolly Roger	A. *That infernal man always on the VHF radio.*
	B. *Pirate flag.*

JC noticed that nearly all the knowledgeable clients answered the wrong or anautical answers on purpose – and quite rightly for such a facetious test, he thought. But they were on vacation, and anyway, it was all in fun and everyone had a good laugh.

On Tuesday morning Harold arranged a meeting at the GSC office to discuss the company's insurance policy. All the necessary surveys had been done and Caribbean Mutual Benefit had drawn up a rough proposal. Harold, Mike Broadrite and Sonia Hodge were present on behalf of the company. Reuben Winston, Charles Mcguire and their lawyer, Adolf Reephoff of solicitors Bigsum, Hannover, Reephoff and Blarney represented Caribbean Mutual Benefit. After introductions and general small talk, they sat down around the polished conference table. Harold opened the proceedings by welcoming everyone. His short speech outlined the repairs, renovations and improvements, and he was pleased that the surveys had been so favourable, even describing the locations of all the fire extinguishers on the property. "And I hope that our business will be of mutual benefit as your name implies," he concluded.

Charles Mcguire responded. He was a grey man – he was wearing a grey suit, a grey tie, he had thinning grey hair and his complexion looked grey – probably from drinking too much port or claret. "It is with great pleasure that I offer the services of our company to you," he began and smiled ingratiatingly around the table, showing expensively capped front teeth. "You have made an excellent choice since all our policies are underwritten by National Allied Insurers of New York and they are immensely well-funded. We have their balance sheet here for your perusal." Broadrite raised his eyebrows at the word "choice" – there had been no choice.

"As you know we are experts in the field of island insurance and have years of experience to draw from, particularly in the area of marine insurance. Our premiums are very reasonable for the coverage offered. For example, the yacht premiums average a little over $3,000 per annum for full coverage – there being a small deductible payable by the charterer and an individual collision damage policy can be taken out by them at the time of booking." Mcguire went on to discuss insurance for the property and buildings; life, accident and health coverage for the employees and a pension plan based on earnings and length of service that Harold had insisted on. As he talked, Winston handed out copies of the proposal: pages and pages of writing and figures, some of it in small print and the text liberally sprinkled with legal jargon to make it all but impossible for the layman to understand. The bottom line, though, was what interested Harold most and he was stunned to see the estimated premiums were almost six figures.

It would be Broadrite's job to go over the content of the policies and scan for loopholes but he had an immediate question that needed confirming. "We must be quite certain that the property and yachts are fully covered for tropical storm, hurricane and related damage," he said. "After the last two severe hurricane seasons our yacht owners are somewhat concerned. Many yachts are leaving our waters and heading south to the safer latitudes from July to November. If our owners decided to do the same, we would lose a lot of business."

Winston responded with a comforting smile. "You may rest assured that your policies will cover hurricane and storm damage," he said. "Unlike a lot of Caribbean insurance companies who have considered the risk too great, we believe that it is our public duty to stand firmly behind our clients on this issue, especially those whose main business activity is the rental of yachts. And don't forget, we have a very solid underwriter." What a silver-tongued salesman, thought Broadrite, but the coverage had been included, as he could see clearly on page 14 of the proposal.

Sonia Hodge had been busy taking notes, but now she spoke up. She looked directly at Winston and with a challenging smile said, "With such a large overall premium, the company would expect favourable terms and a minimum 10 per cent discount on the total." Harold turned and stared at her open-mouthed. Broadrite was startled, too.

"Well – ahem, ahem – " (Reuben Winston was not prepared for this), "our premiums are carefully worked out by computerised formulas," he said, "and there's not much room for maneuvering here."

"You are aware, I think, that my family owned this property until recently and I have the previous insurance premiums right here. Now, even considering the adverse changes in weather phenomena and the property improvements and upgrades, there is little justification for an increase in premiums of over a hundred per cent!" Sonia's voice rose to a crescendo.

"We are always prepared to work out compromises and terms with our valued customers," said Mcguire smoothly. "When the policies are finalised, I will personally make sure that you are satisfied and I believe that a 25 per cent down payment with the balance payable in quarterly increments can be arranged."

The meeting came to a close and Reephoff, who had been silent during the meeting, approached Harold. "Zat was very cleffer how you arranched ze mermaid incident. Now zee whole island knows about GSC. Very cleffer, very cleffer." He walked away smiling his crooked smile and shaking his head. Harold didn't answer, and walked out to the patio in front of the office.

Sonia approached, a little out of breath, her high heels clicking on the tiled floor. "Mr Mcphereson, I hope I didn't overstep the mark challenging those sharks like that, but I was so angry – they've almost doubled the premiums in the last two years."

"You made a bold move at the right time and it worked. They promised a compromise and terms which will be beneficial to us. The problem is that where there is no competition there is no room for bargaining – you either buy their insurance or you don't have any at all. It's an unfortunate situation and on a small island it's sometimes inevitable – just look at the telephone company. Next time, though, notify the members of your team in advance so they know what to expect. Well done, Sonia, good work."

Just then JC came running up with Shirley in tow. "I've just had a call on the VHF. All three of our new catamarans have just cleared customs formalities in Roadstead and should be arriving at the marina in about half an hour."

"Oh, that's excellent news. Make sure there are a couple of men on the dock and ready to help them with the lines. Shirley, I hope you're well rested after your trip." Shirley had arrived back the day before yesterday, and Harold had let both her and JC stay in the lodge, until they could move onto *Sunfun.*

"I'm jutht fine thankth," she said, "and I can't wait to help make *'Thunfun'* the finetht luxury yacht in the Caribbean." Harold had a feeling that she would too; she had the enthusiasm, was grateful for the opportunity and had had formal training. Also, she was anxious to please JC, who had first suggested the idea to her when she was feeling hopelessly depressed about her future.

The official opening of GSC was that Friday, and it seemed that activities were reaching a peak – a crescendo of energy that would end in the climax of the grand opening party. All the tickets had been sold for dinner at the lodge and a large crowd was expected at the Rusty Pelican. Just then, Sonia called out from the office – Jackie and Anne Cleary were at the airport, back from their shopping expedition in Miami, with eight large boxes. Would Harold meet them? "I'm on my way," he shouted.

Harold jumped into the new Land Cruiser and 20 minutes later he was parked outside the airport. He pushed his way through the glass door and came face to face with Godfrey Allbright. The young journalist looked red-eyed and tired. Over his shoulder was slung a worn and tattered carry-all and in his other hand he was holding a rather battered portable typewriter. It took several seconds for Harold to recollect the young man's face and then to connect him to the mermaid incident. But when he did he started to boil with rage. Harold pointed his forefinger right at Allbright's nose and said, "Your disgusting piece of sensationalism in the last issue of the *Island Times* has tarnished my image forever. I hope you're proud of your work!"

The apprentice journalist replied defensively in a whining voice, "I just misinterpreted an islander's dialect, that's all. I didn't write the article, but because of it, I've been fired. I'm sick of journalism and I'm sick of editors. I'm going home to study marine biology." Allbright shuffled away. He looked so despondent that Harold immediately felt compassion.

"Now, wait a minute." Harold ran after the lad. "If you didn't write the article, then who did?"

"I handed my cassette tape over to Neil James and he used it to write the story. I believe he knew the story was open to criticism, that's why he used my by-line. That way he had a scapegoat." He shuffled off towards the ticket counter whilst Harold stood there feeling nothing but contempt and loathing for the editor of the *Island Times.*

"Look," said Harold, "this incident has had unfortunate results for both of us and I'm sorry that Neil James has treated you so badly. Please keep in touch – perhaps I can help you in the future." They exchanged business cards.

"Harold! Harold!" Jackie was waving from the other end of the concourse, surrounded by packages and boxes. Harold waved back and soon the ladies were eagerly describing their trip and their purchases whilst Harold had a porter load all the boxes into the vehicle.

"We brought with us the essential items that will be needed for the opening, the rest is being shipped and should arrive in time for Christmas. I found some beautiful Italian crystal water jugs shaped like mermaids for the bar. And Anne's inventory for the boutique provides plenty of tropical variety." Jackie was obviously excited.

"Not only that but we have a huge selection of T-shirts. They're big sellers and high markup," said Anne knowledgeably.

"Well, I'm glad the shopping expedition went well," said Harold, "but the drawback is that the boutique won't be finished in time for the opening. In fact it probably won't be finished until sometime in January, what with the approaching holidays."

"Perhaps we could display some of the T-shirts and sarongs in the Rusty Pelican," said Anne, always enthusiastic about her little niche in the business.

George Cleary was at the office waiting for them when they returned from the airport. All three catamarans were securely tied up stern-to at the end of the marina, but apparently there was a problem concerning import duty, which had to be paid within 24 hours of arrival. Harold confirmed that he would deal with it first thing in the morning. George and Harold were still on friendly terms, but Harold sensed that the previous owner was finding it difficult adjusting to his new role as departmental manager rather than over-all owner.

After the boxes were unloaded, they all went into the office to discuss the details for the opening. "I want to leave the marina floodlit for the whole evening," began Harold. "This will not only help with security but will highlight the yachts for the benefit of those wandering by. The main attraction at the marina will be the catamarans, of course. I'm going to put JC and Shirley in charge there and they can give guided tours if necessary.

"The Rusty Pelican will be the centre of activity and Memnon will be in charge of the barbecuing. The barmaids should be able to handle the drinks until after dinner, then some of the lodge staff can go down there to lend a hand.

"Up at the lodge Jackie will be in charge of the kitchen with the able assistance of Beulah and Lynette, and I will supervise the Mermaid Bar. I would like to offer the job of host and hostess of the lodge restaurant, for this special opening night, to you, George and Anne. You will know most of the guests and I had a confirmation today that the governor and his wife, the Clement-Joneses, will be attending."

Anne looked at George, who stared back, expressionless. Then they both smiled broadly and Anne said, "It would be a privilege and an honour. And thank you."

Friday morning broke with dark clouds scudding across the Tortuga sky. Intermittent squalls and gusty winds did not auger well for an opening day party, much of which was planned for outside. By lunchtime, Harold was beginning to make contingency plans to move the dinner party indoors, but the clouds separated and a weak sun peeped through. It is seldom that Caribbean weather remains bad for more than a few hours and on this occasion the clouds dispersed throughout the afternoon. Everyone breathed a sigh of relief and the last-minute preparations continued at a feverish pace.

Harold and Jackie and the Clearys were up at the lodge. "I've had commemorative menus printed, embossed with gold leaf," began Harold. "The name for the lodge restaurant will now be the Sunset Terrace. Jackie has decided that the menu will be island style and she and Beulah have been working hard selecting dishes that incorporate local ingredients and lend themselves to international flair."

"Yes," said Jackie, "the menu is as follows – Callaloo Soup or Smoked Marlin; Tropical Salad Vinaigrette; Lobster Thermidor or Medallions of Lamb; Whipped Sweet Potatoes and Asparagus Spears; Mango Ice

Cream; Coffee, Santo Domingo."

"Mmmm, it sounds absolutely scrumptious," said Anne, and the men nodded and murmured in approval.

"I'll explain the dishes so that you'll be able to answer any questions the guests might ask. First, Callaloo Soup is an old island speciality. It is made from the spinach-like leaves of the dasheen plant, a root vegetable and common staple in the islands. The other main ingredients are smoked ham, okra, salt fish and coconut milk. Our version will combine the cooked leaves, milk and other ingredients in the blender and the dish will be finished off with a little cream and nutmeg.

"Old Calvin Woods up at East End caught a black marlin last week and he's smoked most of it. I ordered a five-pound chunk and this will be thinly sliced and served with lemon wedges and a horseradish cream, with brown bread accompanying.

"Steamed crystophine – cold of course, sliced avocado and tomato will make up the salad, and the vinaigrette is my old favourite with soy sauce, honey and English mustard giving it the unique flavour.

"I don't expect there to be many orders for lamb when lobster thermidor is the alternative. The lobsters are boiled to just cooked and halved lengthwise. The meat is removed from the tails, taking care not to damage the shells and the contents of the head space is discarded. A thick bechamel is mixed half and half with heavy cream, a quality grated gruyere is added to taste and the sauce finished with a dry sherry. The lobster chunks are gently folded into the sauce and placed back in the shell and the head cavity is filled with the whipped sweet potato and made decorative by using a star nozzle in a piping bag. The dish is popped under the grill before serving.

"The medallions of lamb are cutlets or chops with the fat and bone removed. They are impregnated with garlic and rosemary and seared in hot olive oil and finished in the oven. They are served with a Madeira sauce.

"The rest is pretty self explanatory . . . Oh, the mango ice cream is homemade. I managed to get some beautiful grafted mangoes from the Dominica boat when it tied up alongside the jetty in town yesterday and they were ripened to perfection. And last, but most important, chilled champagne will be served throughout the meal."

At that moment Beulah and Lynette came round the side of the building on their way down to the Rusty Pelican. They were carrying huge trays of par-cooked baby back pork ribs and quartered chicken for the barbecue. Beulah had her hair tied up in a red and white polka-dotted scarf and her forehead was beaded with sweat. She approached Jackie with a concerned expression. "I worried 'bout Jonas, Miss Jackie. He drinkin' rum an' singin' away but de rate he goin' he ain' goin' to last de evenin'."

"Jonas?" enquired Harold, "who's Jonas?"

"He's a temporary worker I hired to help with the preparation and to do the dishes," explained Jackie, "but drinking on the job is forbidden. I'd better go and see him."

"I done tol' him aready," said Beulah, "but he ain' listen to me. He say he drinkin' tea but I seen de bottle in he back pocket.

"Come chil'," she said to Lynette, "we bes' get dese tings dung to de Rusty Pelican afore de flies does lay dier eggs on dem."

Jackie walked around to the kitchen. Jonas was sitting on a stool and bending over peeling a large pan of sweet potatoes. He looked up cheerfully. "Good aft'noon, Miss Jackie." He was a big man in his late thirties or thereabouts and he wore a rather scruffy cloth cap. His face was unshaven and his eyes were rheumy, but his speech was clear enough.

Without preamble Jackie said, "I want to make it quite clear, Jonas, that drinking on the job is strictly forbidden."

"Oh, yes ma'am, I unnerstan'." He smiled and started peeling a little faster.

"What is that bottle in your back pocket?" said Jackie, pointing accusingly.

"Oh, dat be a bottle o' mauby, ma'am, an' very healty it is too. You ever try it?" He offered the brown pint bottle. "It made from tree bark; plenty o' we does drink it dung islan'."

Jackie was taken aback. She didn't want to get near the bottle of rather nauseating looking liquid with bubbles floating on top that perhaps was saliva. She decided to be diplomatic. After all, would he have offered the bottle if it contained rum – perhaps Beulah had been mistaken. She gave Jonas the benefit of the doubt. "No thank you, Jonas," she said rather awkwardly, "I prefer tea in the afternoon."

Jackie went back out to the terrace and when she saw Beulah returning from the Rusty Pelican she explained what happened. "Aaaaaayeeeee, dat shaw one crafty niggah," said Beulah shaking her head and disappearing back into the kitchen. Jackie looked at Harold with raised eyebrows. She had an uneasy feeling about Jonas and Beulah's use of the forbidden 'N' word.

By 7 p.m. tropically attired dinner guests were climbing the steps to the Sunset Terrace and absorbing the opulence of the brand new restaurant decor. The mermaid was particularly conspicuous: Elroy had cleverly built a mock ship's stem above the door to the

Mermaid Bar and then mounted the mermaid onto it. Spotlights had been arranged to accentuate the beautiful full breasts and the head with flowing golden hair and Mona Lisa smile. The piercing blue eyes looked down on the diners on the terrace in an almost disarming way.

The centrepiece of the restaurant, though, was the three-tiered fountain. In the large bottom reservoir, the lilies and freshwater ferns decorating the edges provided a home for some miniature tree frogs. No-one knew how they got there but Harold had vowed to get rid of them – he was afraid that tadpoles would restrict the water flow. The jets of water that rose from the circumference of the bottom pool were staggered in alternate high and low jets and cascades of water from the next tier up and falling to the bottom level gave a most dramatic effect. Similar cascades fell from the top layer to the second and the whole spectacle was highlighted by blue, green and red lamps that shone through the spray. The two cherubs were peeing down from the top to the bottom level relentlessly in fine Florentine tradition, without a care in the world.

Among the first guests to arrive was old Mr Hodge, the previous owner of the property. He was accompanied by his daughter Sonia, who looked stunning in a yellow and black striped, ankle length dress, slit up the side just high enough to reveal a tempting bit of thigh. She wore a matching turban and large gold circular earrings.

They strolled across the terrace and into the bar, the old man taking a long look at the voluptuous figurehead above the door. "Congratulations, Mcphereson," said the white-haired old patriarch. "You've done a fine job renovating the property."

Harold was standing behind the bar arranging some cigars in a glass cabinet. He was freshly showered and "casually elegant" in an off-white linen suit, open neck shirt and blue paisley cravat with matching pocket handkerchief. Beaming, he leaned over the bar and extended his hand. "It is a privilege and a pleasure to welcome you to our little opening ceremony, Mr Hodge. You gave me very sound advice when you recommended your daughter for employment in our company. Now, what'll it be? The drinks are on me."

Sonia spoke up. "I'd like a planter's punch, but daddy can't drink alcohol – it's his gout."

"Nonsense," said the old man. "Give me a shot of white rum and a beer chaser. Can't let a grand party like this go to waste." Sonia looked disapprovingly at her father and made a sucking noise through her teeth.

When the drinks were served, Hodge said to Harold, "An interesting story about the mermaid in the cellar. I read the whole thing in the weekly Beacon. One thing they didn't mention though, but perhaps it was irrelevant, was that my grandfather was mate on a sailing ship, a barquentine, and her name was '*The Mermaid*.' She often called at Tortuga."

"Really!" said Harold, immediately interested. "Do you remember what were the years of his service?"

"It was around the turn of the century and I think he served for quite a few years on her. As a child I can remember listening to him telling sea stories on a Sunday afternoon. He'd often end up by saying 'Ahhh, the Mermaid were an ill-fated ship . . . yep, she were ill fated.'"

"Why do you suppose he said that?" asked Harold.

"Can't say," said the old man. "Could be that she ran onto a reef. But I can't say for sure." Harold made a mental note to follow up on the mermaid story.

Sonia leaned over the bar and whispered to Harold. "We are being joined by Memnon's uncle, Mr Vernon

Brathwaite and his wife. He's the minister of tourism and very influential, so make sure we get a good table." She smiled and winked conspiratorially.

By now, the Mermaid Bar was filling up and outside on the terrace the island's socialites were mingling. The cool night air was filled with laughter and conversation. Expensive French perfume wafted on the evening breeze. The mermaid and the fountain were the two focal points out on the terrace, and inside the bar the rows of antique wooden casks from Spain were being much admired. Harold had had them cleaned and varnished and the hoops had been de-rusted and painted black.

Just then Harold was dismayed to see Adolf Reephoff and Charles Mcguire walk, in accompanied by two very over-dressed and bejewelled ladies. They sat down at a table and Reephoff immediately shouted towards the bar, clicking his fingers. There were two bar tenders, both extremely busy, and Harold was standing by. There was no waitress service, it being the English pub style of help yourself. After a couple of minutes of making himself conspicuous, Reephoff got up and stalked over to Harold. "You are tryink to run a posh place 'ere but I can't get any service," he said, with the corner of his mouth twitching.

"Good evening, Mr Reephoff," said Harold politely. "It's self service in the bar. What can I get for you?"

"Self service," said Reephoff, and then loudly, "self service! – how very second class. Give me a large Black Label on the rocks, a double Tanqueray and tonic and two pina coladas."

Harold was incensed but he kept his cool and poured the drinks. Reephoff carried them over to the table without paying and without a thank you. "Put it on the bill," he said, in a superior manner.

Reephoff's table was within earshot of the bar and

Harold heard Mcguire and Reephoff making disparaging remarks about the service almost immediately. But what was more disconcerting was the subsequent conversation, of which Harold caught snatches in between the laughter and general hubbub of the bar. "Made a killing on this place," said Mcguire, and then, "Another like this and I'd buy that 55ft. Bertram."

Among other guests who came into the Mermaid Bar was Roger Clement-Jones, with his wife Margaret and Mike Broadrite. All three ordered dry martinis. "Congratulations on a fine job of restoration and I wish you every success," said the governor, shaking Harold's hand warmly. "What an extraordinary find you made in the cellar."

"It certainly was," said Harold, "and what a ridiculous job the *Island Times* did of reporting it. By the way, thank you for your concern when the article first appeared and thank goodness the rumours were quickly dispelled."

Then George Cleary came dashing in and after greetings and handshakes all round informed Harold that dinner was ready. Harold cupped his hands and put them to his mouth. "Ladies and gentlemen, dinner is served." George went out to the terrace and with the assistance of Anne, helped seat the guests.

The bar was almost empty and Harold was installing a Vivaldi CD that would provide dinner music when he heard a commotion out on the terrace. He poked his head out of the bar room door. Reephoff was standing and angrily shouting at George, who was trying to seat him at his table. "I vill not be so inzulted," he shouted, "to be zeated at zuch an inferior table." The table was quite acceptable but it was at the back of the terrace and rather near the entrance to the bar and kitchen.

Charles Mcguire was already seated as were the

ladies, but now he readily joined in. "We would prefer a table overlooking the harbour," he said, "or alternatively over there by the fountain." He pointed at an empty table.

"I'm afraid all the other tables are reserved," said George, lacking the necessary diplomacy. "We are booked solid for this evening's occasion. Now you may be able to get a barbecued meal down at the Rusty Pelican if you find this table unacceptable." George was being inflexible on purpose. He had never liked the cunning lawyer.

"Zis iz abzurd. I vill not dolerate . . ."

Anne came running up. She had overheard some of the conversation, as had many of the other guests. "We could move the whole table down there next to the fountain and then you would have a view of the harbour as well," said Anne with a wide smile. "George, would you get two of the boys to help?"

"Zank God somebody has some brainz around 'ere," said Reephoff, thankfully out of earshot of George, who had gone off to get help. Finally and after a lot of fussing by the overly plumed and manicured ladies, the Reephoff party settled down.

There were about 15 tables in all, mostly parties of four or six and everyone seemed in a festive mood – it was almost Christmas, after all. Champagne corks started popping and soon the level of gaiety and laughter had increased to a merry abandon, whilst enticing smells emanated from the kitchen.

The first course of steaming callaloo soup arrived, and the guests were just beginning to enjoy the famed West Indian treat when the lights flickered once, then twice and then the whole terrace was plunged into darkness. Power outages were not uncommon on Tortuga – but for this to happen tonight of all nights! There were several audible groans and a couple of ribald comments when, just as suddenly, the lights flickered back on, but this time with a more severe intensity than before: now the power was surging. Several light bulbs exploded, the Vivaldi violins sounded like a comic pop opera, and the fountain which had died leaving an eerie silence sprang back to life with renewed vigour – the jets reaching new heights.

The cherub that had been peeing down from its lofty position on the top tier to land in the bottom pool now shot its stream out beyond the environs of the fountain, and as circumstances would have it, straight into the steaming bowl of soup that had just been placed in front of Reephoff. The thick green soup splattered Reephoff liberally and, too late, he jumped back, but not far enough to avoid the attention of a little green frog who showed a keen interest in the liquid. One giant leap landed the frog straight into the appetising mixture, but the little reptile soon found the temperature of the soup to be too hot for his liking, and immediately jumped out and onto the lawyer's white dinner jacket, where several hops later it left a pattern of little green, webbed footprints. Reephoff wildly swatted at the frog with his napkin which, trying to make good his escape, landed back on the table which was now swimming with a green watery liquid, and then onto the lap of one of the ladies who immediately screamed and jumped up, knocking the table to the floor with a resounding crash. Several footprints later, on her white, sequined Armani evening gown, the frog bounded back into the fountain. Then, just as quickly as it had happened, the power supply returned to normal.

Those dinner guests sitting in close proximity to Reephoff's party saw immediately what was happening and burst into uncontrollable laughter, several pointing at the cherub at the top of the fountain. The cherub peeing into someone's soup was a most comical sight, and perhaps it was a trick of the light, but on this occasion the cherubic smile seemed tantamount to mockery. At the first gale of hysterical laughter, the rest of the guests rose and crowded around laughing and clapping. Several guests thought the episode was staged, as bizarre as it was.

George, who had been helping serve champagne, saw the incident from the beginning and he instantly burst out laughing, but quickly composed himself when he saw he was being watched. Harold, though, had been in the bar arranging the liqueurs for the after-dinner crowd and had stepped out just in time to see Reephoff being peed on by the cherub. At least that was what it looked like from his vantage point, and he felt a huge surge of joy well up inside him – a feeling of wellbeing that perfect revenge can sometimes bring.

"This," he said to himself, "is divine intervention." He let no emotion cross his countenance and started to walk over to the scene of the accident, but Anne had got there first and was trying to console the lady who looked the most distraught. Then a waiter appeared with a mop and a bucket.

When Harold got there, Reephoff was still dabbing hopelessly at his green spotted dinner jacket. He looked up as Harold approached but Harold was determined to have the first word. "I am terribly sorry," he said. "This has been a most unfortunate accident. I am afraid, though, that we have no control over the island's utility services."

"Yah," said Reephoff, "and I zuppose you have no control over those vucking vrogs." He stopped dabbing and threw his napkin on the floor. "Come along," he said irritably to the rest of his party. "Ve are not stayink 'ere another minute." He stalked off down the steps

156

with the others trailing. "You have not heard the last of this," Reephoff shouted back. Harold had to agree. He was sure it would be the subject of gossip, tales and jokes for years to come.

The mess was soon cleared up and the dinner continued. Those with tables near the fountain moved a little further away and the puddle made by the other cherub, which fortunately had missed everybody, was mopped up.

The dinner proceeded without further incident, much to Harold's relief, but the kitchen staff were rushed off their feet. There were over 70 guests and they had all been seated at once. This meant that subsequent courses were required simultaneously as well. Jackie made a mental note to see that it never happened that way again – staggering the seating would make it easier on everyone. To add to the pressure in the kitchen, a helper had come up from the Rusty Pelican for more ribs and chicken. Apparently it was jumping down there already.

After dinner many of the guests returned to the Mermaid Bar – the coffee was being served there on a help yourself basis and liqueurs were available from the bar, as were cigars. Roger Clement-Jones leaned towards Harold and, in a moment of atypical frivolity whispered, "You couldn't have provided a better cabaret if you'd tried." He chuckled again at the memory of the cherub and the frog.

Margaret, at Roger's side as usual, said to Harold, "That was an excellent meal, in fact you couldn't find better cuisine on the island. I must congratulate Jackie personally." Just as she'd uttered the words, Jackie came in, looking rather flushed but obviously relieved that the main event was over. She had tidied her hair and put on fresh make up but had forgotten to take off her apron. She immediately got into an animated discussion with Margaret about recipes and tropical ingredients. The governor's wife avoided all mention of the fountain; she had found the incident rather embarrassing and had been one of the few who had not joined in the merriment.

Finally everyone dispersed from the bar. Many guests lingered with coffee and liqueurs and enjoyed the cool, evening breeze on the terrace. Others wandered down to the Rusty Pelican where the dance was just beginning and some went down to the marina to look at the new facility and admire the new luxury catamarans that had just arrived.

Harold and Jackie were alone in the bar, tired but elated; their opening night dinner party had been a success, apart from the episode surrounding the fountain. Jackie had been up to her elbows in callaloo soup and lobster thermidor when the power had gone off but by now she had heard the story at least three times. "Darling," she said, holding his hand, "we're going to have to get rid of those frogs as soon as possible."

"Get rid of the frogs!" he said, incredulous, "I wouldn't dream of getting rid of the frogs. I love frogs. We have a certain bond – frogs and I. In fact I was wondering if there was any special food they liked . . ."

"Harold, you were only saying this morning that you would have to get rid of the frogs because you were afraid that tadpoles might block up the jets in the fountain. Anyway we can't have frogs jumping all over the restaurant."

Harold put his arm around his dear wife's shoulder. "Sometimes, during the course of events in life, we have a change of mind," he said, philosophically, "and in this instance I would like to leave them there – at least for the time being. They seemed to appear from nowhere as though our fountain was their destiny.

Besides, they'll eat all the mosquito larvae."

"Well, if we get sued because a frog jumps into someone's plate of food, I hope you remember this conversation."

"I've already thought of that," said Harold, "I'm going to place a sign for all to see right on the edge of the fountain. It'll read, 'Please don't feed the frogs.' Then, when a frog jumps into someone's soup we can say – 'you were warned.'"

Jackie looked at Harold sideways, and then they both burst out laughing.

Just then Beulah came running into the bar. "Quick, come Ms Jackie, I catch Jonas messin' wid my Lynette an' I shut him in de cold room. Now I can't get de door open." The poor woman was out of breath and obviously distressed.

"Now wait a minute," said Jackie, walking back towards the kitchen. "Explain everything slowly, just as it happened." Jackie was tired – it had been a hectic day and a busy night and she really didn't want to deal with any more catastrophes. She turned to Harold. "You'd better come," she said wearily.

"Well, I jus' come back from putting away some leftovers in de pantry an' I walked past de dishwashing area an' I ain' see Jonas nowhere but de sink still full o' dirty dishes. Den I walk out de kitchen door an I see dem standin dere in de shadows an he have him hands up under her skirt an dey real close. De worse ting – it look like she don' mind at all – it look like she enjoyin' it. Dat my li'l girl an she barely pas' 16 years an' it done make me mad. So I run into de kitchen an' grab de firs' ting I see an' it a rollin' pin an I go after him an' he run into de col' room an' I slam de door. Now de door jam shut. Min' you – it should cool off he overheated ass – but I don' want him to freeze to death even though he wuthless."

Harold walked over to the cold room door and gave it a couple of tugs but the spring mechanism on the handle had broken. "I'm going to need a crow bar and a sledge hammer," said Harold. "Call JC on his boat phone and ask him to bring them from the workshop."

Lynette was sitting down at the kitchen table whimpering and snivelling. Her mother had given her a good scolding. "Get over dere and start on dose dishes," said Beulah. "You de cause o' all dis trouble." The girl ambled over to the sink, head down, looking really sorry for herself. "Next ting you know you be pregnant. I done tol' you before – messin' arung wid fellas ain' nuttin but trouble."

It was about 40 minutes later when Harold and JC finally managed to pry open the cold room door. There was no doubt that Jonas' ardour had been cooled. As he stepped, rather wild eyed, from the cold room into the warm kitchen, his body started steaming. One by one he looked into four pairs of hostile eyes and when he finally saw Beulah staring daggers at him, he took to his heels and ran out of the kitchen door and into the black night.

"Well, I hope dat be de end o' he," said Beulah. "First, he half drunk, den he foolin' arung wid my li'l girl . . . wuthless, jus' wuthless." Beulah shook her head in disgust.

The party down at the Rusty Pelican was in full swing. Harold had walked down there with JC, leaving Jackie and the Clearys to finish tidying up the Sunset Terrace and kitchen. The crowd had finished eating and now serious drinking and dancing were in progress. Memnon was helping the bartenders, now that the barbecue was over, and Harold went over to talk to him. "How's everything going?" Harold shouted above the noise of the band and the excited revellers.

"Everyting jus' fine, Mr Harold. We served over a

100 barbecued dinners. Only one ting – we gettin' low on Heineken and Bud."

"No problem," said Harold. "Keep up the good work. I'll see you get some more beer." He spoke to JC and off he went with a helper for replenishments.

The band was in high gear and they were loving the crowd who, in turn, were loving them and dancing to every tune. Each was feeding the other – a true symbiotic relationship. The band's name was the 'Hot Dogs' and they were a fungi band. There was a miniature ukulele in the lead played by a tall, very dark man with two gold front teeth and wearing an undersized trilby. Next to him was a short, stocky man with a shaved head playing a one-string base on an upturned washtub. They were so strikingly different that they made the focal point of the band and were continuously playing to the crowd. An expert spoons player and a bongo drummer added to the percussion whilst a guitar and saxophone completed the melody section.

Harold recognised a lot of familiar faces in the crowd. The Rasta man, Toshi, was over by the band dancing with a ravishing local girl, his dreadlocks flying in all directions as he whirled around. Alan Stanborg, the architect, was there too, dancing rather stiffly in a British 70s style, with a slim brunette woman that Harold took to be his wife. He saw Harold looking at them and waved. Then he noticed, standing at the bar, Bob and Virginia of Carefree Yacht Vacations. It seemed ages since they had had that wonderful sailing vacation that had influenced them so heavily in re-locating to the Caribbee Islands to start a business. Harold walked over. "Nice to see you again," he said amiably. "You having fun?"

"This is a great party and hearty congratulations on your opening. You have a first class setup here."

"Thank you, yes, so far so good. The bookings are looking quite good for our first season but as you once reminded me there are many variables that are impossible to predict in this business, so I'm not counting my chickens before they've hatched."

"Very wise," said Bob. "We've had to increase all our prices this season. The insurance premiums have almost doubled. Of course, Caribbean Mutual Benefit has it all sewn up."

"Well, one of my objectives is to see an end to that monopoly. Something smells bad there." Harold screwed up his nose.

"Yes, well good luck. Be careful not to tread on the wrong toes – sometimes it can do you more harm than good." Bob wasn't prepared to compromise himself and Harold thought he knew more than he was admitting to.

"Oh, come on you two," said Virginia, "this is a party. Let's dance." She pulled Bob onto the floor just as the band started playing the 'Ram Goat' song. It began like this:

> *"De only time de ram goat laugh*
> *Is when he smell de ewe goat tail,*
> *De only time de ewe goat laugh*
> *Is when she feel de ram goat nose."*

Chorus:
> *"Ba ha, ha ha; Ba ha, ha ha,*
> *Ba ha, ha ha; Ba ha, ha ha."*

It was a typical bawdy West Indian lyric and the crowd loved it. And what a diverse crowd it was. There were locals from all walks of life, boat bums, yachtsmen, tourists and some of the elegant crowd that had previously attended dinner at the Sunset Terrace. It was this type of eclectic mix that made West Indian parties so wildly successful; along with the music, the rum and the star studded sky, of course.

Harold was rejoined by JC, who had just finished restocking the coolers for Memnon, and they continued on down to the marina where Shirley was all alone fielding questions on luxury sailing holidays aboard catamarans. The three yachts looked impressive – they were not only illuminated by the dock lights, but each had its own deck light and cockpit light. Polished stainless steel, waxed fibreglass and tinted ports sparkled. As they approached the first boat, they could hear Shirley.

"We usually thail in the morning to a calm lunchtime anchorage, after lunch thome thnorkelling, and then thet thail again in the afternoon. But our itinerary ith flexible and dependth on the needth and dethires of our guestth." Shirley was standing in the spacious cockpit of *Sunfun Calypso II*. She turned and saw Harold and JC, and she visibly relaxed. Her listeners were none other than the Honourable Vernon Brathwaite and his wife.

"I see you're being given the grand tour," said Harold. "How do you like our new yachts?"

"Very impressive," said Brathwaite. "I can hardly believe the level of comfort and this young lady seems very knowledgeable regarding yachting holidays." Shirley blushed and swelled with pride.

"Oh yes," said Harold, "Shirley's an old hand and a qualified Cordon Bleu cook to boot." Harold turned and winked at her discreetly. It was hard to believe that she had been puking up all over the deck of *Sunfun Calypso* less than six months ago.

"We have had a wonderful evening," said Mrs Brathwaite. "The mango ice cream was delicious – I have been making it for years and yours was up there with the best."

"I thoroughly agree," said the minister, "and the renovations to the lodge are entirely in keeping with West Indian architecture and decor; and the property and facilities are a credit to Tortuga and the Caribbee Islands." He put his arm around Harold's shoulder and together they strolled slowly up the dock. "My office is in the process of putting together a tourism directory for international distribution. I would like to include a two-page spread of GSC. I think it would be a considerable benefit to you."

"Well, thank you for your kind words," said Harold, "and of course we would welcome the free advertising."

"I have in mind a full page accentuating the lodge with its colonial style architecture. A photograph of a portion of the hip roof with the rafters and the stone walls with their unique masonry and arches. Definitely one shot of the terrace with the fountain and the flowers and another of the entrance to the Mermaid Bar and the figurehead.

"The other page would be dedicated to yacht chartering. I believe the flagship of your fleet is the catamaran we were just looking at, the *Sunfun Calypso II*. An interior shot of the magnificent honeymoon suite, and one of the boat under sail with spray flying would give a nice contrast. Then we would include some scantily clad pretty girls in colourful swim wear – palm trees, turquoise water – that sort of thing." It was obvious that Brathwaite had given his promotional scheme quite a bit of thought.

"Now," he said, authoritatively, "I'll provide a photographer and some pretty girls and your contribution will be to provide the yacht with crew for a few days. Your pretty little blonde hostess would be excellent and the captain, JC, will do if we smarten him up a bit. As it happens, I have to organize a tour for a group of writers coming down who represent international travel magazines, and I'd like to schedule the whole shebang for sometime around the middle of January. Three days should be adequate – that will allow for a buffer in case of inclement weather."

So that was it. Harold knew that travel writers always enjoyed junkets and the crafty politician was planning to use the opportunity to include his own promotional material. Still, he had no doubts that the advertising would produce results. "I'll have to see what dates are available," said Harold, noncommittally.

"Excellent!" said Brathwaite, with exaggerated enthusiasm, "I knew you'd love the idea. Never underestimate the power of advertising. It can do wonders for any business." They had walked up to the end of the dock and were now back at *Sunfun* standing by the gangplank. "Come along, my dear, it's getting late," he said to his wife, who was still chatting to JC and Shirley on board. Then he turned to Harold and shook hands warmly. "We have had a most enjoyable evening. Thank you again, and we'll be in touch." He took his wife's arm and together they strolled back towards the car park.

Harold walked up the gangplank and on board *Sunfun.* "Well done, you two," he said. "That was the minister of tourism, and he was impressed with our operation. He wants you both to take out a group of travel writers and promoters sometime in January to showcase the Caribbee Islands." Harold had a quick look around the interior of the yacht. There was a huge tropical fruit bowl in the main salon – there were flowers discreetly placed here and there and on every pillow was a pink sprig of bougainvillea – Shirley obviously had a flair for creating the right ambience. The evening was winding down now, though, and Harold was exhausted. He said goodnight and returned to the lodge.

Some days later Harold was delighted to see that GSC's opening had made the front page of the Christmas edition of *The Beacon*. The centre pages were almost entirely dedicated to photographs of the island's luminaries who had attended but what caught Harold's eye was the cartoon page where an artist had cleverly depicted the fountain and four guests sitting round a laden dining table, one of whom was unmistakably Reephoff. Sitting in the middle of the table was a large grinning frog, and the caption read, "Waiter, waiter, there's a fly in my soup! – Don't worry sir, the frog in the fountain will get it." The joke was to become an island classic, much to the chagrin of Adolf Reephoff.

7

Christmas

Christmas time was a hive of activity for Golden Sunset Charters – everything was booked. You couldn't get a table for dinner, all the yachts were out on charter and all the rooms at the lodge were full. So when Roy arrived, unannounced, the day before Christmas, there was a panic to find somewhere for him to stay.

It was lunchtime on Christmas Eve and the Mermaid Bar was full when Roy made his appearance, looking rather unsteady and relying heavily on a stout walking stick. But there was no doubting his pleasure at being back. He walked straight up to the bar and bear-hugged Harold, who was slightly taken aback, and then he shouted, "A round for the whole bar." Everyone soon knew that he was one of the new owners of GSC and many came over and patted him on the back and congratulated him on the success of the renovations.

Harold was being upstaged but he didn't mind. He had to admit that Roy and his construction crew had done a great job with the property. When Jackie walked in with a huge tray of nibbles, she was as surprised as everyone else at Roy's sudden arrival. She wasn't quite sure how to greet him. "How do you do" was too formal, "Welcome" was perhaps inaccurate, so she settled on "Happy Christmas" and a rather awkward peck on the cheek. It wasn't as though she disliked Roy, it was just that his uncouth manner could be embarrassing. But there was nothing she could do about it – Roy was a partner in the business.

It was Jackie who first broached the subject of Roy's accommodation, and he seemed offended when Jackie told him that all the rooms were booked and had been for weeks. "You should have given us notice that you were coming, Roy. We would have reserved a room for you." She phoned the Calabash but they were fully booked – in fact there wasn't a room on the island until the day after Boxing Day.

"No problem," said Roy, "I'll sleep on the chaise longue in the library until there's a vacancy."

"I'm sorry, Roy, but that is out of the question. We're not running a doss house here. Wait a minute – I have an idea." Roy raised his eyebrows and sighed as though she was making a mountain out of a molehill.

Ten minutes later back she came with Memnon in tow. He had been down at the Rusty Pelican with his guests having Christmas Eve drinks. Memnon was now captain of GSC's second luxury catamaran, *Wet 'n Wild*. This time there was a real bear-hugging welcome for Roy.

In five minutes it was all arranged – Roy would stay at Memnon's house in the spare room. Memnon was out with his guests on *Wet 'n Wild* for another six days but that didn't matter. Roy could have the key and make himself at home until a room became vacant at the lodge. Memnon lived alone so there would be no-one to trouble him – Memnon was a widower, his wife having died some five years ago of severe fish poisoning, and his three children were living with his mother in St Kitts, so the house was empty. "Mind you," whispered Memnon into Roy's ear, "Big Mary comes over every now an' again for servicin,' so don' be surprise if you hear someone creepin' in at two in de marnin', heh, heh, heh."

They sat on the terrace for a while drinking cold Heinekens, telling stories and laughing about old times. Roy was fascinated with the mermaid story and he almost fell off his chair when he heard about the cherub and the frog in the fountain. There were newspaper clippings and photographs in the bar and Roy was surprised at how much GSC had been in the news.

Eventually the conversation shifted to yacht chartering, and Memnon explained how much he loved sailing *Wet 'n Wild*. "De people, dem does love it," he said exuberantly. "She fast, mon. She real fast. Me sail she to 15 knots on a broad reach de udder day an de people, dey sittin' up on de trampolines wid de spray flyin' and laughing an' shoutin'. She so stable nobody get sick – dere ain' no heelin' on a catamaran.

"By de way," continued Memnon, "my uncle Vernon – he de minister o' tourism – he organizin' a couple o' sailin' trips wid models an' photographers an' such. It for promotion. JC an' Shirley be runnin' de boat."

"Really," said Roy, suddenly very interested. "When is this happening?"

"It in 'bout two weeks. You should go – den you can see for yose'f how fast is de boats." Roy nodded his head in agreement but it was not the speed of the boats that had interested him, but the word "models."

They finished their beers and strolled down to the Rusty Pelican, where Memnon's guests were on their third round of rum punches. After brief introductions and the swapping of season's greetings, Roy excused himself on the pretext of urgent business and walked off to inspect the property. With the consent of George Cleary, he commandeered his old pickup truck that was parked behind the boat shed and drove back up to the lodge.

Harold and Jackie were both sitting at the kitchen table drinking after-lunch coffees when Roy walked in. "Pull up a chair," invited Harold, "have you had lunch yet?" Jackie fixed him a huge plate of roast leg of lamb with boulangère potatoes and broccoli branches, and he dived in hungrily.

"Well, you seem to have the place running like clockwork," he said, as he dabbed at a dribble of gravy on his chin with a napkin.

"It runs like clockwork until some unexpected calamity arises to throw the place into disarray," said Harold. "I have never been to any other place where the unexpected lurks around every corner. If you haven't got the constitution of an ox, nerves of steel, the patience of Job or comedic appreciation of almost daily events, you'd soon turn into a blithering idiot."

"Well, nobody said it would be easy," replied Roy, "but some calamities can be averted by careful planning. I was reading an article about the cherub and the frog in the fountain," he chuckled to himself and then burped loudly. "It reminded me that our operation here needs surge protecting regulators. Expensive electric motors can be severely damaged by power surges and God knows we have enough costly equipment. There's the refrigeration and air conditioning, numerous pumps, TVs and videos, and don't forget the office equipment, computers and printers. Surge protection must be a priority. That leads to the necessity of a back-up generator that would automatically kick in if the island's power supply went down. I'll have to calculate our maximum requirements, but in order to service the hotel, the offices as well as the marina, and the needs of power-hungry mega-yachts that may tie up there, I'd anticipate a minimum 350 KW plant. Then of course there'd be the diesel storage tanks for the engine."

Harold glanced across at Jackie and then back to Roy. "You're quite right, of course. Surge protection must be a priority if only to protect our diners from being urinated on by the cherubs." Harold tried to make light of the matter but frankly he was amazed. Roy had arrived back on the island a partial invalid, had spent only a couple of hours on the property and half of that had been spent horsing around with Memnon and drinking beer, yet he seemed to have a handle on GSC's most pressing needs. "We'll have a room for you on the day after Boxing Day. I'll arrange a meeting for that very afternoon and I'll call on George Cleary and Elroy Stevens to attend."

"We also need to discuss the pros and cons of a reverse osmosis desalination plant," said Roy, who was now digging into a large plate of home-made apple pie and ice cream. "The grounds need constant watering to keep the landscape green and vibrant, especially in the dry season. Then of course there could be sizable retail sales. We have one of the few deep-water facilities for fueling and watering yachts in the islands. We should take advantage of it."

"I'll put that on the agenda for the meeting," said Harold. "Financing always becomes a problem for large capital projects. We'll have to examine the figures closely. I'll have Sonia join us."

Roy let out a satisfied sigh and replaced his dessert spoon. "That was a fine meal," he said, "no wonder the restaurant is always packed." He got up and stretched and then winced as his back gave him a nasty twinge.

"There's a new orthopedic therapist in the medical complex in town," said Jackie, noticing Roy's obvious pain, "Perhaps it would be worth a visit. She even practises acupuncture."

"I don't want anybody practising on me," he said. "It's nothing that a little of the horizontal mambo won't put right." It took Jackie a second or two to catch his meaning, but when she did, she dropped the subject immediately. It was exactly the sort of coarse comment she had come to expect from him and it alienated her.

Harold immediately changed the subject. "Roy, we're having a Christmas dinner tomorrow at 3 p.m. on the terrace after all the guests have been served. There'll be about 20 of us all together and you'd be welcome to join us, of course."

"Wouldn't miss it for the world," he said. "Count me in." He walked out of the kitchen leaning heavily on his stick.

Ten minutes later, Roy was winding his way up the steep hill to the other side of the island. The sea was a shimmering blue and the bright green off-lying islands looked like emeralds, the colour intense after the heavy summer rains. Brightly painted, pastel coloured West Indian homes peeped out at him from behind banana groves or coconut palms and sometimes an islander waved, taking time from hanging out the washing or tending to the garden. And, of course, there was the breeze. Roy loved the caress of the tradewind breeze that cooled the intense afternoon sun.

He navigated around a straw-hatted old man astride

a donkey, panier baskets full of "ground provisions," and two corners later he was at the summit. He drove along the ridge a short distance before the road began to descend to the village where Memnon lived. Roy had been enjoying the ride and pondering GSC as the pick-up truck bumped and swerved its way along, avoiding as many pot-holes as possible. Undoubtedly his friends Harold and Jackie were doing a fine job. A bit prudish, a bit pompous perhaps but they had taken the bull by the horns and were definitely succeeding under difficult circumstances. He was happy to be a major player in their team.

He pulled up in front of Memnon's house – it was just the way he had described it. He found the spare room on the second floor and threw his duffle bag and tattered briefcase onto the bed. His thoughts turned to Big Mary and his imagination began to run wild.

It was about 1 p.m. on Christmas day when Roy walked, stick in hand, into the Mermaid Bar. He thought that about two hours for pre Christmas-dinner drinks was about right and anyway he had nothing better to do. He had slept quite well at Memnon's house – he had left the front door unlocked all night and the light on in Memnon's room – but rather to his disappointment, no mystery callers had surfaced.

He ordered a large scotch on the rocks and sat at a bar stool listening to the Christmas music playing on the stereo. The decorations were tastefully done and a small gold tree twinkled at him from a corner. The bar was about half full and guests were coming and going from bar to terrace. He noticed that there was a lot of talk and laughter concerning the fountain and then he remembered that the cherub peeing into a guest's soup was still current news. Just then Harold came rushing in with several bottles of wine. "Got to let these reds breathe for at least half an hour," he said, reaching for a corkscrew. "A merry Christmas to you Roy."

"A merry Christmas and a rollicking Boxing Day," replied Roy, imitating a British expression he'd heard somewhere. "Here, I brought you a little something from America," and he handed over a neatly wrapped package.

Harold was caught completely by surprise. He hadn't expected a Christmas present and he felt even more embarrassed when he realised that he had not reciprocated – but how could he have known that Roy would turn up, he thought to himself. "Thank you very much," said Harold, "very thoughtful of you." He put down the wine bottle he was opening and unwrapped his gift. It was a quality pair of 7 - 50 nautical binoculars in a varnished wooden box. The lenses were German and incorporated in the binoculars was a compass for taking bearings. But the most unusual feature was the night vision facility. Islands, coastline and even ships at sea could be seen even on the blackest night. It was a wonderful present, both appropriate and useful. Harold examined them closely, trying out all the features.

"They'll be great for bird watching," said Roy furtively, with a wink and a leer.

"This is a very handsome present," said Harold, avoiding the remark, "and will undoubtedly come in very useful. Thank you again." He leaned over and they shook hands warmly. "Now if we'd had this technology during the war, the tide of events . . ."

Roy was not interested in "the tide of events." He handed Harold another smaller package and interrupted, "This is for Jackie. I don't want to bother her if she's busy in the kitchen. I'll leave it under the tree."

Later when Jackie opened her present she found a rather cheap necklace of imitation pearls. She said a gracious thank you but the disparity in the two gifts reflected Roy's rather demeaning attitude when it came to women.

The long Christmas table was laid in traditional festive style and it was just a little after 3 p.m. when everyone took their seats. There were cut glass bowls of nuts, others of sugared Turkish delight and yet others of glacé fruits. Christmas crackers interspersed with sprigs of holly that must have been flown down specially, decorated the centre of the table. Two huge turkeys were carved on side tables and bowls of roast potatoes, vegetables, stuffing, sauces and gravy were arranged on the buffet for people to help themselves. Roy had just settled down with a full plate when Beulah came running out from the kitchen. "Dey callin' GSC on de radio. It sung like an emergency."

George Cleary responded immediately. He threw his hands in the air in despair. "Right in the middle of Christmas day lunch! Unbelievable!" He stormed into the kitchen where the VHF radio was installed. He had left his portable one down in the boat shed. 10 minutes later he returned, shaking his head in disbelief. "They're out of anchors," he said to Harold.

"What?" replied Harold. "Sorry, I didn't catch that."

"The young couple that chartered *Dreamin'*. They've used up three anchors in three days and they called up to find out where the other four were stowed so they'd have enough to complete their week." There were chuckles around the table but Harold still hadn't caught on.

"That's terribly bad luck," he said, "to get three anchors fouled in so many days."

"They didn't get any anchors fouled," said George in exasperation, "they just untied them from the boat and threw them off when they left an anchorage – just like you would with a mooring. How could anybody be so stupid? That's about $2,000 worth of equipment they've thrown overboard."

"Good Lord!" said Harold. "Didn't they have a yacht briefing?"

"They had a very thorough briefing that I gave them personally," said George, somewhat embarrassed. "Not only did I go over all the details of anchoring – depth, amount of scope, setting the anchor etc., I also showed them the operation of the anchor winch in great detail. You would think they might ask themselves why."

"We'll have to examine their resumé. This will cost them their security deposit and some," said Harold, finally getting suitably annoyed.

"In the meantime, I'll have to deliver them two more anchors with ground tackle. I'll take the rescue boat, *Speedy*. They're in Great Bay – should take me about half an hour to get there. Leave the radio on Channel 16. Enjoy the plum pudding and mince pies." George was understandably irritable.

"I'll come with you," said Roy, "I'm sure you could use a hand."

"Be grateful for it," said George. "I'll get you a foul-weather jacket from the boat shed. It could be a wet ride."

"Mind if I try out your new Christmas present?" said Roy to Harold, who waved his hand in consent. Roy grabbed the binoculars from the bar and they both headed for the boat shed.

It was 20 minutes later when they finally located *Dreamin'* up in the northeast corner of Great Bay, tied off behind a 50-foot sloop. The ride over had been fast and wet in *Speedy* – she had twin 225 hp outboards and a V bottom for slicing through the waves. The seas had been on the quarter, and the "Christmas winds," blowing at close to 30 knots, had piled them up to eight feet with white caps. Between December and February strong winds in the northeast Caribbean were common, caused by the frontal systems that rolled eastward off the continental U.S.

The wind was gusting into the bay but the sea was flat. George maneuvered up alongside *Dreamin'* and tied up. "Anyone aboard?" he shouted.

A rather pudgy young girl poked her head out of the hatch. "Hi guys, hey thanks for comin' out. I tol' him we should haul up them anchors. Did you bring us some spares?"

"Yeah, we did," said George, trying to keep calm. Then he added, with just a hint of sarcasm, "Where's the captain? We're going to have to try and dive up those lost anchors. You'd better mark on the chart where you dropped them and tomorrow we'll go and look for them."

Just then a freckle-faced youth came up from below and said sheepishly, "I'm sorry, I must have misunderstood. We sail from a dock at home. By the way, just deduct the cost from my credit card. Save everyone a headache."

There was nothing more to be said. These were paying guests and you had to be courteous and patient. As George stowed the two replacement anchors in the bow locker he was seething. He was soaking wet from the ride over; he was missing his Christmas pudding and brandy butter and when he'd finished he'd have to wave and smile and say "have a nice day" instead of giving the bloody idiot the cat o' nine tails as he deserved.

He gave the young man another complete lesson in the use and operation of the anchor windlass and when George was confident he understood, they fired up the big outboards.

"You're so lucky to be able to live here," said the girl. "It's so beautiful," and, just in time, before George could make some caustic reply, she handed over two ice-cold beers.

They untied and headed out of the bay. "Have a nice day," said George, smiling and waving.

As they rounded the point and set their course for Rum Cove, the seas were forward of the beam and the boat started pounding so much that they had to slow down. Every fourth or fifth wave covered the boat in spray from stem to stern and by the time they approached the entrance to Rum Cove it was dark.

Roy got the night vision glasses out and he could see clearly the headland on one side and a rocky outcropping on the other. He handed them over to George who was at the helm. "Fantastic," he said, "I can make out Whale Rock on one side and Rum Point on the other. This should be a piece of cake." They motored in without any trouble and as they were tying up, George told Roy the story of Whale Rock.

"It used to be called Heron Rock but one day the police boat was out doing maneuvers and hit the rock, holed the boat, and smashed the steering gear. They had to be towed in and the boat almost sank. The police department couldn't stand another blow to its already shaky reputation, so the official story in the newspaper that week was that the police boat had hit a whale. Well, the coconut telegraph soon spread the real story. Now the whole island knows the rock as Whale Rock and the cops are ridiculed more than if they'd never made up the tale."

"A tale of a whale and a whale of a tale," said Roy chuckling. "It sounds as though it really backfired on them."

"Yes, and every year the conservation department, which monitors the migration of whales, requests the public to call in any sightings. And every year some smart Alec calls in a sighting off Rum Cove which is always used as the basis for a comical article in the paper." George was laughing now too, the tension of the afternoon easing.

They walked up to the Rusty Pelican. After a quick beer, they said good night and went their separate ways.

8

The Problems

It was the 17th of January and as luck would have it, it was one of those picture-perfect days – sunny and clear with a gentle breeze. JC and Shirley were putting the last-minute touches to the preparations of *Sunfun Calypso* for the arrival of the journalists and photographers who were scheduled to go out for a day of sailing, snorkelling and sightseeing.

Vernon Brathwaite, who had arranged the day, was the first to arrive. He would normally have been described as a handsome man, tall and slim as he was, but today he was dapper. He wore an immaculately pressed, light-coloured tropical suit with an open neck silk shirt, and a wide-brimmed fedora with orange hat band which matched the bird of paradise blossom pinned to his lapel. He swaggered ever so slightly as he walked down the tiled walkway towards the yacht and not surprisingly – on each arm was a long-legged bronzed beauty that could have graced the front cover of any international fashion magazine.

JC had seen them coming and straightened up his "uniform." Harold had told him to wear white shorts and complementing this was a navy blue polo shirt with the logo "Golden Sunset Charters" emblazoned above the breast pocket in white and gold. The only scruffy part of his attire was his shoes – but they were regulation battle-weary topsiders. No self-respecting Caribbean captain would wear new yachting shoes – they had to look as though they'd done at least one circumnavigation.

They came to a stop at the bottom of the gangplank and JC came down to greet them. The first girl, whose name was Pearl, had her hair done in corn rows and the long plaits cascaded down her neck to her shoulders. She was wearing a mini-length white blouse that exposed her midriff and with nothing on underneath her nipples stuck out provocatively. The other girl, Desiree, wore a brief bikini top and skintight scrubbed denims that showed every contour of her perfect body. She smiled and batted her eyelids at JC as they came aboard. He handed them over to Shirley who took the girls below to show them the master stateroom where they could "freshen up." Brathwaite was shown into an aft cabin.

Next to arrive were a couple of reporters from the British *Sunday Times*. One was a staff writer, the other a photographer, who came aboard with two metallic boxes of equipment and a large shoulder bag. The reporter, Justin Jennings, was quite famous and often wrote features for the magazine. He carried a mini tape recorder, standard kit these days, it seemed.

Finally, a motley group from the AWA (American Writers Association) arrived. The association was comprised of free-lance writers and photographers and Brathwaite had personally invited only those that were regularly published in top travel magazines. There were six of them in total and two of them were obviously and unashamedly gay. They all climbed aboard, chattering away like excited schoolchildren.

Brathwaite emerged from the cabin and welcomed everybody – he had changed into shorts and a colourful cotton shirt. He explained briefly that the day's events would include an exciting sail to one of the islands' premier beauty spots, a walk through the Emerald Pools, lunch, snorkelling and an exhilarating sail back.

JC fired up the engines and was just beginning to untie lines when he saw Roy hurrying down to the dock as fast as his stick would carry him. The gang plank was still in place and JC went down to help the big man up. Vernon Brathwaite was at the rail frowning when Roy came aboard, but he quickly explained, "I'm here to represent the company and answer any pertinent questions," and since no-one had paid a penny for the day's outing, that was the end of the subject.

The real reason for Roy's late arrival had been the heated discussion he had had with Harold up at the lodge. Harold was terribly afraid that Roy's presence would be the cause of a disaster on this important day and he tried earnestly to dissuade him from going along, but Roy's will, fueled by super-active hormones, prevailed.

They motored out between Rum Point and Whale Rock and when they were clear of the channel JC raised the big, fully battened mains'l and rolled out the genoa – it was a perfect day for full sail and *Sunfun* sped along at close to 10 knots in the 15 knot breeze.

Introductions were made all the way round and the two models, both wearing colourful sarongs over their bikinis, stayed around just long enough to be polite before going forward to lounge on the trampolines. The rest of the group stayed in the cockpit whilst Brathwaite pointed out islands and told stories. The two gays were talking animatedly to anyone who would listen. The butch one was tall and well built with a fashionable day's growth of beard; his name was Hank. The slim, effeminate one was Stacey, and he was a photographer.

The *Times'* photographer went forward and got some shots of the models whilst they were unaware. Then he got some lying on his back, looking up through the sails. Then he noticed another boat approaching fast and, changing lenses, prepared to take a few shots. She was a classic wooden yawl and in good trim. Suddenly Stacey said, "Ooooooh, look at the buns on that," as he looked at a crew member on the yacht through his telephoto lens, and almost instinctively JC and Roy both craned their necks around to get a good look. All they could see was a bearded deck ape in a pair of tight trunks tweaking the main halyard. JC smiled to himself but Roy was mystified. He hadn't caught on yet.

They sped on their way towards the Emerald Pools and the ride on the large cat was fast and fun. Shirley offered cold beer or pop from a cooler and Roy, already on his second beer, gave her a friendly pat on her little bottom for old times sake; she recoiled and backed away so quickly she almost slipped. As they sailed by Peg Leg's Landing, JC told the journalists the story of old Mr Cooper and the pirate's wooden leg. Some of the writers took notes and some clicked on mini tape recorders.

When they approached the anchorage at the Emerald Pools, Brathwaite assumed the role of director. He conferred with the photographers and JC and finally they all agreed on an anchorage with a perfect backdrop of palm trees and sandy beach with favourable light behind them. The girls went below to change and make up whilst JC managed to nose the big cat right up onto the beach.

Stacey now took charge of the girls – Desiree had on a brief Brazilian bikini, more commonly known as a dental floss swim suit, and Pearl wore a partially see through white crochet bikini. Both of them had oiled their bodies so they glistened in the morning sun. "OK, honey," he said to Pearl with a singsong voice that had a slight lisp. "Stand over there. Hold on to that rope – one hand above your head – bend your knee. OK, perfect – look over there – pout the lips – perfect." He snapped off a roll, bracketing the exposures. Then he did another roll with Desiree and Pearl lying on the trampolines. Then he called Hank, who had now become Hunk, "Hunk, sweetie, go over there and lie next to Desiree – rub some cream on her back. Make sweet talk, yeah, great, click! click! smile some more, yeah good, click! click! I love it – Desiree, bra strap off, yeah, droop it over the shoulder." He ran off another two rolls.

Brathwaite interrupted. "OK," he said, "we're not doing material for Playboy. I want some more tourist oriented material. Roy, I'd like you to sit at the cockpit table with Shirley and pretend to be tourists. Pearl, you can serve two exotic drinks to them from a tray. Go and put on a colourful sarong and put a hibiscus in your hair. Let's have some flowers and a fruit bowl on the table." The scene was quickly set and the photographers positioned themselves.

Roy was mesmerised by the beauty of the two models and he couldn't keep his eyes off their luscious bodies. "Roy, look at her face as she bends down to hand you the drinks and smile as if you're saying thank you." Roy had been staring at her cleavage. "OK, everyone happy?" said Brathwaite as the photographers finished taking shots from different vantage points.

Stacey had noticed Roy's almost hypnotic state when he looked at Pearl's attributes and the effeminate photographer felt a bit jealous – he had inexplicably taken a liking to Roy himself. "I got some great shots of you, honey," he said coming close and putting a hand on Roy's thigh, "you're very photogenic." Roy ignored the familiar comments, still oblivious.

JC now took charge. "There will be time for a hike through the Emerald Pools and a snorkel before lunch," he said.

They all collected up their things, and with Vernon Brathwaite in the lead, they stepped off the boat at the bow into knee high water and away towards the beginning of the trail.

By three in the afternoon they were under sail and heading back to Rum Cove. The snorkelling expedition led by Shirley had been a great success and many of the party were talking about the reef and the colourful fish. JC had put up the spinnaker, a red, orange and yellow sunburst, and as it billowed out it provided a wonderful backdrop for spectacular photos, especially with a wide angle or fish eye lens. The writers and photographers were in a jovial mood – they had had a great day and now Shirley was handing around frozen rum punch from a large pitcher. Only Roy was feeling somewhat subdued – his advances towards Pearl had been spurned and once he had caught the girls whispering and laughing at him behind his back.

Just then Stacey grabbed Roy by the hand and said, "Come on honey. Let's me an' you have our picture taken together." And as they stood there posing, Stacey slipped his arm around Roy's waist and tilted his head to rest ever so slightly on Roy's shoulder. "Mmm, I like your aftershave," he said.

It was like a thunderbolt of realisation, an awakening, a dawning of truth. Suddenly Roy's face flushed red and he looked aghast. "You . . ." he spluttered, "You . . . , you're a godamned faggot!!" He stepped back and shoved Stacey hard and the slim homosexual fell back and tripped over a chair, crashing to the floor. Hank, who had been preparing to take the picture, dropped the camera and came at Roy with lightning speed and fist clenched, but JC was even quicker. He sprang across the few feet of deck space and with a bear-hug maneuver pinned both Hank's arms to his side effectively immobilising him and probably saving Roy from a black eye. Hank and Roy stood staring at each other for a few seconds, seething.

Hank spoke first. "You are not only a bigot but a rude and crude oaf. You don't call a black person 'nigger.' You don't call a white person 'honky' and you don't call a gay person 'faggot.'" Hank was from California and he knew all about "political correctness."

"Well," said Roy, not in the least bit fazed, "tell your 'honey' to keep his hands to himself. Then he shouldn't get into any trouble."

Whilst this fracas had been going on, nobody had been at the helm and *Sunfun* had steered herself almost broadside to the wind and the spinnaker was flapping dangerously – a headstay wrap imminent. JC raced to the wheel, cursing under his breath, and a quick correction just saved a disaster. The rest of the party had suddenly gone quiet and JC asked Shirley to put on a Jimmy Cliff tape to enliven the group and then to refill the glasses. Fortunately Vernon Brathwaite and the two models had been up on the foredeck and had missed the altercation, but JC knew that there was one photographer and one writer who

186

could not now be relied upon to produce a good review. Stacey had picked himself up and was sitting miserably in a corner on his own, but he seemed to recover quickly and soon he was chatting away.

By the time the boat was docked, the group had forgotten the incident and everyone was in good spirits – except Roy. He muttered to himself, "Snubbed by two beautiful women, insulted by a guy as queer as a three dollar bill and everyone thinks it's my fault." He'd have a few beers at the Rusty Pelican and then maybe tonight he'd visit the whore house in town . . .

The final part of the day's tour was a visit to the lodge, the Sunset Terrace restaurant and the Mermaid Bar. Brathwaite, resplendent in his finery once again, led the way.

Most of the party either wandered around the attractive grounds or sat down at tables on the terrace, but Justin Jennings went straight into the bar and ordered a cold beer. Harold was the only one in the bar and he introduced himself to the reporter. "Justin Jennings, *Sunday Times*," replied the reporter, shaking hands. "This is a very attractive inn you have here."

"Thank you," said Harold, "I hope you enjoyed your excursion today. The *Sunfun Calypso* is one of our newest charter yachts."

"We had a wonderful day and some great sailing," said Jennings. "I've been doing travel pieces for various magazines for almost 20 years. It's good 'bread and butter' work but there's nothing to really get your teeth into."

Harold leaned across the bar and looked at Jennings seriously. "If you want a good story and don't mind doing a bit of research I think you could find one right here." He began by telling the reporter how they had acquired the property, the cellar and its contents, and the mermaid. Jennings chuckled to himself when

Harold explained the difficulties they had had in getting the mermaid out of the cellar.

He walked over to where the mermaid was mounted above the front door to the bar and examined the figurehead closely. "I'll get my colleague to run off a couple of rolls of film on that," he said. "What a magnificent carving. And you believe it's almost a hundred years old?"

"The original building dates back to the early 1800s," replied Harold. "We know that for certain from copies of original records. We also know that renovations were made in the 1920s from drawings dating back to that time and this is the most likely time for the cellar to have been sealed off. It would mean that the mermaid was probably placed in there about 80 years ago. Assuming that it was several years old when it was 'interred,' then around a 100 years would be a safe guess. Why the mermaid was placed there is the mystery – and then there's the question of the rum in the sherry casks."

"Rum in the sherry casks?" enquired Jennings.

"Yes," said Harold, and he pointed to the handsome, varnished casks lined up in a row. "These casks were also found in the cellar – in a much worse state than they are now – and full of a very fine rum. What is strange, though, is that the casks were originally intended for sherry," and he pointed to the Spanish words engraved into the wood, 'Jerez,' 'Produto de la Frontera.'"

"Mmm," said Jennings, thoughtfully, "I wonder if there could be a connection between the rum in the cellar and the name of this bay. It's called Rum Cove, isn't it?"

"Yes, I have had precisely the same thoughts," said Harold. "There were some other items in the cellar that may throw light on the mystery. We found some crates of wine and although the wine had spoiled, I saved the bottles. There were 42 altogether and they may be able to be dated. A pair of ship's running lights were also brought up and I had them cleaned and polished and there they are." He pointed to each end of the top row of bottles behind him on the bar shelf. "Unfortunately there's no inscription or any other identifying markings." Harold reached up and passed one of the lamps to Jennings. "Are you interested yet?" said Harold, with a grin and a twinkle in his eye.

"Am I interested?" said Jennings with feigned surprise. "This is a writer's dream. I can incorporate this story with my already planned promotional piece and then do a follow-up when the story unfolds." He turned the lamp around in his hands, examining it carefully. "Can I look at one of the wine bottles?"

Harold handed the reporter a wine bottle. It had a shoulder like the bottles used for Bordeaux wine, but there were no other distinguishing marks on it except that the top of the neck had an unusually pronounced lip. "Would you mind if I kept this for a while and take it back with me to England? It could be a valuable clue."

"By all means," said Harold. "And I have something else to show you. Excuse me, I'll be back in a couple of minutes." Harold went upstairs to his suite and was soon back with a packet of photographs, each carefully preserved in its own damp-proof envelope. "This was the cellar just as we found it." He handed Jennings the pictures that JC had taken on that exciting day just a few months ago.

"Some of these photographs are excellent and the eerie glow of light really adds to the mood of a dark and dingy, long undiscovered cellar. This one even highlights a cobweb in the corner." He handed Harold a picture to look at, and they both chuckled. "If my magazine uses any of your photographs you will be paid well," he said, replacing the photos in their protective envelopes and handing them back.

"If only we knew the name of the ship that the mermaid belonged to, it would make the whole research effort so much easier," continued the reporter, shaking his head.

"Well," said Harold, "the fact that the ship's figurehead was a mermaid may very well mean that the ship was named 'Mermaid.' Of course it may be a long shot but there is some evidence to back up the theory." He told Justin Jennings the story that old Mr Hodge had told him on the night of the grand opening.

"It sounds like a very plausible story," said Jennings, thoughtfully. "A barquentine named *The Mermaid* that made regular stops in Tortuga and then the fact that it was an 'ill fated ship.' Could be that the ship hit a reef and sank and the figurehead, the casks of rum, the running lights and other sundry bits and pieces were all salvaged from the wreck and placed in the cellar."

"That is really the problem," said Harold. "There are so many maybe's and could be's. I have a vested interest to know the truth – I decanted almost 30 cases of rum from those barrels and if I can prove that it is of a grand vintage then the value will be substantially more than if I have to sell it off only as an old rum."

Harold reached for a bottle up on a high shelf and poured two small shot glasses of light golden spirit. "This is 'Mermaid's Gold,'" he said. "Here's to your investigation." They both sipped the golden elixir and Jennings was the first to smack his lips in appreciation.

"By God," he said, "that is smoother than the finest single malt whisky I've ever tasted. I wonder what proof it is."

Harold laughed, "I suppose you're going to tell me you'll need to take a bottle back with you for testing."

"Well," said Jennings, "since you've mentioned it . . ." They both laughed now, the rum warming them. Harold topped up both glasses.

"I'm sure, with all your years writing newspaper stories, that you are quite familiar with research. But if I may be so bold as to make a suggestion, I think this particular subject begs an enquiry with Lloyd's register of shipping. Not only have they been registering shipping for donkey's years, but Lloyd's of London are the oldest insurance underwriters in the world."

"Sound advice," said Jennings, "and a good place to start."

By now quite a few customers had wandered into the bar for "happy hour." Jennings was staying at the lodge, having taken a suite together with his partner, and was ready for a long, refreshing shower before dinner. He made a move to get up and leave but Harold hadn't finished. "If, in the course of your enquiries, you need to do some investigating on this side of the Atlantic, I will provide a room at the lodge for you free of charge. I find the whole mystery fascinating and compelling and would love to see a solution to the puzzle. And if you need a research assistant in the U.K. this young man may be useful." He handed Jennings a card. It contained Godfrey Allbright's name and address.

"What more incentive could a man ask for," said the reporter, smiling. "Tomorrow I'd like to see the cellar. Even in its clean and renovated state, I'd like to get the feel of the mystery hiding place."

"By all means," said Harold. "We'll talk later." Jennings had another long, hard look at the mermaid as he walked out of the barroom door to the terrace.

As the season progressed through February and into March, both Harold and Jackie were delighted at the success of the business. The yachts were going out with frequent, quick turnarounds and the lodge and Sunset Terrace restaurant were busy. The advertising campaign had really paid off and Betty with her travel agency network had sent down a lot of business.

Roy had returned to Florida at the end of January to organize the acquisition of the new generator and all the components for a water desalination plant. The bank manager had approved the necessary loans as long as the plant and equipment were insured, and Charles Mcguire had not hesitated to provide a supplementary policy. When Harold had looked at the additional premium he imagined Mcguire's dream power-yacht would soon be a reality. Before Roy's departure, he had installed power surge protection units on all the important equipment and on all the power outlets on the dock.

Harold had finally been persuaded to have all the frogs removed from the fountain. It had been an effort but Jackie's continued badgering had finally had its effect, helped by the fact that one night a waiter, with a full tray of entrees, had slipped on a dead frog and come crashing to the floor. That and a dead cat that had been found floating in the fountain with half a frog in its mouth.

It had been a job getting rid of them because, just as Harold had originally feared, they spawned like there was no tomorrow and tadpoles had soon filled the fountain. New frogs had appeared almost as quickly as the old ones were removed. Finally they had had to empty all the water out and leave the fountain dry for 10 days. The tadpoles died and any remaining frogs migrated to wetter climes.

But although the business was running very successfully, it was immensely hard work with long hours. Harold and Jackie had originally moved to the

Caribbee Islands to enjoy the climate, the waters and the related activities such as sailing, diving and snorkelling, but so far they had had little time for any of this. The success of Golden Sunset Charters was compensation though, at least for now. They had been very fortunate in acquiring a good nucleus of staff. Even Roy, with his sometimes distasteful ways, was invaluable.

Even though Harold and Jackie had anticipated well the problems and potential pitfalls of their fledgling business in Tortuga, there were oddities and peculiarities that they had not planned for. The incident of government bribery, the erratic behaviour of the utility services, the decline in the island's roads where pot-holes seemed to appear more quickly than they could be repaired – these were problems endemic to the islands. It was also a peculiarity of the islands that nobody seemed to care very much – after all, it had been that way for years and tomorrow was another day! There was another unfortunate oddity that was peculiar only to the Caribbean islands, and it was during the first week in March when Harold and Jackie found out about it.

The Sunset Terrace had been so busy during February that Jackie had run an advertisement in *The Beacon* for a kitchen helper. Poor Beulah and Lynette were so exhausted at the end of every evening that a helper was needed and no-one was more surprised and horrified when Jonas ambled into the kitchen the next day, cap in hand, to apply for the job. It took Jackie about three minutes, with the help of a few choice words, to send the reprobate from the property. But a week later she received a letter from the island's labour office, under the direct control of the chief minister, Lionel Bradshaw, that GSC must hire, without further question, Mr Jonas Stoutt, to fill the advertised position. He was a citizen of the territory with all the necessary qualifications – end of subject.

Jackie wrote back explaining the events that had happened during the opening night dinner, but it was all to no avail – the manager of the labour office was adamant and wrote that Jonas was to be hired. "A citizen of the territory takes preference over all other persons if he can fit the job description. An employee must have had three warnings of misconduct before he/she can be terminated," the letter read. Word of the letter with the instructions filtered from the office to the restaurant kitchen and it was a tearful Beulah who handed in a letter of resignation on behalf of both her and Lynette the next day.

"I ain' workin' wid dat animal fo' all de tea in China," she said. "Anyhow, it only my daughter he after."

When Harold heard of the catastrophe, he soon deduced that there was only one real solution to the problem. He would have to fill the kitchen helper vacancy immediately so that the position was no longer available. He couldn't possibly lose Beulah and Lynette – they were the backbone of the Sunset Terrace restaurant. He went to Sonia Hodge for advice.

"You're right," she said, "you can't possibly hire Jonas now. He would make a laughing stock of you in front of all the other staff. He would brag that he had managed to over-ride your authority by going to the labour office and that he had forced you to hire him. It would undermine your authority towards the rest of the staff. The only way is to find a kitchen helper immediately and I think I know someone who can fill in, at least temporarily. It'll give us a bit of breathing room."

By that evening there was a new kitchen helper. Sonia had saved the day. She explained to Harold how the labour office had become so misguided. "The labour office tries to protect the interests of the islanders and make sure they get employment. Sometimes business owners want white or foreign employees and advertise impossible requirements for a position in order to eliminate an islander from getting work that he could easily do. So the labour office leans towards ensuring locals get all the possible chances at a job. That's only fair, don't you think?"

Harold nodded in agreement. "Yes, I certainly do," he said.

"But a problem sometimes arises when a local is hired, and then through misconduct or poor job performance a manager tries to replace him. All the employee has to do is report the firing to the labour office and complain of discrimination, and the business is forced to rehire the delinquent person under threat of trade licence withdrawal. Then the management is ridiculed by the staff who feel immune from discipline. This makes for ineffectual management and poor and careless job performance. It's why service is so bad in many of the island's hotels – the management is powerless." Sonia shrugged her shoulders with a helpless expression.

"We must try not to let this problem affect us," said Harold, with a worried expression.

"The only way to guard against it is to make absolutely sure, when you initially hire an employee, that you have a good, honest, and dependable person with references. It's not always easy with a limited labour force to draw upon. Unfortunately, Jackie, who originally hired Jonas, didn't examine his past history very carefully – but of course he was only a temporary helper at first."

The next morning, which was Monday, Jonas called up and asked when he should start and Harold told him, in no uncertain terms, that the job had already been filled. No vacancies now existed. Harold thought that the incident was over but the next day he received a call from the manager of the labour office.

"Mr Mcphereson," said the manager, "you have directly and purposefully contravened the instructions coming from my office concerning the employment of Jonas Stoutt."

"Well," said Harold, "between the time your letter arrived and Monday morning we had already hired someone, an islander who badly needed the job and who was suitably qualified. We were in desperate need of someone immediately and Mr Stoutt didn't call back until Monday morning."

"This incident will be reported to the minister," said the manager angrily. "We are not used to being ignored." He slammed the phone down and Harold sighed in frustration. He was a fair man, a reasonable man and this petty bureaucrat was getting under his skin.

The volcanic island of Montserrat was about 250 miles south of the Caribbee Isles and had seen very active seismic eruptions for the past 18 months. Lava flows had actually reached the sea and formed new land masses, and nautical charts were having to be reviewed and changed accordingly. Large areas of the island had been evacuated already and a British warship was stationed offshore to evacuate the remaining population should a red alert be sounded by the seismologists.

Tortuga and the Caribbee Isles were on the same fault line as Montserrat and as a result they often experienced tremors and "shakes" but nothing much over 5.5 on the Richter scale. But 5.5 was enough to shake things up and cause items to fall from supermarket shelves, rattle windows and doors and render a scream or two from frightened humans. It was a quake such as this that rocked the island of Tortuga one weekend in April. The tremor was particularly severe at GSC.

It was lunchtime and the Mermaid Bar was about half full when the shaking began. Almost immediately, several bottles toppled from shelves behind the bar counter and these knocked more off as they fell to the ground. Some glasses fell and a wall clock crashed to the ground whilst several women screamed and others sat, open-mouthed and paralysed.

It took several seconds for most people to realise what was happening and that a minor earthquake was in progress, but the noise of breaking glass and the all pervasive shaking soon had people to their feet. In textbook fashion, some ran to the outer walls of the room, while others ran to the door to get clear of the building.

It was an overweight, grey-haired American visitor who had just passed through the door who became an unlucky victim. The mermaid chose that moment to come crashing down and she caught the man a glancing blow on the back during her descent. The tourist went down like a sack of potatoes and almost certainly saved the mermaid from serious damage.

Harold, who had come out from behind the bar at the first tremor, saw the whole incident from where he was standing, flat against an outer wall. He rushed up to the scene of the accident and bent down to examine . . . the mermaid!! . . . to see if any damage had been done to his beloved figurehead.

Meanwhile, the man was writhing in pain on the floor and looking at Harold in a beseeching manner, completely bewildered. Why was this buffoon examining an inanimate object when he was lying there dying, he thought. Harold, who had been in something of a trance, was quickly brought back to reality by the strange, guttural noises coming from the man next to him and he quickly turned his attention to the visitor. Harold was well versed in first aid from his army days and knew enough not to move the man, who seemed to be in great pain. The tremors had stopped now and the man's wife came over. "Don't move him," ordered Harold, "I'm going to call an ambulance."

Someone brought a sheet to shade the man's body from the sun,and inadvertently covered his whole body, including his head, and this set the woman to crying hysterically. "He's not dead yet, you moron," she cried, and bent down and mopped her husband's forehead with her handkerchief. "Everything will be fine, honey," she said comfortingly, "you're in good hands." The man looked at her doubtfully.

The mermaid had fallen in such a way that she was lying on her side and facing the hapless tourist. Her half smile looked almost leering and the piercing blue eyes stared unrelentingly. The man inclined his head towards his attacker. "Black glue," he said, again in a choking, guttural fashion. The woman looked mystified, but Harold, back from making the emergency call, and kneeling beside the unfortunate American, got the meaning immediately – 'fuck you,' he had said to the mermaid.

Away in the distance, an ambulance siren could be heard and Harold breathed a sigh of relief – at least the ambulance service was prompt, he thought. He looked down at the man lying there with glazed eyes. "I'm going to remove your shoes. OK, can you wiggle your toes?" he said. Toes were wiggled. "Wiggle your fingers." Fingers were wiggled. Harold breathed another sigh of relief – there was no evident sign of paralysis.

The man then pointed to his throat and made

another choking noise and Harold said, "Open wide." There was something lodged deep in the man's gullet and Harold, not in the least bit squeamish, dived in and with a pincer-like movement of thumb and forefinger fished out a huge plug of chewing tobacco.

"Oooh, that feels better," said the big man. "My back feels on fire," and he tried to get up. Harold pushed him down.

"It's best not to move until you've been examined and possibly X-rayed. Back injuries can be exacerbated if you move about. Have you ever had any back injuries or pain before?"

"Don't answer that," said Adolf Reephoff, bending down and offering the man a business card. "I am a lawyer – you will need representation here to secure compensation. Save all other comment for court. Just sign here . . ."

At that moment two ambulance men arrived with a stretcher. "Give us room, here. Mind the way." They pushed through the crowd and set down the stretcher beside the victim.

"Well, I guess we will need a lawyer," said the injured tourist and, somewhat confused, signed the piece of paper, against the protestations of Harold.

As the man was whisked to hospital the crowd dispersed and a general cleanup began. Harold shook his head in disbelief – to add to the rest of Reephoff's dubious attributes was "ambulance chaser."

Harold turned to examine the mermaid again and ascertain the cause of the accident. The mermaid had been affixed to the imitation ship's bow by two bolts that protruded from the wooden structure and the vibrations caused by the tremor must have caused the nuts to work loose. They had rolled clear of the mermaid and were lying on the floor of the terrace. Harold got onto Broadrite right away to make sure the company was covered. "Did you feel the tremor in town?" asked Harold.

"Yes we did," answered Broadrite, "it lasted for almost a minute here. No damage, though. Everything all right at GSC?"

Harold explained what had happened. "I just wanted to make sure that we were covered by our insurance policy."

"Yes," said Broadrite, "GSC is covered against anyone claiming damages for injuries sustained on the company's premises."

"Pheeeew!" said Harold, "I'm pleased to hear that. I think Reephoff's out for blood."

"It'll be an interesting case if he does sue – he represents the insurance company, too. Definite conflict of interest there. Crafty bugger's working both sides of the fence."

"And another thing . . . I received a letter from his office this morning. He's asking for $200,000 for acute embarrassment at GSC's opening night dinner. He also included a cleaning bill for $225. I'd advise paying the cleaning bill with apologies for the island's utility services. Also explain that you can take no responsibility for the island's wild life. Can you imagine what might happen if you paid any kind of compensation for the action of those frogs? Soon people would be suing for mosquito bites or an annoying fly!" he laughed out loud. "Don't worry, it'll never get to court."

"You seem to have a pretty good handle on the situation," said Harold, relieved. "Why don't you reply to the letter and pay the cleaning charge. Just add the amount to my account." He put the phone down just as Jackie came walking into the Mermaid Bar.

"Is everyone all right?" she said, worriedly, looking at the mermaid lying on the terrace floor just outside the barroom entrance. "We lost a few plates in the kitchen, but nothing serious. What happened to the mermaid?"

"Everything's fine," he said, and explained about the man being knocked down by the mermaid. "I've already been on to Broadrite and he knows all the details. The mermaid's undamaged – I'll have Elroy re-install it first thing in the morning – this time with 'locktight' glue."

"Look what came in the mail this morning. A copy of Exotic Islands and we're featured. I haven't read the story but the pictures are fantastic!" She handed Harold the copy of the glossy magazine.

Harold walked over to the coffee machine and poured himself a strong, hot cup and settled down by the picture window to read the story. It was by Hank Krichek with photos by Stacey Lane. The article was so evocative of a fun day of sailing and snorkelling in the islands that Harold determined that he would set aside a weekend in the near future when one of the luxury cats was not booked and take Jackie sailing for a well-deserved break – after all, that was why they had moved to the islands in the first place.

He had almost finished the colourful article when the last paragraph caused him to stare hard at the lines to see if he had read correctly. It said, "In these islands of sun, fun and colour there is a cloud that casts a shadow of unease. An old statute that remains on the law books allows immigration officials to deny entry or expel members of minority groups, including Rastafarians and gays 'forthwith and without explanation.' This writer personally experienced discrimination, being a member of the latter minority group, not at the hands of the government, but by one of the owners of Golden Sunset Charters, Ltd. This deplorable action would not be experienced, however, by heterosexual, well-heeled WASPs, the vacationer that the Caribbee Islands welcomes with open arms."

Harold jumped out of his chair and stormed into the kitchen where Jackie was preparing some swordfish steaks for dinner. "Remember those writers that came to visit the property and go sailing on *Sunfun* last January? What on earth did you say to them to evoke a response like this?" He threw the magazine onto the kitchen table. "Read the last paragraph."

"I can assure you that this has nothing whatsoever to do with me. In fact I didn't even meet the writer in question. You'd better go and check with JC and see if he can shed any light on the incident – he took them all sailing that day."

Harold was so riled that he immediately went down to the marina to find JC, who was busy hosing down the deck, having just completed a charter that morning. After small talk about the just completed charter and the morning's tremor, Harold came to the point. "Read the last paragraph and tell me anything you know about it," he said.

JC glanced at the article and pictures and then read the last paragraph. His eyebrows arched in surprise as he read. "There was a bit of an argument between Roy and the photographer and a bit of shoving took place," explained JC.

"That bloody fool," said Harold, "I might have known he'd start something. I remember trying to dissuade him from going that very morning."

"It really wasn't Roy's fault," said JC. "The guy was being very familiar with him and Roy didn't catch on that he was gay for a long time. When he finally did, he blew his top – but even then – he only shoved him away. I'd say the magazine article is a gross exaggeration, at best. Of course the bit about the government and its discriminatory law is true. I wonder how the writer found out about it."

"Well," said Harold, "I'll have to write to the magazine and explain that the company's policy is the same for minority groups as it is for everyone else. All are welcome. I must say, though, that I'm rather surprised that the magazine's editor allowed the paragraph."

About a week later, Vernon Brathwaite stopped by the Mermaid with the sexy Pearl on his arm. Harold was behind the bar and a copy of the current Exotic Islands magazine was lying on the counter. "Magnificent article in Exotic Islands," said Brathwaite, and Harold nodded, wondering what was coming next. "I loved the pictures and the story was so colourfully written. It's why we organize those writers' junkets. The last paragraph was perfect, don't you think? We don't want a bunch of Rastas and 'antiman' infesting the islands. Might ruin our thriving tourist industry." So that was it, thought Harold. Brathwaite himself was prejudiced and had perhaps orchestrated the article, or at least the last paragraph.

9

The Pines

It was towards the end of June when the bookings for *Sunfun* eased a bit that Harold arranged a weekend for himself and Jackie to go sailing. Shirley stocked the boat with gourmet provisions and some nice wines and on a sunny Friday morning they departed Rum Cove for the Isle of Pines. "They say history repeats itself," said JC. "Here we are sailing a yacht called *Sunfun Calypso* just as we were nearly a year ago – minus Roy, of course."

"We should be thankful for small mercies," said Jackie. "I'm going up to the foredeck to relax on the trampoline. Shirley, would you bring a bottle of cold Chardonnay and two glasses?"

Shirley had turned into an excellent hostess and yacht chef, all signs of seasickness having disappeared, and her relationship with JC was mostly smooth and trouble free, except when she was too tired to make love. Living on board the boat they were able to save most of their salary and so far that season they had made excellent tips. JC was also happy with his lifestyle: There was nothing he liked more than sailing the Caribbee Islands and he felt that Harold and Jackie were not only his employers but also his personal friends. He had to admit that, during that first sail all those months ago, he thought that Harold was something of a bumbling and pompous ass but his first impressions had changed radically. He admired the way they had attacked all the problems concerning the business and brought them under manageable control, and he showed both of them all due respect.

JC popped the beautiful yellow and orange chute and they cruised downwind on a flat sea, the wavelets sparkling in the noonday sun. Shirley arranged a tray of paté, cheese and fruit and took it forward to accompany the wine. Just then a turtle popped its head out of the water. "Look, a turtle," said Shirley but, as often happens, it sounded before Harold and Jackie could crane their necks around to look.

"I'm going to spend at least an hour this afternoon snorkelling," said Jackie.

"I'd love to join you," replied Shirley. "There's a beautiful reef at the Isle of Pineth."

"And I'm going to spend at least an hour having a nap," said Harold, and nobody could deny that he'd earned it. By the time they anchored in Grand Harbour he was already snoring.

The evening meal was a challenge for Shirley. Both Harold and Jackie had told her to keep it simple but Shirley was cooking for her bosses and one of them was a professional chef; she was determined to do a good job. After a refreshing swim and a snorkel she headed straight to the galley. Before leaving Rum Cove she had managed to buy four red snappers of about 16 ounces each and these she proposed to pan fry whole, very slowly in butter, and serve with fresh squeezed lime – some things needed to be kept simple, she reasoned. But to accompany this she had planned "Island Breadfruit." A cruising yachtsman had given her a recipe from the Pacific islands, "to die for," he had said. The breadfruit was peeled and cored and cut in slices and then covered in freshly squeezed coconut milk. This was simmered slowly until all the milk was absorbed and then seasoned to taste.

To begin the meal she had prepared a hummus dip with lots of garlic and olive oil, fresh squeezed lemon juice and a little tahini. A sinful dessert would be a rich vanilla ice cream with chocolate Cointreau. This was where she cheated a bit: she would melt caramel chocolate confectionery in a double boiler and add the liqueur at the last moment – there had never been any complaints before.

And there were no complaints that night either. The four of them sat around the huge cockpit table; Shirley served the food and JC took care of the drinks and wine. It was a wonderful break for both Jackie and Harold.

In the morning they decided to go ashore and stroll the beach. There were one or two gift shops and Bimbos famous bar was at one end. Jackie wanted to compare the gift shops with GSC's and then have a look at the well-known watering hole. They dinghied ashore and tied up at the rickety dock by the government building.

As they walked they were surprised that they recognised several faces and even more surprised by how many people knew them. "Mornin' Ms Jackie, Mr Harold,' and 'Welcome to de Pines," and "Nice to see you on de islan'." As they walked, they attracted a following of kids ranging from about three to about 10, so that when they arrived at Bimbos they had quite a crowd around them. The island children were a happy bunch – laughing, jumping and running, splashing into the sea with screams of delight and generally causing mayhem.

"Well, well, well, and a very good mornin' to the Pied Piper of Hamelin," said Rocky, with a laugh. He was gently swinging in a hammock and slowly got up to meet the new arrivals. "A pleasure to see you visitin' dis part o' de world, Mr and Ms Harold." Rocky had been to the opening night party at the Rusty Pelican and thoroughly enjoyed himself on the "big islan'." "I thought I recognised de boat. Dat be *Sunfun Calypso*. Yeah, JC and Shirley does bring deir people here all de time. He reckon it de highlight o' de week for he tourists."

They sat around talking about boats, sailing and island life. Jackie ordered cold juice drinks for all the children and Rocky laughed, "You got friends for life now – hope you got plenty o' room on dat boat."

Just then an old black dog flopped down under the hammock and Rocky said, "Dat's a island dog. You know how I can tell he a island dog?" They both shook their heads. "Well – he black, he sit on he ass all day, an' he don' know who he fadder is." Harold chuckled at the way Rocky told the joke, obviously one he told tourists almost daily, but Jackie was more circumspect.

"You can get away with telling that joke because you're black," she said, finding it hard not to smile. "If I told it I'd be accused of racism."

"Yeah, you right," said Rocky. "People shaw get all bent out o' shape dese days 'bout racism, colour an' terminology. In de States de black people want to be called 'African American' instead o' black. Before dat it were 'coloured.' Well I tell you – I 'black,' I like 'black' an' I proud o' 'black.' Anyhow it de white people dat coloured when you really get down to it. When dey get sunburn dey does turn red, when dey sea-sick dey go green, when dey freezin' col' dey turn blue, when dey 'fraid dey go yellow an' when dey dead dey go purple. Me, I stay black."

"Well said," said Harold, laughing out loud. "You forgot about jaundice – can turn a man as yellow as a daffodil." Rocky looked vacantly at Harold – he'd never heard of a daffodil.

"Well, come along," said Jackie to Harold, "we must get back, we've got some sailing to do."

Rocky lay back down in his hammock. "Come back soon," he said. They smiled and shook hands.

Harold and Jackie strolled off down the beach and back to the dinghy followed by an even bigger crowd of children and the 'island dog' bringing up the rear. When they pushed the dinghy into the water they had about 15 young helpers, and six of them, some wearing nothing more than raggedy shorts, scrambled into the boat whilst others started to swim out to *Sunfun.* Harold started to shoo them away but Jackie admonished him. "Let them come out to the boat for a little while – they mean no harm." Then a little girl of no more than two years grabbed hold of Harold's hand and looked up at him with big brown eyes and said, 'Boat . . . go boat,' pointing to the yacht. His resolve melted. Just as Rocky had predicted, they had made some new friends that were not anxious to leave them.

They reached the yacht and the six "stowaways" scrambled out and onto the big catamaran and two or three of the older children who were strong swimmers were fast approaching. JC came out on deck to see what all the pandemonium was about, and Jackie explained that their visitors were guests for about half an hour. The children started diving off the bow and then swimming back to the stern ladder and forward again to the bow and round and round. These island kids were so full of energy and down to earth fun, pushing each other into the water and shouting and laughing. There was Bugeye with large bulging eyes; there was Tall Boy, a skinny, gangling youth, and Tutu, or Two Tooth, who had only two visible incisors, his front teeth missing.

"I gonna be a captain one day," said Tutu.

The others laughed. "You gonna be a cabin boy," they chorused, "an' after a lot o' trainin' you might make it to deck scrubber." They doubled over with laughter while Tutu ran to the bow and dived in.

This gave JC an idea, and he organized a deck cleaning team with buckets and scrubbing brushes, but he soon ended that game when he saw the resulting mess. He thought that a knot tying lesson might go down well and cut 10 lengths of thin line. He started with the most useful knot a seaman must know – the bowline – and after about five minutes, Tutu had learned it.

"You must be able to tie that knot in the dark with one hand, on a rolling deck with cold water spraying in your face," JC said in a swarthy, piratical voice and the motley young crew screamed with delight at his antics. When it became time for them to leave, JC had to chase several reluctant ones up to the bow where they leapt off into the water, again with screams of delight.

That afternoon they sailed to a small cay and anchored off a white sand beach. They spent an hour snorkelling on a nearby reef and later JC launched the two double kayaks and they paddled around the island. It was another fun day and they all went to bed early that night, quite exhausted.

The following day, after a late breakfast, they sailed back to Rum Cove, tacking up the south side of

Tortuga in brisk 20 knot winds. Harold and Jackie lay on the trampolines up forward, watching the briny deep go flashing by beneath them.

"You know, I've been thinking about those kids back on the island – they seem happy but they have so little to do."

"I don't know about that," said Harold, "they have the water, boats, snorkelling, fishing. I'd say they are better off than a lot of kids, especially those raised in big cities."

"Well, you're right about the environment being more healthy, but I didn't see a boat available to them. I didn't see any of them with snorkelling equipment or fishing tackle, either. I just don't think their parents can afford luxuries like that."

"You may be right there, judging by their raggedy clothing, anyway."

Jackie got up on one elbow and looked at Harold earnestly. "What do you think of this idea? We have an open day for island kids one day a week on the little beach next to the marina at GSC. We already have some kayaks, dinghies, snorkelling equipment and windsurfers – we'd hardly have to spend a penny."

"It's an excellent idea in theory," said Harold, nodding and smiling at his dear wife's unselfish intentions, "and I'd be all for it, except that supervisors and teachers would be required and we're already under-staffed."

"I don't think that would be a problem," said Jackie. "We just ask around for volunteers from suitably qualified people and parents. Half the people on the islands have jobs that are marine-related. Would you sanction the use of GSC's equipment if I can find personnel to staff the project?"

"I certainly would. The quicker children learn about the sea and related activities, the sooner they become worthy workers in the industry. It would have benefits all the way round, I think it's a great idea." He leaned over and kissed her on the cheek. "I bet JC would be a willing volunteer – he seems to have a knack with kids – but the trouble is that he's out with guests on charter so often."

On that sunny Sunday, on the deck of *Sunfun Calypso*, the idea was born for a voluntary organization whose object would be to teach children about the sea. It was officially named CLATS: Children Learn About The Sea, but soon became fondly known as "Cluts" as the antics and mishaps of these "beginner" sailors became more well-known.

When the yacht was tied up back at the marina, Harold and Jackie both swore to make similar trips at least once a month; it had been such a fun-filled and entertaining weekend.

It was on Monday morning whilst Harold was going over the previous week's accounts with Sonia, when the fax machine rattled out a particularly long message. It was from Justin Jennings in London and he began by explaining that the *Sunday Times'* magazine wanted to run a six-page spread on Tortuga and the Caribbee Islands highlighting the Sunset Lodge, the Mermaid Bar and GSC in a future edition. He hoped to follow this up with an interesting story about the mermaid and he described his research progress.

"I began by accessing the Internet and found no fewer than eight 'Mermaids' in the maritime archives. For further information the computer advised me to look through the comprehensive records at the Board of Trade and their files are all on microfilm. I spent days searching reels and reels of film for the years 1880 to 1920. Then in the very last box of rolls, I came across a barquentine of 420 tons, 140 feet in length and named *The Mermaid*! She was built in Glasgow in 1859 and was involved in the Caribbean trade for 20 years from 1900 to 1920. Her ports of call were listed as Portsmouth (Homeport), Cadiz, Spain; Gran Canaria; Port of Spain, Trinidad; St Eustatia; Virgin Islands; Caribbee Islands; San Juan, Puerto Rico; and New York. She would do two trips annually and often carried passengers. She was registered by Lloyd's of London – I'm going there tomorrow to see if they have a record of her registration papers. I am optimistic that this is our ship. I'm very excited about this and hope for some revelations soon. Godfrey Allbright, who was unemployed, has turned out to be very useful. He spent hours at the Department of Trade records office going through the files with me.

"I took the wine bottle to an antique dealer and he immediately said: 'French, turn of the century.' He showed me a picture from a reference book. It looked identical and it fits in with the dates of the vessel. By the way, he said the bottles are worth about 50 pounds each if they're in good condition."

Harold read the fax through twice and was so delighted he rushed up to the kitchen and showed it to Jackie. She read it through and nodded and smiled but secretly thought that Harold was being perhaps a little extreme with this mermaid research. She was well aware that the age of the rum that had come from the casks had to be verified before it could be sold as a fine old vintage, but Harold had a fixation on the mermaid, she thought.

When Memnon returned from a week's charter on *Wet 'n Wild* the following day, JC told him about the proposed CLATS programme. Memnon was immediately enthusiastic. He knew of at least half a dozen kids from his village who would not only benefit from the programme but who would jump at the chance. "Safety at sea, den basic navigation an' compass readin',' rules o'de road an' boat operation. De kids will love it – keep dem out o' trouble, too."

"Oh yeah, and dinghy sailing, races and windsurfing lessons. It'll be so much fun they'll be lining up to join," agreed JC.

A committee was formed to decide issues concerning the running of CLATS and Memnon was elected President for the first term of one year. There would be weekly classes and Saturday was the obvious day for them, not only because the kids would be off school but Memnon and JC would, hopefully, be between charters on that day. To begin with, they were the only two instructors. George Cleary hadn't come forward as they had hoped, but Shirley volunteered to be the organization's secretary and keep the books. A corner of the boat shed was designated as a classroom and Harold said the company would donate 20 plastic chairs and a blackboard.

In the weeks that followed, the CLATS programme became increasingly popular and almost half of the participants came from the Pines.

The month of August did not begin well for GSC. To begin with the weather was particularly hot and humid, and business was slow. A lot of yachts had already left the Caribbee Islands and headed south to latitudes that were considered safe from tropical hurricanes. Yacht charters were down because of bad press – the previous two hurricane seasons had seen above average activity, and potential visitors to the islands were reluctant to come.

But the real icing on the cake of despondency was a demand for money from a Mr Cyril Longfellow for compensation for a "severe accident caused by negligence" that had happened on the premises of

Golden Sunset Charters, more particularly the Sunset Terrace. The letter went on to explain that a large wooden fixture, namely a carving, had fallen onto the innocent bystander and caused "permanent back injury" as well as "enduring pain and suffering." What with medical tests, X-rays and finally scans, it was ascertained that Mr Longfellow had suffered from a fractured vertebra, but that the injury had not been diagnosed correctly initially, and the backbone had been allowed to heal crookedly with calcium buildup at the point of fracture. Now there was irreversible damage. A lifetime of debilitating headaches and backaches was likely and weekly therapy with pain-relieving medications was the only remedy. This would be the necessary treatment into the foreseeable future and a half million dollars was sought as reasonable compensation in order to avoid litigation. The letter was signed on behalf of the plaintiff by a Mr Adolf Reephoff of A. Reephoff and Associates. The letter was accompanied by a copy of a neurologist's report that stated: "An evaluation with a high resolution CT scan of the cervical spine and MRI showed protrusion of the C4-5 disk with some impression in the thecal sac. A healed C4 fracture was also evident." To Harold, it all sounded very serious, very technical and very expensive. He phoned Mike Broadrite and explained his dilemma.

"Send a copy of the letter to the insurance company and instruct them to deal with it," explained Broadrite. "They will be well aware that on that day there was an earth tremor of medium magnitude and will probably use that to deny the claim. It was an 'act of God' that I'm sure is not covered in the standard policy, unlike the hurricane coverage that we stipulated be included, and was an 'extra.' Reephoff may try to sue GSC if the insurance company rejects the claim, but we can use the 'act of God' clause too, and claim no responsibility. At that stage we would need to send in our own medical experts to verify the alleged injuries. In any event it will be a hard one for him to win. Reephoff seems to have an insatiable desire to harm GSC."

"Yes, two threatened lawsuits in as many weeks," replied Harold. "Did you notice that he signed the letter 'A. Reephoff and Associates'? The usual letterhead of the partnership of Bigsum, Hannover, Reephoff and Blarney was absent."

"You're right," said Mike. "Reephoff has started his own practice. He was never very well liked in his old partnership – ethics were always a bit doubtful. From all the rumours flying around, I believe he was asked to curtail his questionable methods – ambulance chasing, for one – and it was then that he threw in the towel and decided to go it alone. Personally, I believe that the conflict of interest in the Longfellow case may have had something to do with it. He desperately wants to 'get even' with you so he sided with Longfellow to sue the pants off you, and quit the partnership. You know the frog incident turned him into the laughing stock of the whole island and then the cartoon in the paper was like rubbing salt into the wound. For some reason he blames you for everything. I'm sure he would love to see the successful GSC come tumbling down."

"The man must be obsessed," said Harold. "The frog incident was hardly a planned event. I wonder how he managed to start up on his own so quickly. Normally it takes months for the trade licence to come through and all the paperwork to be processed by the government."

"Reephoff's been here long enough to know the right palms to grease. I just read in the paper that he's representing the chief minister's office in a libel suit. He may have traded expertise for favours. He's a slippery customer, as you well know."

Harold felt uneasy about the whole affair but sent the letter off to the insurance company that, until very recently, had had Adolf Reephoff as its lawyer.

10

The Hurricane

In a network of meteorological centres in the U.S.A. there is one in Colorado that, every year, predicts tropical storms and hurricanes for the Caribbean. Using data as diverse as temperatures of the sea-water off the coast of Peru and the amount of rainfall experienced in tropical Africa, fairly accurate forecasts can be made as to the number and intensity of storms likely to occur that year – as proven by the five preceding years. Now, in 1998, an above average number of named storms were forecast to traverse the tropical Atlantic and Caribbean Sea, and the beginning of August was the time to start taking the necessary precautions. Indeed an early hurricane in July '96, Hurricane Bertha, had caught everyone off guard in the Virgin Islands and damage and losses were greater than need have been. Now the satellite images of potential tropical storms and hurricanes were carefully monitored by TV stations and beamed down to the islands from the States.

On August 5th, Harold and Jackie were sitting in the library, enjoying a late breakfast, when Harold switched to the weather channel on the new big-screen TV, complete with its own satellite dish. There were a string of dense cloud masses, almost like a necklace, stretching all the way from the west coast of Africa to the Caribbean, and one in particular had already developed into a tropical storm with the dreaded circular wind pattern. The present location was still 1,200 miles east southeast of the Caribbee Islands, so there was no immediate cause for alarm. The system was travelling at 15 m.p.h. so it was at least three days away, but the meteorologist said that conditions for strengthening were extremely favourable. The Bermuda 'High,' a high pressure anticyclone that is an almost guaranteed feature somewhere in the central north Atlantic, was unusually intense and this was of some concern because it is the difference between very high and very low pressures that produces the steep gradients that cause strong winds.

"This forecast looks very ominous," said Harold. "We'll have to watch the situation carefully."

"What a shame," said Jackie, "they may have to cancel all the carnival plans. This year looked as though it was going to be such a grand event, with so many people participating." The annual carnival was a highlight of the year for many of the locals. It was a celebration of the emancipation of slavery and had been revived as a tourist attraction some 20 years before.

"I'm going to start hurricane preparations immediately down at the docks. Then we'll make sure we have all the necessary materials for boarding up and securing the buildings. I think it would be wise to notify the guests – they may wish to fly out."

"We only have six guests staying in the lodge at present," said Jackie, "but I think there are about 10 of our yachts out sailing amongst the islands. Thank goodness we took adequate insurance."

"Yes," said Harold. "We must contact each yacht and have them monitor the weather station and Channel 16. If necessary, we will have to recall all vessels back to base and give the charterers the option to fly out as well. You'd better prepare all the rooms for occupancy and check our food supplies. Thank God we had the emergency generator installed – now at least we won't lose our frozen foods if there's a power outage. I'm going down to the marina to make arrangements with George." Harold got up and, leaving an unfinished bowl of prunes and bran flakes, walked briskly down to the marina. He silently thanked his partner for his foresight; it had been Roy who had persuaded them to install the generator for just such an impending situation.

George Cleary was in the boat shed doing inventory when Harold entered. "Good morning, George," he said to his marina manager, "there's a large storm about three days away with every indication that it will soon become a hurricane. Did you see the weather forecast this morning?"

"I did," said Cleary, "but I don't think it's anything to worry about. The sea temperature is too cold for any major development – besides, it's still pretty early in the season. By the law of averages, September is the dangerous month."

Harold stood there aghast, his mouth hanging open. "You can't go by averages when it comes to something as potentially dangerous as a hurricane! We must start making preparations immediately."

"As you wish," said George Cleary, sulkily, "but you may be sounding a false alarm and then all the work will have been for nothing."

"Look," said Harold, "I'd rather have 10 false alarms that were properly prepared for than overlook one that turned into a hurricane." Harold walked over to George and put his arm around his shoulder. "This is our first season of business and I'm relying on you heavily. You have more experience and expertise in the marine field that anyone in the company – that's why I was so pleased to give you the job. I know you won't let me down."

"No, no, I won't let you down," said George, rather half-heartedly.

"Good man!" said Harold, and slapped him on the back to try and cheer him up. "Now, do you think we should get all the yachts down to 'The Pond' and tie them to the mangroves?" The Pond was a completely landlocked lagoon except for a narrow entrance and was only seven feet deep. It was surrounded by mangrove bushes whose roots were very strong and spider-webbed into the bottom – perfect for "good holding." A yacht would be secure tied to the roots of such a tenacious plant although conservationists sometimes made noises of disapproval.

"Oh, no, that won't be necessary," said George. "We'll take off all the sails, awnings and dodgers, stow all loose deck gear and then tie each vessel securely in the centre between two finger piers with double lines and extra strong chafing gear."

"All right. Well I'm sure you'll make the best decisions for the safety of life and property," said Harold, not feeling very sure at all. "We'll know a lot more about the severity of this storm and its proximity to us by this time tomorrow. We must notify all of our charterers and tell them to stand by on Channel 16.

'Prepare for the worst and hope for the best,' was the motto of my old commanding officer, and I must say I couldn't agree more in this particular instance."
Harold walked out of the door and down to the docks, leaving George muttering to himself about overzealous novices. About a year ago he had held the reins of power at GSC – now he felt he was just another employee.

There were four yachts tied up at the slips and two of the three new, luxury catamarans were tied stern-to the bulkhead with the bows secured to two moorings. Memnon was not aboard *Wet 'n Wild* and it took Harold a moment to remember that he was off, taking his two-week annual vacation. Memnon loved carnival and he always took his holidays to coincide with the riotous celebrations. Now it looked like it would have to be postponed.

Shirley and JC on *Sunfun Calypso* were out on a two-week charter, but Harold had every confidence that JC would make sensible and effective decisions if and when the situation warranted them.

The following morning the predictions were even more ominous. The tropical storm had just been upgraded to a hurricane, which meant sustained winds of 75 m.p.h.. It was called Ben, the second named storm of the season, and its course, if unchanged, would take it right through the Caribbee Islands. "Conditions are favourable for strengthening and all islands in the Leewards and Windwards are advised to keep a close watch," said the radio announcer. The only slightly positive note in the whole broadcast was that the system had slowed to 12 m.p.h. which meant that people had more time to fly out of the island or more time to prepare for it – but, as everyone knew, when a hurricane slowed it usually intensified.

That morning a lot of pundits hung around

theorising, but not Harold. His first thought was that if the property and buildings were secure, then people would be safe. He rang up Elroy and asked him to come over to GSC and bring Toshi and Isaac if they were available. He wanted all apertures and windows boarded up; all loose equipment, dinghies, deck chairs, flower pots, etc., secured or brought inside. The Rusty Pelican was only about four feet above the high water mark and the boutique was about six. Harold decided to empty the contents of both buildings and take them up to the lodge by Range Rover. The buildings would then be protected by sand bags around the perimeter to a height of a further six feet. There would be plenty of work for the construction crew and Harold was aware that each man had his own property to protect. It would have to be a team effort with timing being the key.

Hurricane warnings were issued at noon on the 8th August for the Caribbee Islands. The eye of the hurricane, which was about 40 miles in diameter, was expected to pass just north of Tortuga mid-morning of the 9th August. "All persons should be completing final preparations for the onslaught of this powerful storm," said the radio. "Marine interests must take special precautions since the barometric pressure at the centre of Ben is unusually low at 954 millibars and the sea level could rise by as much as 10 feet. This coupled with a storm surge, could result in severe flooding of low-lying areas. Maximum sustained winds of 130 miles per hour can be expected with gusts approaching 200 m.p.h.."

"Lawd help us," whispered Beulah, who was sitting at the kitchen table. "Dis gonna be sometin' else. We bes' prepare some big pots o' stew an' rice. Come girl," she said to Lynette, who was nervously fidgeting with a cold cup of tea, "we bes' start peelin' potatoes an' onions."

"What gonna happen to all o' we, Mummy?"

"Dat be in de hands o' de Lawd," said Beulah. "We done secure everyting bes' as possible up at de house an' de animals have deir food an' shelter. Me an' you, we gonna stay here through the storm an' help out bes' we can."

Harold, who had also been listening to the latest hurricane update in the kitchen, said to Jackie, "We'll make the kitchen our centre of operations whilst the storm lasts. We can make up some temporary beds on the floor in the pantry, and we'll leave the VHF radio on Channel 16 as usual. Elroy and his crew have done an excellent job securing the property but I want to let them go home now to make their own preparations. I'm still rather worried about the boats. I'm going down to the marina now to help."

Just as he was leaving JC and Shirley walked in with Memnon behind them. "Here we are," said JC cheerfully,."Just show us what needs doing – we're here to help."

"First, tell me what you've done with *Sunfun* and your guests," said Harold.

"*Sunfun* is secure down at The Pond," said JC, "and the guests managed to fly out this morning. I tried to call with the information earlier but I couldn't get through. They were all happy, said they'd really enjoyed their cruise. They were due to fly out tomorrow anyway, so they only lost one day of their charter. But I didn't see any other GSC boats at The Pond – where have you taken them all?"

"They're all right here in the marina," said Harold, "George is down there now supervising all the last-minute arrangements."

"Oh, good," said JC, "that must mean that the latest weather update has reported some favourable changes to the situation."

"To the contrary," said Harold. "The hurricane is now a very dangerous Category Four storm with wind gusts of 170 miles per hour. The eye is expected to pass just north of us tomorrow morning."

JC and Memnon looked at each other quizzically. Memnon said, "Dat ain' make sense at all – I mean wid de boats. If de storm goin' to pass to de nort' den we can expec' winds from de north through wes' and den sout.' Rum Cove expose to de wes' an' sout'. It de worse place to leave de boats."

"Well, George is confident that the boats will all be secure in the marina. He is spider-webbing each boat between two finger piers. I was just on my way down there when you walked in. Let's go and check on his progress."

The three of them walked down to the marina, leaving Shirley to help at the lodge. They walked past the Rusty Pelican which was now almost invisible behind a six-foot wall of sandbags. George, who was supervising the tying of the catamarans at the marina, saw them coming but ignored them. Harold walked up to him and said, "I hope we're making the right decision to leave these boats here. The latest hurricane update forecasts a severe storm that will pass very close to us."

"By noon tomorrow, the path of the hurricane will have changed to a more northerly direction," said Cleary confidently. "You'll see that this will have been largely a false alarm."

JC, standing next to Harold, could hardly believe his ears. "The latest update on the TV showed that we are in a position for a direct hit. You can't disregard evidence like that at this late stage. By tonight we'll be feeling the first effects of the outer bands of the storm. The safest place for these boats would have been down at The Pond."

George's face turned red and he spoke quietly at first, slowly building to a crescendo, "So . . . It sounds like you think you know more about the situation than me. Well, let me tell you something: I was down here in the Caribbean dealing with boats and the weather whilst you were still dribbling food down your shirt front and pissing in your pants!!!" JC took a step back, as Clearys trembling finger was pointed an inch from his nose. Then he turned to Harold. "As for you," he said, "I would expect a proprietor to support the decisions of a manager. But even that won't be necessary much longer, because I am giving you one month's notice of my intention to terminate my employment at GSC. You'll have it in writing by tonight!"

"Now, now," said Harold in a soothing tone, "there's no need to make hasty decisions at a time like this. Everyone's feeling a bit tense – we must concentrate on the job at hand. Anyway, it's too late to move the boats anywhere, and The Pond is full. Let's finish rigging the dock lines with backups everywhere and secure chafing gear."

George Cleary stalked off towards the boat shed, shaking his head and mumbling something incoherent. "He ain' t'inkin' right," said Memnon, "I t'ink he maybe gone tropo."

"Tropo" was an expression given mainly to white expats who had become mentally deranged or peculiar due to the effects of too much rum, other booze or dope, or too much sun, and lack of patience with "island time" where everything took twice as long as usual to get done. It was more common amongst long-time residents, the effects being cumulative. The making of irrational decisions is the start of the condition. Confirmed sufferers end up wandering around town, naked, staring vacantly into space.

At 5 o'clock that evening, they all walked wearily back up to the lodge. There was still some tension in the air, but everyone was talking amicably once again. Everything humanly possible had been done to secure the yachts, and all the guests were either up at the lodge or in alternative accommodation in Roadstead. As Harold closed the kitchen door, the first northerly zephyrs rustled the leaves of the nearby coconut palms.

Anne Cleary rushed up to meet the men as they entered the kitchen. "Is everything all right down at the marina?" she asked, worriedly, and then continued without waiting for an answer. "I've secured the house, everything's boarded up," she said to George, "I've brought our overnight things. Jackie has invited us to stay here. There couldn't be a better hurricane shelter on the island." George nodded his head wearily, and sat down in a corner. He looked thoroughly depressed.

Memnon volunteered to stay the night too, in case he was needed. The hurricane was not expected to hit until next morning, but the large pan of bubbling beef stew and dumplings was a powerful incentive.

JC and Shirley left to return to *Sunfun* down at The Pond. Harold went into the Mermaid Bar – he had decided to close it early, though, to allow everyone to get some rest in anticipation for the storm. There were now 12 guests staying at the lodge, and Jackie hoped that they would all eat early. It had been a stressful day and she was tired.

At first light about 5:30 a.m. Beulah and Lynette were up making tea. They were soon joined by George and Anne, and a little later Harold came in. No-one had slept well; the sound of the increasing wind, coming in howling gusts, had unnerved the hardiest sleeper, even though the lodge was one of the most solid and sturdy buildings on the island. Harold walked to the window and peered out through a crack in the boards; during gusts the upper limbs of bushes and small trees were bent over almost horizontal, and leaves, branches and oddments of rubbish were flying through the air. The sky was leaden, with low cumulus scudding north to south. He walked over and switched on the portable radio – the 6 a.m. news and weather update was imminent.

"Hurricane Ben, a dangerous Category Four hurricane, is approaching the Caribbee Islands," said a sombre radio announcer. "The centre of Ben was located 80 miles east of Tortuga at 5 a.m. and is travelling west northwest at 15 miles per hour. Hurricane force winds extend 75 miles from the centre in all directions and gale force winds 200 miles. Maximum sustained winds are 130 miles per hour, with gusts at the higher elevations to 180 miles per hour. A gradual turn to the north-west and north is expected today." George, who was sitting at the kitchen table drinking tea, looked up with a little smile, but was smart enough not to say anything.

Harold was poring over a nautical chart of the area and calculating Ben's probable course. "We can expect hurricane force winds for the next 8 to 10 hours," he said grimly. "All we can do is wait it out and hope for the best. Unfortunately, the anticipated change in direction will be of little help." He glanced over at George, but his smug expression had gone. He was eating a piece of toast and staring vacantly at the wall.

The radio broadcast droned on. It was linked to the island's hurricane shelters, and live reports were coming in. One old lady who was being interviewed sounded quite distraught. Her goats had been turned away from the shelter. "Dem goats is God's creatures too," she said, "but de superwisor he did'n let dem in. Dat ain' right at all. If dey does run off or get blown away me goin' sue de govmint. Dat's right, somebody goin' to pay!"

Another woman seemed to believe that the end of the world was imminent. "Hell-fire an' brimstone," she said, "pestilence, storm an' flood, it all in de Bible an' it mean dat de human race goin' pay for deir sins. We mus' all pray now an beg for His humble forgiveness."

An old man blamed it on the government. "Dat ol' weather station been operatin' since jus' after de war. All dat equipment need replacin' years back – it no wonder we gettin' more hurricanes. It high time de govmint come up to date for de people's safety."

Then there were more warnings – people were warned not to panic, not to go outside, not to engage in looting of damaged or destroyed businesses and homes once the storm abated. Then the power went off. At the lodge there was a momentary blackout and then the emergency generator kicked in automatically. In most homes on the island, though, this was one of the most depressing times of an intense storm. When hurricane force winds reached a dangerous level, the power was intentionally shut down to minimise damage and hazards and to facilitate re-activating it after the storm. For a household it meant no lights, no hot or even cold water since the pump and heater could not function, no shower, no toilet, no TV and no fans or air conditioning. Cooking on the island was almost exclusively gas, so at least people could make hot food and drinks. Most families huddled around kerosene lamps or candles, listening to a portable radio.

By lunchtime the hurricane had reached its most intense phase. Miraculously, the portable radio was still broadcasting. The radio station had managed to get hold of one of the two Roman Catholic priests on the island and they put him on the air. "In this time of trial and suffering," he said, "we beseech thee to show thy mercy. We acknowledge your almighty power and humbly beg for succour . . ."

The monotone of the preacher's voice, combined with the eerie howl of the wind was too much for Beulah. She dropped to her knees, and clasping her hands in front of her ample bosom, she looked to the ceiling with eyes wide and prayed out loud, "Lawd have mercy on my soul an' my li'l Lynette. Forgive all our sins especially de time when I let Norbert into my bed, an' Calvin, an' Bernard, an' Zachary, an' de big fella from de distillery . . . An' de time I done cuss out me sister on de phone an' de time I forgot to pay for de cake at de bazaar an' . . ." She was oblivious to anyone else in the room, it seemed, and certain that the end of the world was nigh.

Lynette listened, open-mouthed and dumb-founded.

The VHF had been broadcasting messages all morning, and it was clear that there was substantial damage island-wide. Then suddenly a message came through for GSC. It was from a house up on the hill overlooking Rum Cove. "Breaking waves are sweeping right across the docks and two yachts have washed up on the opposite banks and a large catamaran is hanging on by one line. Visibility is patchy but I'll get back to you with more detail when I can, over."

"Please keep us informed," said Harold, solemnly, "GSC out." Harold's face was ashen when he replaced the mike.

George, who had been sitting silent for most of the morning, got up and, foul-weather jacket in hand, rushed for the door. "Wait!" shouted Harold, "don't go, it's too dangerous!" But before anyone could stop him the door slammed shut and he was gone.

Memnon stood up, "I'm going too," he said, "I'll try and bring he back if it look bad." He grabbed a foul-weather jacket from behind the kitchen door.

"Take this," said Harold, handing him a portable VHF radio, "and keep in touch on Channel 9. Be careful – I mean that!" Harold slapped him on the back and watched him disappear into the tempest.

The force of the wind was incredible. As soon as Memnon emerged from the shelter of the side of the building, he felt himself being blown along with branches, leaves and other assorted debris. He crouched down and ran from one sheltering structure to another, like a man avoiding gunfire in a movie. He pulled up the hood of his jacket and tied it tightly around his face to help against the stinging of the horizontally driving rain, and continued down the path. He climbed over two fallen palm trees and almost stepped on a dead dog whose face was contorted in a gruesome rictus.

When he finally got to the Rusty Pelican he was two feet deep in sea water, and breaking waves were crashing into the protective barrier of sandbags. He rested for a little while behind the building in the lee of the wind, the driving rain having beaten his face till it felt like a pincushion.

The most unnerving thing was the sound. There were six to eight feet breaking waves roiling into Rum Cove and the wind was shrieking through the trees and the rigging of the yachts, coming in varying bursts of intensity. It was a primeval, angry roar and it was terrifying.

Memnon tried to peer around the side of the building to get a glimpse of the docks but when he faced the weather the wind tore at his breath and the needles of rain beat at him like hailstones, making it impossible. It was then that he had a brain wave: if he could get to the boat shed, only about 30 yards away, he could get hold of a snorkel and mask. Then he would be able to see and breathe.

He chose his moment carefully, and crouching low and with his back to the onslaught, he made a dash. About half way, he was picked up by a gust and dropped again 30 feet downwind. He crawled on his hands and knees for the last 10 yards, through mud and debris, but it mattered little; he was filthy anyway and soaked through to the skin. He yanked the back door of the shed open and staggered inside, but a brief feeling of respite was soon gone when a gust of wind rocked the building. He clambered to the box of snorkelling equipment and dug out a set that he thought would fit. Adrenaline was pumping through his body as he wondered what had happened to George. He put on the equipment and tied an old towel around the exposed skin on his face, securing the whole with the drawstring on the hood of his foul-weather jacket. Again he stepped out into the maelstrom.

Walking crab-like, backwards and sideways, and keeping his body low, he made his way slowly to the docks. He had only fair visibility because the mask kept steaming up and the driving rain and spume continued relentlessly. When he reached the bulkhead he saw the terrible damage. There were now three yachts washed up on the banks and a further three were sunk at their slips with just parts of their masts and rigging visible. Of those yachts still floating, one had been dismasted and the rest were heeling dramatically with every gust, their dock lines taught as piano wire.

The quick survey of the marina in its storm-bound condition made it obvious to Memnon that there was little anyone could do, but just then, through his fogged up snorkelling mask, he glimpsed a speck of yellow at the end of the bulkhead near the catamarans. He slowly made his way along the bank above the bulkhead dock which was three or four feet deep in water, and then he saw George in his yellow jacket. *Wet 'n Wild* had broken away from the dock, its two stern lines having chafed right through, and was pitching and tossing wildly, its stern crashing into the vessel next to it. It was only a matter of time before both vessels were holed. George, who had somehow managed to get on board, was trying to get a line from the catamaran to shore, but the task was hopeless. He was being thrown around like a rag doll, and anyway the line was heavy and waterlogged and the wind would have taken it as soon as any attempt was made to throw it. They made eye contact about the same time and waved, with Memnon gesticulating frantically for George to come back ashore, but he took no notice – conversation was impossible in the howling wind, but George was anxious to talk to Memnon and cupped both hands to his mouth to convey a message. At that moment, a huge roller caused the boat to pitch dramatically and a wave of green water came over the bow, sluicing aft, and washed over the whole deck. George was caught off balance by the jerky motion and was swept up in the torrent of water. He bounced twice on the stern boarding steps and disappeared into the water. His head came up once but another wave smashed him against the stern of the adjacent vessel. Memnon jumped down onto the submerged bulkhead and looked for him just as there was another rending crunch. Both vessels came together again at their sterns, slowly annihilating each other.

Memnon scrambled back up the bank. He was practically paralysed with fear and worry, and at a loss to know what to do. Then he remembered the radio, and struggled to get it out of his jacket pocket. He glanced back down at the scene of the terrible accident. Out of the corner of his steamed up mask, he caught sight of a green but blurred object. It was the top of a palm tree, complete with coconuts, and one of these nuts glanced off Memnon's head as the whole tree top flew by at 50 miles an hour. All his problems were temporarily solved, as blackness enveloped his being.

Back in the kitchen of the Sunset Lodge concern and worry started turning into anguish and fear as the afternoon wore on. Harold continually berated himself for not stopping the two men from going outside. "They went entirely voluntarily," comforted Jackie. "At the moment we know nothing of their whereabouts so don't be pessimistic. They are probably sheltering in the boat shed." Little did Jackie know that the boat shed was now a twisted mass of wood and galvanised sheeting lying some 50 yards away from its foundations.

By 4 p.m. the wind had backed into the southwest and the sustained winds had dropped to about 60 m.p.h. although stronger gusts still howled and rattled the kitchen windows. The latest weather update put the hurricane's centre northwest of the Caribbee Islands by about 90 miles. It was maintaining its strength, but, for the little archipelago that had just been the victim of its wrath, the worst was over. The swath of destruction, though, was only now being perceived by a population just emerging from shelter.

Harold grabbed a foul-weather jacket with instructions to Jackie to listen in to Channel 9 on the VHF "and don't hesitate to call me if anything comes up. I'm going to make my way to the marina." Harold strapped a portable VHF radio to his belt and went outside.

The sky was a little less menacing as Harold made his way down the path, which had turned into a stream, towards the offices. There were fallen trees, palm fronds, branches and leaves everywhere, but the lodge, terrace and fountain seemed to have suffered no damage. When he got to the company offices, he noticed the large tamarind tree that had shaded the car park had fallen on the building's roof. He continued on to the Rusty Pelican and saw that although the sandbags had kept most of the water out, all the roofing had gone. But when he got to where the boat shed had been he caught his breath: there were boxes of equipment, outboard motors, dinghies and miscellaneous yacht inventory scattered about in pools of water. One wall of the building was twisted and bent, crazily swaying in the still-high wind. The rest of the building was strewn across open ground in pieces. Jackie had suggested that George and Memnon might be sheltering here and a shadow of doom made him shudder. "George, Memnon," called out Harold loudly, but no reply came.

He carried on down to the docks and was appalled and horrified at the amount of damage. There were four yachts washed up on the banks, four yachts were sunk at their docks and debris was strewn everywhere. The sea had receded a bit, and the bulkhead and docks were just awash. He called out again, but still no reply, and then he noticed a prostrate form, clad in yachting jacket, lying on the bank opposite the catamarans, some distance ahead. He ran up and knelt down next to the outstretched form of Memnon, still wearing a mask and snorkel and with a VHF radio clutched in his hand and tuned to Channel 9. Harold rolled him over and noticed a huge bruise and swelling on his right cheek and eye. He put his ear to Memnon's nose and mouth and detected solid, steady breathing. "Memnon, wake up," he shouted, whilst patting his good cheek sharply with the palm of his hand.

Memnon groaned and his eyes flickered open. "Wh'happen?" he said groggily, and then his eyes focused on Harold, "Wh'happen to George?"

"When and where did you last see George?" said Harold, looking intently into Memnon's eyes.

Memnon pointed to *Wet 'n Wild,* that was miraculously still floating. He tried to sit up but groaned and held his head in his hands.

"Don't get up," instructed Harold. "Just lie there until we can get help." Harold started to take off his jacket to help keep Memnon warm, but the stout islander would have none of it.

"No, no I jus' fine. It a bit of a headache, dat's all. Listen, George were on de boat yonder an' a wave carried he into de water. It were blowin' like hell, den a coconut tree knocked me dung an' out. I were tryin' to contac' you but de coconut tree contac' me firs'."

"Oh, my God!" said Harold, and slithered down the muddy bank to the bulkhead where *Wet 'n Wild* had been tied up stern-to. "How long has he been in the water?"

"Well, dat must o' been close to a couple o' hour back," said Memnon groggily, "but I can't say for sure – I were out col'."

Harold peered into the opaque brown water: it was littered with debris and rubbish. He ran back to the first finger pier and out to the end searching frantically, then to the second, then the third. Between the third and the fourth a sunken yacht's upper rigging and mast were all that was visible, but at the end of the port lower spreader, that was just submerged, Harold glimpsed a yellow fabric, somehow caught on the protruding end. It looked like a foul-weather jacket. Harold strained to get a better look but just then a small wave obscured the yellow cloth. But as the water settled again it became obvious that it was a synthetic, yellow foul-weather jacket and from the end of an arm hole was a hand. At first his mind refused to accept it, but as he stared more intently, he saw a head slowly bob to the surface, the grey hair waving like the tentacles of a sea anemone.

Harold was momentarily overcome with grief and as he crouched there staring, he quietly said a few words of prayer as a lump swelled in his throat. He looked up and there was Memnon approaching him. One look at Harold's face told him that his worst fears were a reality. They both stood there on the dock, locked in an embrace of shared grief as the remnants of the killer storm gusted and flurried and the gloom of the encroaching night enclosed around them.

"We must get the body from the water," said Harold in a subdued tone when he had regained his senses. Memnon nodded and walked away, returning in a moment with a boat hook. They managed to pull the submerged body closer to the dock and with great effort, with each man grabbing an arm, they heaved the waterlogged corpse up and onto the dock. They stood up, weak from the exertion, and suddenly the body rolled sideways and let out a loud burp. Harold and Memnon looked at each other in amazement – could George still be alive? They knelt and examined the body more closely, but their fears were confirmed. The back of his head was smashed and a pink translucent jelly oozed out between white fragments of skull and bloody, matted hair. The backbone seemed to be broken in several places too.

They covered the body with a piece of blue awning that had been torn from one of the boats. Then quietly and silently they walked back up towards the lodge in the waning light. Rum Cove looked like a war zone: Three boats in the harbour had strands of tattered jib snapping horizontally in the last gusts of dying wind. Another yacht's mast had bent in two and hung like a broken bone, whilst other vessels had been thrown haphazardly ashore with other debris, their anchor chains or moorings unable to hold them against the powerful winds. Many palm trees were now no more than tree stumps and some buildings were roofless or lay in a twisted mass of wreckage.

For Harold it was one of the darkest moments of his life. As he looked at the destruction on his property, he couldn't help feeling partly responsible for the tragedy. Now he had to break it as gently as possible to George's wife Anne. He kept telling himself that George had been a hero – unselfishly going out in the middle of a hurricane to secure company property, and this was the way he would explain it to Anne. But in his heart of hearts he knew that George's action had been the last desperate attempt of a man trying to correct a serious error in judgment . . . and he had paid a terrible price.

They approached the kitchen entrance. "I'll do all the explaining," said Harold to Memnon.

"Yeah, dat de bes'," said Memnon, still sad and with head bowed. "Good luck, Mr Harold." Memnon knew that breaking tragic news to loved ones was never easy.

Everyone in the kitchen was eagerly awaiting their return and they were bombarded with questions as soon as they entered. But Harold took charge immediately. He asked Beulah to make some strong tea and bring it through to the library and then he ushered Anne Cleary and Jackie into that peaceful room and made sure they were comfortably seated. Then he told the awful story.

11

The Funeral

The funeral was held six days later at the Roman Catholic church in Roadstead. The reason for the delay was that the roof had been blown off the church and a temporary one was taking rather a long time to build because the power had not been turned back on – apparently some lines were still down.

The power outage was causing a major problem at the hospital's morgue as well – after 48 hours its temperature was a very comfortable 90 degrees and the smell was attracting an increasing number of flies. This led to maggots which made autopsies rather difficult to perform – according to the morgue's administrator, who had called Harold and pleaded with him to make contingency plans for his corpse. It wasn't as though the morgue didn't have an emergency generator, it was just that it was broken down, still awaiting parts to arrive from the States. For this reason, George had to be stored in the lodge's cold room, along with a side of beef and three legs of lamb.

It was a relief indeed when the service finally took place. At last the roads had been cleared and utilities had been restored to 90 per cent of the island. But many residences were roofless, and bright blue plastic sheets over makeshift framing were the temporary solution and they dotted the island's landscape. The church had been repaired in a similar manner, and a large crowd of sombrely dressed mourners were gathered outside on this sunny Saturday morning.

Amongst the notables present were Roger and Margaret Clement-Jones, Vernon Brathwaite, old Mr Hodge and the pre-eminent lawyer on the island, Mike Broadrite. They were all waiting outside whilst the Father made last-minute preparations for the service. Finally, a congregation of more than 150 people began filing into the church. Right on cue, Harold, Jackie and Anne pulled up in the new Range Rover. All were smartly attired in dark clothing, Anne with black hat and veil. Harold escorted Anne into the church and to the front row of the congregation.

In front of the altar rested the coffin, with George lying there decked out in his Sunday best. There had been a slight problem: even with the precautions that had been taken George was beginning to go off. Extra embalming fluid and the liberal use of an aerosol "fresh air" had helped a bit, but every now and again a noxious whiff offended an unlucky nostril. The Father was anxious to get on with it.

The service opened with a hymn welcoming George to heaven and the congregation sang with a vigour unknown anywhere but in the Caribbean islands. This was followed by a ceremony known as "placing of pall and symbols." The pall was the white garment, or a replica, used at the time of baptism. The symbols were usually items that represented the life work or occupation of the deceased. A bible and the pall had already been placed into the coffin when a GSC dock employee came forward and placed a coil of rope and some rigging shackles into the casket as a symbol of George's association with boats. There were a few murmurs of disapproval, but the Father stood back piously with a sanctioning nod and the moment passed.

On this occasion the Father was dressed in a rather grand white cassock, similar to the one worn at Easter and other religious festivals. He was a short man and his shiny bald head glowed with a blue aura that looked almost saintly, until you realised that it was just the reflection from the bright blue, temporary roof covering. It was his new philosophy that death was a celebration rather than a time for sorrow, and his "first reading" exemplified this.

Life on earth was nothing but trial and tribulation, a continual fight between temptation and the true path and the devil lurked around every corner just waiting to drag down the tempted, the undevout, the disbelieving heathen. Death was a welcome release from this eternal merry-go-round of pain and suffering and the devout churchgoer would float effortlessly up to paradise in the company of angels, to the sound of a thousand harps . . . When he finished the reading, there were a few envious glances towards the coffin.

The first hymn was "The Lord's my Shepherd" and nearly everybody knew this one. The volume of the singing was almost enough to wake the dead, though it didn't. But it was typical that the native population really enjoyed their singing. It seemed that the louder you were, the more pious you must be, and competitions between individuals or groups of the congregation sometimes took place, much to the delight of the pastor.

"From ashes to ashes, from dust to dust," was the line in the next prayer that brought out cries of grief. Anne was comforted by Jackie as wet sobs gushed forth, and then Beulah, ever emotional, joined in. The crying was contagious and soon other close friends of George and Anne were sniffling. "This is good," whispered a solemn Mike Broadrite, who was standing next to Harold. "It helps to purge the grief."

Harold was then called upon to read a prepared eulogy, and this he did with great aplomb, finally praising the heroic deeds of both Memnon and George in going out into the tempest to try and alleviate an almost impossible situation. Then the pastor gave a second reading. Life on earth was sheer purgatory, he explained, and again he emphasised that the body was no more than a temporal thing – mere flesh and blood and simply a vehicle for the soul that continued on through infinity. Our lives on earth were a test and the results dictated our future existence – if our souls gained points we moved to a higher plane, but if we fell back then more purgatory awaited. "Whilst our souls travel through time forever, our earthly bodies simply rot away," said the Father to nods of agreement from those members of the congregation in the first few rows. The obnoxious odour was becoming increasingly offensive in the warmth of the church.

The service was curtailed considerably and finally the congregation filed out to exuberant organ music. The interment in the lovely meadow high above Roadstead was accompanied by most of the congregation. It was a beautiful setting, and tall almond and tamarind trees provided shade from the hot afternoon sunshine – fortunately they had mostly survived the ravages of Ben. Margaret Clement-Jones and Jackie both stood beside Anne, giving her support and comfort as the coffin was lowered into its final resting place. At the end of the ceremony, the number of flower arrangements placed on the grave was testimony to the recognition given both George and Anne on the island.

Jackie had arranged a funeral wake in the form of a tea at the Calabash, and Harold had called earlier in the day to ensure that the bar would be open. A procession of cars now headed to the quiet resort hotel. The area by the pool had been reserved for the funeral party and tables were laid with plates of delicately prepared sandwiches, biscuits, cakes, iced lemonade and several large pots of tea. Anne was the centre of attention, of course, and many went to offer condolences, sympathy and best wishes for the future. She didn't stay long, having found the day particularly strenuous, and soon departed to one of the previously reserved hotel rooms, accompanied by Margaret. She had arranged to stay here for the remaining few days she would spend on the island, before returning to Bermuda.

Whilst the ladies mingled by the pool, consuming cucumber sandwiches and tea, many of the men repaired to the bar for slightly stronger refreshments. The conversation centred around Hurricane Ben. It transpired that Rum Cove and Roadstead had been the two worst-hit areas on the island, although there were pockets of severe damage in other areas. JC and Shirley had come out of it unscathed on *Sunfun Calypso*, as had nearly all the yachts that had been anchored at The Pond. Thankfully, they were discreet enough not to emphasise this.

Roger Clement-Jones and Harold were standing at the bar trying to cool themselves off with large gin and tonics – their black suits not helping in the afternoon heat. "If there's anything at all I can do to help with regard to reparations, don't hesitate to ask," said the governor. "I shall be asking Her Majesty's government for assistance in the form of aid when we have the damage tally in. You may be entitled to a grant."

"I shall keep your offer in mind," said Harold, "and thank you, but all the yachts and property are insured, so as soon as they have assessed our damage, we should have the finances to rebuild."

"I don't wish to be nosy," said Clement-Jones, being just that, "but how extensive was your damage?"

"A rough estimate of our property damage is $250,000, but our yacht damage could be three million. We lost our boat shed with most of its contents, the roof was blown off the Rusty Pelican and a tree came down onto the office building and damaged the roof. Amazingly our new boutique escaped undamaged, as did the lodge, but the grounds will need extensive work – we lost several trees, too."

"Most unfortunate," said Clement-Jones. "The botanical gardens were severely damaged as well. Margaret is devastated, but I have assured her that some of the aid money will go towards their restoration."

Harold turned towards the bartender to order another round, just as Memnon approached, chatting amiably with the pastor, who was on his third glass of port. "Would you both join us for a drink?" asked Harold, and introduced them to the governor.

"I understand that you were the hero of the day during the terrible hurricane. You are to be commended for your bravery," said the governor to Memnon, who stood there looking rather embarrassed.

"You were extremely lucky," enjoined the pastor. "I

can't imagine what must have induced George to go outside in the midst of such a melee. You could have ended up just like him." Memnon nodded but he was becoming confused. Just an hour ago the Father was preaching that life on earth was pretty bad and that George was indeed fortunate to be on his way to paradise. Now it was Memnon who was the lucky one. He thanked Harold for the beer and excused himself from the company. He needed something to eat to take his mind off religion.

12

The Insurance Company

On Monday morning, Harold called Mike Broadrite at his office and asked him to get hold of Caribbean Mutual Benefit. "We have three separate claims. First I want to get George Cleary's life insurance claim settled so that Anne, who is leaving for Bermuda tomorrow, can have the security of knowing that her money is in the bank. Then I need an assessor to ascertain our property damage, and I'm hiring Alan Stanborg to do an independent damage report and assessment on our behalf. Lastly, they must send their marine surveyor to start analysing the yacht damage. Four yachts are already down at the boatyard, hauled out, and we are presently raising four that are sunk at the marina. One yacht has severe rigging damage and two catamarans will need work but are in no immediate danger. Again, I will hire an independent marine surveyor to represent us."

"Right," said Broadrite. "Of course they'll have their hands full at the moment but the life insurance claim should be straightforward. I'll get back to you."

Harold walked down to the docks to see how the raising of the sunken yachts was going, and was pleasantly surprised to see the first one already floating. It was a relatively simple matter to raise a yacht that was sunk in only 20 feet of water. It was all done with air bags. Divers took deflated air bags made of strong Hypalon or similar durable fabric, and tied them, evenly spaced, to the sunken yacht's topsides. Then the bags were filled with pressurised air, either through tubes from the surface or with scuba tanks and . . . hey presto!! the yacht floated. Then the holes were patched temporarily, usually with thin plywood, after heavy duty pumps had evacuated the water.

By the following afternoon, all four of GSC's sunken yachts were hauled out at the Tortuga Yacht Services yard, awaiting survey and repair.

When Harold got back to his office that evening to close up, he noticed a fax waiting for him. It had come directly from Caribbean Mutual Benefit:

With reference to your claims for insurance compensation we are pleased to inform you that Mrs Anne Cleary will be eligible for compensation in the amount of $270,524 on account of Mr George Cleary's life policy No. 35887400. This amount is the final and total amount due and will be paid by us on our receipt of the death certificate of the said Mr Cleary by the registrar's office.

Thank you for your valued business and we look forward to being of service to you again in the future.

Yours faithfully,
Reuben Winston

Harold read it through twice but there was no mention of the other important business outstanding. He left the office with a nagging feeling of foreboding.

The first thing he did next morning was call the insurance company direct. "Harold Mcphereson here, Golden Sunset Charters – Mr Reuben Winston, please," he said to a receptionist. The junior partner came on almost immediately.

"I need to have the claims for property and yacht damage at GSC processed as soon as possible," said Harold without preamble. "When can I expect your marine surveyor and property damage assessor?"

There was a long pause and then a muffled noise like someone talking with a hand placed over the mouthpiece and then, in a smooth, even voice, "Good morning Mr Mcphereson, Charles Mcguire here. First let me offer my condolences to you and your dear wife over your recent loss, and let me just repeat that the life policy funds for Mrs Cleary are being processed at this moment." He paused, as if waiting for a verbal pat on the back, but none was forthcoming.

"Now with regard to hurricane damage on property and yachts, I have just explained the whole situation to your lawyer, Mr Broadrite. I am very sorry to have to inform you that I'm afraid you were not covered. At least, not according to the policy that I am holding here in front of me. But perhaps there was a subsequent policy that I am unaware of."

Harold sat there in his office chair. For a second he was speechless and then he said, slowly and deliberately, "Mr Mcguire, we paid a small fortune in premiums for a fully comprehensive insurance policy that specifically included hurricane damage for yachts and property. There is no *subsequent* policy – only the one that we discussed in detail here at GSC less than a year ago. Reuben Winston clearly and unequivocally stated that our policies would cover hurricane damage. He also said that your company regarded it as a 'public duty' to stand behind the chartering industry. I remember his words as if it were yesterday. You'd better re-examine our policies more closely. I'm sure you'll find I'm correct."

"Aah, I believe I see where our misunderstanding has developed," said Mcguire sagely. "Do you have a copy of the policy in front of you?"

"Well, actually no," said Harold. "Mr Broadrite handles all our insurance business. But what misunderstanding are you talking about?"

"As I explained to Mr Broadrite, there is an addendum to Subsection 14, the one that includes hurricane damage compensation, and that clearly states that coverage will be limited to damage and loss caused by windstorms and hurricanes up to and including Category Three storms as defined by the National Hurricane Centre in the U.S.A. Any storm damage caused by very severe hurricanes in excess of Category Three will not be covered. Hurricane Ben was Category Four, as I'm sure you're aware. I'm afraid it's right here in black and white." Mcguire's voice held a false tone of sympathy.

"I shall have a meeting with Mr Broadrite as soon as possible and will get back to you," said Harold, impatiently.

"I believe the governor is applying for aid from the British government. You may be eligible for something from that quarter," said Mcguire, but Harold had already put the phone down.

Harold scratched his head. How could Mike have missed an important addendum that affected their complete hurricane insurance policy? It was unthinkable. He was just about to call the lawyer when a brief knock on the door announced the arrival of Mike Broadrite. Harold invited him to take a seat and then he called for one of the girls in the outer office to bring coffee.

"Mike, this is a very serious matter. Mcguire says our insurance policy doesn't cover severe hurricane damage because of some addendum that precludes intense storms of a Category Four or greater. What do you make of it?"

"He told me the same thing this morning – that's why I'm here. I can assure you, Harold, that there never was an addendum attached to our policy with regard to intense storms. I would never have sanctioned such a provision if there were. I always deemed full coverage to be essential. This strikes me as a lowdown and evil way for Caribbean Mutual Benefit to escape their obligations."

"Let me see the policy," said Harold, all business. Broadrite handed it over and Harold leafed through the document until he came to Subsection 14. He read it through slowly and then nodded his head. "Everything is covered for tropical storms, windstorms and hurricanes – specifically by name. There is no addendum or reference to an addendum. What the devil is the man talking about?"

"On the title page under the subtitle there are some notes in very small print. Note number 5 says 'Addendums to some subsections may apply.' But I repeat – I did not receive any addendum with the policy." The lawyer was becoming irritated.

"Right," said Harold. "We'll go and pay Mr Mcguire and his 'Mutual Benefit' a visit right now. We have to get to the bottom of this. Will you come with me in my car or take your own?" Mike chose to take his own vehicle.

Half an hour later, two very serious and determined

men walked up the steps and into the offices of Caribbean Mutual Benefit. They brushed past a receptionist, who was busy doing her nails, and in through a door marked "President." A startled Charles Mcguire looked up from his chair, did a double take, quickly composed himself and rose to greet his intruders with a forced smile. "Gentlemen, what an unexpected pleasure," he said. "Please . . . have a seat."

"We are not here on a pleasure visit," said Harold, "but on the very serious matter concerning an addendum that you say invalidates our insurance against the recent hurricane damage. We have never seen or heard of an addendum and want to see a copy right now."

"Absolutely," said Mcguire. "That will not pose any problem at all. Of course, you had a copy included with your policy. I wonder what became of it." He opened a file and handed Harold a single sheet of paper with the title "Addendum to Subsection 14." It was printed on quality paper with the title printed very formally in old English lettering. The subject matter clearly indicated that hurricanes were classified into five categories and that the policy was invalid for the most severe hurricanes – those of Category Four and Five, with sustained winds in excess of 114 knots.

Harold handed the document to Broadrite, who examined it carefully. "Mr Mcguire, I have never seen this document before. I would like to take two copies with me, if that could be arranged." Broadrite could see nothing to be gained by arguing the point.

"It's easy to overlook details in comprehensive documents," said Mcguire, smiling and directly implying an oversight on Broadrite's part. "Have my receptionist run off two copies on your way out." The meeting ended as quickly as it had begun, and with the same lack of civility.

Out in the car park, Broadrite turned to Harold. "There is something underhanded going on here. I am certain that this addendum was not included with the policy when I first received it almost a year ago. I can remember the chain of events clearly because the policy was sent over to my office by messenger directly from the insurance company. I spent part of the next two days examining it closely – sitting at my coffee table in the bay window. I can remember it so well because on the first morning I spilt some coffee on the document. Then I locked it in the safe with all GSC's important documents." Broadrite was clearly perturbed.

"Well," said Harold. "I'm going to make some discreet enquiries amongst some other customers of Caribbean Mutual Benefit. Then if necessary, a private investigator may have to be hired."

They parted company with something less than their normal camaraderie.

The following Monday morning, at the office, Sonia was working on budget figures for the upcoming season, when the loud hammering and frequent clouds of dust finally became too much to bear. The damaged roof caused by the fallen tree was being repaired by Elroy's crew of workmen. They had strung up a tarpaulin on the inside of the building to catch any falling debris but it did not stop the noise and dust. Harold had contemplated moving out of the office whilst the repairs were being done, but Elroy had estimated that only about four days would be needed to complete the necessary work, so the office staff had decided to soldier on. Sonia, though, was now on her third attempt at writing out a report when a cloud of dust and loud banging again distracted her. She pushed back her chair and stalked outside.

The fallen tamarind tree had been removed. All the branches had been sawn off and the trunk had been lifted off the roof with the help of a backhoe. Toshi and Isaac were up on the roof fitting some new frames whilst Elroy and the machine operator were piling the tree sections in a corner of the car park. But all work stopped when they saw the voluptuous figure of Sonia heading their way. She was always a smart dresser, but today she was devastating. She was wearing a gold and green two-piece suit with the tight skirt several inches above the knee. Her high heels clicked as she approached the workmen. "You fellas makin' so much nize I can't t'ink straight," she said angrily, reverting to dialect.

"Dat's right darlin'," said Toshi from the roof, "dis kind o' wuk make nize."

She walked over to where Elroy was standing, but before she could vent her spleen Toshi called down. "De boomsie lookin' sweet, honey. You need a date, le' me know."

Sonia ignored the remark and spoke to Elroy. "Dis nize gonna have to stop. Ain't no wuk gettin done in de office an' we behin' aready. De hurricane done hol' us back."

"Ain't nuttin I can do 'bout dat," said Elroy. "It like Toshi say, dis kinda wuk does make nize."

"Well, you gonna have to try to keep it dung. It for everybody's benefit." Sonia was getting nowhere but she realised that it was hardly the fault of the workmen.

"It kinda hard to bang nails quietly, Ms Hodge," said Elroy politely, "but we should be finished in 'bout de nex' two days."

"Well, do your bes'," she said, somewhat appeased. "Dat hurricane were hard on everybody." She turned and walked back, her buttocks undulating. All eyes were on her sexy figure.

Whilst the short conversation had been going on down below, Toshi and Isaac had been discussing Sonia's physical attributes. "You won't get nowhere wid she," said Isaac, "she a loner."

Toshi glanced at his friend in disbelief. "What a waste." He looked down from his perch on the roof. "Remember," he shouted down, "if you doesn't use it, it goin' grow over." Ribald laughter erupted from the rest of the crew.

"Mind your manners," shouted back Sonia, looking annoyed but secretly pleased at the attention. "Ya ain't nuttin but disgustin'." She was over 30 and still unmarried – many of the island men found that her managerial position and academic qualifications made them seem inferior.

No sooner had she sat back down at her desk than Harold called her in to his inner sanctum and explained the whole story of the insurance company's rejection of their claim. She was flabbergasted. She knew of pockets of corruption in the government and of deals cut between rich businessmen and those in positions of authority to grant permits and licences for handouts, but these paled compared to the audacity of this apparent insurance scam. She had the ears of certain friends and acquaintances in positions of power, she said. She promised to make some enquiries of her own.

They discussed the financial aspects of the necessary repairs and rebuilding. By the end of the day it had been agreed that all property damage would be repaired at the company's expense, including new inventory and fixtures and fittings where necessary. All invoices and receipts would be saved and presented to the insurance company at a later date when the problem had, hopefully, been resolved. The yachts would have to wait, though. In any case they were not the property of GSC, but were held on lease agreements. Harold had little doubt that if the insurance problem was not resolved, it would be the end of GSC. His credibility would be suspect.

The other important business of the day concerned the renewal of GSC's business licences and the work permits for Harold and Jackie and those employees who were not Caribbee Islands citizens. This time it would just be a formality, explained Sonia – renewals were granted automatically, except in rare cases. Harold thought he had heard "just a formality" before when dealing with bureaucrats, but he nodded and smiled anyway. It had been a long day and he was tired. Sonia would have the necessary applications completed and ready for signing by tomorrow, she said.

"When those applications have been completed, I am closing the office until the repairs are finished," said Harold. "I don't know how you've managed to work in that dusty, noisy environment but I'm full of admiration for you. You and your assistant may have the next two days off." Sonia smiled to herself. Harold's intrinsic feeling for situations was one reason she liked working for GSC.

About two weeks later, on the first Monday of September, Harold received a call from Mike Broadrite. "The missing addendum has turned up," he said. "A cleaning lady at my office found it under a cushion on one of my easy chairs. It was rather crumpled up, as though it had been there for some time."

"Are you sure?" said Harold, incredulous. "But you were certain that you'd never seen an addendum. Do you mean to tell me that an addendum was part of the original policy and that somehow it became misplaced and found its way under a cushion where it has remained for the best part of a year?"

"That is the way the scenario is supposed to look," said Broadrite, "but I am certain that there was no addendum with the initial policy. Not only has my office been cleaned on a weekly basis for the past year and nothing was found during any of that time, but there was coffee spilt on the policy when I originally examined it. There is no coffee stain on the addendum. I questioned the cleaning lady, but she stuck to her story, although she wouldn't look me in the eye."

"You'd better bring it around right away," said Harold, "so that we can compare it with one of the copies we got from Mcguire."

Later that afternoon, Mike, Harold and Sonia closely examined the two documents and found them to be identical, but it was Sonia whose sharp eyes picked out a peculiarity in the printing on both documents: the tails of the 'y' and the 'p' were both partially missing. "Well, that doesn't prove anything," said Broadrite.

He was right – it didn't prove anything but on examination it was found that the policy and the addendum must have been printed separately – the "y" and the "p" on the policy were normal. Again, there was nothing really suspicious about this, but the observation had caught the imagination of Sonia. "Let me keep a copy of the addendum," she said. "I'd like to do a little investigating."

Although repairs were being undertaken to much of the property, the operation of the lodge, the Sunset Terrace and the Mermaid Bar continued in customary fashion, without hindrance. Even though it was the height of the "off-season" the restaurant and bar were particularly busy. The mermaid had gained notoriety island-wide and the food at the Sunset Terrace was now known to be the best on the island. Harold was often questioned on the origin of the handsome figurehead above the barroom door, but he had to disappoint patrons when he told them that it was still in the research stage. Even so, he often felt that he should get a commission from Kodak – hundreds of photos were taken monthly.

So when Justin Jennings faxed a ream of information on what he described as "solid evidence on the history of our lady the Mermaid," Harold was delighted. The fax read as follows:

I continued my research at the Maritime History Archive, more specifically Lloyd's List. This is a marine newspaper that was first published by Lloyd's of London in 1741 and continued through until 1927. I found the *Mermaid* both registered and insured by Lloyd's of London from the year 1859 to 1923. The information tallied with the previous information that I'd obtained from the microfilm at the Department of Trade.

Then I accessed the General Registry of Shipping and Seamen and concentrated on the years 1900 to 1920. I found crew lists for each voyage, particulars of voyages, crew agreements and official logbooks. The captain of the *Mermaid* for most of this time was Scott Finlay, and from 1903 to 1915 the Master's mate was Nathaniel Hodge, whose given address was Roadstead Harbour, Tortuga, Caribbee Islands!!!!! Can you imagine how I felt? This was the solid evidence that I was really looking for to confirm that I was on the right track.

From the logbooks, I gleaned some information about certain voyages. She regularly did two transatlantic voyages annually and seemed to have more than her fair share of bad luck. There was a fire on one voyage, three deaths by poisoning on another, a dismasting on another and a mutiny.

There was not much detail, though, regarding these events, so on a mere hunch I decided to look for surviving relatives of Captain Finlay. His address at the time of his service was given as 16 Kilmarnock Crescent, Glasgow, and I was surprised and elated to find the family name in the Glasgow telephone directory with just such an address. I called and explained my mission to a retired gentleman with a strong Scottish accent, and after explaining that he was indeed the grandson of Captain Scott Finlay, he invited me to tea the following day.

Apparently the Finlay family have been mariners since the 1700s and the old man was so full of sea stories that our afternoon tea graduated to pints of draught beer at the local pub. By closing time, I'd heard so many fantastic and implausible anecdotes that I felt his *Mermaid* stories must have been a result of many years of immoderate consumption of fine Scottish ale. I took the night train back to London and although I was rather disappointed, my mind was full of visions of a square-rigged ship sailing between tropical islands with that striking mermaid figurehead on the ship's bow.

It was about 10 days later when I received a phone call from the old man. He'd been rummaging through an old sea chest in the attic and had come across a pile of logbooks from the voyages of his grandfather. If I was interested he would let me read them – but only right there in his house. Yes, I replied, I would be most interested and I returned to Glasgow that evening and booked into a small but comfortable hotel.

The following day, back at 16 Kilmarnock Crescent, Mr Finlay produced 12 rather weather-beaten private logbooks, written by nibbed pen in now rather yellowed ink from the hand of the old captain – "not for publication," insisted Finlay, "without permission."

From Captain Scott Finlay's logbooks I took extensive notes and I have outlined a brief description of the voyages and excerpts and summaries where applicable . . .

When Captain Finlay was master, the *Mermaid's* homeport was Portsmouth. Here she'd board passengers for all ports, but mostly for the Caribbean and New York. Household goods were much in demand in the Caribbean and these were loaded along with clothing and spools of cloth, foodstuffs, tools, marine and building supplies. Sherry and wine were loaded in Cadiz and again, building materials for the previously Spanish colonies, particularly tile for roofs and floors.

The Canaries were a last watering and victualling stop before the transatlantic crossing. In Trinidad, bales of cotton, hardwoods like mahogany, teak and lignum vitae, and tropical foodstuffs were loaded, along with sugar, molasses and rum. There was also a certain amount of inter-island passenger traffic.

St Eustatia and St Thomas in the Danish West Indies were both international market places for the entire region, and again, rum, molasses, sugar, spices, almonds and tropical foodstuffs were sold, whilst household goods, iron and other metal manufactured goods, kitchenware, distillery goods, cart-wheels, equestrian tack and tools were always in demand. Tortuga and the Caribbee Islands provided a supply of rum, sugar and molasses and what they lacked in quantity, they made up for in quality. Puerto Rico's San Juan provided a market for the Spanish goods and was a good place to re-victual the ship for the long voyage to New York. Here there were always passengers for Europe, along with numerous and diverse cargo, as well as a ready market for rum, molasses and sugar, and tropical fruits, particularly pineapples.

These round-trip voyages were always lucrative and profitable and Captain Finlay became a wealthy man, never failing to negotiate a percentage of the profits. But his destiny that led to his early retirement could be foreseen by no-one.

From the log of the *Mermaid:*

4th January, 1915: Departed Gran Canaria at 0600 hrs and well clear with all sail set by 0700 hrs. Fair south east trades of 25 kts. 15 passengers all settled in, but some complaints that the bleating goats in their house on deck amidships will keep them awake. Passengers are a necessary evil on a trading ship . . . but they pay well.

5th January: Noon position puts our day's run at 260 miles. Sighted a steamer at 1600 heading west, hull down by nightfall.

6th January: 0900 hrs. Sickness reported in the passengers' accommodation. Mr Sedgwick, the ship's doctor, found a Mr Roberts of London to be hanging to life by a thread and when I examined him I could scarcely believe my eyes. His body was bloated, white and moist with perspiration. His breath was coming in laboured gasps and the whites of his eyes were all that showed on his agonised face. On occasion he would shudder with convulsions and heave up a white froth-like sputum. Then a delirium set in from which he never recovered. The doctor was powerless even though he administered poultices and encouraged cold water consumption as best he could. The victim expired at 1400 hrs. Mr Sedgwick diagnosed poisoning but no poison was found. Some passengers blamed the food, but this was dismissed since everyone had partaken of the same meals.

Noon position 520 miles west of Gran Canaria. Easterlies at 25 kts.

7th January: Burial at sea at 1000 hrs. We had no chaplain aboard, so I held the service. Mrs Roberts was overcome with grief when the body was committed to the deep, and had to be revived with smelling salts.

Noon position 725 miles west of Gran Canaria. Easterlies moderated to 15 kts.

8th January: Ship's passengers heavy with grief and suspicion. The crew having it easy with constant trade winds. Noon position 920 miles covered and just north of the rhumb line. Pole star latitude confirmed daytime latitude.

9th January: Wind increasing to force 7 with squalls. 1100 hrs struck the main tops'l, 16 kts reported by the bosun. Day's run 295 miles.

10th January: Another passenger sick. Mr Stockton of Trinidad in bed with fits and convulsions. Dr Sedgwick endeavoured to examine the patient's throat and lost the tip of his forefinger in the process. By 1600 the doctor was fearing for the victim's life, him being in a delirious state and losing control of his bodily functions. Finally the eyes' pupils rolled up into the victim's head and he expired at 1830 hrs.

Wind moderated to force 6. All sail set. Another good day's run of 280 miles. Total distance covered by noon 1,200 miles.

11th January: Burial at sea and whilst the ceremony was in progress a tropical downpour sent an eerie pall over the proceedings. Mutterings of discontent, of witchcraft and evil spirits from the passengers. The crew are in a sombre mood as well. The doctor is sure that the symptoms are identical with poisoning but none can be found and no motive for foul play suggests itself. Both passengers were seemingly strangers until the start of the voyage. Later in the day a spokesman selected by the passengers asked to see me and suggested that the mate, Nathaniel Hodge, being the only black man aboard, be incarcerated for fear that he may be practising voodoo. I immediately dispelled this ridiculous idea and explained that this fine seaman has done many voyages with me and is totally reliable.

Trades are steady at 20 kts. Weather fair. Day's run 260 miles. Distance covered 1,460 miles.

The voyage continued uneventfully until the 18th January. Captain Finlay decided to make landfall in Barbados to report the deaths. Only a day before their arrival, disaster struck again.

20th January: Passenger sick. Mrs Mckilroy from Aberdeen is suffering from burning pains and severe headaches. Doctor Sedgwick pronounced, with grave concern, another poisoning. The patient went into fits and convulsions after only three hours of the onset of the disease. Swelling of face, arms and legs and constant perspiring were only alleviated with cold compresses. The victim went into delirium at 1300 hrs and expired at 1430.

The passengers' quarters were evacuated and the corpse, suitably covered, was placed in the cargo hold. The said quarters ('tweendecks and amidships) were being swabbed when the seaman on duty there gave such a scream that it was heard by the helmsman aft. He came up on deck holding a dead scorpion the length of a man's hand, its curved tail still twitching– a messenger of death. Tension on board somehow eased at this discovery – the shadow of skulduggery and suspicion gone.

Mrs Mckilroy was given a Christian burial at Bridgetown, Barbados, where the *Mermaid* dropped anchor the following afternoon, the 21st January. The local coroner had confirmed death by poisoning.

Will fax more details at a later date – my computer has developed an internal problem and my notes taken at Finlay's residence are barely legible. I am very enthusiastic with my progress here, and I think a picture is emerging.

Kind regards, Justin Jennings.

Harold read the complete fax through twice and then called old Mr Hodge to verify the name of the *Mermaid's* mate.

"Yes," said the white haired patriarch, "Granpappy Nate, we used to call him." Harold's emotions were mixed. On the one hand he was delighted with Jennings' obvious progress, but he was impatient to know the end of the story, and how the mermaid had arrived in the cellar, along with the precious rum.

The repairs to the roof were finished only two days later than had been promised by Elroy, and Harold was now so accustomed to island time that he was actually pleased at such a short delay. Sonia and her staff were back at work and it was a mid-week morning when she called Harold in his inner office on the intercom. "I need to talk to you as soon as possible," she said, excitedly. "It's about the insurance scam."

"Well, come in right away," said Harold. "We must get to the bottom of this without delay."

Sonia walked over to Harold's office with a spring in her step and a confident air. She knocked once and walked in. "I have solid evidence of fraudulent conduct by Caribbean Mutual Benefit." She placed a file on Harold's desk and sat in the proffered chair.

Harold looked at her with raised eyebrows – he'd been discussing the situation with Broadrite on and off for the last week and they had both come up empty-handed. "I must call Mike Broadrite," he said. "He is the company lawyer and should be present if you have come up with some revelations. Have a cup of coffee while we wait."

Twenty minutes later the three of them were sitting around Harold's desk expectantly, whilst Sonia explained her discovery. "It was pure luck, really," began Sonia. "They won't have a leg to stand on after it's made public."

"What on earth are you talking about, Sonia?" said the frustrated Broadrite. "Let's have the details."

"Well," continued Sonia, "my investigation began with the printing abnormality on the copies of the addendum. On the copies that we got from Charles Mcguire and the copy that 'turned up' in your office," she said, looking at Broadrite, "there was an abnormality on the tail of the 'y' and 'p', as you already know.

"One day last week I phoned up the receptionist at Mcguire's office and asked her if she'd join me for lunch at the Pink Hibiscus – 'Business managers should get together for informal, social meetings on occasion,' I explained, inflating her position a little, and she agreed. So I made a point of meeting her at her office. While there, I asked if she'd mind printing out another copy of our addendum 'for my personal files' and she did without hesitation. I glanced at it and noticed the abnormality, just as I'd expected, but I also noted the type of printer used. It was a 'Laser Jet All Star 4250.'

"We started lunch with planter's punch and I made sure that hers was plenty strong," Sonia smiled at the memory, "and then I ordered a bottle of Chablis with our food. By the time the main course was finished, she was talking 19 to the dozen. She told me that there have been a lot of distraught customers in her office lately and several requests for copies of addendums to policies. It seems that two other large charter boat companies are being denied their claims or are being put on a 'waiting list.' On the other hand, some customers are being paid out fairly promptly. Most of the clients whose claims are being processed for payment are government employees with individual boats, but the large customers being denied payment are those with many boats and large claims.

"We chatted on about the island's business boom over the last 10 years, and who was getting the best jobs and the most pay and blah, blah, blah, and then she said that this year, business has been so busy that her office has had to buy all new business machines: faxes, telephones with answering machines, copiers and printers. 'Oh,' I said, sounding surprised, 'that must have been an added chore, having to get used to all new equipment,' and she replied that it was and that she still wasn't used to it even now, because it was only four months ago that the new equipment had been installed." Sonia sat back in her chair beaming and looked expectantly from Harold to Broadrite. But both men sat in their chairs frowning.

"Don't you see?" said Sonia, exasperated. "We bought the insurance policy one year ago but the printing machine that the addendum was printed from is only four months old. Therefore the addendum couldn't possibly have been a part of the original policy."

Harold looked up, his eyes opening wide. "By George," he said, "I think you've hit on something here. This is the sort of break we've been hoping for."

Broadrite, though, was more circumspect. "It looks good," he said slowly, "but there are possible loopholes and certainly some facts that need proving beyond doubt. First, there is the possibility that all Laser Jet All Star 4250 printers have an abnormality with the 'y' and 'p.'"

"Negative on that," said Sonia exuberantly, "I checked two other identical machines at 'Island Business Equipment, Ltd.' The 'y' and the 'p' were normal. Then I checked whether Caribbean Mutual Benefit had purchased its new equipment from IBE and . . . Bingo! The sales clerk obliged by showing me the receipt. It was dated June 12th, this year and two Laser Jet All Star 4250s were listed. Here," she said, opening the file, "I took a copy of the receipt." Sonia leafed through the papers and produced the damning evidence.

"Well done! Well done," said Harold. "Excellent work, Sonia, and beyond the call of duty."

"I agree," said Broadrite. "A thorough and praiseworthy investigation. But we must tread lightly and make sure that not a word of our discovery reaches Caribbean Mutual Benefit. If they destroy that printer our case loses all credibility."

"We may be able to cover ourselves on that point," said Sonia. "When new office equipment is bought it always comes with a guarantee of usually 12 months. On the warranty card, the serial number of the equipment must be recorded, along with the address of the buyer, of course. We can check the manufacturer's records."

Right then and there Harold made a phone call, pretending to be an employee of Caribbean Mutual Benefit to check on all that company's business machine warranties, and a very helpful clerk verified all the serial numbers.

"We need to get hold of the printer with the abnormality so that we can can use it for evidence," said Broadrite. "We have a good case already, but that machine in our possession would make it water-tight."

"Mmm, I agree," said Harold. "But we can't very well just steal it."

"I know!" said Sonia. "The manufacturer could recall the two printers presently in use by Caribbean Mutual Benefit under the guise of some 'substandard components installed in error' and supply them with two brand new machines."

"And I will happily pay cash, with a bonus, to our helpful clerk if he sends them directly to CMB and returns the defective ones to me," said Harold, triumphantly and smiling appreciatively at Sonia.

Broadrite stood up. "Well," he said, " thanks to your work, Sonia, I think we can go to court with this. For my own satisfaction, though, I'd like to interview the cleaning lady who found a copy of the addendum under the cushion of the easy chair in my office."

This he did with Harold present, and it only took 10 minutes before the tearful woman admitted placing it there for a $200 payment. Who had paid her? asked Broadrite. All the instructions had been given by phone and the document to be planted had been placed in an envelope in a tin by a tree with the money, she said. But the poor woman was in a terrible state of distress because the man had threatened terrible things would happen to her three children if she told anyone.

It was about a week later when Harold received a large box via Fed Ex with the printers, one being the important evidence. During this time, Broadrite had been making discreet enquiries amongst the other charter yacht companies, and he had discovered that something like 10 million dollars worth of claims were being rejected by the insurance company, almost all on the basis of an addendum that had 'suddenly appeared' with no-one's prior knowledge. He began to savour the moment when he could confront the crooks at Caribbean Mutual Benefit. When Harold notified him that the printer had been delivered, he knew that that moment had arrived.

Broadrite called Caribbean Mutual Benefit to make a personal appointment, but he was quickly brushed off. "The company is being inundated with calls and enquiries," said a receptionist. "You must understand that this is a very busy time for us." Broadrite put the phone down and decided that the direct approach was the only way to deal with the situation. He called Harold, who in turn contacted Sonia, and the three of them, in a manner that was becoming customary, walked into Caribbean Mutual Benefit's offices and in through the familiar door marked "President."

Mcguire was sitting at a computer and Reuben Winston was leaning over his shoulder, pointing out something on the screen. This time Charles Mcguire went white and stammered that the intruders were trespassing – and had no prior appointment.

"That may be," said Broadrite, "but it is hardly as severe an offence as fraud. And we at Golden Sunset Charters have solid evidence that your company is denying payment on hurricane damage claims by false pretences. Your 'addendums' are as phony as silicone breasts!" His voice rose as his anger increased.

Mcguire's forehead beaded with perspiration even though the office was air conditioned. His hand trembled slightly. "If you propose litigation," he said, "you can serve the papers with A. Reephoff and Associates. I have retained that firm for all hurricane related legal matters."

"Good," said Broadrite. "We shall sue for three million in damages, three million in punitive damages and there will be thousands in expenses. And we have no doubt of the outcome." The three of them walked out of the office with a sense of relief. The ball was now in Mcguire's court. Broadrite would serve the papers within the month.

Harold invited Sonia and Mike for lunch back at the lodge. He had a lot to thank his two companions for, and although there was certainly no victory to celebrate he felt a small triumph – as though he was in control of his life again. They had drinks in the Mermaid Bar. Jackie joined them and was brought up to date on the latest developments. Lunch on the terrace was a spinach and cheese quiche, warm straight from the oven, accompanied by a tossed salad. An exotic cheese tray and baguette followed, and an ice-cold Chardonnay complemented nicely.

They were just finishing the meal when a group of local kids straggled across the terrace and one of them pointed at the cherubs in the fountain and started laughing. Soon they were all laughing until Memnon, bringing up the rear, warned them to be careful. "You never know what dem li'l statues might do," he said solemnly, and then laughed as the kids looked at him gravely and then across to Harold's party. Most of the children were from the Pines and they knew Harold to be the boss. They were over on Tortuga for the weekly CLATS session, a highlight of the week for most of them, and one that had been cancelled for the previous six weeks due to the hurricane damage. For Harold and Jackie, they were a welcome sight and another sign that things were getting back to normal.

But normality didn't last long in the Caribbee Islands. It was about a week later that an official looking brown envelope arrived at GSC with the red seal of the chief minister's office and the words "Department of Trade and Labour." Sonia had collected the mail and after knocking and entering Harold's office, said cheerily,

"Looks like your business licences and work permits have come through." She threw the package of mail onto Harold's desk and walked out.

Half an hour later, she was back in his office sitting in the chair opposite a deflated and dejected Harold reading a document that would change all of their lives. The contents of the brown envelope had revealed a letter, signed by the chief minister, stating that the request for renewal of all work permits and business licences for GSC had been denied. The immigration department would graciously allow the applicants to stay in the territory for a period of one month from today's date in order to terminate all business activities and domestic affairs. Then they would have to repatriate to their countries of origin. Sonia read the letter through and just sat there shaking her head in disbelief. "This is impossible," she said, "they haven't even given a reason. I can't believe it." Then after a stunned pause she said, "I'm going to call the chief minister – he must have some kind of explanation."

"Thank you for your concern," said Harold, wearily. He came round the side of his desk and squeezed Sonia's shoulder. "We'd better let Mike deal with it. There may be legal implications." He called Broadrite and explained what had happened and then sent him a fax of the document.

"I'll deal with this immediately," he assured Harold, "and get back to you right away. This smells of a conspiracy – stay by the phone."

Broadrite got back to Harold in more than 15 minutes. "I got hold of Bradshaw almost immediately. He said he was expecting my call and very quickly told me that under Subsection 43A of the immigration law, a person or persons can be extradited for being 'undesirable in temperament or manner' – he quoted that part.

"Then he said that it was not obligatory for the trade and labour department or the immigration department to give a reason for their actions, but since I was a longtime friend, he would fax me a list of reasons why GSC's business licences were not being renewed. He must have had it all ready, because he faxed it immediately. I'll fax it on to you and then we should arrange a meeting. How about tomorrow morning?"

"That'll be fine," said Harold. "Let's make it for 9 a.m. sharp." He put the phone down and almost immediately a fax came rattling through. It was on plain, unmarked paper and on it was a numbered list. It read:

1) Complaints of a disturbance and possible drug use at the Calabash hotel by one Roy Blake, a shareholder in GSC, October last year.

2) Notice of an investigation in the U.S.A. of an IRS enquiry into the affairs of one Roy Blake.

3) Sex scandal reported widely in the local press involving Harold Mcphereson and a female known as 'Mermaid.'

4) Direct contravention of an order made by the labour office to hire Caribbee Islands citizen, one Jonas Penn.

5) An article written in an international magazine directly concerning the tourist trade reporting evident discrimination in the Caribbee Islands. The article was written as a result of a day excursion on board a GSC yacht.

RENEWAL OF ALL GSC TRADE LICENCES DENIED.

Next morning, Harold and Jackie, together with Mike Broadrite and Sonia Hodge, sat around the small conference table in the company's office. Sonia poured coffee for everyone – Jackie was too distraught, she'd been up most of the night crying and her eyes were red and puffy.

They had all had a chance to examine the five points of contention between the government and GSC, but it was Broadrite who came straight to the point. "I believe that the refusal of the chief minister to grant your business licence renewals is directly linked to the insurance scam. Caribbean Mutual Benefit is terribly afraid that we know their fraudulent secret, as indeed we do, and they would like nothing better than to see you quietly disappear. The five points that describe GSC's 'undesirable' conduct, though, need examining. What do you make of points 1) and 2)?"

Everyone looked blank and Jackie shrugged her shoulders. "They could be fabricated or, knowing Roy, they could be true. I think you should call him right away and try to get to the bottom of this." Jackie looked across at Harold in worried anticipation.

Harold stroked his chin thoughtfully. "I like the conspiracy theory. The five 'undesirable' points are just a smokescreen. Unfortunately, the government is not bound by the law in cases of immigration and 'trade and labour,' as the chief minister so clearly pointed out. They can throw us out under the heading of 'undesirable', and that's that."

"You mean they can just kick us out after 12 months of working our fingers to the bone?" said Jackie softly, with a forlorn expression. "It seems so unjust."

"It is unjust," replied Broadrite, "and we will fight tooth and nail to the end."

Harold had been pondering the situation and again he spoke up. "It just doesn't make any logical sense that the government would want to get rid of us," he said. "We have generated a lot of business that is beneficial to the islands, increases government revenues and creates jobs. We have opened a small hotel that provides fine food and service and is frequented by top government officials. Our charter yacht division has expanded and flourished. In fact we have helped put Tortuga on the map. No, I believe there is something sinister going on here and it seems as though we only have a month to find out what it is."

As usual, Sonia was on the ball. "We must look for a connection between the insurance company and the department of trade and labour with Bradshaw as its leader. I think it's too much of a coincidence that as soon as we uncover the insurance fraud the government wants to kick you out. There must be some sort of collusion here."

"Exactly!" said Harold, with Broadrite nodding vigourously. "In fact there is one connection that is patently obvious – Reuben Winston, the junior partner in the insurance company, is the brother of Talbot Winston, the sleazy assistant to Chief Minister Bradshaw. I think that is a lead that should be followed up without delay."

"The insurance business in the Caribbee Islands is a monopoly which Caribbean Mutual Benefit has enjoyed, surprisingly without the threat of competition, for many years," said Mike. "I wonder why. Perhaps we should make enquiries with the Federation of Caribbean Insurers to see if any companies have applied to do business here in the past and been denied a licence."

"I think we should go to the governor and explain the whole situation," said Jackie, pragmatically. "It is so obvious that Caribbean Mutual Benefit is run by a bunch of crooks – they should be forced to pay out all they owe and then be kicked off the island."

The meeting was heating up, but it was time to make

some decisions on a plan of action. Finally it was decided that Mike would follow up with the Federation of Caribbean Insurers. Sonia would quietly make enquiries with her contacts in government circles and Harold would write a long letter to *The Beacon* exposing the insurance company fraud. Jackie was not given a particular assignment – she was too busy anyway running the lodge. But Jackie had a plan up her sleeve – she was going to call Margaret Clement-Jones in the morning.

Things were at their lowest ebb ever at Golden Sunset Charters. It seemed futile to try and fight such an all-powerful government – and just when it appeared that things could get no worse, they did. A letter arrived from Roy to say that indeed he was being investigated by the IRS. He was fearful of fines and confiscations – his "Mr Fix It" stores might be seized. He needed to sell his share of GSC . . .

Harold was the only member of the upper management who refused to become despondent. Justice would prevail in the end, he kept telling everyone, but no-one really believed him – time was too short.

13

The Mermaid's Demise?

Next morning, while Harold was in the middle of writing a very descriptive letter to *The Beacon*, a lengthy fax came through from Justin Jennings in London. It was entitled, "Final Installment on the Adventures of *The Mermaid*." It read:

Hello everyone at Golden Sunset Charters, and first let me apologise for the delay in sending this fax; my computer has only just been returned from the manufacturer. I am delighted to be able to send you this final episode that not only reveals some of the extraordinary history of *The Mermaid* (the ship) and the demise of the mermaid (the figurehead), but also verifies that the rum found in the cellar is indeed of a very old vintage.

From Captain Finlay's personal log and other

documents concerning the same voyage but on the leg from Trinidad to St Eustatia, I have pieced together the following story:

The Mermaid was reaching towards St Eustatia with yards, clews and jib sheets hauled tight on the port side. The evening meal had just finished when a white squall increased the 25 knot trades to 55 knots and caused the vessel to heel considerably. The cook was cleaning the galley, the cookhouse being on deck, when an oil lamp that was hanging from a beam swung off its hook and landed in a pan of cooking fat. A fire erupted spontaneously and with the fresh winds fanning the flames, spread rapidly.

Captain Finlay, who was called on deck almost at once, ordered an immediate chain of buckets. First-mate Nathaniel Hodge courageously put himself at the fire end of the chain, in the position of most risk, but after only a few minutes he fell and twisted his leg and had to be replaced. From then on he retired to the deck and contributed to the fire-fighting effort by giving orders and shouting encouragement. After nearly an hour, the fire was finally brought under control but not before the crewman who had replaced Hodge had succumbed to smoke inhalation and had fallen into the fire. Almost half the cargo was lost, with barrels of sticky sugar and leaking molasses creating a mammoth cleaning task.

The next day, there were murmurs and mumblings amongst the crew that perhaps Hodge had invented his twisted leg story in order to relieve himself of fire-fighting duties. The intrepid Hodge, though, upon hearing the insulting rumours, challenged any man amongst them to a duel with either bare fists, knives or guns, right then and there on the deck of the rolling ship, if they so wished to be rid of him but not a man jack of them took up the challenge.

On the 15th of February 1915, *The Mermaid* put into Rum Cove on Tortuga and two significant things happened. Nathaniel Hodge signed off the crew list, never to go back to sea again. He was back at his homeport and, reflecting on the incidents of this voyage so far, it was hardly surprising. Secondly, the crew began an uprising that almost developed into a mutiny. It started when one of the hands suggested that the vessel's bad luck was a direct result of the ship's figurehead, with its Mona Lisa smile and piercing eyes. Ever since the Canary Islands, with first the poisonings and then the fire, the crew had become more and more disillusioned – "the ship was jinxed, no doubt about it," the men said. Not one of them would touch the capstan nor climb to the yards until the mermaid was removed. No matter how much Captain Finlay exhorted them to listen to reason instead of superstitious mumbo-jumbo, they were steadfast in their demand – the mermaid must go!

And so it was . . . the beautifully carved figurehead was removed from its place beneath the ship's bowsprit and taken ashore, right there in Rum Cove. Captain Finlay also ordered that all alcoholic beverages, including the cargo of precious rum that could not be stored in the lock-up. be moved ashore. He was afraid that his now-hostile crew might drink themselves into a frenzy . . . That in a nutshell is the answer to the enigma of the mermaid and I have all the documents to prove it!

It is interesting to note that *The Mermaid* continued the Caribbean trading runs for a further five years without incident.

Captain Finlay retired from duty at the end of the 1915 season – steamships were beginning to monopolise the trade.

My editor is interested in running a serial on this extraordinary story and Allbright and I will fly out soon to do a final wrapup.

Kind regards, Justin Jennings.

Harold read the fax through twice, slowly nodding to himself, as reality dawned on him. Ever since the mermaid had come into his life bad luck had dogged him, often as a direct result of the beautifully carved figurehead. There had been the initial finding of the thing in the cellar and as soon as it had been removed, he had been libelled in the paper, in fact accused of gang rape. Although the charges were completely false, the chief minister was now using them as a reason for denying him his trade licences and work permits.

Then, during the tremor last summer, the mermaid had fallen from its mounting above the bar and come crashing onto a tourist who, with the help of Reephoff, was suing him for a small fortune.

There had been lots of other unfortunate incidents that had happened in their first year on the island, not least of which was the death of George Cleary. and now, most recently, the crooks at Caribbean Mutual Benefit were trying to deny their hurricane insurance claims. Could it be that the mermaid was in some way responsible for all their misfortunes? The crew on the ship had certainly thought that the figurehead had been responsible for theirs.

Harold was a realistic man, a logical man who normally waved superstitious theories aside, but the latest revelations about the mermaid and its effect on the ship, coupled with his experiences of the past year, had his mind spinning.

Up at the Sunset Terrace, Memnon was busy breaking

open coconuts, outside the kitchen door, with a long machete. The large catamaran *Wet 'n Wild* that normally was under his command was now in the boat yard awaiting repairs, so in the meantime he was helping out around the property. Just then, Harold walked up and raised his eyebrows at the unusual sight of all the coconuts.

"Ms Jackie makin' fish with coconut cream," explained Memnon, "and Ms Beulah jus' gone to de bar to bring some white wine."

Harold smiled to himself. Here they were, on the brink of a cataclysm, and Jackie was busy preparing a gourmet meal, hardly missing a step. He felt very proud of her – in his time of need she was giving him strength.

But Harold didn't have much time for contemplation. Just then, Beulah came dashing around the corner of the building, flustered and out of breath. "De obeah in dat mermaid and dat for true. I seen it wid me own eyes an' I tellin' you – I ain' goin' near dat ting ever again." She removed her red spotted scarf that held her hair up and dabbed at her face.

"Now, now, it's all right," said Harold, approaching the distraught woman and placing a comforting arm on her shoulder. "Explain what you mean."

Beulah, who was trembling slightly, explained between deep breaths, "Dat mermaid full o' devil spirit. It voodoo magic for shaw. I were walkin' out de bar an' I felt a drop o' water on me back an' I look up an dere's de mermaid lookin' dung on me real funny an' she cryin' . . . dat's right, she cryin' wid real tears streamin' dung she face and drippin' on de flaw."

"Go and rest up in the kitchen and make yourself a cup of tea," said Harold. "Come, Memnon, let's go and see our crying mermaid." They walked around to the front of the Mermaid Bar and Harold's tone of amused derision soon changed to one of incredulity. Sure enough, the mermaid was crying and stains of tears were clearly visible down the pink cheeks. Again, Harold's mind went into a spin. With all the recent events that pointed to the mermaid having magical powers was this yet another unexplainable phenomenon. After all, the newspaper reporter Jennings had only just discovered the demise of the mermaid and its interment in the cellar some 83 years ago and now the resurrected mermaid proudly watching over the Sunset Lodge was crying – perhaps feeling guilty for past sins. It was uncanny.

It was Memnon who finally clarified the matter. He had fetched a ladder from behind the building in order to get a closer look and was now standing next to the mermaid, which protruded out on its support above the doorway.

"Termites is attacking the statue," he shouted down. "Dey comin' across de wall in dis crack an den down by dis pipe an' into de mermaid." He pointed to the pencil-thick trail that the termites had made. "What happen is de termites dem eatin' into de head o' de mermaid and make a hole. Den de rainwater collectin' and it drippin' out de eyes . . . Ain' no obeah man cause dat," he laughed. "It jus' de dam termites!" He climbed down and faced Harold. "We can fix dat wid resin an' sawdust an it be good as new. Don' worry, we ain' goin' lose our famous mermaid."

"Burn it," said Harold, his face flat and expressionless.

"What?" said Memnon, unsure of Harold's meaning.

"Just burn it," repeated Harold. "Termites can spread like wildfire. I don't want to risk any of the wooden parts of the building or the furnishings." He was masking a nagging feeling that perhaps the mermaid was afflicted with demons and supernatural powers.

"Dat ain' necessary," said Memnon. "We can jus' call up de exterminator an' he spray up de place an' spray de mermaid till ever'ting jus' fine."

"Memnon," said Harold, slowly and deliberately, "call up JC to help you. Take the mermaid down and around to the back. Cut it up in pieces with the electric 'sawsall.' Make a bonfire and burn it!!"

"Yes suh, Mr Harold . . . no problem." Memnon walked away somewhat despondently. He had never been spoken to like that from Harold. He wondered if perhaps the man was going tropo. Little did he know that Harold was under great strain and in grave danger of losing his hard-won business.

14

The Party

Sonia did not find it difficult to nose around in inner government circles. Not only was she from one of the old, respected families on the island, but she was also an attractive, available young woman. When she walked into a government office with an enquiry, she usually found that there was at least one rather bored male civil servant anxious to help her out.

She soon verified that all government members who had maritime insurance claims due to hurricane damage were being paid out and that not one of them had heard of an addendum referring to severe hurricanes. From the immigration department she found out that the Winston brothers were not citizens but only residents and originally from Antigua, although they had both resided in the Caribbee Islands for 20 years plus. Whether this would be of any help to her she didn't know, but she noted it anyway. From the police department, she could find no evidence of wrongdoing by either of them.

She was in the passport office continuing her research when a slim, handsome young man smelling of a musky perfume came sidling up to her to offer his assistance. After he had given her the information she had requested, which turned out to be of little use, he began offering information by way of informal chat. "I know Reuben real well," he said. "He nearly always goes to the weekly party."

"Weekly party?" replied Sonia. "What's that all about?"

"Every week, on a Friday night, a department head hosts a party either at his house or at a hotel or villa rented for the occasion. It's a lot of fun, with plenty of food and drink," and then quietly into her ear, "and other things too, if you feel inclined."

"Really?" said Sonia, pricking up her ears. "Who goes to these parties?"

"Well, usually top civil servants, sometimes well-off business people, always a lot of pretty girls. It's a real blast – goes on all night long. The only thing is they're a bit fussy about who goes in – it's by invitation only and there's always a security guard at the door. This week's party should be one of the best ever. It's up at the Mill House on the hillside overlooking Distillery Bay. If you'd like to go, I'll invite you as my guest. My name is Zach Bundy." He held out his hand and smiled at the voluptuous Sonia with just a hint of a leer. He was already imagining how cuddly she would be between the sheets.

Sonia took the proffered limp hand and smiled a falsely seductive smile to encourage him. "Yeah," she said, "sounds like fun." This party, she felt, might lead to something in her investigation.

The Pink Hibiscus was about half full that Friday, as Sonia sat alone at a corner table with a glass of sparkling water awaiting the arrival of Zach Bundy. Their rendezvous time of 10 p.m. had now become 10:20 and Sonia was about to give up when she heard a screeching of tyres by the front entrance. Seconds later, a highly perfumed and colourfully dressed Bundy stood in front of her, smiling. He was wearing a lime green suit with flared trousers, a pink tie and a wide brimmed black fedora with pink hat band. Gold rings and a gold chain shone ostentatiously. Sonia didn't know whether he looked more like Jimi Hendrix or a 1940s gangster. "Island time," he said, palms up and shrugging. "C'mon baby, let's go."

Sonia climbed into Bundy's red Mazda sports car and the would-be playboy accelerated away from the popular bar with the required burning of rubber, and soon they were twisting and turning their way up the hillside. When they were almost at the top of the hill Bundy pulled off the road and lit up a fat marijuana joint. He took a couple of long drags whilst installing a rap cassette into his tape deck. Then he passed the cigarette over to Sonia. "Here baby," he said, "this'll put you in the mood."

"Oh, no thanks," said Sonia, "I'm already in the mood." She let out a rather unauthentic laugh.

"Goooood," said Bundy, "I liked you as soon as you walked into my office." He edged over and put a hand on her thigh, simultaneously reaching over to kiss her neck. Sonia cringed and squeezed up against the car door. "Look, are you sure you want to go to this party?" said the rejected young man, angrily. "It's for fun-loving people who want to get loose and be cool."

"Oh, yes," said Sonia, "I'll be fine when I've had a couple of drinks. I'm just not quite ready yet, that's all."

Bundy started the car and they sped away, again with wheels spinning. He turned up the stereo and increased the bass to max, at the same time opening his window. He wanted to be sure that everyone he passed could hear how 'cool' he was. Also. the volume ensured that no conversation could take place.

They pulled up outside the walled residence and Sonia immediately noticed all the flashy cars parked in the small parking area and winding haphazardly by the roadside, until they disappeared out of sight She could tell that the place must be crowded. Bundy got out of the car, paying no attention to Sonia, and walked up to the front gate, where a uniformed security guard stood. He said something to the guard, who opened the gate and let them both through. Well, thought Sonia, if Bundy was going to ignore her for the rest of the evening that was just fine with her.

They walked up a beautifully tiled garden path lined with palm trees and in through the front door to a large reception area. The high-ceilinged rooms were painted white and open arches allowed access to different parts of the grand residence. Sonia heard music playing and walked through to a large living area where an oak dining-table was spread with a variety of food. She looked around and saw with relief that Bundy had gone off in a different direction.

Along the back wall was a buffet table with drinks, ice buckets and glasses, and she immediately walked over to it and poured herself a drink so as not to appear conspicuous. She stirred her tall vodka and cranberry and then slowly strolled across the room and down a circular stairway to a lower level, where a swimming pool was illuminated by underwater lights and some people were swimming. She passed several acquaintances who smiled and nodded. Everyone was dressed up to the nines and small groups mingled, chatting amiably. She walked along a path and then down to another level where a second pool, also illuminated, seemed empty. She stopped to gaze at the view down the hillside to the tiny sparkling lights of Distillery Bay. A gibbous moon shone a silver path on the black sea and the stars twinkled in a cloudless sky. She was so absorbed by her surroundings that she didn't hear the footsteps come up quietly behind her.

"Sonia Hodge, what a pleasant surprise," said Talbot Winston. The chief minister's assistant smiled at her with a row of perfect, white teeth. "I've never seen you at the weekly parties before."

"I came with Zach Bundy," she said, and then added. "He's not a friend, just an acquaintance."

"I see," he said. "Well, Zach just happens to be a good friend of mine."

"I suppose you know that he not only smokes marijuana but pushes himself rather aggressively onto unsuspecting ladies," said Sonia, self-righteously. She was still annoyed at Bundy's behaviour in the car.

"So, what else is new?" said Winston, sarcastically. "There's usually someone smoking the stuff at most parties."

Sonia decided to change tack. "Did your brother make it to the party this week? I haven't seen him here."

"Aah, so that's it. You've got the hots for Reuben. Well, you'll have to join the queue. My brother uses the best of all aphrodisiacs and the girls are lining up. In fact I have some as well . . . Wanna try it?" He held up a small plastic bag containing a white powder.

"Hey, I'm here for the dancing," said Sonia, knowing that she was on dangerous ground, but also sensing that she was onto something.

"Let's go back up to the party. I could use another drink and then we can dance." He grabbed her hand

and they returned to the party room. Reggae music from Jimmy Cliff came booming out of the speakers:

"You can get it if you really want. You can get it if you really want. But you must try, try and try, try and try. You'll succeed at last."

They were by the first pool and several couples were dancing. Talbot took Sonia in his arms and joined in, rather to her displeasure. Well, it's all in the line of duty, she said to herself. As they spun around she noticed a couple emerge from the archway leading to the upstairs – the beautiful dark-skinned girl was wearing only a bra and mini skirt and one bra strap had slipped from her shoulder. Then another girl appeared from the same entrance wrapped only in a sheet. She went straight to the bar, poured a drink and then returned upstairs. Nobody seemed to pay much attention.

During the next half-hour, Sonia noticed a steady traffic between the bedrooms upstairs and the living area downstairs. Many of the girls appeared to be rather young, perhaps only 15 or 16 years old, and seemed dazed or drunk. She excused herself from Talbot by saying that she had to go to the bathroom and, when no-one was watching her, she slipped upstairs. Almost immediately a girl came out of one of the bedrooms and walked across the landing towards the bathroom. Sonia stopped her and asked if she'd seen Reuben Winston but the girl looked down her nose arrogantly and continued on without replying. Then a couple came up the stairs and Sonia knew the girl, a secretary for a well-known trust company on the island, and she asked the same question.

"He's probably in the master bedroom," she whispered. "It's that one at the end of the passage – but he's probably occupied," she nodded in the direction of the room, and then chuckled furtively. Sonia walked quietly over to the closed door and put her ear to the door jamb. She could hear some slow soul music and then the regular creaking of a bed, as though love-making was in progress. She felt in her hand bag to make sure that her camera was still there and then she tried the door. It was not locked and she opened it about three inches and peeped in. She could see the end of the bed and some of the furniture and she could tell by the increased intensity of the love-making that now was her opportune time. She pushed the door open about half way and peered in. The couple on the bed were so involved with themselves that they didn't notice a thing and Sonia had a chance to observe the room closely. There were several glasses on a bedside table next to a portable stereo and a half full bottle of brandy on the floor. Next to this was a small bathroom mirror and on it what looked like the remnants of lines of cocaine and a small heap of white powder. Her heart started beating faster– she was very nervous, but she steeled herself. She desperately wanted photographs showing the drugs, the naked couple and the general debauchery, so she had to position herself perfectly, but she would have only seconds; a clean getaway was imperative.

With her mind focused and her body tensed, she ran into the bedroom, simultaneously snapping pictures as she went. She managed to shoot about six frames and then she was running out of the door, along the passage and down the stairs.

Reuben Winston was taken completely by surprise. It wasn't until about the third flash of the camera that he realised they were being photographed. Even then his first reaction was that it must be some kind of prank or practical joke. When finally he tried to get off the bed he couldn't, the girl's legs were clamped around his torso. Eventually he got up, wrapped himself in a towel, and walked to the landing where he could see the living room below. "What the hell's going on?" he shouted down, irritably. "Can't a man get any privacy around here?" No-one took much notice of him and he walked back into the bedroom to continue what he hadn't finished. It wasn't until much later that he started worrying.

Meanwhile, Sonia had made a clean escape and was now running down the road to a house she had noticed on their way up. She kept turning her head to look behind her but could see no-one. She imagined footsteps fast approaching, running and catching her up. But soon she was at the driveway to the house and she ran to the front door and rang the bell. She explained to the old man who answered the door that she urgently needed to call a taxi and could she please wait until it arrived.

She finally got home at 1:30 in the morning completely exhausted. Her eyes were swollen and red and dried tears had made streaks down her cheeks. Instead of feeling elation at having succeeded in her mission she was angry and upset: The girl who had been with Reuben Winston was her 15-year-old niece.

Four days later, Harold called a meeting in the company's small conference room in the office. Present were Harold and Jackie, Broadrite, Sonia, Memnon, JC and Shirley.

By now everyone knew of the insurance company scandal and the government's efforts to close down Golden Sunset Charters by denying the renewal of their licences. Harold's letter to *The Beacon* had been published in its entirety and all the irrefutable facts were there. There had been a retaliation the next day on the radio: Adolf Reephoff, who was representing

Caribbean Mutual Benefit in all hurricane damage related matters said during the broadcast, that they would be suing GSC for libel, but Harold had just laughed. He had watertight evidence.

After they'd all poured themselves glasses of water or cups of coffee, they came to order, and Harold threw the meeting open to anyone who had a good idea on how to challenge the government. Broadrite spoke up first. "I contacted every member of the Federation of Caribbean Insurers – there were 26 of them. Eight of them had applied to the Caribbee Islands government to do business here and every one of them was denied permission. Very strange on an island where there is such a need for insurance. Something stinks there."

"Your comments are noted, Mike, and thank you for your effort," said Harold. "Anyone else with any ideas?"

Memnon looked up, coughed and then said, "Personally, I tink it nuttin but disgustin'. De govmint done treat you real bad an' I ashame o' dem. But I tell you one ting – you got a lot o' support on de islan'. People dem behin' you big time. Even de kids at de CLATS programme. Dey wants to have a demonstrashun in tung wid placards an signs an' marchin' trew de main street. Yep, dat for true, de people dem behin' you big time."

"Thank you for your support, Memnon," said Harold. He looked around the table and saw that Jackie looked dewy-eyed at Memnon's emotional response. "Anyone else?"

Up to now Sonia had been quietly listening, hoping that some revelation might come to light. She didn't really want to expose the sordid details of the party, with her family involved, but now she knew she must. "Over the past few days I've been making some enquiries," she said, looking around at the others who were all ears, "and I have found out some interesting facts that should help the predicament of GSC.

"My first objective was to try and find a connection between Caribbean Mutual Benefit and the government and I started with Reuben and Talbot Winston. First, and very important, is the fact that they are not citizens of the Caribbee Islands, but only residents. This means that they can be deported if the government should so desire.

"Secondly, I found out about a party that takes place on the island in different luxury residences on a weekly basis. It is attended by notables from government and private business. During my enquiries I found out that Reuben Winston was a regular guest, and as luck would have it, I managed to get myself invited. These parties are all very hush hush – by invitation only and a security guard at the door – and you know why?" Sonia looked at her audience as they sat there expectantly. "These parties involve sex with school girls, drugs and underage drinking, and our friend Mr Winston was right there in the thick of it. I have photographs of him in bed with a young girl, with drugs by the bedside." There were murmurs around the room and several raised eyebrows.

Then, after a pause: "It seems as though you have uncovered a rather sordid business," said Harold, "but for all your diligent efforts, I don't see how it can help the dire straits that GSC finds itself in." Harold was being a little slow on the uptake, so Sonia went on to explain.

"Reuben Winston is a partner in Caribbean Mutual Benefit and as such has a position of power, prestige and prominence in the community. Not only that but he is probably very well off and would undoubtedly be loath to lose his position. What we now have is evidence that Reuben Winston is an immoral pervert and if this information were made public it would destroy him. So in other words, what we have here is leverage. We can threaten to expose him unless he admits that Caribbean Mutual Benefit was in collusion with the government."

"May I see the photographs?" said Broadrite.

Sonia held up a roll of film between thumb and forefinger. "They haven't been developed yet," she said. "These pictures are lewd and crude and I wouldn't want the identity of the girl to be made public knowledge. For that reason the pictures should be developed off-island and even then, they must be held in strictest confidence. I would like to entrust them to you, Mike, for safekeeping." Sonia desperately wanted to keep her elder sister's daughter out of public scrutiny.

"Of course there is no guarantee that Winston will admit to anything," said Jackie. "I mean he's damned if he does and he's damned if he doesn't."

"That's true," said Broadrite, "but a sex scandal involving drugs and children is much more serious than a lawsuit claiming fraud by a company in which he is only a junior partner. I think we have a chance here of getting him to acknowledge government involvement in the insurance fraud, especially if we add a sweetener – like agreeing to reduce the amount of our damages claim. The question is – how do we go about it?"

"There is only one avenue open to us," said Harold, "and that's the governor. In fact he phoned me yesterday and suggested we have an official meeting. He had not only read my article in the paper but he seemed to know a lot about our situation." Jackie looked at the floor. It had been she who had surreptitiously told Margaret Clement-Jones the whole story.

A few days later, Charles Mcguire was busy working at a computer when his receptionist knocked on his door and handed him a letter, delivered in person, from the office of the governor. He ripped it open and read that both he and Reuben Winston were requested to attend a meeting at the governor's office the next morning. Mcguire walked across to the adjoining office and went in. "What do you make of this?" he said to Winston, throwing the letter onto his desk.

"I have no idea," replied his partner. "Does anyone up at the governor's residence have a claim in?"

"I don't know, but that's what I want you to find out. I want you to search the files thoroughly for information concerning anyone connected with the governor who has current business or outstanding claims. We should be well prepared." Mcguire returned to his office.

After two hours of searching through the files Reuben could find nothing. He scratched his head and wondered what on earth a meeting at the governor's office could be about. His guilty conscience drifted to the weekly parties, but only for a second. No-one even remotely close to the governor's office would ever be invited there.

At five to nine the next morning, Miss Primby answered the door and ushered in Harold and Mike Broadrite, who were shown into the conference room. A couple of minutes later the governor walked in and shook hands cordially. They chatted briefly, but there was tension in the room. They all knew that they were involved in a very serious matter.

While they were waiting, Harold admired the room. There was a large picture of the Queen at her coronation adorning one end of the long room and on either side were two antique corner cupboards with a silver tea service in one and silver salvers in the other.

Along one of the long walls was a massive bookcase and opposite was a walnut sideboard with three ornate lamps behind it. At the other end were large picture windows looking out onto the grounds, the burgundy-red, velvet curtains drawn back and tied with gold and tasseled ropes.

It was almost 9:15 when Mcguire and Winston were shown in and it was suitably late to visibly annoy the governor, who greeted them perfunctorily and bade them sit at the long, polished table.

The five of them took up less than half the table, the governor sitting at the head. The Queen's representative opened the meeting and without any preliminaries came to the point. "It has come to my attention that Caribbean Mutual Benefit is rejecting claims on marine related damage caused by recent Hurricane Ben. Four different companies have contacted me on this matter and all report the same findings, namely that a disclaimer in the form of an addendum suddenly appeared long after initial insurance contracts had been signed and premiums paid. Mr Mcguire, would you care to respond to these allegations?"

"Well, I do believe this matter should be accorded due process in a court of law," said Mcguire confidently. "We in the insurance business spend half our lives dealing with matters of litigation. There are many who fill out questionnaires untruthfully. Then there are those who sometimes fake valuations. And then there are those who omit relevant details when seeking medical coverage. Why, just last week I had a case where a man insured his life for millions and then suddenly dropped dead from a heart attack. He was a non-smoker, he said on his application, but at the autopsy his lungs were so blackened with tar from cigarettes there was just no oxygen getting to his blood.

The case went to court, and of course, we won." Everyone in the room knew that Mcguire was blowing a smokescreen.

"Mr Broadrite, would you respond please," said Roger Clement-Jones.

"Mr Mcguire," began Broadrite in a voice of exaggerated patience, "we have concrete evidence that Caribbean Mutual Benefit is fraudulently rejecting honest claims. We know the addendums are fake. What we need to know is the government's connection in all this because it is trying to remove Mr and Mrs Mcphereson from the island."

"First let me say that concrete cracks and then crumbles under pressure. My lawyer, Mr Reephoff, will be delighted to challenge your claims in court. Secondly, Mr and Mrs Mcphereson are being kicked off the island for unseemly conduct: the scandal with the mermaid girl and several incidents of questionable behaviour by Roy Blake, a partner in the business. One involved drugs, another was a case of tax fraud and yet another involved an altercation with travel agents on board a yacht."

Mcguire's voice rose in pitch at the end of his diatribe to emphasise the "atrocious" behaviour. Harold was flabbergasted. These were exactly the reasons he had been given by the chief minister but no one else was privy to the information. It was further proof that a conspiracy was afoot between Mcguire and Bradshaw.

"Please explain, Mr Mcphereson?" said the governor formally.

"Your Excellency, everyone on the island now knows the truth about the mermaid and its discovery. It was irresponsible reporting by the editor who has since apologised, even in print, on the front page of the paper. As far as the allegations against Mr Blake are concerned there is no evidence to substantiate them whatsoever, and there are no charges against Mr Blake at the police station either. It should also be noted that Mr Blake is a minor shareholder in GSC and visits the islands infrequently. To penalise the whole of GSC, Ltd solely on some doubtful transgressions of his would be totally wrong and unjust."

Mcguire responded immediately. "I hope you'll agree, then, that allegations against Caribbean Mutual Benefit should not be summarily decided until we've had our day in court."

There was a short silence and Broadrite knew it was time to pull his trump card. "Mr Winston, you are a junior partner with Caribbean Mutual Benefit. Do you know anything about the alleged fraud?"

"No, nothing at all," said a worried looking Winston, who started fidgeting with a notebook he had in front of him.

"If you did know anything about fraudulent dealings, then as the junior member of the partnership you could hardly be expected to take the blame." Broadrite tried to sound like a sympathetic father.

"Don't say a word," said Mcguire. "This sounds like some sort of trickery."

"All right," said Broadrite. "I'll change the subject. Mr Winston. Have you ever heard of what is popularly called the weekly party?"

Winston visibly blanched. "Well, yes, I've heard of them," he said timidly.

"Have you ever attended them?"

"Well, let me see . . . yes I did attend one once." Winston didn't elaborate and Broadrite knew he was telling only half the truth. According to Sonia, he was a major player every week.

"Let me tell you what I know about the weekly parties," said Broadrite in a strong and accusing tone.

"These parties are held at private and secret luxury venues in order to seduce and sexually use and abuse underage girls after intoxicating them with alcohol and hard drugs such as cocaine. Drug offences and statutory rape such as this could put someone away for 30 years."

Reuben Winston started shaking but it was Mcguire who said, "Don't say a word – defend yourself in court!"

"You seem to like the courts, Mr Mcguire, but I'm afraid even the courts can't refute this evidence." He pulled an envelope from his inside jacket pocket and produced six postcard size photographs. These are very explicit, Mr Winston." Broadrite looked at them slowly, one at a time, shaking his head despairingly. Then he passed them across to Harold. "We would be prepared to tear these up and forget about the whole incident in exchange for information about the fake addendums and the government involvement."

Winston looked frantic, his eyes wide with desperation. He couldn't imagine how Broadrite had got hold of the photographs but it was too late now. He remembered Broadrite's words of a few minutes ago: "a junior partner wouldn't be held responsible." Thirty years in jail was unthinkable . . . Then the truth came tumbling out. Yes, Caribbean Mutual Benefit produced the addendums just after Hurricane Ben in order to save themselves millions. The government department of Trade and Labour under Chief Minister Bradshaw kept all other insurance companies out of the islands to ensure CMB's monopoly. In return, Caribbean Mutual Benefit paid Bradshaw 10 per cent of all premiums and 10 per cent of annual profits. All transactions were done through special assistant Talbot Winston, his own brother.

"You fool," cried Mcguire. "Shut up! Don't you see what you're doing?"

Harold handed the photographs back to Broadrite but Mcguire leaned across and snatched them. "Let me look at these photographs."

Mcguire leafed through the photos one at a time and then looked up in disbelief. Every one of them was blank. For some reason not one of them had come out.

15

H.M.S. Boxer

A_s they departed that all-important and revealing meeting, Roger Clement-Jones came up to Harold. "It is now obvious that you have been the victim of very serious fraud and government corruption", he said. "I shall take steps immediately to correct the situation – and don't worry, your immigration status and your business licences will be restored. I'm extremely sorry all this has happened, but our meeting today was very worthwhile. It's all on videotape."

Harold and Broadrite left the meeting with a sense of relief. Thanks largely to Sonia's efforts, the government's corruption had been exposed. Sonia was delighted, later that day, when she heard of the successful conclusion.

"Now I can have the photographs back," she said,

"I'm going to burn them."

"No need for that," said Harold, "they didn't come out. You must have had the lens cover on." Sonia hesitated for a minute and then laughed out loud at her stupidity. Her anxiety about the photos melted away. Providence had been on her side; her secret was safe.

Ten days before the Mcpheresons were due to be expelled from the islands, a Royal Navy warship of the frigate class, H.M.S. Boxer, was scheduled to arrive in Roadstead harbour. It had only been announced two days previously that an official visit was in the offing and speedy arrangements had to be made to provide the ship's company with the right kind of hospitality and extra-curricular activities. A rugby match was arranged. Someone suggested a boat trip, but that was thought to be inappropriate, so a beach barbecue was organized instead.

The official reason for the visit was that a senior Foreign Office minister and a junior civil servant would be on board and were coming to assess the recent hurricane damage. The governor had put in a request for aid. It was not normally the job of the Royal Navy to transport members of the British government around, but this was a special circumstance: The two had just been to the volcano-ravaged island of Montserrat where H.M.S. Boxer was on standby duty in case of the need to evacuate.

The unofficial reason that H.M.S. Boxer was visiting the island was that Governor Clement-Jones had reported to the Foreign Office the serious exposé of government corruption at the highest level and that he would be asking Chief Minister Lionel Bradshaw to step down under threat of impeachment. He felt that the presence of a British warship would add stability to the situation. After rigorous questioning, his request was met with approval.

That evening H.M.S. Boxer, painted the steely grey of the Royal Navy, and with the frigate bird painted on a blue background and encircled in gold, prominently displayed on the superstructure, tied up to the dilapidated commercial pier in Roadstead harbour. Just as the two gangplanks were rolled out and secured, the governor's three-litre Rover pulled up alongside the ship. The governor, in civilian dress, and his wife alighted and the captain came down to meet them, followed by the minister and his assistant. It was all very informal and they greeted each other with smiles and handshakes. There was to be an official party with dignitaries and ceremony the following Friday but for now, the governor wanted to make sure the captain was aware of the sequence of events for the next day.

At noon on the following day the mid-day news announced: "The Honourable Lionel Bradshaw, Chief Minister of the Territory of the Caribbee Islands, has resigned from office forthwith. There was no reason given for this sudden decision, but it is thought that failing health or family concerns must rank high on the list of possible reasons. The Honourable Minister was not available for comment. The Deputy Chief Minister, the Honourable Alexander Smith, will be sworn in as Acting Chief until elections are held as soon as possible."

It had been an unpleasant duty for Governor Clement-Jones. He had asked the chief minister to attend him at Government House at 9 a.m. that morning concerning a matter of grave importance and the government head had arrived an hour late. The meeting, behind closed doors, had lasted nearly an hour. The chief minister was told that his grave misconduct and corrupt activities had been exposed and that evidence was recorded on film. There was no denying it. He was given two choices – step down and resign immediately or go through long legal battles with all the accompanying revelations displayed to the public before being impeached. The shrewd Bradshaw hadn't taken long to decide his fate. He wrote a letter of resignation there and then, stalked out of the official residence and down to his waiting car. Clement-Jones instructed his office to issue a press release immediately.

The governor was relieved to be done with the unpleasant duty but was still not happy with the outcome. Bradshaw, having resigned, would be eligible not only for a full pension but for some expenses and perks as well. He had probably salted away a small fortune in ill-gotten gains during his tenure and he would still retain a certain stature among the people. But this was the way it was in politics and if the man had stayed in power to fight to the end, he could have sewn seeds of distrust and discontent amongst the people against the Crown – like a rotten apple in a barrel, he could have quickly contaminated the rest. The territory was well rid of him.

The resignation was on the radio again that evening and on the local TV where it was the subject of a talk show. One of the brighter interviewees drew a correlation between the royal navy warship and the chief minister's departure and this raised the question of whether Britain was meddling in the islands' internal affairs. This in turn brought about a heated discussion on independence, a topic always simmering just beneath the surface of many a proud islander's skin.

The next day there was a small demonstration in town, mostly with people from Bradshaw's district, campaigning against the Crown. But it was insignificant and short lived. A lot of politicians and island residents knew of Bradshaw's dealings, in fact his nickname in some circles was "Mr Ten Per Cent." Many were glad to see the back of him and at several expat cocktail hours, the governor was toasted for finally having done something useful for the community.

Harold and Jackie were overjoyed at the news. A few days later, all their business licences were back in order, having been renewed without further ado. The next day a polite call from the immigration department asked them to come in with their passports. They were then stamped in as permanent residents.

That day, after the conclusion of their paperwork, they decided to have lunch at the Pink Hibiscus. They were seated outside on the terrace and Harold was just beginning to dig into a spicy beef roti with a large helping of mango chutney when he heard three blasts from a ship's horn. He looked out across the harbour to see H.M.S. Boxer pull away from the pier and steam southwards.

During the following week there was considerable fallout from the cataclysmic event that had erupted in the government's hierarchy. Chief Minister Smith's immediate job was to quieten everyone down and get things back to normal. There had been headlines and front page stories in both newspapers – and even inside page stories in London and Stateside editions. By the weekend everything had leaked out and the British Sunday tabloids were reporting stories of drugs, underage sex and high-powered government ministers bingeing in a tropical paradise under the British flag. In one paper there was a picture of the governor in his white uniform, complete with shiny buttons, ceremonial sword and feathered Wolsey helmet, standing erect but with eyes gazing at a bikini clad young island girl lying suggestively on a sandy beach.

The photograph had obviously been doctored, but the meaning was clear.

Damage control was essential. The Caribbee Islands' economy was based on tourism and offshore financial services. These services involved legal methods of secretly hiding money in international business corporations and trust companies, for the purposes of tax avoidance, or "tax management" as the administration liked to describe it. An ethical and stable reputation around the world was paramount. Tourism could weather a scandal all right, but the offshore financial services industry was a bit more fragile. Its success was attributed to its ties with Britain, a bastion of solid corporate and banking principles and ethics. A picture of top government officials, drunk and high on drugs, frolicking in a tropical paradise with nubile young girls was not desirable. Neither was government corruption. The acting chief minister issued a carefully worded press release:

"It is with great sadness that the Honourable Chief Minister Lionel Bradshaw has had to resign from office. But after long, honourable and dedicated service, we wish him well in his future endeavours and hope that a richly deserved retirement will bring him peace and happiness.

"It has also been reported in the tabloid press that certain acts of a salacious and unsavoury nature have taken place in private residences on the island of Tortuga. We in our democratically elected government strongly support the 'right to privacy' and do not condone investigation into the practices and goings-on in people's homes unless serious crimes are being committed and we do not act on hearsay and rumour. However, if serious allegations unfold, necessary steps will be taken to see that justice prevails.

"It must be unequivocally understood that this

British territory remains committed to providing fair, honest and legal services in our fast expanding financial sector."

This bold statement was widely reported and had the desired calming effect . . . but not for long. The very next week Charles Mcguire hanged himself. The exposé of his corrupt business practises coupled with his fall from social respectability had been too much for him.

Then the former chief minister's general assistant Talbot Winston was personally escorted to the airport by the Caribbee Islands' police and summarily deported. From his home island of Antigua he sold his story to a British weekend national newspaper. This brought a deluge of reporters to the island, ironically improving tourist revenues temporarily. But the damage done to the offshore financial industry was severe and it was months before investors started trickling back.

16

The Carnival

It was now the second half of October and there was general relief on the island that the hurricane season had not produced any more threatening storms. It was announced on the radio that the islands' carnival would be re-scheduled to take place during the first two weeks in November, having been postponed in August due to Hurricane Ben.

The Autumn, even up until the middle of December, was a quiet time in the Caribbee Islands and Harold was wondering how he could generate some business from the upcoming festival. He decided that a fancy dress party at the Rusty Pelican would suit the occasion, and penciled it in on his calendar for the second Friday in November. He was just musing over what the theme should be when the phone rang. It was Justin Jennings from London. Could he and Godfrey

Allbright come out the following week to wrap up the mermaid story? His editor wanted to run the first episode around Christmas when he felt his readers would like a colourful, tropical story to cheer them up at the beginning of winter. Harold agreed whole-heartedly – he could see that the spotlight on the Caribbee Islands would not only be good for the islands but very useful advertising for Golden Sunset Charters. He replied to Jennings that, yes, he would be most welcome . . . and then he added that the islands' carnival was taking place during the first two weeks in November, culminating with the parade on the second Saturday. That would be the time to come. Jennings agreed.

The Caribbee Islands, like most islands and island groups in the Caribbean, are situated well inside the tropics, which are delineated by the tropic of Cancer, at 23 degrees and 27 minutes as the northern boundary, and the tropic of Capricorn with the same degrees and minutes of boundary in the southern hemisphere. The weather is always hot but during the months of July through October, especially around mid-day, the heat becomes oppressive and the pace of life slows to a crawl. Many blame the natives for being indolent, but the climate is at least partly to blame. The attitude is "Why over exert yourself? Tomorrow's another day."

But now, with carnival just 10 days away, indolence was replaced by exuberance. There was just so much to be done there weren't enough hours in the day. Top priority was given to the construction of the Carnival Village in the town square.

The village consisted of a ring of booths that sold food and drinks and surrounded a large central stage where nightly acts, contests, shows and bands performed. Individuals rented spaces from the carnival committee and erected their own booths so individual styles and varieties of food and drinks were ensured.

Next to the village a travelling fair was being hastily erected with swings, roundabouts, stalls and sideshows. The children would certainly not be left out.

And then there were the events. A beauty pageant was planned with local dusky maidens competing for prizes that guaranteed them all-expenses-paid, world-wide travel for bigger and better accolades up to Miss Caribbean, Miss World, Miss Universe . . .

The calypso contest was always a favourite and charismatic, strong-of-voice contenders vied for the title 'Calypso King.' A calypso is characterised as a story of topical interest, sometimes spontaneous, put to music. The winner was one with a catchy tune and meaningful lyrics, sometimes with an underlying innuendo of sex. A full brass section often accompanied a calypso singer's rendition, making it vibrant and alive. A good calypso contest could rival any show on earth for entertainment value.

There were other shows at carnival time too – a fire eater, perhaps; or an Indian sadhu walking on hot coals or broken glass.

And then there were reggae bands and steel bands and scratch bands and fungi bands and . . . well, in short, a Caribbean carnival means music . . . and music means dancing.

It was into Tortuga's carnival village that Justin Jennings and Godfrey Allbright walked during that second week of carnival celebrations. They were there specifically for the Calypso King Contest which was due to start at 7 p.m. but now at nearly 8 p.m. they were still waiting. "Let's get something to eat and another beer," said Jennings, "it seems like we're on island time." They walked over to a booth and Allbright ordered a rack of ribs with spicy West Indian barbecue sauce, and Jennings went for the "Fry fish and Johnny cake." They were served two heaping plates and two ice-cold beers and as soon as they sat at a nearby table, Jennings started dousing his food with hot sauce as though it were ketchup.

"Take it easy with that stuff," said Allbright. "It'll take the skin off the roof of your mouth."

"Nonsense," said Jennings, "I like plenty of sauce. Gives the food some flavour." He took a large bite and after a couple of seconds he was spluttering and choking and reaching for his beer. "Aaaaaaaaaaaah," he said, as tears started streaming from his eyes. He downed his beer and was about to say something when he again coughed and choked. He reached across and grabbed Allbright's beer and downed that in one gulp as well.

"I told you to take it easy," said Allbright, smiling.

"What do they put in that stuff, gunpowder?" said Jennings. He scraped the remains of the pepper sauce from his food and from then on carefully examined each mouthful. Allbright chuckled to himself – he might forget about the incident that evening but in the morning he'd have a painful reminder.

"I guess it's your round," said Allbright, with a twinkle in his eye, as he looked at both empty beer bottles. Jennings looked at him sideways, knowing he was being mocked.

On the stage, band members were organizing themselves, mikes were being tested, speakers adjusted and instruments fine-tuned. Just then an announcer came onto the stage. "Thank you for your patience, ladies and gentlemen. The contest is about to begin . . . and the first calypsonian is Tortuga's own . . . Lord Pompey!" The calypsonian ran forward onto the stage. He was dressed in black trousers, white shirt, black bow tie and a multi-coloured jacket with tails, covered with sparkling sequins. A shiny top hat set at a jaunty angle but with the top sliced open, like an open tin can, completed his attire.

The announcer then went on to explain all the previous achievements of his career and that his first-time rendition, specially written and composed for this year's Calypso King Contest was . . . "De Politishun." It started like this:

> *"All o' we done vote ya into power*
> *All o' we our wishes dem gone sour*
> *De pledges an' de promises ain' here*
> *We plans, we dreams, all done disappear*
> *De taxes, all de money, where it be?*
> *It shaw ain' here, helpin all o' we*
> *It in a bank belongin' to de Swiss,*
> *We should o' never vote a man like dis."*

Lord Pompey was a real showman. He pranced across the stage, gesticulating, pointing. He strutted, he danced, he contorted, he cavorted and the crowd loved it. The horn section were brilliant too, carrying the catchy melody to its conclusion.

Jennings and Allbright loved the show and watched every performer, Jennings managing to shoot two rolls of slides. The contest was decided by six judges, who picked the winner based on lyrical content, showmanship and musical style, but listened carefully to audience response as well. Sometimes a performer won simply on crowd appeal, and favourite calypsonians often won time and time again.

But tonight was Lord Pompey's night, because he won the contest by a unanimous decision. He won a statuette, a cash prize, a recording contract and a guaranteed following. The band struck up and out he came to perform his winning calypso once again – this time louder and more vigorously than before. By now the crowd had swelled to several thousand and it seemed as if the whole of the Caribbee Islands' population was there. They were all in a festive mood, too and beer, rum and mixed drinks were being consumed like there was no tomorrow.

When the two journalists eventually flopped into bed back at the lodge it was 3:30 a.m.

JC and Shirley were up early on the day of the carnival parade. Harold had asked them to prepare *Sunfun Calypso* for up to 10 guests for a day's outing to watch the parade. He asked Shirley to prepare a finger buffet for lunch and not to forget white wine and champagne on ice, along with an assortment of the usual beverages – beer, pop, iced tea and sparkling water.

"I'm going to anchor the boat just off The Waterfront," shouted JC, as he emptied a case of Heineken into a giant cooler in the cockpit. "That's the best place for a great view of the parade."

"I hope it won't be too choppy," replied Shirley, from the galley below decks. She was busy mixing minced conch with flour and eggs for the conch fritters.

"Not only is it one of the calmest spots in the bay, it is also very close to the dinghy dock for town, in case anyone wants to go ashore. The weather forecast is good too – light southeasterly breezes."

"Ooooh, I'd love to go athore at thome time during the parade," said Shirley. "I've never theen a carnival before." She appeared at the companionway with both hands covered in batter and approached JC with arms extended, threatening to smear him. At the last minute, she simply dabbed him on the nose with a blob of batter and then licked it off, playfully grinning all the while. He engulfed her in his big arms and leaned down to give her a long wet kiss. He was just wondering whether he should carry her down to their cabin to continue when he heard a familiar voice.

"Now, now you two love birds. I know it's love that makes the world go round, but you two might bring it to a stop. How are the preparations coming along?" It was Harold, and he was half an hour early. Their departure time from the GSC dock had been planned for 11 o'clock.

"Right on schedule," replied JC, and Shirley smiled and waved, disappearing back to her conch fritters.

"Good," said Harold, "I've just come to tell you that, at the last minute, the governor and his wife have unexpectedly decided to accept our invitation and join us. So you'd better wear your whites and Shirley should wear something a little more formal than usual. I'd suggest whites as well. And don't forget to have gin and tonic available."

"Right," shouted JC to Harold, who was still standing on the dock. "How many guests can we expect all together?"

"There should be about eight: the governor and his wife, Mike Broadrite, myself and Jackie, Allbright and Jennings and old Mr Hodge. Allbright and Jennings will dinghy ashore when the parade starts, but they didn't want to miss the sail down to Roadstead."

It was 11:15 when they departed the dock. A ninth guest had joined the party, Annabelle, a pretty Trinidadian mulatto. Justin Jennings had met her at the calypso contest and invited her to spend the day with him.

Once they had cleared the bay and left Whale Rock safely to starboard, JC hoisted the sock that contained the beautiful yellow cruising spinnaker with its orange sunburst. There were audible gasps when it ballooned forth, huge and awe-inspiring, with the sun's rays reflecting a golden sheen onto the white decks. "Bravo," shouted the governor clapping. "Magnificent effort." He was applauding the seamanship of JC and Shirley who had handled the setting of the large sail perfectly.

Once the sail was trimmed, JC engaged the auto pilot and was just about to tidy up the lines in the cockpit when the governor approached and asked if he could examine the navigation station. Explaining all the instruments and their operation was one of JC's favourite pastimes, and he welcomed Roger Clement-Jones's enthusiasm. He ushered the governor inside the main salon. "The central navigation station is here; outside the instruments are repeaters." The depth sounder and knot meter were already on, as were the VHF radio, auto pilot and wind instruments. Now he switched on the global positioning system, or GPS, the radar, weather fax and single sideband radio. The nav station, with the different instruments glowing with their subdued lighting, was intended to prevent loss of night vision in the dark. The radar shone green, the GPS blue, the speed, depth and wind red and the engine instruments orange. It was an impressive display.

"This GPS is one of the most advanced on the market," explained JC. "You insert a tiny chip into the instrument here," he pointed at the side of the unit, "and the screen will display the chosen geographical area. Then you press 'position' and in less than a minute a small symbol of a boat marks your position on the screen. Then you programme in your destination and a course line shows up marking the most direct route. You can zoom in and zoom out either to enlarge or diminish the geographical area." JC pressed a button and the screen zoomed out to show the whole Caribbean with portions of north and south America. Then he zoomed in and they could both see *Sunfun* sailing down the coast of Tortuga.

"That's fantastic," said Clement-Jones. "It must be hard to get lost with one of these on board."

"Yes," said JC. "It was technology like this that raised so many eyebrows during the Gulf War. Do you remember that famous clip shown on TV when a guided missile was fired at an Iraqi target? It was fired towards the town, then it was diverted down a street, along an alley and through a window into the target building."

JC programmed in the destination co-ordinates just off The Waterfront, and as *Sunfun* sailed down the coast it was plain to see that they were slightly off course. "Now as the vessel departs from its course line, we can correct it by altering the auto pilot a few degrees port or starboard – in this case starboard." JC hit the button and the symbol on the screen visibly turned and after only a few minutes they were back on track. "Now we have to trim the sails to correspond to our new course."

"Amazing to think how fast the human race is rushing towards its destiny," said the governor philosophically. He was standing there looking up, deep in thought. "When Columbus sailed to the 'new world' just over 500 years ago there were many who thought he would fall off the edge. And less than 300 years ago they were still searching for the chronometer so that mariners could find their longitude. Now we can navigate ourselves around the world by pushing buttons."

"Not only that," said JC, "but we can also communicate around the world, too." He opened a drawer and inside was a lap top computer. "This is plugged into our own satellite antenna. We have Internet access and E-mail communication."

Just then Shirley called from the cockpit. "Small boat on a collision course off the port bow. Some way off at the moment."

"Well, that just proves it," said JC. "We'll never eliminate the human being completely." The governor laughed and they both returned to the cockpit where the rest of the guests were enjoying an exhilarating sail downwind with the tropical coastline providing beautiful scenery. The little powerboat came closer and someone on the bow took several pictures before it zoomed off, the three or four occupants laughing and waving.

They dropped anchor just off The Waterfront at 12:45 and the parade was due to start at 1 p.m. That meant 2:30 p.m. island time. Shirley appeared with a tray of glasses and an ice bucket and right behind her was JC with a bottle of rum, gin and several tonics. They set up a small bar, Shirley displaying her artistic flair by producing a decorative table with tropical flowers and ferns. "Since people will be coming and going during the afternoon, food and drinks will be available on a help-yourself basis. Cold beer is in the cooler here," said JC pointing to the large cold box.

"Very sensible," said the governor. "And thank you for the exciting sail and guided tour of the nav station. You certainly know this boat inside out."

JC nodded and smiled. "Thank you, sir. It was a pleasure." He liked the governor. The coconut telegraph had spread the word that he had been instrumental in exposing the insurance company fraud and the government involvement.

It was the white-haired Mr Hodge who was the first to take advantage of the refreshments. He had been sitting, looking out to sea with quiet contemplation during the short sail, but now he spoke up. "Young lady, would you please be kind enough to pass me a cold Heineken?" he called out to Shirley who was just coming through the door with a plate of jerk chicken.

"Oh, and just a thimble full of dark rum – strictly because it's a celebration."

Hodge turned to Clement-Jones. "Surprising that the chief minister should resign with such short notice." He cocked his head and looked askance at the governor.

The Queen's representative often had to field ticklish questions and, like the best politicians, he had become an expert at diplomacy. He had hoped, though, that this trip would be strictly pleasure. Of course he was mistaken. "Yes, well he probably thought the timing was right. But I agree, it was rather sudden."

"I've known Bradshaw since he was a boy. Came from a good family, good education, religious background. But it is the power that corrupts – the ego that comes when a person thinks the whole world revolves around him. It can be very dangerous – can make a man too greedy." Old Mr Hodge obviously knew of Bradshaw's shortcomings. Just then, Shirley arrived with Hodge's beer and rum and Clement-Jones headed to the bar. He needed a large gin and tonic with plenty of ice, the afternoon sun was beginning to get oppressive.

Soon everyone was in the spacious cockpit chatting, drinking and enjoying the delicious finger food. The hot conch fritters were an instant success and Annabelle, who was an expert on West Indian cuisine called for "some o' de real hot sauce from Trinidad." Jennings, though, who was constantly at her side, told her to keep the stuff well away from him and she playfully berated him for "bein' a cold Englishman."

Harold, who had been chatting to Broadrite on the foredeck about the origin of carnival, suddenly changed topics. "I'm very worried about the Caribbean Mutual Benefit affair. Although we have evidence and an admission of guilt from the insurance company, it's going to be months or perhaps years before we have our claims settled, and the finances to repair the damaged yachts. As the company lawyer, Mike, can you suggest a course of action to speed things up?"

"Well, you're quite right. It will take several months for this case to get to court, especially with Mcguire's suicide. But it would seem that it's an open and shut case, what with the admission of guilt from Winston and the videotape from the governor's security camera. National Allied Insurers of New York were the underwriters for Caribbean Mutual Benefit and they will probably be liable for at least half of the claims, the amount of which could be as much as 10 million. I checked on their credentials even before we bought our insurance policies over a year ago. They are very solid with billions in assets and huge annual revenues. But even so, I'm sure they will delay payment for as long as possible. There is one avenue open to us and that is that we could offer to accept . . . say 15 per cent less than our claims are worth if payment is made immediately. I think they might go for that. After all, they'll have to pay out sooner or later anyway."

Harold didn't have to think long. "Offer them 10 per cent first and as a last resort, 15 per cent. When you write to them you might mention that with Bradshaw's resignation, there will likely be plenty of competition in the future. They may wish to be nice to us if they feel that their lucrative Caribbean business might slip away."

"I can see that immediate funds are essential to rebuild the yachting division – especially with the season just around the corner. And you were telling me that Roy Blake is in financial trouble with his business in the States and wants to sell his stake in GSC."

"Yes," said Harold, "some difficulty with the tax department, I believe."

"Well," said Broadrite, "I would be interested in buying his share if the price was right. Not only that, but I would be prepared to loan GSC at least a portion of the funds necessary to get the yacht chartering division back on its feet – for a fair return, of course. I have great faith in GSC and I believe it has a bright future."

Harold could hardly believe his ears. Mike Broadrite would be a perfect partner. His legal expertise and his stature in the islands would be a tremendous benefit to GSC and its management team.

"Are you two talking about business again?" It was Jackie and she came up to Harold and slipped her arm through his affectionately. Her glass was almost full from a freshly opened bottle of bubbly and she was thoroughly enjoying the day out on the boat.

"Mike, we must talk more about this later," Harold smiled and nodded as though in affirmation. "For now though, I think champagne is in order." He walked over to the bar and opened another bottle with a resounding "pop." He filled six glasses and handed them around to all those without, and was just wondering whether he should make a welcoming speech, when old Mr Hodge stood up.

"A toast," he said, and then louder, "I wish to make a toast," and with a theatrical pause he said, "To the emancipation of slavery!" He held his glass high and then, almost religiously, drank a deep draught.

There was a perceptible pause. No-one had expected the rather saturnine subject of slavery to be raised. It was a topic that was embarrassing to both whites and blacks because the descendants of both oppressors and oppressed felt guilty. The former for having subjugated a race – the latter for being unable to extricate themselves for so long.

The governor was the first to raise his glass. "To

emancipation," he said.

Everyone followed suit and Margaret Clement-Jones said in a whisper, "May mankind never forget its mistakes."

Allbright, who had been down in the galley, arrived in the cockpit with a fresh plate of steaming conch fritters. "I heard you drinking to the abolition of slavery," he said. "Is there any connection between the carnival and slavery?"

"The emancipation of slavery is celebrated every year by carnival," replied Hodge. "That is why we have it. The trouble is that so many people these days, especially the young, don't appreciate the origins of carnival and the struggle that our ancestors had in order to attain freedom. To them it's just an excuse for drinking, wild cavorting and free love." Hodge sounded somewhat bitter but Allbright thought that the young people's attitudes were pretty normal.

The governor, though, had some words of wisdom. "It was a shameful episode in history, and like all past events, when men abused their fellow men it must be remembered so that it shall not be repeated."

Just as the mood was getting sombre, Jennings with Annabelle on the foredeck shouted, "The steel band is playing and the first truck in the parade has started along The Waterfront." Sure enough, when they all stopped talking, the sound of the steel drums came echoing across the water – an unmistakable West Indian rhythm. The tune was *'Back to back, belly to belly'* and every drum was in unison.

Harold walked across to the navigation station and reached for his new high-powered binoculars. "Yes, you're right. The parade is finally under way." At the head of the procession a beautiful, brown-skinned girl dressed in a white gown and adorned in a bejewelled crown sat on a raised platform on the back of a black convertible. She was the Carnival Queen and she smiled and waved – an attendant holding up a white parasol to shade her from the sun. Next came a big Mack truck, slowly making its way, with the band playing furiously on the flatbed under the protection of a large yellow and white striped awning. Alongside the truck, revellers danced with gay abandon, some holding bottles or cans of beer.

Behind the truck the first troupe was from the High School. About 16 teenage girls called the Majorettes were marching in time to the steel band music. Dressed in shiny blue, one-piece mini skirt and tank top combo, white socks and sneakers, each girl was performing to the max. They wore white pompoms at ankle and wrist and expertly twirled batons, the leader throwing hers skyward on occasion, never missing a perfect catch.

The first "float" or theme group, again on the back of a flatbed, was "The Coral Reef." This was an artfully decorated display with papier maché staghorn and elkhorn coral and rocks. On one end of the float was a cave partially obscured by sea fans and tube sponges. Colourful cardboard cutouts of tropical fish hung from threads from a canopy that was painted to look like the sea, complete with breaking waves. There were large cardboard models of undersea flora and fauna and interspersed with these models were people in clever costumes. It was hard to tell the people from the models until they moved. A very lifelike octopus that had remained stock still for minutes suddenly moved four of its eight legs and shrieks of delight from spectators could be heard on *Sunfun*, even above the noise of the band. Then a lobster emerged from the cave, waving its tentacles. "What an amazing float," said Harold, still gazing through the binoculars.

The carnival queen at the head of the procession was now adjacent to *Sunfun* and all on board had a magnificent view. Jennings, though, was anxious to get a closer look. "Can you run us ashore?" he asked JC. "I must get some pictures of this."

Jennings, Allbright and Annabelle all tumbled into the dinghy and they were just about to cast off when Shirley appeared with a pleading expression and JC gestured for her to jump in. They sped off, the fast inflatable arcing a frothy wake.

Margaret Clement-Jones turned to Jackie. "What a wonderful crew you have for your yacht – so friendly and polite."

"Yes, Shirley was with us on our first sailing holiday in the islands. In fact we first met her in England when she came to stay at The Coach and Horses with Roy Blake. They seemed an unlikely couple and I think she's much happier with JC . . . It seems ages ago now." Jackie's thoughts drifted back to an earlier life.

The main part of the carnival parade was now slowly making its way down The Waterfront and all the floats, troupes and bands were clearly visible from the yacht. A troupe of colourful butterflies, with wings made of translucent material stretched over wire frames and gilded with silver and gold, danced to the sounds of a reggae band in front. Then a group of mocko-jumbies came striding by. These colourfully dressed clowns on stilts, sometimes 15 feet off the ground, were a real crowd pleaser and one particularly happy clown with extra deep pockets was striding along and throwing handfuls of sweets to the children, who shouted and screamed with glee.

Harold was busy explaining to the governor that he had learned that a 'jumbi,' to the West Indian people, was an evil spirit, when he glanced up and scanned the length of the parade. He was just taking a sip of champagne when his glass dropped with a smash onto the deck. "Great Scot!!" he exclaimed, reaching for his binoculars. "This is incredible. I mean it's unbelievable, I must be seeing things." Harold slumped down onto a seat. Then he got up again and raised the binoculars to his eyes once more. "Look over at the float just emerging at the beginning of the procession."

There was no mistaking it. On the front of a large flatbed a mock prow of a ship had been erected and proudly staring forth was . . . the Mermaid!! resplendent with golden hair, piercing blue eyes, pink cheeks and the mouth with the Mona Lisa smile. Harold stared at the float, open-mouthed. The rest of the flatbed resembled an old sailing ship, complete with cannons, rigging, masts, spars and a big ship's wheel. Climbing all over it were mini swashbucklers and buccaneers with eyepatches and silver, cardboard cutlasses. They were the local kids from the CLATS programme and they were having the time of their life. Tutu and Tall Boy were going at it hammer and tongs . . . or, more accurately, sword and dagger. The leader of this motley pirate band was a rather dark-skinned Blackbeard. His long, matted ringlets were partly covered by a black, three-cornered hat and on bandoliers were slung two brace of flintlocks. A long sabre hung from a belt. It was impossible to recognise who it was behind the clever costume, but Jackie knew instinctively. Even the swaggering gait and occasional 'Yo ho ho's' could not disguise the wily figure of Memnon.

"Harold, my dear fellow. Are you all right? You look rather pale." The governor put his hand on Harold's shoulder. "Come, you'd better sit down. You look quite ill."

"No, no, I'm fine . . . really. It's just that I can't believe that the mermaid – our old mermaid – is in the carnival procession. You see – I gave Memnon strict instructions to burn it."

"Really," said Roger Clement Jones, "why on earth would you wish to burn the talisman that has brought such notoriety and prosperity to the Sunset Lodge?"

"Well," said Harold rather weakly, "it was full of termites." He would not admit to the governor that the possibility of the mermaid being possessed by supernatural powers had influenced his decision.

As the mermaid passed *Sunfun*, Memnon, acting his part to the letter, shouted through a bullhorn, "We shall give no quarter nor do we expect any!! . . . AAAAAttack!!" The pirate band began slashing imaginary adversaries and firing wooden flintlocks and soon, blood was running. Nobody noticed a gallon ketchup jar roll off the platform into the gutter.

The spectators lining the road sent up a loud cheer and the small group on *Sunfun* echoed the applause with shouts of encouragement and clapping. "Keep your powder dry," called out the governor, getting into the spirit of things. Harold, though, was too stunned to participate. He walked over to the bar and fixed himself another drink.

The front of the procession had just reached the media platform and commentary could now be heard from a PA system. Two TV stations were filming the parade and commentators were roving the crowd getting audience reaction. There were writers and correspondents and a bevy of photographers, many with high-powered lenses. As the carnival queen passed the platform her previous intermittent grin was replaced with an ear to ear, teeth exposing, camera ready smile that she managed to maintain for minutes, whilst waving and batting her eyelashes simultaneously. Having been well-rehearsed, she was obviously looking for greater stardom in the future.

The different bands struck up their latest hits and played with gusto as they in turn passed the rostrum.

The float depicting the reef got a huge applause as they passed the cameras. One young boy in the crowd poked at the slippery-looking octopus with a stick and was rewarded with a squirt of black liquid. This had the crowd in an uproar and the cameras quickly moved to capture the drama.

Alongside and behind the floats revellers danced to the reggae beat. One girl was "win'ing" or slowly gyrating down onto an imaginary phallus, others were lewdly imitating the sex act with sweat pouring from their bodies in the afternoon heat.

Once ashore Jennings, Annabelle and Allbright had rushed from one end of the parade to the other taking notes, recording interviews and taking pictures. But they soon realised that the best place was on the media platform, and Jennings managed to get the three of them up there by flashing his press card. The presence of the TV cameras, commentators and photographers elicited the best performances from bands, floats and troupes alike. Godfrey Allbright was standing on the far end of the platform focusing his camera when a tap on the shoulder caused him to look around. The smiling face of Neil James stared at him. "Welcome back to the island," said the shady editor of the *Island Times*. "I hear you're on assignment for the *Sunday Times* with Justin Jennings."

It took Allbright a moment for his feelings to tune in. It had been a while since his wrongful dismissal but the venom of hatred he had once felt had not completely subsided. "It's no thanks to you that I'm back on the island," he said with an icy glare, "in fact I'm surprised to see you still here after your libelous journalism."

"Now, now . . . no need to stir up ancient history. By the way, how's that old fart Mcphereson? I hear they're going to kick him off the island."

"For a newspaperman, you're extremely ill-informed. Not only that but you are rude as well. Now get out of my sight before I lose my temper." Allbright left the platform and Jennings and Annabelle followed.

"What was all that about?" asked Jennings, who had heard snatches of the conversation.

"That is the editor of the *Island Times*. I don't want to go into it right now, but he's a nasty piece of work."

"Look," cried Annabelle, "the mermaid and the pirates are coming."

"I want pictures of this," said Jennings, "come on! Let's get closer." They ran the hundred feet or so towards the float that had temporarily stopped and Jennings shouted to Memnon and the pirate crew. "These pictures are for the press," he said. "Can I have a good show?"

Memnon obliged: "Right, me hearties, prepare to repel boarders," he said in his swarthiest accent. The little pirates stood defiantly, cutlasses at the ready.

"Quick Annabelle, climb up there . . . show us some leg . . . skew your hat . . . perfect." Jennings shot off a roll as Annabelle cocked her wide brimmed sombrero to a jaunty angle and parted her sarong to show a sexy bit of thigh. The procession moved forward again and there was heightened activity as the mermaid approached the media platform and an announcer loudly praised the CLATS' float whilst TV cameras were trained on the pirate band. Suddenly the flatbed lurched and rocked sideways as one of the truck's front wheels sank into a deep pot-hole, and burst its tyre. The mermaid leaned sideways and, together with the ship's prow, somehow tore loose from its mounting. With a rending groan, it crashed onto the platform scattering media persons, TV cameras, tripods, microphones and speakers in all directions. To add to the confusion sparks and smoke came pouring from a smashed amplifier accompanied by a sharp crackling. The impact caused the mermaid's head to detach itself from its body, and it rolled off the platform to land on the pavement below, where it came to a stop, face up, still smiling its weird half smile.

There was absolute pandemonium. Jennings and Allbright, who had been only yards away, were first onto the platform to help the injured, dazed and distraught. Annabelle helped those with only minor injuries to leave the stage, and others ran to help them be seated in a shady area nearby. Allbright had just helped two injured v˙ ⹀ns – one had concussion and he had told her to lie still until the ambulance arrived, the other had severe back pain and the young journalist had advised him not to move as well. The third victim looked the worst – there was blood pouring from a head wound and he was making a choking, guttural noise with a dribble of blood coming from the corner of his mouth. The mermaid had scored a direct hit on . . . Neil James.

Only seconds after the accident, the parade came to a stop and all the bands ceased. The kids from the mermaid float, miraculously unhurt, were led away to safety by Memnon, just as two mounted policemen arrived to take charge. An ambulance siren could be heard in the distance but it didn't seem to be getting much closer – the crowds and the procession, now at a standstill, impeded its progress.

JC and Shirley, who had been watching the parade from a pub balcony nearby, fought their way through the crowd, and finally met up with their three guests. It took JC a while to get Jennings away from the scene – being a true journalist he wanted to record all the details. But soon they were away from the bedlam and wizzing their way back to *Sunfun*.

There was animated discussion about the incident

all the way back to Rum Cove. Harold was now only too willing to expound his theory on the mermaid's jinx, backed up by Jennings' and Allbright's historical findings where the rebellious crew of the sailing ship *Mermaid* had removed the figurehead and placed it in the cellar of what was now the Sunset Lodge.

"One thing that is worrying me is that I told Memnon, in no uncertain terms, to burn the mermaid when we found that it was being attacked by termites. I had just received the final fax from you, Justin, outlining the extraordinary circumstances surrounding the mermaid's history. I am not normally a superstitious man but I must say that your revelations certainly influenced me. Then and there I considered it prudent to burn the thing and the termite problem gave me a logical excuse. But for some reason Memnon decided against it . . . Of course he was unaware of your findings." Harold shrugged his shoulders in despair.

"And now the mermaid has caused another accident with serious injuries," said Mike Broadrite. "It's uncanny. Mind you, Neil James didn't seem particularly concerned when he caused you serious injury with his libelous reporting. You might say the wheel has turned full circle."

"Exactly what I was thinking," said Godfrey Allbright. "Poetic justice."

"You are being very harsh on a man who has just sustained serious injuries and is probably in great pain," said a compassionate Margaret Clement-Jones. "Revenge is never really the answer. As Ghandi said, 'An eye for an eye only makes the whole world blind.'"

Nobody spoke for long seconds as everyone pondered the words of wisdom. Then suddenly, "Stand by, everyone. We're going to furl the jib." It was JC. They had just arrived at the entrance to Rum Cove. Shirley took the helm as JC winched in the huge head sail. The mains'l followed and Shirley, at the helm, headed the large craft into the wind whilst JC released the halyard. The sail dropped neatly between the lazy jacks in one easy movement. They motored in and the captain expertly reversed into their slip as Shirley secured the bow.

As the guests filed down the gang plank, there were thanks and words of praise for a wonderful day. Both JC and Shirley, still looking very smart in their whites, shook hands with the governor and his wife and the rest of the guests. When they had all gone Shirley breathed a sigh of relief. It had been a demanding day. She stepped up to JC. "Now, where were we before all thothe people arrived?" she said with a mischievous glint in her eye.

"Well, if I remember correctly, you were smearing my face with conch fritter batter whilst I was getting as horny as an antelope," and with a chuckle, grabbed his little nymph by the hand and led her below. It had been over a year that the couple had been in lust and the fire showed no signs of cooling.

Two days after the parade, Memnon was sitting in the kitchen of the lodge enjoying a mid-morning cup of tea when Harold walked in. He had a few questions he'd been dying to ask his elusive friend, but Memnon got up and headed for the door, sensing he might be in trouble. Harold, though, was in good spirits. "Congratulations on your prize-winning float," he said, going over to the big man and putting his arm on his shoulder. "You and the CLATS kids put on a fine show . . ." After a slight pause he continued, "Amazing that you found a mermaid identical to the one you burnt, though!" Harold's British sense of humour never lacked in sarcasm.

"Dat mermaid were too to good to burn," said Memnon. "She were a real work o' art . . . and to tink

327

o' all o' de wuk we done to bring she up out o' de cellar. No suh, I couldn't do it."

"Memnon, that mermaid is jinxed. I should have told you before but it contains the spirit of the obeah." He explained about the ship and how the mermaid had been placed in the cellar to avoid a mutiny.

Memnon's eyes opened wide and he stared at Harold. Then after a long pause he said, "You mean dat Beulah were right? De jumbi in de mermaid?"

"No question about it," said Harold. "In the old days it spooked a whole ship's company, and since we brought it up from the cellar, it almost had me charged in a rape case. Now it has again caused some terrible injuries. By the way, whatever happened to the thing after the carnival?"

"Well, dat's a funny ting," said Memnon, "I were jus' comin' back through tung after seein' off all de kids when I see de mermaid still layin by de side o' de road. You know dat de head done bust off after it fell off de float. Well, dere it were layin' dere in two pieces an I were jus' gettin out o' my mini-bus when dis big black car pulls up an' two white fellas gets out. Dey goes straight over to de mermaid's body an tries to pick it up an' I see dat dey're wantin' to put it in deir car. Dey does see me watchin' an' calls out for me to help. So I ask dem what dey goin' to do wid it and dis one fella he say he goin' to mend it an' put it in his garden. So I say to he dat maybe it don't belong to him and he say dat it belong to anybody cos it in de gutter. Den he says dat he knows it from de Sunset Lodge an' it serve dem right if dey never gets it back. Well, I doesn't help dem at all but finally dey gets it into deir car an' drives off . . . an' shoutin' rude ting at me too – but I don't care – I didn't want de ting anymore anyhow. It were only for de carnival dat I wanted it."

"Did you recognise these two rude people,

Memnon?"

"Yeah, I recognised one o' dem – de one dat goin to put it in his garden. Dat lawyer wid de funny accent and de twitchin' eye. I tink dey calls him Reephoff."

Harold couldn't prevent a sardonic smile from slowly spreading across his face, "Come Memnon," said Harold, "it's no time for drinking tea." Harold led the way into the Mermaid Bar and reached for a bottle of Mermaid's Gold. He poured two healthy shots and handed one to Memnon. "To carnival," he said, and raising his glass, he drank.

17

CLATS International

The Christmas edition of the *Sunday Times'* magazine was almost entirely devoted to the Caribbee Islands, Tortuga and Golden Sunset Charters Resort. The handsome figurehead lording it over the terrace and bar was displayed proudly on the front page, a sherry cask and a bottle of Mermaid's Gold inset. The story of the mermaid and the Mermaid Bar were described with flare and colour and the whole story was cleverly augmented with pictures of the carnival, *Sunfun Calypso* with spinnaker flying, the fountain, the lodge with the flowers and grounds, scantily clad girls and palm fringed tropical beaches. Harold had persuaded Justin Jennings to include a pitch for Mermaid's Gold in the feature. The unique eighty-year-old vintage rum was now packaged in a "Collector's Set," complete with a descriptive booklet and two shot glasses in a carved mahogany box. Price . . . $250. Some of the proceeds would go to CLATS, it said – but better hurry – there were only 340 sets left of this limited-edition antiquity.

The article, in such a prestigious and widely read paper, did wonders for Golden Sunset Charters. Enquiries and bookings came flooding in the very week after the edition was published, adding to an already well booked season.

Golden Sunset Charters' second year under the Mcpheresons' ownership was looking better than the first, despite the damage caused by two hurricanes. Mike Broadrite was now a partner in the business and to everyone's surprise, he had volunteered to manage the yacht chartering division as operations manager. He had been a keen sailor for over 20 years but had become more and more office-bound with his lawyer's practice. He had felt that it was time for a change and Harold had readily agreed to his offer. He kept his practice and hired two replacement lawyers with himself acting as consultant. The only problem was that now he couldn't represent GSC since there would be a conflict of interest, though there weren't any pressing legal matters on the horizon.

The insurance company had taken advantage of GSC's offer and paid all their claims less 15 per cent for immediate payment. By the end of January all of GSC's yachts were operational and bookings were good for the remainder of the season.

Memnon was no longer captain of *Wet 'n Wild*. One day he had come back from a particularly trying two-week charter and had stopped Mike on the dock. "Do the islands go all the way to the bottom?" he said, casually.

"What was that?" said Broadrite, busily examining the innards of a large outboard motor.

"Do the islands go all the way to the bottom?" repeated Memnon, keeping a straight face.

Mike stopped what he was doing and stared at Memnon inquiringly. Was the normally exuberant islander going "tropo"? Suddenly Memnon burst into laughter and slapped his thigh: Mike's face was a picture of confusion. "Dat's just one o' de questions I had to answer dis past two weeks. I were confused too but de lady – she serious! I done tol' she, 'Yeah de islands go all de way to de bottom exceptin' de ones goin' by at 5 knots.' She looked at me straight-faced, completely satisfied, nodded and said, 'thank you.'" Memnon shook his head and sighed deeply. "I sick o' de job. I can only take tourists in small doses. I prefer to wuk here on de dock an' go home every night. It less money but better fo' me soul."

So Memnon became foreman on the dock and everyone was happy. He got along well with the dock staff, had a ready smile and a good attitude with the guests.

By the end of April the season began to slow down and Jackie and Harold made plans to take *Sunfun Calypso* for a cruise of the Windward and Leeward islands. For the first time in a year and a half Golden Sunset Charters was running like clockwork. Jackie had hired a new chef, straight out of catering college, and had taught him all her secrets. He was as keen as mustard too and had proudly shown Harold a new sample menu. "Fine," said Harold, "but take the Frogs Legs off the menu." The young man looked bewildered but was savvy enough not to ask any questions. He got along well with Beulah and the restaurant maintained its high standard. There was also a very bright young woman from Jamaica who had been hired as assistant manageress for the lodge and Sonia Hodge was appointed overall General Manager.

Both Harold and Jackie's original intentions had been to come to the Caribbean, not only to start a small hotel, but to explore and enjoy this beautiful part of the world. Now it seemed that the time was right: After months of impossibly long hours and often frustrating and backbreaking work, the business was running well. JC and Shirley were thrilled when they were told of the plans. Previously booked charters were shuffled onto *Wet 'n Wild*, and stocking and provisioning of *Sunfun Calypso* began in earnest for a three-month trip. By the second week in May, they were ready.

On the morning of their departure a crowd of the hotel's staff gathered on the dock to wave them off. "Min' you, kiss de groun' for me when you reach St. Kitts," said Memnon. "Dat's my islan'."

"And don't forget to try Blue Mountain coffee if you reach Jamaica," said the new manageress, "and Salt Fish Akee – it's de bes'."

JC maneuvered the big cat out of the slip and soon they were sailing fast on a close reach with spray flying and the sails pulling to a steady tradewind of 20 knots out of the east northeast. Their destination was Grenada, and *Sunfun Calypso* romped along at 10 knots. At this speed they'd be there in about 48 hours. When all the sails were trimmed to maximum performance, JC set the auto pilot and after inserting the appropriate chart chip, watched the catamaran's position on the GPS. Only a slight adjustment was needed to maintain the course to the rhumb line.

Harold was busy rigging fishing lines with flesh-coloured squid lures and double hooks. Jackie went over to him and kissed him on the cheek. "Good luck, Hemingway." She disappeared below to lie down in the spacious aft cabin in air conditioned comfort. To her, cruising was visiting interesting anchorages and island hopping to pretty snorkelling spots – the passage making was just a necessary inconvenience. Meanwhile Shirley, in the galley, finished preparing two days of healthy meals and put them in the fridge. She didn't intend to spend hours in a hot and pitching galley getting seasick.

Keeping watch was just that and JC organized watches on a four-hours-on and four-hours-off rotation. JC and Shirley spent the first part of their watch snuggled up together on the trampoline until a rogue wave had them scampering back to the shelter of the cockpit. The auto pilot did all the steering and the steady trades made sail trimming unnecessary but not even the radar could eliminate the human eye. They filled in the logbook, noted passing ships and kept an eye on the yacht's systems. The main had to be reefed once when an ominous black cloud mass loomed directly to windward of them, but *Sunfun* outran it and it passed harmlessly behind them. Both evenings had all of them staring skywards into the sparkling, star filled heavens; first in awe and then inquisitively trying to pick out constellations and planets. On the second day, Harold reeled in a huge mahi mahi and just as he was hauling it on deck, another one hit on the other lure. Thirty pounds of dolphin fillets went into the fridge.

They arrived in the pretty, crescent shaped harbour of St Georges, Grenada on a clear and almost windless morning. The first to spot the island had been Shirley, whose excitement at the adventure had never waned. "I thee it, I thee it . . . Land ahead!" she cried, as she turned up the collar of her track suit against the early morning chill.

The small silhouette on the horizon was crowned with fluffy cumulus and as they got nearer, the lush green, wooded slopes yielded to their tired eyes. Whilst the sky changed from orange through green to blue, the morning haze, the plumes of smoke from early fires, the exotic smells of a new land as they approached from downwind had them all eagerly searching for the harbour entrance. JC went below and zoomed in on his GPS screen. "Right on course," he announced. Just as they rounded the point to enter the harbour, the sun emerged from behind the bluff, as if in welcome. They motored into the Careenage and the anchor chain rattled out to mark the end of the first leg of their cruise.

No sooner had the anchor hit the bottom than an armada of boat boys descended, swarming around *Sunfun* like flies on fresh meat, in all manner of craft, from dugout canoes to barely floating corregated tin dinghies. "You need de customs an' immigration? I show you, I you guide," said one boy dressed only in raggedy shorts.

"I take de laundry fo' de Missus," said another.

"You like some limes?" shouted a little girl, holding up a basket. "It 10 fo' dolla'." She looked up expectantly with big brown eyes, her hair a mass of tightly woven braids. "An' I got mangoes too. Dey sweet an' ready." She pointed to a basket in the bottom of her dinghy.

"Right," said JC, taking control whilst the other three leaned over the rail gaping, "we're going to launch the tender and go to the dock. We'll need some help and we'll buy some limes there," he said pointing to land and trying to disperse the mob of unruly kids, some of whose dinghies were scratching the yacht's topsides.

No-one moved – his words drifted past deaf ears. He turned around and there was Jackie with a bag of sweets and a box of cakes. JC quickly took her to one side. "Don't give them those now," he said in a whisper, "or we'll never get rid of them."

"But they look so poor, so skinny and dressed in rags like that."

"That's just the way island kids are," said JC. "Really, they're as happy as sandboys. Look," he said nodding at the children. They were laughing, shouting and splashing each other, a few drifting away back towards the shore.

JC went to the stern and lowered *Sunfun*'s inflatable tender. He grabbed the ship's papers, passports and clearance documents from the cabin. To the kids that were left he shouted, "Sweets and cakes on the dock. First one there takes all!" A starting gun to a race had never been more effective. A flotilla of motley craft splashed, paddled and otherwise propelled themselves towards land, as JC sped to the dock.

The *Sunfun* crew thoroughly enjoyed Grenada. They explored the Grand Etang lake, swam in the cool, freshwater pools at Concorde waterfall and hiked along scented trails bordered by clove and nutmeg, cinnamon and bayleaf. Shirley and Jackie stocked up on fresh fruit and vegetables at the most colourful marketplace they'd ever seen.

Wonderful brisk sailing took them through the magical isles of the Grenadines. The Tobago Cays was a place Jackie would never forget: The snorkelling there was the best ever. At Bequia they explored Friendship Bay and saw whaling boats from pre-tourist days. The ramp and whale slaughtering area on Petit Nevis, a neighbouring cay, completed the picture. When they sailed into Admiralty Bay a newly built local schooner was being launched and a crowd was on the beach enjoying the spectacle and imbibing in no small way. They launched the dinghy, whizzed ashore, and joined the happy revelry, Harold snapping pictures like a tourist, which of course he was.

Later, back on board, they were enjoying rum drinks

with freshly squeezed lime when a young Rasta paddled up alongside *Sunfun* in a tiny 'two bow' – a dinghy with two pointed ends. "You like a souvenir o' Bequia?" he said, putting two model coconut shell boats on the deck.

They were simple affairs made from half a coconut husk, gaily painted and with colourful striped sails. Harold immediately took a liking to them and examined one, turning it around in his hands. "How much?" he enquired.

"Dem is tree dolla' a-piece," he said and then added, "Yankee dolla,' dat is."

Harold turned to Jackie. "I have a place for these in the Mermaid Bar," and then turning to the long-haired youth he said, "I'll take eight, but all must be with different coloured sails."

"Shaw boss," said the happy salesman with a wide grin. He hadn't had such a good sale all day. "You really does like boats, I can tell." Then, after a pause, he added, "My fadder build dat boat over yonder an' it jus' launch today." With the goods exchanged for cash the boy paddled away, standing up and sculling with one oar. "I bring you some conch tomorrow," he shouted back, still grinning widely.

JC grabbed the binoculars and looked across at the newly launched vessel floating serenely in the soft evening sunlight, its elegant sheerline and raked transom a pleasure to behold. "That schooner is 85 foot long and the whole thing, from the first frame to the last plank, was built by eye – nothing on paper, not a plan anywhere," said JC, shaking his head incredulously. "Hard to believe, but two people told me the same story."

"All the natives seem to be of mixed race," said Jackie, changing the subject.

JC explained that the people of Bequia were

descended from New England fishermen and whalers, Scotsmen, some French renegades and African slaves. "An unlikely potpourri but they are the best boatbuilders in the Caribbean."

By now the *Sunfun* crew had settled into a pattern of friendly co-existence. Although Harold and Jackie were owners and the employers of JC and Shirley, their different roles often overlapped. Harold was an early riser and often took it upon himself to swab the decks in the morning. Jackie loved to explore the local shops and markets and so often would accompany Shirley on her re-provisioning trips. It was working well, but JC reminded Shirley not to become too familiar – it was still necessary to maintain a "guest and crew" relationship.

About a week later and a month into their cruise, they arrived at the Pitons in St Lucia where again they were inundated by island boys who tied the yacht's stern lines ashore to palm trees in exchange for dollars. The volcanic monoliths rising out of the sea were shrouded in a misty haze and they had read that ashore, bubbling coloured mud, a "devil's cauldron," was a "must see." But, the report said, the same volcanic activity also provided therapeutic, hot sulphur spring baths. "Come Harold," shouted Jackie, already waiting by the dinghy with towel and cosmetic bottles, "let's roll around in some hot mud."

Harold decided that this was not quite his cup of tea so declined the offer whilst the other three left for nature's skin tune ups in what Harold thought would probably be smelly surroundings.

When they returned from their healthful wallowing they were followed by the ubiquitous armada of small boys begging for dollars or pestering for non-existent jobs.

"It's such a shame," said Jackie. "They really need

branches of CLATS all through these islands." Her brainchild of Children Learn About The Sea was such a success in the Caribbee Islands and the kids loved it. Not only that but they learned so much about their marine environment and many would later benefit from it.

Harold was sitting in the cockpit enjoying a fresh cup of coffee, early in the morning of their third day in St Lucia, when the telephone rang. It was Mike Broadrite. Could Harold fly back immediately. It was a matter of great importance. No not serious, not bad news, nothing untoward . . . no, it couldn't be discussed on the telephone . . . but it needed immediate attention. Harold finally concurred. Both he and Jackie would fly out in the morning.

That afternoon they sailed up to Rodney Bay and secured a slip in the marina and the following morning Harold and Jackie took a taxi to the airport. After several delays at islands en route they finally arrived at Tortuga only two hours later than scheduled. Mike Broadrite was at the airport to meet them.

After initial pleasantries, Mike came straight to the point. "We have some guests staying at the lodge and they want to discuss a business proposition. They are very serious and they led me to believe that money is no object. That's why I urgently called you back. I have taken the liberty to arrange a meeting in the company's offices for tomorrow at nine – the two of them and the three of us. They spent all of yesterday nosing around the docks and the lodge. I think they're going to make an offer to buy the place."

"Well, it's not for sale," replied Harold, immediately.

Broadrite gave him a shrewd look. "Everything's for sale . . . at the right price."

During the next four days meetings took place in the company's offices. Broadrite had been right – the two businessmen represented a consortium of companies that owned luxury corporate mega yachts. They were searching for a marina with facilities for a club with first-class accommodations. GSC and the Sunset Lodge were perfect. But Harold was adamant that the property was not for sale . . . he had fallen in love with the place, had built it up with blood, sweat and tears. It had survived two hurricanes, albeit with one death, it had a profound history; the mermaid had come and gone . . . When the offer was suddenly increased to five million dollars, Harold wavered.

That night, Harold and Jackie retired to their suite early. They were both confused by mixed emotions – they loved the place but it was hard work and a big responsibility. They had overcome so much to get to where they were . . . but 5 million!!

It took them less than an hour to work out a satisfactory compromise in the way of an agreeable counter-offer. Their proposal would be presented at yet another meeting in the morning. Finally they both fell asleep in an ambivalent mood, confident that whichever way the pendulum swung they would be content.

It was one of those picture-perfect days when they awoke next morning, still and clear with not a cloud in the sky. It was early when Harold went into the kitchen to make a pot of coffee, but Beulah had already arrived for work. "Mr Harold," she began, breathlessly, "de word is dat you an' Ms Jackie sellin' up de place an' I want to tell you right now dat all o' we on de staff ain' happy wid dat at all, an' we ain' guarantee dat we goin' to stay wid any new owners an' all o' we in favour o' you all stayin' . . . dat's all." Beulah walked back to the stove and gave a couple of loud sniffs.

"Well, that's very kind of you to say so," said Harold. "We're having another meeting today and I want to assure you and all the staff that whatever happens we are not going to abandon you. Everyone will be informed. The one thing that has made Sunset Lodge so successful is the staff."

"All o' we bin worried, Mr Harold . . . I'll bring your coffee an' breakfast out to de terrace. You want bran flakes an' prunes, right?"

"Thank you, Beulah, and a pot of tea and a croissant for Ms Jackie."

The meeting began in its usual cordial manner with everyone helping themselves to coffee or iced water from the sideboard. The air conditioner was switched to a comfortable 80 degrees, and Mike Broadrite handed out folders of documents to all the participants. Harold and Jackie were confident that they would emerge triumphant – they knew that what they had was what the other side wanted, they were holding all the cards and if the other side backed down – well that was fine, too.

After an intense morning, by lunchtime, everything had been agreed. The price tag had been dropped to 4.5 million dollars but Harold had persuaded the new buyers that he and Jackie would retain a 10 per cent holding in the new company. Also written into the agreement was the proviso that there would be a permanent slip available for *Sunfun Calypso* at the GSC dock.

There had been a long, hard battle fought over the question of staff. But Harold had remained steadfast and insisted that all staff must be retained for a minimum of one year, as long as they chose that option, and as long as they performed their jobs properly. The new owners had ummed and aahed over that one, saying that several changes were planned and some staff might not be necessary. It was finally resolved when it was agreed that staff could be terminated at a month's notice as long as a year's severance pay was awarded.

But it was Jackie who had the hardest job. Before the meeting she had persuaded Harold that under no circumstances would GSC be sold unless access and use of the little beach at the end of the property along with the sailing dinghies was granted to CLATS in perpetuity. Then they both had to persuade the potential new owners.

These starched and suited men who represented the mega yacht millionaires just couldn't fathom the importance of this demand and the tenacity with which Harold and Jackie held on to it. Were they really ready to jeopardise a multi-million dollar sale because of a few raggedy island kids . . . ? As it turned out, they were. Finally, with much shaking of heads and raised eyebrows, the agreement was signed with the written stipulation that CLATS could use that specific area of the property three days a week. Unbeknown to the buyers, this paragraph in the contract was to stand them in good stead when their applications and transferral documents went to the government for approval.

When Harold and Jackie walked out of the company's offices and into the warm sunshine they breathed huge sighs of relief – the ordeal was over. In a single week of business meetings and intense negotiations, their lives had been irrevocably changed, and even though they had secured a wonderful deal for themselves, they were sad that they had lost control of the place they had come to love. Slowly they walked up the path to the lodge, between the flowering bougainvilleas and red and pink hibiscus. When they reached the terrace they stood by the fountain holding hands and looked down onto Rum Cove. Jackie's eyes filled with water and she swallowed hard a couple of times.

The next day at 5 o'clock in the evening Harold called a meeting in the library to explain the developments to the staff. "We are still shareholders in the company," explained Harold, "but now we will be silent partners. We expect to spend time here every year and we are going to keep *Sunfun Calypso* at the dock. The new owners have promised that you will all be well looked after, and I have ensured them that they have inherited a happy, hard working and honest staff. So don't let me down!

"Most important, though, is that now Ms Jackie and I will have time to expand and develop the CLATS programme throughout the eastern Caribbean from Trinidad to Cuba, a dream we have had for some time. We plan to initiate clubs for the kids, perhaps in conjunction with the islands' yacht clubs, in all the islands. We want to encourage sponsorship and donations and in time, inter-island competitions and regattas. We want all the children in the region to learn about the sea."

After the meeting, both Harold and Jackie thanked staff members personally. Beulah, who had managed to contain herself with quiet reserve throughout the meeting, broke into sobs when Harold handed her a thick envelope with his heartfelt thanks. "We always be rememberin' you all," she said, "an' our prayers be wid you."

Memnon was more logical. "Dis ain' goodbye," he said. "Dis only a change o' course." Even so there was much hugging, kissing and shaking of hands.

Then Sonia Hodge called for quiet and made a short eulogy praising the Mcpheresons for maintaining GSC in island tradition whilst upgrading its amenities and increasing its success financially. "And there can be nothing more honourable," she concluded, "than giving of one's time and energy to those in need, like many of the islands' children. I know I speak for all of us here when I wish you well." There was energetic applause and then Harold announced that the Rusty Pelican would be serving complimentary drinks for the rest of the evening. Several staff members wandered down there for a thirst quencher but most people slowly drifted home – this was not a party occasion, but rather a sombre farewell.

A week later all the loose ends had been tied up and Jackie and Harold were on their way to the airport to continue their island cruise on *Sunfun Calypso*. They asked Quickly to take them along the ridge road; the view from that elevation was always magnificent. They rounded a corner on the wrong side of the road and almost hit another mini cab coming at them fast. Quickly swerved into a ditch and came to a stop against a large tamarind tree. "Mudderscunnnn!" he shouted. "Dat fella lookin' fo' God! Now look what he done to my vehicle."

They all got out and examined a long scratch and dent along the offside of Quickly's minibus. Worst of all, though, two tyres were burst and Quickly only had one spare. "My cell phone ain' wukin an' I need to call home so my brudder can bring me a nudder wheel. Look at my poor bus – it ain' even half paid off." He shook his head despairingly.

"We just passed a driveway on the right-hand side," said Harold. "Let's go up to the house and see if we can borrow the telephone."

Quickly and Harold left Jackie to watch the things and walked up the steep and pot-holed drive in the heat of the mid-day sun and Harold noticed that the grounds of the stately residence were in a terrible state of disrepair. They were both sweating and out of breath when they reached the portico. Harold rang the bell.

A matronly lady answered the door, a domestic servant. Her face was dark and lined and she spoke with a hint of a Spanish accent. "Mr Reephoff is unavailable, I'm afraid. What can I do for you gentlemen?"

Harold stood there for a second, agape – quite by accident they had stumbled onto the private residence of Adolf Reephoff. "Our minibus has broken down on the ridge road and we'd like to make a phone call if possible," said Harold politely.

"Well I suppose it'll be all right – since it's an emergency," said the elderly lady, looking around nervously whilst showing Quickly to the phone in the hall. Then she moved closer to Harold and said in a lowered voice, "Mr Reephoff's been getting very moody lately. I think he's coming down with a sickness."

"Would that be Mr Adolf Reephoff, the lawyer?" asked Harold innocently.

"Yes, you must know him. You're the gentleman from the Sunset Lodge, aren't you?"

"Correct on both counts, I've had certain dealings with Mr Reephoff in the past." said Harold.

"Well," said the old maid, "ever since he brought back a wooden carving of a mermaid from the carnival and put it in the garden we've had problems. All his plants, shrubs and trees have died. We've got termites running all through the building and dead rats have contaminated our cistern water. Then, last week after the heavy rain, we had an infestation of tree frogs and Mr Reephoff took great exception to them – running around like a madman trying to step on them and squash them all. Right now he's sitting in the drawing room drinking neat vodka. He's been going through a bottle a day!"

"You should get rid of the mermaid – it contains evil spirits – the obeah is in it. Whilst it is here you will have problems – you must get rid of it," Harold said urgently. He didn't owe Reephoff any favours, but still . . .

The matron's eyes opened wide and her knuckles flew to her mouth. Then Quickly came out. "My brudder comin' jus' now wid he pick up. Les' go."

They turned to go. "Thank you for your help," said Harold. "Remember . . . get rid of the mermaid!!"

They walked back down the driveway and Harold climbed the bank to see if he could see the mermaid. There it was, right in the middle of the unkempt lawn. Its head had been glued back on but the job had been done poorly and the head was now crooked. Dribbles of glue ran down the neck onto the breasts, looking quite gruesome, like blood from a slashed head, and the whole thing was covered in a film of fungus. But even so the strange half smile and piercing eyes were menacingly visible. Harold shuddered at the sight.

Soon they were bouncing along the pot-holed road towards the airport. They had allowed two hours for checking in, but that had now been reduced to half an hour and they were still 10 minutes away. Then a herd of goats chose that moment to cross the road in a leisurely line, and Quickly's honking on the horn just elicited noisy bleating. Finally they hurried to the check-in counter and were told that the plane was late . . . 'island time' has its blessings, they thought.

"Mr Harold, Ms Jackie," someone shouted from a distance away up the concourse. It was Memnon and he approached them puffing. Behind him ran Tall Boy, Bugeye and Tutu. "We so glad to catch you," said Memnon, "de boys have someting fo' you."

Tutu handed Jackie a large cardboard box, his wide grin showing the gap between his two incisors. "What on earth is it?" she said, surprised.

"Well, open it and see," said Bugeye.

Jackie unwrapped the box, with Harold helping with the difficult bits. Inquisitive tourists and passers-by stopped and peered into the involved circle. Finally out it came – a magnificent model of *Sunfun Calypso*, complete with mast, sails, rigging and wheels, even the colour of the spinnaker with its orange sunburst matched the original. Harold was the first to speak. "This will take pride of place in the main salon," he said proudly, "and it will have a small spotlight that can shine on it. Magnificent!!"

"It have CLATS written right here too," said Tall Boy, and he pointed to underneath the name where the home port would normally be written.

Jackie seemed too overwhelmed to say anything much. "Thank you, boys . . . very much. This has special . . . meaning." She swallowed hard, then the loudspeaker announced their flight was boarding.

Hugs and claps on the back were exchanged by Harold and Memnon, who was grinning widely. "All o' we be seein' you again soon," he said. He shook Jackie's hand and nodded, smiling. "Good flight and good sailin' . . . an' keep your powder dry."

THE END

To order copies of *Sunfun Calypso:*

In the Virgin Islands:
Julian Putley, Virgin Island Books,
PO Box 8309, Cruz Bay, St. John, USVI 00831
Tel/Fax: (284) 494-0726
E-mail: putley@caribsurf.com

Elsewhere Orders to:
Cruising Guide Publications,
PO Box 1017, Dunedin, FLA 34697-1017
Tel: (800) 330-9542   Fax: (813) 734-8179
E-mail: cgp@earthlink.net